Anglo-Saxon Studies 51

REMAINS OF THE PAST IN OLD ENGLISH LITERATURE

Anglo-Saxon Studies

ISSN 1475-2468

General Editors
Andrew Rabin
John Hines
Catherine Cubitt

'Anglo-Saxon Studies' aims to provide a forum for the best scholarship on the Anglo-Saxon peoples in the period from the end of Roman Britain to the Norman Conquest, including comparative studies involving adjacent populations and periods; both new research and major re-assessments of central topics are welcomed.

Books in the series may be based in any one of the principal disciplines of archaeology, art history, history, language and literature, and inter- or multi-disciplinary studies are encouraged.

Proposals or enquiries may be sent directly to the editors or the publisher at the addresses given below; all submissions will receive prompt and informed consideration.

Professor Andrew Rabin, Department of English, Bingham Humanities 315, 2216 1st Street, University of Louisville, Louisville, KY 40292, USA

Professor Emeritus John Hines, School of History, Archaeology and Religion, Cardiff University, John Percival Building, Colum Drive, Cardiff, Wales, CF10 3EU, UK

Professor Catherine Cubitt, School of History, Faculty of Arts and Humanities, University of East Anglia, Norwich, England, NR4 7TJ, UK

Boydell & Brewer, PO Box 9, Woodbridge, Suffolk, England, IP12 3DF, UK

Recently published volumes in the series are listed at the back of this book

REMAINS OF THE PAST IN OLD ENGLISH LITERATURE

Jan-Peer Hartmann

D.S.BREWER

© Jan-Peer Hartmann 2025

All Rights Reserved. Except as permitted under current legislation
no part of this work may be photocopied, stored in a retrieval system,
published, performed in public, adapted, broadcast,
transmitted, recorded or reproduced in any form or by any means,
without the prior permission of the copyright owner

The right of Jan-Peer Hartmann to be identified as
the author of this work has been asserted in accordance with
sections 77 and 78 of the Copyright, Designs and Patents Act 1988

First published 2025
D. S. Brewer, Cambridge

ISBN 978-1-84384-736-6

D. S. Brewer is an imprint of Boydell & Brewer Ltd
PO Box 9, Woodbridge, Suffolk IP12 3DF, UK
and of Boydell & Brewer Inc.
668 Mt Hope Avenue, Rochester, NY 14620-2731, USA
website: www.boydellandbrewer.com

A CIP catalogue record for this book is available
from the British Library

The publisher has no responsibility for the continued existence or accuracy of
URLs for external or third-party internet websites referred to in this book, and
does not guarantee that any content on such websites is, or will remain, accurate
or appropriate

Contents

List of Illustrations	vi
Acknowledgements	vii
Abbreviations	ix
Introduction: Old English Literature and the Archaeological Imagination	1
1 Excavating the Cross in *Elene*	25
2 Ruins and their Multiple Temporalities: *The Wanderer* and *The Ruin*	83
3 The Perils of Anachronism: *Beowulf* and the *Legend of the Seven Sleepers*	142
4 Visions of the Holy Cross: *Elene, The Dream of the Rood* and the Ruthwell Poem	192
Conclusion: Conceptualising Time and History through the Remains of the Past	252
Bibliography	258
Index	275

Illustrations

1   Detail from Cotton Tiberius B.v, fol. 56v, from the British Library archive, Cotton Tiberius B. V, Part 1, f.56v. © The British Library Board.   77

2   W. Penny, engraving published with Henry Duncan's 'An Account of the Remarkable Monument in the Shape of a Cross, Inscribed with Roman and Runic Letters, Preserved in the Garden of Ruthwell Manse, Dumfriesshire', *Archaeologia Scotica: or, Transactions of the Society of Antiquaries of Scotland*, 4 (1857), 313–36 (Plate XIII). Image © National Museums Scotland.   233

3   The Ruthwell Cross, crucifixion panel. Image © Crown Copyright: HES.   241

The author and publisher are grateful to all the institutions and individuals listed for permission to reproduce the materials in which they hold copyright. Every effort has been made to trace the copyright holders; apologies are offered for any omission, and the publisher will be pleased to add any necessary acknowledgement in subsequent editions.

Acknowledgements

This book has been a long time in the making. It was written while I was a research fellow at the Collaborative Research Centre 'Episteme in Motion' (Sonderforschungsbereich 980 Episteme in Bewegung) at the Freie Universität Berlin, funded by the German Research Foundation (Deutsche Forschungsgemeinschaft), whose sponsorship I gratefully acknowledge. My research in general and my understanding of the issues I deal with in this book have benefited greatly from discussions with my colleagues, past and present, both at the CRC and the Institute of English Philology, especially (in alphabetical order) Mira Becker-Sawatzky, Thies Bornemann, Simon Brandl, Sarah Briest, Şirin Dadaş, Isabelle Dolezalek, Sven Durie, Jutta Eming, Anne Eusterschulte, Jan Fusek, Matthias Grandl, Stephan Hartlepp, Kristiane Hasselmann, Iris Helffenstein, Armin Hempel, Elisabeth Kempf, Beate Ulrike La Sala, Lea von der Linde, Peter Löffelbein, Michael Lorber, Miltos Pechlivanos, Nikolas Pissis, Falk Quenstedt, Tilo Renz, Claudia Reufer, Margitta Rouse, Kostas Sarris, Regina Scheibe, Nora Schmidt, Nora K. Schmidt, Wilhelm Schmidt-Biggemann, Ulrike Schneider, Hanna Zoe Trauer, Martin Urmann, Sophia Vassilopoulou, Christian Vogel, Katrin Wächter, Volkhard Wels, Helge Wendt and Kai Wiegandt. I would also like to thank our former student assistants Steve Commichau, Elisabeth Korn, Mats Siekmann and Christoph Witt. I have been very fortunate to have been part of several international and interdisciplinary projects that allowed me to discuss aspects of my research with scholars whose work has been inspirational to my own. In particular, I would like to mention (again in alphabetical order) Joshua Davies, Miriam Edlich-Muth, Naomi Howell, Philip Schwyzer, the late Ladislav Šmejda and Estella Weiss-Krejci. In addition, I would like to express my gratitude to Irina Dumitrescu, Roberta Frank, Alaric Hall, John Hines, Marijane Osborn, Katherine Starkey and Uta Störmer-Caysa for their generous support at various points during the past years. I also thank my teachers at the Institute of Nordic Languages and Culture (Nordeuropa-Institut) at the Humboldt-Universität zu Berlin and the Institute of English Philology at the Freie Universität Berlin for awakening my interest in medieval languages, literature and culture, in particular Jurij K. Kusmenko, Wolfram Keller and Andrew James Johnston. To Andrew, I owe my greatest debt: his unfailing loyalty and encouragement have accompanied me from my time as an undergraduate and throughout my entire professional life; without him, this book would not have been written. Together with Wolfram, he supervised my PhD, and both read the entire manuscript of the present book (in Andrew's case, more than once), making countless invaluable comments and suggestions. Numerous improvements were also suggested by my friend and former colleague, Martin Bleisteiner. Their collective efforts saved me from many errors and misjudgements. Those still remaining are, of course, solely my own. At Boydell and Brewer, my thanks go to Caroline Palmer and Laura Bennetts. Outside academia, I am deeply grateful to my parents, Urs and Monika Hartmann, whose moral and financial support during my undergraduate and graduate studies, not to mention baby-sitting, enabled me to pursue academic projects like the present one; as well as to my brothers, Nils and Falk Hartmann, who have shared in many of my hobbies and interests. Most importantly, I thank my wife, Kirsten Middeke, a professional historical linguist, who not only shared the care work and family responsibilities with me while having her own book to write, but was always ready to answer my queries concerning Old English (and, occasionally, Latin) grammar. Finally, I thank my children, Jakob and Luise, who have had to put up with endless academic babbling when they would have much rather talked about their many areas of interest, immeasurably more fascinating than my own.

Abbreviations

ASC	*The Anglo-Saxon Chronicle: A Collaborative Edition* (Cambridge, 1983–)
ASPR	*The Anglo-Saxon Poetic Records: A Collective Edition*, ed. George Philip Krapp and Elliott Van Kirk Dobbie (6 vols, New York, 1931–53)
ASE	*Anglo-Saxon England*
BL	British Library
BT	Joseph Bosworth and T. Northcote Toller (eds), *An Anglo-Saxon Dictionary Based on the Manuscript Collections of the Late Joseph Bosworth* (Oxford, 1898); *Supplement*, ed. T. Northcote Toller (Oxford, 1921); *Revised and Enlarged Addenda*, ed. Alistair Campbell (Oxford, 1972), online edition <https://bosworthtoller.com> [accessed 26 February 2024]
CH	John R. Clark Hall, *A Concise Anglo-Saxon Dictionary for the Use of Students*, 2nd edn (New York, 1916)
Douay-Rheims	*Holy Bible Douay-Rheims Version, with Challoner Revisions 1749–52* (Baltimore, MD, 1899), <https://www.drbo.org/index.htm> [accessed 15 December 2023]
EETS OS	Early English Text Society, original series
EETS SS	Early English Text Society, supplementary series
HE	Bede, *Bede's Ecclesiastical History of the English People*, ed. and trans. Bertram Colgrave and R. A. B. Mynors (Oxford, 1969)
JEGP	*Journal of English and Germanic Philology*
JMEMS	*Journal of Medieval and Early Modern Studies*
NM	*Neuphilologische Mitteilungen*
RES	*Review of English Studies*
Weber-Gryson	Robert Weber and Roger Gryson (eds), *Biblia Sacra iuxta vulgatam versionem*, 5th edn (Stuttgart, 2007), <https://www.bibelwissenschaft.de/bibel/VUL/GEN.1> [accessed 25 February 2024]

Parts of Chapter 4 have already appeared, in an earlier form, in my article 'The Ruthwell Cross and the Riddle of Time', in Jan-Peer Hartmann and Andrew James Johnston (eds), *Material Remains: Reading the Past in Medieval and Early Modern British Literature* (Columbus, 2021), 172–90.

Introduction:
Old English Literature and the
Archaeological Imagination

This is a study of the archaeological imagination in Old English literature; that is, in texts produced in the English language as it was written between the early seventh and mid-eleventh centuries. The term 'archaeology' may seem oddly incongruous in the context of the early Middle Ages – after all, archaeology in the modern sense only started to develop in the seventeenth and eighteenth centuries and had no direct equivalent in early medieval Britain. Neither archaeology as an institutionalised academic discipline nor most of its methods and technologies existed during the early Middle Ages. And yet, premodern societies were by no means unfamiliar with material traces of the past, nor were they shy of offering explanations for these traces, or of using them to support their own versions of history. In a well-known passage of his *De civitate Dei*, Augustine offers what may be described as archaeological evidence for the supposedly greater body size of earlier human generations:

> Sed de corporum magnitudine plerumque incredulos nudata per vetu-statem sive per vim fluminum variosque casus sepulcra convincunt, ubi apparuerunt vel unde ceciderunt incredibilis magnitudinis ossa mortuorum. Vidi ipse, non solus sed aliquot mecum, in Uticensi litore molarem hominis dentem tam ingentem ut, si in nostrorum dentium modulos minutatim concideretur, centum nobis videretur facere potuisse. Sed illum gigantis alicuius fuisse crediderim. Nam praeter quod erant omnium multo quam nostra maiora tunc corpora, gigantes longe ceteris anteibant, sicut aliis deinde nostrisque temporibus rara quidem, sed numquam ferme defuerunt quae modum aliorum pluri-mum excederent. Verum, ut dixi, antiquorum magnitudines corporum inventa plerumque ossa, quoniam diuturna sunt, etiam multo posteri-oribus saeculis produnt.

> [As far as the size of bodies is concerned, however, sceptics are generally persuaded by the evidence in tombs uncovered through the ravages of time, the violence of streams or various other occurrences. For incredi-bly large bones of the dead have been found in them or dislodged from them. On the shore of Utica I myself, not alone but with several others, saw a human molar so enormous that, if it were divided up into pieces to the dimensions of our teeth, it would, so it seemed to us, have made a hundred of them. But that molar, I should suppose, belonged to some

Remains of the Past in Old English Literature

giant. For not only were bodies in general much larger then than our own, but the giants towered far above the rest, even as in subsequent times, including our own, there have almost always been bodies which, though few in number, far surpassed the size of the others. [...] But, as I have said, the size of ancient bodies is disclosed even to much later ages by the frequent discovery of bones, for bones are long-lasting.][1]

The passage highlights some of the key issues addressed in the present study: when and to what ends do texts reference material traces of the past – regardless of whether they are fictional or actually exist? What can such passages tell us about the texts' attitudes towards the past and about the ways that they conceive of the temporal processes that separate it from the present? How do different perceptions of the material and the temporal intersect in descriptions of the material remains of the past? It is the principal aim of this study to show how literary depictions of 'archaeological objects' have the capacity for foregrounding different perspectives on the passing of time, thereby testifying to the complex ways in which premodern people – in this case, early medieval authors in Britain – imagined their own place in history.

Augustine's description of 'giant bones' found in ancient tombs occurs in the context of a discussion of the truthfulness of the Bible, which doubters called into question on the grounds of the perceived implausibility of its historical accounts. He presents prehistoric remains as evidence for the tallness of earlier human beings, and thus obliquely supports the Bible's narrative of their equally longer life span: the latter, Augustine admits, cannot be proven by material evidence,[2] but if there are ancient remains that corroborate the Bible's report of the former existence of giants, why should we not believe its account of the longevity of prediluvian humans, too?

The molar tooth that Augustine says he saw may well have been that of a prehistoric mammal, and when he refers to bones as 'long-lasting', he may in fact be thinking of fossilised skeletal remains. Yet from the perspective of the present study, the question is not whether Augustine's explanation is historically accurate; the much more intriguing thing is that, besides quoting authorities such as Virgil, Pliny and Homer, Augustine

---

[1] Augustine, *De civitate Dei* xv.9. Text and translation are from Augustine, *City of God*, Loeb Classical Library, 411–17 (7 vols, Cambridge, MA, 1957–72), vol. 4, trans. Philip Levine, 456–9. Throughout this book, unless otherwise indicated, translations are my own.

[2] Augustine, *De civitate Dei* xv.9: 'Annorum autem numerositas cuiusque hominis quae temporibus illis fuit nullis nunc talibus documentis venire in experimentum potest' [On the other hand, the longevity of individuals in those days cannot now be demonstrated by any such tangible evidence; Augustine, *City of God*, 458–9].

Introduction

draws on material evidence to support his claim, and that he appears to be granting some material artefacts the same or even superior evidential status compared to written texts: where ancient authorities (to say nothing of the Bible) fail to convince, material objects are deployed as proof to persuade the incredulous. In this respect, Augustine's strategy resembles the way that modern historians frequently cite archaeological evidence to substantiate their claims. As Philip Schwyzer has demonstrated in the context of the 2011 excavation of Richard III's remains, the ascription of greater evidential weight to items of material culture than to written texts is characteristic of popular perceptions of present-day archaeology, according to which material evidence does not lie, whereas texts may distort and misrepresent the historical 'truth'.[3]

It is interesting to note that Augustine refers specifically to bones that have re-emerged from ancient burial sites; that is, to what are perhaps the most visibly human traces of the past. For Augustine, said bones are not merely evidence of the existence – and, more specifically, the body size – of earlier generations of human beings, they are also intimately linked to other material indicators of past cultural activity. Collectively, the passage demonstrates, these traces have the capacity for opening a window to the past – in this case, a biblical past where men were taller and giants walked the earth. Moreover, they invite further reflection on the temporal processes that divide past and present: as Augustine's description implies, the monuments he has in mind had been around for a long period; they were untended, perhaps hidden and unknown to the people of the present, until the forces of nature and the wear of time revealed their existence and their contents. In their present state, the sepulchres are visibly damaged, dilapidated; they are, in a sense, ruins. And yet, it is precisely their ruined state that lends weight to Augustine's argument as the most compelling evidence for the bones' great age.

Bede's *Historia ecclesiastica gentis Anglorum*, one of the most influential texts produced in early medieval Britain, likewise mentions items of material culture to substantiate its historical account. Speaking of the Roman occupation of Britain, Bede names 'cities, lighthouses, bridges and roads' ('ciuitates farus pontes et stratae') as evidence of Rome's former presence in the British Isles.[4] As in Augustine's discussion, reference is made to material culture in order to corroborate written authority; and, again as in Augustine, specific kinds of structure are highlighted that, for Bede and his audience, were recognisably ancient and recognisably Roman rather

---

[3]   Philip Schwyzer, 'The Return of the King: Exhuming King Arthur and Richard III', in Jan-Peer Hartmann and Andrew James Johnston (eds), *Material Remains: Reading the Past in Medieval and Early Modern British Literature* (Columbus, OH, 2021), 78–100.

[4]   *HE* i.11 (ed. and trans. Colgrave and Mynors, 40–1).

than 'English' or 'British' (whatever meaning they may have associated with these terms).[5]

Both Augustine and Bede display an apparent trust in the capacity of ancient objects to provide information about the past, a trust that the texts discussed in this study do not always share. Schwyzer has observed that the 'vision of the perfectly preserved body or artefact that, touched by the living, dissolves suddenly to dust' – often without disclosing its secret – recurs 'in a remarkable range of late medieval and early modern texts'.[6] This timespan can be extended in either direction, the disappearing blades of the giants' sword in *Beowulf* (discussed in detail in Chapter 3) and the Ringwraith's Morgul knife in *The Lord of the Rings* being particularly prominent cases in point. In these scenes, it is not merely the materiality of the object that eludes the grasp of the would-be archaeologist, but also the very past that the object supposedly embodies – here, the fragmented nature of the remains stands emblematically for a past beyond recovery.

Archaeology and Literature

Augustine and Bede both employ specifically 'archaeological' motifs to support their respective historical claims; that is, they refer to items of material culture that they consider to be recognisably human and recognisably ancient in order to make points about preceding eras of human history. If the academic discipline of archaeology is the study of the mate-

---

[5] It is difficult to ascertain the precise meaning early medieval texts such as the *Historia ecclesiastica* attached to terms like *Angli* or *Brittones*, and how contemporary audiences would have interpreted them. Traditionally, these were regarded as ethnonyms; however, recent scholarship has drawn attention to the possibility that these appellations may have been restricted to the aristocratic classes (Nicholas J. Higham, *An English Empire: Bede and the Early Anglo-Saxon Kings* [Manchester, 1995], 218–19, 226, 251), or that they were primarily markers of religious identity and/or legal status (Susan Oosthuizen, *The Emergence of the English* [Leeds, 2019], 70–1). It is partly for these reasons that the established designation 'Anglo-Saxon' as a marker of a certain cultural, linguistic and ethnic identity is no longer undisputed, another factor being its use in racist right-wing discourse. Unfortunately, the widespread substitution of 'English' (or 'early medieval English') for 'Anglo-Saxon' exacerbates rather than solves the problem, as it suggests a historically unwarranted cultural and political (as well as, potentially, genetic) continuity between early medieval polities and the modern British nation state. In the present study, it is by and large irrelevant how the milieux in which the Old English texts under discussion were read and produced identified ethnically. Given that multilingualism was quite common in early medieval Britain, I use the designation 'early medieval (British)' mainly in reference to the texts' historical context.

[6] Philip Schwyzer, *Archaeologies of English Renaissance Literature* (Oxford, 2007), 4.

Introduction

rial remains of the past,[7] a knowledge-seeking engagement with material artefacts *as* traces of the past could in a sense be called 'proto-archaeological'. Indeed, in a discussion of megalithic tombs, archaeologist Cornelius Holtorf has proposed that later engagement with these monuments can be seen as an early form of archaeological research:

> Megaliths have probably at all times been fascinating curiosities in the landscape, and many generations of people are likely to have been excited by the strange mounds containing huge stones and sometimes human bones. [...] Whether from coincidental discoveries of human bones or artefacts, or from deliberate investigations, some people may have suspected that mounds contained ancient finds and were in fact old graves. Subsequent attempts to find out more about these sites and the objects associated with them can be considered as the earliest form of prehistoric archaeological research.[8]

However, it is not the aim of this study to write a history of archaeology *avant la lettre*. Even if people in prehistory did attempt to find out more about the origins and history of certain sites or objects, as Holtorf hypothesises, we cannot ascertain the frame of mind in which such 'research' would have been undertaken, and nor do I wish to suggest that the concern with material culture exhibited by Augustine and Bede is directly comparable to modern archaeological research. While the latter do refer to ancient objects *as* traces of the past, they do not study the past *through* these artefacts, nor do they examine the artefacts themselves; two forms of engagement that, according to John Hines, clearly distinguish the modern discipline of archaeology from its antiquarian predecessors.[9] The historical accounts presented by Augustine and Bede are not constructed from information inferred from material culture, nor are the two authors usually interested in the histories of the ancient objects as such.

---

[7] John Hines, *Voices in the Past: English Literature and Archaeology* (Cambridge, 2004), 9.

[8] Cornelius Holtorf, 'The Life-Histories of Megaliths in Mecklenburg-Vorpommern (Germany)', *World Archaeology*, 30:1 (1998), 23–38, at 28.

[9] Hines, *Voices*, 9–10. Today, the field is remarkably broad, comprising not only professional archaeologists with their various specialisations, but also intersecting with a wide array of other disciplines, including botany, genetics, biochemistry and climate science. The interpretation of finds relies increasingly on complex laboratory analysis and mathematical modelling, while their conservation and curation constitute yet another distinct field of expertise. As a cultural phenomenon, however, archaeology is not confined to academia: spectacular finds such as the Staffordshire Hoard or the skeleton of Richard III engage the attention of large parts of the public, and indeed many of them would not have been made in the first place without the aid of amateur archaeologists and metal detectorists.

Remains of the Past in Old English Literature

Monika Otter notes that 'modern archaeology is inferential', constructing 'historical insights from small finds, and from such finds it claims to piece together an entire past epoch, complete with social structures and a "daily life"'; by contrast, 'medieval diggers dig deductively, not inductively' – their finds merely confirm what is known beforehand.[10] The same would seem to apply to the historical accounts offered by Bede and Augustine, whose approach resembles that of the modern historian who cites archaeological research in support of their claims. Indeed, writing a historical account is precisely what Bede set out to do, however different his notion of history may have been from ours.[11] According to Otter, medieval *inventiones* – accounts of the discovery of a saint's body or relics – usually serve a similar purpose. In many instances, the location and identity of the holy remains are claimed to have been revealed beforehand in dreams and visions, or through the study of ancient texts; the recovery of the relics thus merely confirms what was known (or at least suspected) all along. Otter suggests that the emphasis these texts nevertheless place on the actual act of digging self-consciously mirrors the activity of historical writing: excavation becomes a metaphor for the composition of the text, which performs, on a different level, the very action it describes.[12]

Nevertheless, Otter concedes that some texts display sensibilities much closer to the modern concept of archaeology, citing the example of an episode in Matthew Paris's contribution to St Albans' chronicle *Gesta abbatum*, wherein the tenth-century abbot Ealdred digs in the ruins of Roman Verulamium across from the Abbey in order to unearth building materials, as well as to root out robbers, prostitutes and a bothersome dragon. However, the dig also brings to light historical artefacts, some of which corroborate details found in earlier historical accounts (such as rusty anchors and parts of ships confirming the former presence of a substantial river), while others are noteworthy in and of themselves, transforming the locals' perception of their geographical surroundings.

From the vantage point of the present study, it is especially fitting that this episode in the *Gesta abbatum* is set within the time frame under consideration here. In several of the pre-Conquest texts I discuss, the traces of the past discovered stimulate interest in their specific histories, and sometimes even give rise to imaginative reconstructions of their earlier contexts. This is the case, for instance, in the poetic descriptions of ruins discussed in Chapter 2, most obviously in the way *The Ruin*'s narrator attempts to construct a story of the deserted city's past out of the material

[10] Monika Otter, *Inventiones: Fiction and Referentiality in Twelfth-Century English Historical Writing* (Chapel Hill, NC, 1996), 53.

[11] *HE* Praefatio (ed. and trans. Colgrave and Mynors, 2–7).

[12] Otter, *Inventiones*, 57.

Introduction

traces still extant; the giants' sword and dragon's hoard in *Beowulf*, discussed in Chapter 3, elicit similar responses.

These caveats aside, I share Hines's conviction that archaeology in the broader sense of 'the curation, interpretation, and active use of material remains' constitutes 'a near-constant feature' of human culture in general, with the academic discipline of the same name being only its latest, culturally specific manifestation. Consequently, as Hines notes, 'engagement with the material past was necessarily a feature of medieval English literature, just as it was of the cultural life of medieval Britain and Europe generally'.[13]

What I am interested in, then, is a phenomenon that Schwyzer describes as the 'archaeological imagination' of literary texts (a term he borrows, with somewhat different emphasis, from Jennifer Wallace);[14] that is, the archaeological themes, motifs and metaphors manifested in the works that I discuss. A significant number of texts produced in early medieval Britain – both in Latin and the Old English vernacular – display an acute awareness of, and pronounced interest in, an ancient, pre-medieval past, an interest often expressed through references to material objects that can be described, from a modern perspective, as 'archaeological'. In the context of this study, the term 'archaeological' thus serves primarily as a heuristic to denote items of material culture – or a form of engagement with them – that are highlighted or singled out as specifically ancient, and hence capable of introducing a historical perspective. References to the material traces of the past can range from mere observations, which may in turn give rise to reflections on the mutability of material culture or the world more generally, as in *The Wanderer*, through descriptions of actual acts of excavation, as in *Beowulf* and *Elene*, to instances of reuse or adaptation. The forms of engagement with material objects described in these texts often reflect practices that were characteristic of the cultures of early medieval Britain, but for the purposes of this study, it does not matter whether the respective encounters with material remains really took place or not. I am by no means concerned with the factuality of the 'archaeological' confrontations described in the narratives in question; rather, I am interested in what literary engagements with archaeological objects – objects *from* the past – tell us about these texts' perceptions *of* the past.

---

[13] John Hines, 'But men seyn, "What may ever laste?" Chaucer's House of Fame as a Medieval Museum', in Jan-Peer Hartmann and Andrew James Johnston (eds), *Material Remains: Reading the Past in Medieval and Early Modern British Literature* (Columbus, OH, 2021), 240–57, at 240–1.

[14] Schwyzer, *Archaeologies*, 2; Jennifer Wallace, *Digging the Dirt: The Archaeological Imagination* (London, 2004).

It has frequently been argued that premodernity in general, and the Middle Ages in particular, lacked an understanding of historical difference, that is, the ability to differentiate between the past and the present, as well as between different pasts, except in terms of mere chronological priority. Peter Burke's discussion of the development of a sense of anachronism illustrates this position quite succinctly: medieval people, he maintains, 'thought that the world had always been the way they saw it'.[15] Often, such views are founded on cursory interpretations of medieval chronicles, as well as on a simplistic notion of Christian salvation history as the historiographical master narrative of the Middle Ages, a *grand récit* whose teleology was based on divine providence and intervention rather than progress and historical development.[16] However, as Renée Trilling reminds us, 'not all historical consciousness was governed exclusively by an orthodox Christian teleology'.[17] Such a limited view of Christian theology neglects to take into account the variety of different perspectives on history that salvation history allows for, such as, for instance, the simultaneity of linear historical time with typological history, as discussed in Chapter 4. In addition, medieval theology itself was far from stable or consistent; and as Caroline Walker Bynum has demonstrated in her discussion of late medieval materiality, even interpretations that were accepted as orthodox doctrine were frequently contradicted on the level of actual practices.[18] To complicate matters further, literary texts need not necessarily conform to what is regarded as the received theological opinion – in fact, through the medium of representation, they may do the exact opposite, referencing that which eludes more explicit modes of theorisation and thereby opening up other, potentially non-orthodox, perspectives.

Accordingly, we should not burden our interpretations of texts with strict definitions of historical context as that which can and cannot be said or imagined at a given point in time. As Rita Felski observes:

> context does not automatically or inevitably trump text, because the very question of what counts as context and the merits of our explanatory schemes are often anticipated, explored, queried, expanded, or

---

[15] Peter Burke, 'The Sense of Anachronism from Petrarch to Poussin', in Chris Humphrey and W. M. Ormrod (eds), *Time in the Medieval World* (York, 2001), 157–73, at 158.

[16] See, for instance, Zachary Sayre Schiffman, *The Birth of the Past* (Baltimore, MD, 2011), 2–4.

[17] Renée R. Trilling, 'Ruins in the Realm of Thoughts: Reading as Constellation in Anglo-Saxon Poetry', *JEGP*, 108:2 (2009), 141–67, at 152.

[18] Caroline Walker Bynum, *Christian Materiality: An Essay on Religion in Late Medieval Europe* (New York, 2011), 30–1.

Introduction

reimagined in the words we read. The detachment of historical explanation is ruffled, even rattled, once we recognize that past texts have things to say on questions that matter to us, including the status of historical understanding.[19]

There is no single early medieval way of perceiving the past, just as there is no single modern way. As Joshua Davies remarks, 'the archive of the Middle Ages is defined by its diversity rather than its consistency'; medieval texts are 'ambivalent and inconsistent'.[20] Archaeological research similarly suggests that 'relationships between people and ancient monuments were widespread, varied, and long lived' during the early Middle Ages,[21] and this is at least partly reflected in the surviving literature of the period.

That said, I do not believe that there is a one-to-one correlation between literary works and contemporary practices involving items of material culture. Rather, I take the texts under discussion as particular responses to questions of materiality and temporality that may or may not have a counterpart in contemporaneous practices and discourses.[22] What the texts do reveal, I argue, are complex and richly variegated ways of understanding the relationship between past, present and future, and the temporal processes (not all of them linear) that both connect and divide them. Looking at material items from an 'archaeological perspective' allows them to conceive of temporality in potentially new and unforeseen ways, ways that may at times move beyond the established theological and historiographical models of early medieval Christianity. (Although, again, these latter are in themselves complex and allow for multiple perspectives, as will be explored in detail in Chapter 4.)

---

[19] Rita Felski, *The Limits of Critique* (Chicago, IL, 2015), 159–60.

[20] Joshua Davies, *Visions and Ruins: Cultural Memory and the Untimely Middle Ages* (Manchester, 2018), 12, 4.

[21] Sarah Semple, *Perceptions of the Prehistoric in Anglo-Saxon England: Religion, Ritual, and Rulership in the Landscape* (Oxford, 2013), 2.

[22] Alaric Hall similarly criticises the notion that texts can be regarded as straightforward expressions of a specific era's worldview, as this would necessarily entail a monolithic conception of society; Alaric Hall, *Elves in Anglo-Saxon England: Matters of Belief, Health, Gender and Identity* (Woodbridge, 2007), 8–9. The idea that different historical periods (and, by extension, cultures) are characterised by dominant 'epistemic' views or assumptions was most famously proposed by Michel Foucault in *The Order of Things*, although Foucault does admit the possibility of the coexistence of other forms of discourse that do not comply with the respective period's dominant episteme; see Michel Foucault, *The Order of Things: An Archaeology of the Human Sciences* (London, 2004); Foucault, *The Archaeology of Knowledge* (London, 2007).

Materiality and Temporality

There is something particularly evocative in the conjuncture of time and materiality that appears to make 'archaeological' artefacts an especially fruitful starting point for exploring questions of temporality and historical change. This, I suggest, has to do with the potentially greater life spans of many material objects in comparison to those of human beings – as Denis Ferhatović notes, 'artefacts often ensure survival of the trace of the human because they have much longer temporalities'.[23] Yet this does not necessarily mean that such objects provide access to the past; in fact, some of the works that I discuss – including *Beowulf*, *The Wanderer* and *The Ruin* – suggest that the very opposite is the case. In these texts, I will argue, it is precisely the inaccessibility of the past that is foregrounded by the respective material remains: beyond the ascription of great age, these objects signify above all the opacity of a past that refuses to disclose its secrets.

Old English poetry has an equivalent to Augustine's reference to 'giant' bones in the formulaic expression *eald enta geweorc* (and variants): 'ancient work of giants'. To a certain extent, this turn of phrase resonates with Augustine's discussion of the allegedly greater size of earlier human beings and the former existence of giants, and I will return to the question of the latters' identity in Chapters 2 and 3. More importantly, however, the formula is used with respect to ancient objects that are remarkable not only for their superior craftsmanship, but also for their improbable survival into the present. In several poems (*Maxims II*, *The Wanderer*, *The Ruin*, *Elene*, *Andreas*), the expression *enta geweorc* is used predominantly in conjunction with ancient structures built from stone, reminding us of Bede's reference to Roman buildings that were still observable due to the durability of their materials. Other objects, too, are described as 'the work of giants': in *Beowulf*, for instance, the expression is applied to an ancient sword and a hoard of treasure whose exact provenance has become obscured by the passing of time. What links all these items and marks them as 'archaeological' is that their use has been interrupted; they re-emerge in the present after having been, at least for a time, invisible to known history.

By contrast, many objects of everyday use appear to exist in a continual present in the minds of those who interact with them. As Ian Hodder points out, 'the notion that things are stable and fixed, at least inanimate

---

[23] Denis Ferhatović, *Borrowed Objects and the Art of Poetry: Spolia in Old English Verse* (Manchester, 2019), 8. Of course, the statement cannot be extended to material constellations in general, which, as Ian Hodder points out, are often extremely short-lived; see Ian Hodder, *Entangled: An Archaeology of the Relationships between Humans and Things* (Chichester, 2012), 5.

Introduction

material things, is widely assumed'.[24] He quotes Hannah Arendt, who argues that:

> it is this durability which gives the things of the world their relative independence from men who produced and use them, their 'objectivity' which makes them withstand, 'stand against' and endure, at least for a time, the voracious needs and wants of their living makers and users. From this viewpoint, the things of the world have the function of stabilizing human life, and their objectivity lies in the fact that [...] [we] can retrieve their sameness [...].[25]

This is mainly a question of perception, however. As new materialist thinkers such as Karen Barad or Jane Bennett emphasise, the material world is never stable, but itself in a process of continual change. Matter is never inert, it is intrinsically 'lively' (though not 'ensouled') or 'vibrant', and hence subject to the same processes of change as human bodies, albeit on a different timescale.[26] It is only because in the case of some materials, such as stone, these processes happen at such a slow rate as to be practically imperceptible to human observers, that the objects in question are thought of as inhabiting a state of stability:

> The stones, tables, technologies, words, and edibles that confront us as fixed are mobile, internally heterogeneous materials whose rate of speed and pace of change are *slow* compared to the duration and velocity of the human bodies participating in and perceiving them. 'Objects' appear as such because their becoming proceeds at a speed or a level below the threshold of human discernment.[27]

The inertness of certain objects is thus mainly a matter of perspective. Whether we acknowledge the relative age of an everyday object such as a knife or a hammer, or whether it exists for us in an apparent state of timelessness, depends on multiple factors, including said object's design, the presence of signs of wear and our personal relationship with it.

As Carolyn Dinshaw has demonstrated, human perceptions of time are always multiple and complex, and form part of processes of embodiment and subjectivity.[28] This is true also of Western modernity, despite the fact

---

[24] *Ibid.*, 4.

[25] Hannah Arendt, *The Human Condition* (Chicago, IL, 1958), 137.

[26] Jane Bennett, *Vibrant Matter: A Political Ecology of Things* (Durham, NC, 2010), viii, xvii; see also Karen Barad, *Meeting the Universe Halfway: Quantum Physics and the Entanglement of Matter and Meaning* (Durham, NC, 2007).

[27] Bennett, *Vibrant Matter*, 57–8.

[28] Carolyn Dinshaw, 'Temporalities', in Paul Strohm (ed.), *Middle English* (Oxford, 2007), 107–23, 109. See also Carolyn Dinshaw, *How Soon Is Now? Medieval Texts, Amateur Readers, and the Queerness of Time* (Durham, NC, 2012).

that historicism has tried to impose the notion of a single, homogenous and secular historical time, which modern Western subjects take for granted even as it contradicts their everyday experiences.[29] In her article on multiple temporalities, Dinshaw identifies the 'temporal heterogeneities' of a whole range of different experiences of time: first, the continuous 'now' of the fifteenth-century mystic Margery Kempe, which granted her direct access both to Christ's Passion and the future joys of heaven; second, the feeling of connectedness to the medieval mystic experienced by Kempe's twentieth-century editor, Hope Emily Allen; and third, Dinshaw's own relationship with both Kempe and Allen.[30] As bodies within time, her subjects are each tied to a specific 'here and now', but their inner sense of connectedness to earlier human beings makes them feel asynchronous, out of joint with their contemporary world. Dinshaw speaks of a 'sense of simultaneous belonging to one's own time as well as to other times, the balance between contemporaneity and difference, connection and distance', which she identifies as 'very delicate'.[31] These individual and highly subjective experiences of temporal synchronicity clash with the normative understanding of time as a linear process, which posits a temporal distance between the respective persons and events. According to Dinshaw, the discrepancy between the historical situatedness of her three subjects' bodies in linear time and their asynchronous experiences of temporality marks them as 'queer':

> A history that reckons in the most expansive way possible with how people exist in time, with what it feels like to be a body in time, or in multiple times, or out of time, is a queer history – whatever else it might be. Historicism is queer when it grasps that temporality itself raises the question of embodiment and subjectivity.[32]

This 'queerness' manifests itself, for instance, in the sense of alienation that her protagonists appear to feel and sometimes evoke in others. Dinshaw discusses Kempe's account of her own display of grief at seeing a pietà, a depiction of the Virgin Mary holding the dead Christ. A priest who witnesses the scene attempts to console Kempe: 'Damsel, Ihesu is ded long sithyn' ('Jesus is long since dead'). As Dinshaw notes, Kempe and the clergyman are divided by radically different perceptions of time, despite their historical contemporaneity: whereas to Kempe, the scene represented by the pietà is as vivid as if it were happening in the present moment, the

---

[29] Dipesh Chakrabarty, *Provincializing Europe: Postcolonial Thought and Historical Difference* (Princeton, NJ, 2000), 15, 22–3.

[30] Dinshaw, 'Temporalities'; the expression 'temporal heterogeneities' is found at 111.

[31] *Ibid.*, 119.

[32] *Ibid.*, 109.

Introduction

priest's reaction shows that Christian perceptions of sacred history, itself a narrative of historical progress, could easily grasp the distance in historical time separating the present moment from the biblical event. According to Dinshaw, the cleric may be intimating that the Church's preservation of direct access to the body of Christ should be consolation enough for Kempe: 'In the priest's world, time passes but the Church reclaims it; his words separate the past from the present and brandish it as an affirmation of institutional power.'[33] By contrast, Kempe's experience of the temporal immediacy of the historically distant moment of the crucifixion derives from a mystical sense of an eternal *now* that directly connects her to Christ's suffering.

As Dinshaw observes, similar 'asynchronous temporalities' (a term that she borrows from Ernst Bloch via Paul Strohm) can be observed within postcolonial societies.[34] They are the result of Western modernity's view of these societies as backward, archaic, on a lower level of historical development – a treatment famously described by Johannes Fabian as a 'denial of coevalness'.[35] Again, the perception of asynchrony depends on a notion of linear time, here understood as a history of progress according to which not all cultures reach the same cultural level at the same time. For instance, as Dipesh Chakrabarty has argued, due to the specific historical situation in India that led the elites to adopt and 'mimic' a certain version of Western modernity and its concept of a single, homogeneous and historicist time,[36] Indian culture itself is characterised by plural, contradictory temporalities. Drawing on Homi Bhabha's concept of the pedagogic and performative aspects of nationalism, Chakrabarty contrasts nationalist historiography in the pedagogic mode,[37] which 'mimics' Western historicist notions of history (and hence itself perceives Indian culture – or at least its non-elite components – as backward and non-modern), with the plural, 'antihistorical "histories"' of the subaltern classes and their everyday lives and actions. The latter, Chakrabarty explains, are 'organized – more often than not – along the axes of kinship, religion, and caste, and involving gods, spirits, and supernatural agents as actors alongside humans'.[38] From the perspective of nationalist historiography in the

[33] *Ibid.*, 108.
[34] *Ibid.*; Paul Strohm, *Theory and the Premodern Text* (Minneapolis, MN, 2000), 82; Ernst Bloch, 'Nonsynchronism and the Obligation to Its Dialectics', *New German Critique*, 11 (1977), 22–38.
[35] Johannes Fabian, *Time and the Other: How Anthropology Makes Its Object* (New York, 1983), 31.
[36] Chakrabarty, *Provincializing Europe*, 40–1.
[37] *Ibid.*, 10; Homi K. Bhabha, 'DissemiNation: Time, Narrative and the Margins of the Modern Nation', in *The Location of Culture* (London, 1994), 139–70.
[38] Chakrabarty, *Provincializing Europe*, 40, 11.

pedagogic mode, these subaltern practices appear anachronistic, even as they participate in shaping the cultural and political life of the country. However, Chakrabarty argues, this is not so much a conflict between elites and non-elites, but between different perceptions of the subaltern's status:

> The history and nature of political modernity in an excolonial country such as India [...] generates a tension between the two aspects of the subaltern or peasant as citizen. One is the peasant who has to be educated into the citizen and who therefore belongs to the time of historicism; the other is the peasant who, despite his or her lack of formal education, is already a citizen.[39]

Different perceptions of time need not result in a feeling of temporal asynchrony, however. Dinshaw cites Aron Gurevich's notion that all medieval people lived in two spheres simultaneously: the plane of local, transient life with its agrarian, genealogical and cyclical perceptions of time, and 'the plane of universal-historical events which are of decisive importance for the destinies of the world – the Creation, the birth and the Passion of Christ'.[40] Again, this is not simply a difference between elite and non-elite or institutional and private experiences of time, as the Church itself – to name only one obvious example – adhered both to linear, teleological accounts of history (as in the concept of salvation history, stretching from the Creation through the Incarnation to the Last Judgement) and to cyclic perceptions of time, as in the recurrent festivals and the liturgy of the ecclesiastical year.

Depending on the context, one and the same person may thus endorse very different notions of history and temporality, without these being necessarily perceived as being in conflict. Indeed, Hartmut Rosa points out that despite Western modernity's strong adherence to a singular narrative of linear historical development, for most of its subjects, 'everyday time has [...] a mostly repetitive and cyclical character'.[41] Both Rosa and Gurevich implicitly subscribe to the conventional dichotomy of 'linear' versus 'cyclical' time, which has frequently been invoked in narratives of progress, where it serves to contrast the modern with the premodern, pitting advanced versus retarded, Western versus non-Western and/or elite versus subaltern perceptions of time. Moreover, even though Rosa concedes that modern experiences of time, like premodern ones, are not necessarily homogeneous, Dinshaw's analysis demonstrates that the expe-

---

[39] *Ibid.*, 10.

[40] Dinshaw, 'Temporalities', 110. The quotation is from Aron J. Gurevich, *Categories of Medieval Culture* (London, 1985), 139.

[41] Hartmut Rosa, *Social Acceleration: A New Theory of Modernity*, trans. Jonathan Trejo-Mathys (New York, 2013), 8.

Introduction

rience of temporality involves a far greater spectrum of phenomena than linear and cyclical perceptions of time, including, for instance, Margery Kempe's radical sense of synchronicity upon encountering the depiction of the pietà, or the feeling of asynchronicity that pervades her relationship with contemporaneous society.

Multiple understandings and experiences of temporality such as these frequently involve and characterise human interactions with material objects. Bruno Latour has remarked on the essentially 'polytemporal' nature of human behaviour that always involves differently aged objects:

> I may use an electric drill, but I also use a hammer. The former is thirty-five years old, the latter hundreds of thousands. Will you see me as a DIY expert 'of contrasts' because I mix up gestures from different times? Would I be an ethnographic curiosity? On the contrary: show me an activity that is homogeneous from the point of view of the modern time. Some of my genes are 500 million years old, others 3 million, others 100,000 years, and my habits range in age from a few days to several thousand years.[42]

As Latour notes, the essentially polytemporal nature of our actions renders redundant the use of such labels as 'archaic' or 'advanced', because 'every cohort of contemporary elements may bring together elements from all times'.[43] Latour is speaking of object categories ('hammer', 'electric drill') and human interaction with said categories rather than individual arte-facts, but these latter are, of course, characterised by the same polytempo-rality. Topographic features like hills and rock formations are not usually perceived as immensely old, the result of imperceptible tectonic move-ments and drawn-out processes of erosion; instead, they are seen as time-less, unchanging features against which the events of quotidian life are measured. The same can apply, on a smaller scale, to some human-made features as well (such as buildings), whereas other entities, whose pro-cesses of material change occur at a much higher speed, may by contrast appear ephemeral, such as bubbles or many edibles. Different material configurations can thus inhabit different temporalities, even when viewed at the same moment in time. Jonathan Gil Harris discusses the potential discrepancy between the inherent polychronicity of objects – that is, their ability to reference different moments of their own histories – and the ways in which they are perceived by human beings, who may choose to acknowledge only a single one of these different moments. In so doing,

---

[42] Bruno Latour, *We Have Never Been Modern*, trans. Catherine Porter (Cambridge, MA, 1993), 75.
[43] *Ibid.*

he invokes Michel Serres's distinction between the 'polychronic' and the 'multitemporal':

> What may at first seem like a pair of synonyms for 'polytemporal' are, on closer inspection, two subtly different concepts, and this difference points to a significant disjunction in the meanings of 'time'. 'Time' can refer to a moment, period, or age – the punctual date of chronology. [...] But 'time' can also refer to an *understanding* of the temporal relations among past, present, and future. [...] Serres's notion of the polychronic draws on the first, chronological meaning of time in asserting that objects collate many different moments, as suggested by Latour's polytemporal toolbox and genes. By contrast, Serres's notion of the multitemporal evokes the second meaning of time. In its polychronicity, an object can prompt many different understandings and experiences of temporality – that is, of the relations between now and then, old and new, before and after.[44]

It is only when we acknowledge the object's polychronicity, its ability to connect past, present and future in multiple ways, that our perspective becomes multitemporal.

In support of his argument, Harris cites the polytemporal nature of 'Renaissance' objects that 'were not of the Renaissance as such but survivals from an older time',[45] with monastic garments recycled as props in early modern public playhouses and London's still-visible Roman walls serving as cases in point. Such things, Harris goes on to explain, 'are often shrouded in anachronism' – not merely because they are travellers from the past or because they have been coded as temporally obsolete and hence socially unacceptable, but 'because objects of material culture are often saturated with the unmistakable if frequently faint imprints of many times'.[46] In contrast to instances where these imprints are usually ignored in everyday life – as with topographical features or buildings whose relative age is not usually perceived by their inhabitants – the objects discussed by Harris are defined precisely by their distinct historicity, even though that historicity is, in fact, multiple. Alexander Nagel and Christopher S. Wood have metaphorically referred to such objects as 'relics',[47] a category that clearly encompasses the 'archaeological' objects discussed in the present study.

---

[44] Jonathan Gil Harris, *Untimely Matter in the Time of Shakespeare* (Philadelphia, PA, 2009), 3–4; Michel Serres, with Bruno Latour, *Conversations on Science, Culture and Time*, trans. Roxanne Lapidus (Ann Arbor, MI, 1995), 60.

[45] Harris, *Untimely Matter*, 3.

[46] *Ibid.*, 7.

[47] Alexander Nagel and Christopher S. Wood, *Anachronic Renaissance* (New York, 2010), 8.

Introduction

As the foregoing discussion has shown, it is not necessarily the physical characteristics of an object that render it 'archaeological' – although these may play a role, too – but rather the perspective applied to it: the museum exhibit appears as an object of the past not because it is old, but because the context in which it is displayed (usually) suggests to the observer that its main temporal point of reference lies in the past. In contrast to objects in everyday use, which seem to exist in a continuous present until they break or are superseded, historical artefacts are perceived only through the prism of their past uses, their datedness, their fragmentary state. Once the primary point of reference lies in the past, the temporal dimension becomes primary; the object becomes artefact, the structure monument. This mechanism presupposes one of two related but opposing moves on the part of the observer: either a consideration of the temporal processes continually shaping and re-shaping the object, or a (re)construction of a specific point in its past. Both moves are tied to very different views of history: whereas the former is diachronic in a processual sense and depends on a notion of the passing of time, the latter is synchronic in that it privileges a single historical moment over all others. Often (but not always), this will be a moment that is supposed to reflect the earliest or 'original' meaning or usage of the object in question. In essence, this second move stems from a historicist desire to (re)construct an originary moment that, from a diachronic perspective, is never quite tangible: since every object is always in the process of changing, a synchronic perspective can never be more than a simplifying construct or, at best, a snapshot of a mere moment in time.

Nonetheless, historicist modernity has all too often allowed this second perspective to stand as the only one possible.[48] This is reflected, for instance, in philology's search for origins, its attempt to reconstruct an 'original' form, meaning or context,[49] and similar notions continue to haunt other disciplines in the field of the humanities, such as archaeology or art history, despite the advent of theories designed to address this imbalance. Museologists have increasingly begun to take into account the multiple meanings that exhibits may have acquired over the course of their respective histories – through adaptation, reconfiguration and repurposing – as well as the alternative histories suppressed by a narrow focus on a single historical context.[50] As objects travel through time and space,

---

[48] See further Rita Felski's critique of current literary criticism's tendency to delimit discussions of texts to their 'original' historical contexts in Rita Felski, '"Context Stinks!"', *New Literary History*, 42:4 (2011), 573–91, printed in revised form in Felski, *Limits of Critique*, 151–85.

[49] See, for instance, Allen J. Frantzen, *Desire for Origins: New Language, Old English, and Teaching the Tradition* (New Brunswick, NJ, 1990).

[50] See, for instance, Isabelle Dolezalek's discussion of the Ashmolean Museum,

they may be used and reused in different settings, thereby acquiring new meanings. Hence, any perspective that focuses on only one of these settings necessarily supresses others, whereas taking into consideration more than one temporal context draws attention to the respective objects' inherent polychronicity in the sense proposed by Serres and Harris. That said, in the final analysis, the museum exhibit is, of course, always contemporaneous with the observer, even if they may prefer to suspend recognition of the shared moment in order to construct an anachronistic – and thus temporally asynchronous or plural – situation in which the object appears to be speaking from the past. This perspective – that of the modern subject reaching out to an object allegedly still located in the past via its reconstructed meaning, context or appearance – resembles Dinshaw's notion of 'asynchronous temporalities', and it is precisely this perspective that we encounter time and again in the texts examined in this study.

My choice of delimiting the scope of this study to texts written in Old English is in part an artificial one. Not only were Latin and vernacular works copied and read side by side and in the same literary milieux,[51] but Latin texts produced in early medieval Britain arguably display a similar or even greater interest in the material remains of the past. In a different context, I have already investigated the early eighth-century Anglo-Latin *Vita Sancti Guthlaci*'s engagement with such remains, and similar studies could be conducted for other Latin works such as Bede's *Historia ecclesiastica* or the various *Vitae Sancti Cuthberti*. What distinguishes these texts from the ones examined in this study, however, is the way that they link (often explicitly) their discussion of 'archaeological' objects to contemporary religious and political issues. Thus, I have argued elsewhere that Felix's *Vita Sancti Guthlaci* uses the traditional hagiographical motif of the saint's sojourn in what appears to be a prehistoric burial mound as a means of bringing up and problematising Guthlac's relationship as an 'English' saint with Britain's displaced or subjugated 'Celtic' population.[52] The fact that the two Old English poetic retellings of the Guthlac material

---

whose exhibition strategy of 'crossing cultures, crossing time' seeks to overcome the more usual contextual isolation; Isabelle Dolezalek, 'Alternative Narratives: Transcultural Interventions in the Permanent Display of the Museum für Islamische Kunst', in Vera Beyer, Isabelle Dolezalek and Sophia Vassilopoulou (eds), *Objects in Transfer: A Transcultural Exhibition Trail through the Museum für Islamische Kunst in Berlin* (Berlin, 2016), 25–35, at 27.

[51] See Christopher Abram, 'In Search of Lost Time: Aldhelm and *The Ruin*', *Quaestio*, 1 (2000), 2–44, at 42–3.

[52] Jan-Peer Hartmann, 'Monument Reuse in Felix's *Vita Sancti Guthlaci*', *MÆ*, 88:2 (2019), 230–64.

Introduction

– the Exeter Book *Guthlac A* and *B* (not otherwise discussed in the present study) – eschew this sociopolitical context arguably supports my point.

The four chapters assembled here explore different ways of perceiving temporal difference and historical change through literary representations of material objects. Although the texts discussed in this study are, to echo Davies, in themselves ambiguous and diverse,[53] often representing more than one mode of understanding time-related processes, I have dedicated each chapter to one dominant theme, partly building upon the preceding ones and gaining in complexity. Given the notorious difficulties in dating many Old English texts, especially poetic ones, and given that it is not my aim to establish a diachronic perspective on different perceptions of time (let alone a teleological history of mentalities), such a thematic structure (which is, of course, only one among many possible ones) appears to me more advantageous than attempting to construct a chronological order between the texts.

The chapters' themes, then, are based on the different kinds of engagement with archaeological objects that the texts suggest, and on the different perceptions and experiences of time that they foreground.

Chapter 1 deals with the notion of historical change as framed in terms of replacement or supersession, and the political uses to which such a concept of history can be put. The Old English narrative poem *Elene*, I argue, promotes a theory of historical change along the lines of the *topos* of *translatio*, a concept developed in classical antiquity to describe the transfer of an object or an abstract quality from one place to another. In addition to the spatial movement that this term implies, the transfer also has a temporal dimension: it signals a change in the current state of affairs, a transformation that can be construed into a temporal relation of 'before' and 'after'. This is most famously the case with the classical model of *translatio imperii*, which posits successive transfers of political power from one 'empire' to another. *Elene*, I argue, uses its story of the discovery and excavation of the True Cross by Elene (Helena), mother to the Roman emperor Constantine I, to construct a similar transfer of spiritual and sapiential authority from Jerusalem to Rome in parallel with the material transfer of some of the cross's relics to Rome. At the same time, the imperial behaviour displayed by the emperor's mother towards Jerusalem's inhabitants emphasises the political *translatio* through which Rome has achieved its present position of hegemonic power: in *Elene*, the concepts of *translatio imperii* and *translatio religionis* go hand in hand and cannot be separated.

The imperial aspect of Elene's visit is further stressed by the fact that Elene's eastward journey to Jerusalem traces (at least in part, and in reverse

---

[53] See Davies, *Visions*, 4.

order) the westward movement of the *translatio imperii*: according to this concept, imperial rule (*imperium*) had moved, in successive steps, from the Assyrians in the East to the Romans in the West. The poem's allusion to Elene's visits to various historical battle sites (*herefeldas*) is rendered especially poignant by her later reference to the Trojan War – the very event to which Virgil's *Aeneid* traced the origins of the Roman Empire, with many medieval foundation narratives later following suit.

Intriguingly, Elene's reference to the Trojan War gives rise to a discussion concerning the conditions of historical knowledge that implicitly confronts two different forms of 'archaeological' discourse, a 'religious' and a 'secular' one, each characterised by its own form of temporality. Whereas the former, seemingly supported by the poem's plot, posits that human beings are incapable of garnering historical insight from material remains alone and require divine assistance to interpret the traces of the past, Elene's quest for the material remains of the Christian and non-Christian past in furtherance of her son's imperial claims acknowledges, at least implicitly, the possibility of coming to an understanding of historical processes by studying the traces that they left behind – if only to construct historical difference for the sake of political ambitions.

Taking up *Elene*'s themes of appropriation and the potential of material remains to afford historical insights, Chapter 2 examines two highly canonical Old English poems, *The Wanderer* and *The Ruin*, which both portray forms of material reuse and repurposing across different historical strata, albeit without sharing *Elene*'s overt interest in the political utility of appropriated relics. Traditionally, scholarship tended to treat these poems primarily as expressions of the theme of worldly transience, an interpretation supported by *The Wanderer*'s final message that constancy is to be found in Heaven alone. Yet it is my contention that both *The Wanderer* and *The Ruin* project a more complex temporal panorama in which descriptions of material remains used and reused over successive generations and across different cultural contexts open up a temporal perspective that acknowledges multiple layers of pastness.

While *The Wanderer* refers to the possibility of material reuse only obliquely in suggesting that the strange serpentine patterns painted on a wall may stem from a little-understood past, *The Ruin* describes the history of a now-ruined city over a sequence of many generations and successive kingdoms without, however, being able to locate the latter in definite historical moments. Both poems, then, imagine forms of material reuse independent of actual historical knowledge or understanding. As I will argue, the poetic formula *enta geweorc* [the work of giants], which both texts employ in reference to the respective structures' origins, emphasises the alterity of the past, thereby drawing attention to the problematic nature of a historical transmission that leaves later observers to imagine the past in merely the most general and conventional terms. And yet, in spite

Introduction

of the conventionality of the poems' vignettes of imagined past life, the juxtaposition of the present with a historical fantasy not only underlines the notion of change over time, but indeed showcases the architectural structures' inherent polychronicity, their belonging to and being shaped by different moments in time.

Their similar treatment of the fragmentary nature of historical knowledge notwithstanding, the two poems differ considerably in their assessment of the meaning and significance that archaeological remains may afford to the present. *The Wanderer*'s images of ruined and ultimately incomprehensible structures, I suggest, are based on a temporal perspective that is more traditionally Christian in its eschatological focus. Even so, it does not primarily revolve around the central idea of the world's final destruction, but rather sketches a future in which the ruins of the past amount to little more than meaningless jumble. In *The Ruin*, by contrast, an eschatological perspective is present, but plays a minor role at best; here, the poem's appreciation of the aesthetic value of material remains endows the archaeological objects it describes with historical legitimacy despite or, indeed, *because* of the fact that their precise meaning and history are unknown to the present. *The Ruin*'s more empathetic perspective, in which the assessment of archaeological remains is based on an aesthetic sensibility, demonstrates, I argue, that the past can be made meaningful to the present without denying its inherent alterity.

Chapter 3, meanwhile, explores the question of historical alterity through the lens of the concept of anachronism. Many modern historians and philosophers of time locate a culture's historical consciousness – that is, its awareness of historical difference – in its ability to discern and theorise instances of anachronicity. Such an awareness, according to these scholars' understanding, does not become manifest in the creative anachronic imagination that Nagel and Wood observe in Renaissance art,[54] but rather in acts of radical periodisation that divide history into clearly defined segments in which individual phenomena are placed in a sequence defined by their alleged appearance or disappearance. While, generally speaking, medieval texts are not interested in basing their concept of history on such a radical notion of sequentiality, I argue in this chapter that works such as the anonymous Old English version of the Legend of the Seven Sleepers or *Beowulf* are nevertheless capable of grasping and problematising a concept of anachronism based on the notion of 'not belonging to a certain time'. Both texts, I propose, draw attention to the historical and ethical problems involved in the practice of assigning entities to certain historical periods while simultaneously denying them the legitimacy to exist in others.

---

[54] Nagel and Wood, *Anachronic Renaissance*.

Remains of the Past in Old English Literature

When, in the Legend of the Seven Sleepers, the eponymous saints wake from a miraculous slumber that has lasted from the mid-third to the mid-fifth century, they experience a pronounced feeling of asynchrony with the world into which they have been transported. This asynchrony is also expressed in their eventual fate: their theological purpose fulfilled, the saints depart from the sphere of everyday life, effectively becoming relics enshrined in their cave. In *Beowulf*, too, the anachronistic existence of Grendel and his mother, who should have been killed during the Flood, is brought to an end, as is, in due course, the heroic protagonist's own. The poem suggests that in a history based on radical periodisation, the practice of assigning objects and beings to specific historical compartments necessarily entails their eventual obsolescence, and hence the need for them to disappear. *Beowulf*'s monsters, anachronistic already at the point that they enter the narrative, have to be killed off in order for history to progress. In a similar fashion, the archaeological artefacts so famously highlighted by the poem are rendered useless either through the damage wrought by the passing of time, or, more often than not, by the very efforts of the characters to salvage them. Even as the poem's monsters and archaeological objects insist on their polychronic status by forcing their way into the present, this present is intent on keeping them confined to the past by denying them their right of existence in the here and now of the narrative, a parallel treatment underscored by the fact that most of the items in question are either directly or indirectly associated with monstrous creatures.

In both the Legend of the Seven Sleepers and *Beowulf*, the question of anachronistic survival is linked to the preservation of historical knowledge. This is particularly noteworthy in *Beowulf*, which suggests that knowledge of the past is ephemeral and precarious, but can also increase as time goes by – for instance, through the introduction of new cultural ingredients such as the Christian historiography that would have been familiar to the poem's narrator and original audience. Thus, even as the narrator is free to associate Grendel and his mother with the Bible's prediluvian giants, this identification is impossible for the inhabitants of the heroic world depicted in the poem, who, as pagans, are ignorant of biblical history. This leads to the ironical situation that the poem's audience is aware of the fact that Grendel and his mother ought not to exist after the Flood, whereas the characters lack the requisite historical knowledge to realise the monsters' anachronistic state: for them, the Grendelkin constitute an existential rather than a chronological problem. But while in this case, the poem's narrator and audience enjoy the benefit of hindsight bestowed by a more enlightened later period, there are also passages in the poem in which it draws attention to instances where historical information has been lost, for example regarding the giants' sword's original owner or

Introduction

the identity of the people whose treasure was buried by the similarly nameless 'last survivor'.

If anachronistic survival has to end in order for historical progress to resume its course, how does this affect the transmission and preservation of historical knowledge, and in how far is it necessary for new insights to occur? If the past must be shut out and buried, how is historical knowledge possible at all? Even though *Beowulf* ultimately fails to answer these questions, it nevertheless exposes the violent mechanisms by which this kind of historical narrative determines that everything will in time become obsolete and hence anachronistic, including the doomed heroic world it depicts and, ultimately, the poem itself. And yet, even as *Beowulf* through its protagonist manages to bring closure to the past, the fact that the whole plot is characterised by the sudden and unexpected reappearance of long-forgotten objects and beings highlights the problematic nature of periodisation: while on the one hand, the monsters and artefacts, by their very temporal associations, mark the boundaries between past and present, and indeed between the different periods drawn up by the poem, they simultaneously overstep these boundaries and thereby question the validity of the cultural practice of periodisation by drawing attention to the anachronic permeability of its constructs.

Discussing three Old English poetic texts – *Elene, The Dream of the Rood* and the runic inscription on the Ruthwell Monument – along with the different ways in which they exploit the tension-ridden interplay between material-historical and symbolic-representational perceptions, the fourth and final chapter returns to the narrative of the discovery of the True Cross and the attendant temporal perspectives. In addition to the 'secular' and 'religious' forms of archaeological discourse discussed in the first chapter, *Elene* highlights the divergent temporalities of the symbolic and material dimensions of the cross, a tension I attempt to capture through Erich Auerbach's juxtaposition of figural and literal history.

As a polysemous Christian symbol, the cross is not bound to any specific point in time; its relevance to salvation history can be extended to either side of the temporal spectrum from the moment of the crucifixion. From this perspective, the cross's significance can indeed be regarded as timeless in that it forms part of God's extratemporal eternity. By contrast, the discovery of a 'true' cross invokes the material existence of a physical object situated in a highly specific historical time span. The True Cross constitutes a singular material entity, a contact relic hallowed by Christ's blood and therefore granting direct access to God – even in the plurality of the relics produced from it, which nevertheless refer back to the singular object used to crucify Christ. Its existence in historical time makes possible a biographical perspective that is successfully exploited in *The Dream of the Rood*'s first-person account of the history of the cross and its parallel in the Ruthwell inscription. By veiling the speaker's identity, however,

23

the inscription opens up an ambiguous space in which that speaker can be identified both with the absent True Cross and the present monument representing it, suggesting that either identification is, ultimately, only possible through the medium of fiction. The representational character of the Ruthwell Monument draws attention to the symbolic aspect of the cross, which only exists in material manifestations that need not, however, be identical with each other. A figural interpretation of the semiotic relationship between the True Cross and its representation makes it possible to see both entities as historically and materially distinct while also acknowledging the existence of a figural identity or accord between them, thereby allowing the representation to partake in the spiritual significance of the True Cross and thus to become a holy object itself. In so doing, the figural relationship establishes a second, non-linear temporality besides the linear, historical one of the True Cross and its various representations, which it complements but also complicates. The three texts discussed in this chapter acknowledge the existence of these two temporal schemes, but also reveal the tension between them.

It goes without saying that the potential of archaeological motifs and narratives to highlight diverging temporal perspectives is not restricted to the texts discussed in this study, nor is it a prerogative of Old English literature alone. Accordingly, the concluding section traces some of the themes pursued in the preceding chapters into the later Middle Ages in general, and to the Middle English poem *Saint Erkenwald* in particular. As my brief discussion of this text demonstrates, archaeological narratives continued to serve as a vehicle for the exploration of temporal perceptions, drawing heavily on the astounding capacity of archaeological objects to produce meaning in the present. The engagement with the material remains of the past made it possible for medieval texts to negotiate the relationship between past, present and future through aesthetic means, and to develop complex and nuanced responses to questions of materiality and temporality that allowed them to conceptualise not merely history, but indeed the very processes by which historical thought operates.

1

Excavating the Cross in *Elene*

In August 1873, Heinrich Schliemann – businessman, antiquarian, amateur archaeologist – publicly announced that he had found King Priam's treasure during excavations at Hisarlık, a hill in an area that had been identified, since antiquity, as the site of ancient Troy.[1] On 31 May, Schliemann reports, he discovered a sizable copper artefact behind which he could discern the shimmer of gold:

> Behind the latter [wall] I exposed at a depth of 8 to 9 m the Trojan circuit-wall as it continues from the Scaean gate, and in excavating further on this wall, right next to the house of Priam, I came across a large copper object of the most remarkable shape, which attracted my attention all the more as I thought I saw gold behind it. On the copper object lay a stratum, 1½ to 1⅓ m thick, hard as stone, of red ash and calcined debris, on which rested the aforementioned fortification-wall, 1 m 80 cm thick and 6 m high. The wall was composed of large stones and earth and must date to the earliest period after the destruction of Troy. In order to withdraw the treasure from the greed of my workmen and to rescue it for science, the utmost speed was necessary, and although it was still not yet breakfast-time, I immediately had 'paidos' called – a word of uncertain origin that has passed over into Turkish and is here used instead of ἀνάπαυϐις or break. While my workmen were eating and resting, I cut out the treasure with a large knife. It was impossible to do this without the most strenuous exertions and the most fearful risk to my life, for the large fortification-wall, which I had to undermine, threatened at every moment to fall down on me. But the sight of so many objects, each one of which is of inestimable value for science, made me foolhardy and I had no thought of danger. The removal of the treasure, however, would have been impossible without the help of my dear wife, who stood always ready to pack in her shawl and carry away the objects I cut out.[2]

[1] Joachim Latacz, *Troia und Homer: Der Weg zur Lösung eines alten Rätsels*, 6th edn (Leipzig, 2010), 47–8.

[2] 'Hinter der letztern [Mauer] legte ich in 8 bis 9 Meter Tiefe die vom Skaeischen Thor weiter gehende trojanische Ringmauer bloss und stiess beim Weitergraben auf dieser Mauer und unmittelbar neben dem Hause des Priamos auf einen grossen kupfernen Gegenstand höchst merkwürdiger Form, der um so mehr meine Aufmerksamkeit auf sich zog, als ich hinter demselben Gold

Remains of the Past in Old English Literature

In Schliemann's account, the act of archaeological excavation bears all the traits of the heroic: the lone excavator, defying life-threatening adversities to unearth the treasures of the past, saving them from the grasp of his native labourers for later scholarly investigation, aided only by his faithful wife, who supports the clandestine endeavour in appropriately ladylike manner.[3] According to Sarah Salih, 'archaeology lends itself to

---

zu bemerken glaubte. Auf dem kupfernen Gegenstand ruhte eine 1½ bis 1¾ Meter dicke steinfeste Schicht von rother Asche und calcinirten Trümmern, auf welcher die vorerwähnte 1 Meter 80 Centimeter dicke, 6 Meter hohe Festungsmauer lastete, die aus grossen Steinen und Erde bestand und aus der ersten Zeit nach der Zerstörung Trojas stammen muss. Um den Schatz der Habsucht meiner Arbeiter zu entziehen und ihn für die Wissenschaft zu retten, war die allergrösste Eile nöthig, und, obgleich es noch nicht Frühstückszeit war, so liess ich doch sogleich "païdos" (ein ins Türkische übergegangenes Wort ungewisser Abkunft, welches hier anstatt ἀνάπαυϭις oder Ruhezeit gebraucht wird) ausrufen, und während meine Arbeiter assen und ausruhten, schnitt ich den Schatz mit einem grossen Messer heraus, was nicht ohne die allergrösste Kraftanstrengung und die furchtbarste Lebensgefahr möglich war, denn die grosse Festungsmauer, welche ich zu untergraben hatte, drohte jeden Augenblick auf mich einzustürzen. Aber der Anblick so vieler Gegenstände, von denen jeder einzelne einen unermesslichen Werth für die Wissenschaft hat, machte mich tollkühn und ich dachte an keine Gefahr. Die Fortschaffung des Schatzes wäre mir aber unmöglich geworden ohne die Hülfe meiner lieben Frau, die immer bereit stand, die von mir herausgeschnittenen Gegenstände in ihren Shawl zu packen und fortzutragen.' Heinrich Schliemann, *Trojanische Alterthümer: Bericht über die Ausgrabungen in Troja* (Leipzig, 1874), 289–90; the translation is from David A. Traill, 'Schliemann's discovery of "Priam's treasure": A Re-examination of the Evidence', *Journal of Hellenic Studies*, 104 (1984), 96–115, at 101–2. A slightly revised version of the account was published, in English, in Henry [Heinrich] Schliemann, *Ilios: The City and Country of the Trojans; The Results of Researches and Discoveries on the Site of Troy and throughout the Troad in the Years 1871–72–73–78–79, including an Autobiography of the Author* (London, 1880), 40–1.

3   Schliemann describes his wife's role in the excavations: 'I made my way to the Dardanelles, together with my wife, Sophia Schliemann, who is a native of Athens and a warm admirer of Homer, and who, with glad enthusiasm, joined me in executing the great work' (Schliemann, *Ilios*, 21). In this account and Schliemann's later, book-length autobiography (where the same passage is found on page 3), Sophia evinces all the enthusiasm and selflessness initially shown by Casaubon's Dorothea in George Eliot's *Middlemarch*. His second wife, and thirty years his junior, Sophia Engastroménou came to Schliemann's attention when he asked his friend and teacher in Greek, Theokletos Vimpos, bishop of Athens and Sophia's uncle, to help him find a suitable wife who would be able to support him during his excavations. Unlike Dorothea, who despairs over the impossible task of bringing to fruition Casaubon's ambitious project, Sophia Schliemann acted out her role as Schliemann's ever-helpful aide-de-camp to the end, continuing to spread her husband's fame after his death by

Excavating the Cross in Elene

narration in the heroic mode'[4] – a claim she supports by citing archaeologist Cornelius Holtorf's observation that

> making archaeological discoveries is a literary theme that has […] often been employed to tell the stories both of archaeologists' lives and of the history of archaeology. In this perspective, the archaeologist is a passionate and totally devoted adventurer and explorer who conquers ancient sites and artifacts, thereby pushing forward the frontiers of our knowledge about the past. The associated narratives resemble those of the stereotypical hero who embarks on a quest to which he is fully devoted, is tested in the field, makes a spectacular discovery, and finally emerges as the virtuous man (or, exceptionally, woman) when the quest is fulfilled.[5]

Schliemann's self-portrayal fits this type of heroic narrative perfectly. But at the same time, the hero of Schliemann's account is also an enlightened researcher, whose pioneering work is performed solely in the interest of science: indeed, at this point in the narrative, the hero-archaeologist's selfless undertaking has finally yielded indisputable material evidence that Homer's account was 'true' – or at least, that was what Schliemann himself, and great parts of the eager public, wished to believe.

Schliemann's desire to match Homer's description of the Trojan War to the material remains he encountered in Hisarlık is evident throughout his writings. In his autobiography, published posthumously by his second wife Sophia, Schliemann traces his quest to discover and excavate Troy to his childhood fascination with the siege and destruction of the city in his father's retellings of the Homeric epics. He recounts a touching episode in which his seven-year-old self takes an illustration of the burning city's wall in Georg Ludwig Jerrer's *Weltgeschichte für Kinder* [Universal History for Children] as evidence that at least some of Troy's material remains were still visible: how else could Jerrer have been able to depict the scene so accurately? Unimpressed, his father replies: 'Mein Sohn, […] das ist nur ein erfundenes Bild' [My son, […] that is merely a fanciful picture].[6] But

---

giving public lectures about his work as well as completing his autobiography, published in 1892. Intriguingly, the story about Sophia clandestinely removing the artefacts in her shawl is untrue, as Heinrich Schliemann later admitted: Sophia was with her family in Athens at the time; see Caroline Moorehead, *The Lost Treasures of Troy* (London, 1994), 133.

4   Sarah Salih, 'Found Bodies: The Living, the Dead, and the Undead in the Broad Medieval Present', in Jan-Peer Hartmann and Andrew James Johnston (eds), *Material Remains: Reading the Past in Medieval and Early Modern British Literature* (Columbus, OH, 2021), 21–37, at 22.

5   Cornelius Holtorf, *From Stonehenge to Las Vegas: Archaeology as Popular Culture* (Walnut Creek, CA, 2005), 55.

6   Heinrich Schliemann, *Heinrich Schliemann's Selbstbiographie: Bis zu seinem Tode*

Remains of the Past in Old English Literature

Schliemann is undeterred: if Troy did indeed boast such massive walls as the account suggests, he reasons, some remnants at least must have withstood the passage of time; in turn, matching these material remains to the descriptions in the Homeric epics would provide unshakable proof of Homer's truthfulness. More than forty years later, it seemed that Schliemann had finally accomplished his dream:

> It had become Schliemann's purpose in life to uncover the scenes of the Homeric songs with the help of pickaxe and spade. That a wondrous true story had played out at the sites of the legend – of this, his persever-ance had now given full proof.[7]

Contemporary archaeologists were quick to question both Schliemann's methods (which sometimes involved outright forgery) and his conclu-sions (informed less by contemporary state-of-the-art scholarship than by romantic readings of the classics) – and a few years later, Schliemann himself had to admit that the treasure he had found predated the pre-sumed date of the Trojan War by around a thousand years.[8]

Nevertheless, Schliemann's excavation and the way he presented it to the public – in a quick succession of often contradictory accounts – proved to be a defining moment in the history of modern archaeology: the moment when archaeology ceased to be the preoccupation of an exclusive band of gentleman-scholars, and turned into a discipline capable, more than any other, of providing an avid and information-hungry public both with 'facts' about the past and – just as importantly – with stories of adventure, perseverance and reward. Archaeology spawned a whole industry of popular, sometimes sensationalist narratives of spectacular archaeological

---

vervollständigt, ed. Sophie Schliemann (Leipzig, 1892), 5. Schliemann gives the same story in *Ilios*, 3, whence the translation.

[7] 'Schliemann's Lebenszweck war es geworden, mit Hacke und Spaten die Schauplätze der homerischen Gesänge aufzudecken. Dass eine wundersame wahrhafte Geschichte an den Stätten der Sage gespielt hatte, dafür hatte nun seine Beharrlichkeit den vollen Beweis erbracht' (Schliemann, *Selbstbiographie*, 62–3).

[8] For a discussion of Schliemann's manipulation of finds and his at times cavalier attitude towards facts, see David A. Traill, *Schliemann of Troy: Treasure and Deceit* (London, 1997). As D. F. Easton notes, even within Schliemann's own dating scheme, the treasure he had found clearly belonged to a different layer than the wall he had excavated, since it had been 'deposited in the top of the destruction-debris outside it. To Schliemann, who wanted it to belong to Priam's Troy, this must have been troublesome. [...] Schliemann overcame his problem by rationalizing the find-spot a metre or two to the North and saying, in his later publications, that it had been found ON the citadel wall.' D. F. Easton, 'Priam's Gold: The Full Story', *Anatolian Studies*, 44 (1994), 221–43, at 223.

Excavating the Cross in Elene

discoveries, such as Howard Carter's excavation of Tutankhamun's tomb or Hiram Bingham's of Machu Picchu, and provided the raw materials for fictional works from Tintin to Indiana Jones.[9] Accounts such as these – from the well-informed journalistic to the outright fantastic – continue to inform the image of the discipline to the present day.[10] Archaeology's alleged capacity for corroborating – and potentially correcting – written history is deeply engrained in its public perception and habitually reinforced both in contemporary fiction and media coverage, most notably in well-publicised cases such as the discovery of the Nebra Sky Disc in Saxony-Anhalt or the 2012 excavation of Richard III's bones under a Leicester car park.[11]

But it is perhaps just as intriguing to note the degree to which such modern archaeological fantasies – including Schliemann's own – tend to resemble another strand of archaeological narrative; namely, that of the

---

[9] One of the most influential works about spectacular archaeological discoveries is C. W. Ceram's 1949 *Götter, Gräber und Gelehrte: Roman der Archäologie*, which was translated into more than twenty-five languages (including into English, under the title *Gods, Graves and Scholars*) and sold more than five million copies, according to Wikipedia's article <https://en.wikipedia.org/wiki/Gods,_Graves_and_Scholars> [accessed 1 August, 2023]. On Troy's prominent role in the public perception of modern archaeology and its role as a European *lieu de mémoire*, see Latacz, *Troia*, 37.

[10] Leo Deuel notes that Schliemann's 'retouched self-image' as a self-denying idealist 'has by now become so enshrined in the annals of archaeology that it is reverently invoked not just by popularizers but by latter-day archaeologists who have come to look up to Schliemann as one of the masters – and patron saints – of their discipline'. Leo Deuel (ed.), *Memoirs of Heinrich Schliemann: A Documentary Portrait Drawn from His Autobiographical Writings, Letters, and Excavation Reports* (New York, 1977), 1–2. The latter assertion probably does not hold for most professional archaeologists today; still, popularised accounts of adventurous excavations such as Schliemann's at Hisarlık or Carter's in the Valley of the Kings continue to play a role in triggering an early interest in the discipline for some students, just as there are a number of medievalists whose career was launched by reading the works of J. R. R. Tolkien.

[11] The former involved archaeological looting and a spectacular recovery at the hands of the Swiss police, with Saxony-Anhalt's Director of Archaeology, Harald Meller, acting as a decoy (a story Meller recounts to great effect in one of his books about the Sky Disc); see Harald Meller and Kai Michel, *Die Himmelsscheibe von Nebra: Der Schlüssel zu einer untergegangenen Welt im Herzen Europas* (Berlin, 2018), 24–51. Meller and Michel see the Sky Disc as evidence not only for far-ranging cultural contacts (including with ancient Egypt and Babylon), but also for the existence of a Bronze Age proto-state in today's Middle Germany, which would imply a level of cultural sophistication far beyond what is usually ascribed to the region's cultures at the time. For a discussion of how Richard III's mortal remains have been repeatedly invoked as a corrective to Shakespeare's 'biased account' in *Richard III*, see Schwyzer, 'Return', 89–90.

medieval *inventio*.[12] *Inventiones* describe the discovery or rediscovery of a saint's relics, usually related as a brief episode within the larger framework of a hagiographical narrative. The *inventio* is arguably the most widespread archaeological motif in medieval literature. Just like modern popular accounts of archaeological discovery, *inventiones* serve both to authenticate and to entertain, combining (pseudo-)historical facts, divine revelation and gripping narrative with the interpretation of material evidence. At the same time, however, these stories also have a spiritual dimension that modern narratives tend to lack: in most *inventiones*, the actual discovery is brought about or confirmed by divine providence or the direct intervention of God and the saints. That said, many modern accounts highlight moments of coincidence, inspiration and premonition that resemble, in purely structural terms, the miraculous element in medieval *inventiones*, a point to which I will return further below.

As Monika Otter points out, the *inventio*'s core plot elements remained fairly constant over the centuries:

> The relics are found either by coincidence, usually in connection with some construction or renovation project, or by divine guidance, through dreams or visions. The search for the right place and the digging itself are usually much emphasized; it is stressed that the community 'earned' the relic through its intense desire and hard work. There must be an audience present, minimally represented by the bishop or other high clerics in charge, but often described as a large crowd of clergy and laity. There will be some confirmation that the relic is genuine: the body may be incorrupt, or at least emit a pleasing fragrance; sometimes there is an inscription or some identifying artifact. The *inventio* is followed by a *translatio*, that is, the body is brought to a more worthy shrine, and its authenticity is further confirmed by miracles.[13]

In temporal respects, *inventiones* are characterised by a complex interplay of stability and change. On the one hand, relics foster continuity through the ongoing presence of the saint, a continuity that transcends

---

[12] Schliemann is by no means the only scholar whose account is – perhaps subconsciously – based on the medieval *inventio*: as Andrew James Johnston has argued, Stephen Greenblatt's *The Swerve* follows the same genre conventions. Greenblatt, Johnston suggests, is compelled to resort to the miracle structure of *inventio* narratives because the methodological limits of the New Historicism (including its often-criticised penchant for purely synchronic modes of analysis) prevent him from making use of such analytical tools as would allow him to pursue a more complex diachronic narrative; see Andrew James Johnston, 'Das Wunder des Historischen: Stephen Greenblatts *The Swerve*', in *Aufklärung: Interdisziplinäres Jahrbuch zur Erforschung des 18. Jahrhunderts und seiner Wirkungsgeschichte*, 25 (2013), 287–303, at 298–303, esp. 298.

[13] Otter, *Inventiones*, 28–9.

physical changes, including deterioration and fragmentation, and is amply evidenced by the accounts of miracles worked through the relics that usually accompany the *inventio* story. On the other hand, the very fact that a relic needs to be 'discovered' implies some form of rupture, which the relic, through its promise of continuity, is supposed to bridge. Consequently, 'the use of relics to emphasize material continuity is extremely common', Otter observes, further arguing that *inventio* accounts are often 'stimulated by the need to reassert rights and privileges'.[14]

Inventiones thus fulfil a powerful social and political function: they provide communities with a sense of continuity, either with what they perceive as their 'own' past or with earlier phases of use or ownership. To give an example: according to the twelfth-century *Liber Eliensis*, the late tenth-century refoundation of the monastery of Ely, which had been destroyed during Danish raids a century earlier, was accompanied by the discovery of the remains of its original founder, Saint Æthelthryth. When the old church was abandoned, the bones were transferred into its successor, along with other relics and holy objects. As Otter demonstrates, the *inventio* and subsequent *translatio* of the founder saint's relics gener-ated material and spiritual continuity across a phase of disruption in the community's history, thereby helping to facilitate the reconceptualisation of what was originally a double monastery under female leadership as an all-male institution.[15] But relics were also moved over much larger dis-tances: Osbern Bokenham's fifteenth-century Middle English *Vita Sanctae Margaretae*, the first of his thirteen *Legendys of Hooly Wummen*, tells how Saint Margaret's bones were first transported from Antioch to Italy, how they were then transferred from one place to the next as each monastery in turn was destroyed or abandoned, and how, finally, the deceased saint actively directed the discovery of her relics and their transport to a place of her own choosing, where a new church was erected and a new monastic community founded.[16]

Otter argues that 'most medieval *inventiones* are foundation stories, both in a literal sense (they often serve to motivate the foundation of a monastery [...] or the refoundation of a defunct one) and in a larger sense: *inventiones* serve, in many ways, as the foundation of a monastery's cor-porate identity and self-definition'.[17] But the possession of relics provided a community not only with social and spiritual, but also with political and

---

[14] *Ibid.*, 33, 22.
[15] *Ibid.*, 32–3.
[16] Osbern Bokenham, *Legendys of Hooly Wummen*, ed. Mary S. Serjeantson, EETS OS, 206 (London, 1938), lines 974–1379. Note how much space the poem affords to these different *inventiones* and *translationes* in comparison to the saint's 'pre-mortem' life, which occupies lines 241–868.
[17] Otter, *Inventiones*, 30.

economic capital; it signalled to the outside world that the community enjoyed the respective saints' favour, and helped elicit financial benefits in the form of grants and donations from patrons who wished to receive spiritual guidance or support. Hence, *translationes* often involved a political component, which explains the frequent mentioning in chronicles of relics being bequeathed, bartered, or even stolen. One particularly striking example is found in the Peterborough manuscript of the *Anglo-Saxon Chronicle* (Laud Misc. 636). The entry for the year 1013 reports how Abbot Ælfsige travelled to the impoverished monastery at Bonneval in northern France and bought the body of Saint Florentine (minus the head) for 500 pounds.[18] Ælfsige, whose abbacy lasted for fifty years, was also responsible for bringing other relics to Peterborough, including those of sister saints Cyneburh and Cyneswith, which had been kept at the monastery at Castor, destroyed in Danish raids in 870.[19] At Bonneval, he effectively exploited the local community's adverse economic conditions to increase his own institution's status and long-term wealth under the guise of providing much-needed monetary support.

Examples such as these recall the frequent instances in which modern archaeological practices and their objects get caught up in social, political and economic transactions as collectors, museums and entire social, ethnic and political communities negotiate their various claims on the artefacts in question and the values they attach to them, demonstrating that practices involving objects from the past are rarely disinterested. Even when they are directed at investigating the past, that past itself is often the object of conflicting claims and traditions, a point that will come up again and again in this chapter's discussion.

The inventio crucis *Tradition*

Given the fact that *inventiones* are usually transmitted as part of a larger hagiographical narrative that includes pre- and post-mortem deeds, it may come as a surprise that one of the earliest and most eminent examples does not pertain to the remains of a human being, but to those of an object: the True Cross – that is, the cross upon which Christ was

---

[18] 'Ælfsige [...] for to þone mynstre þe is gehaten Boneual þær Sancte Florentines lichama læg. Fand þær ærm stede, ærm abbot 7 ærme muneces, forþan þe hi forhergode wæren. Bohte þa þær æt þone abbot 7 æt þe muneces Sancte Florentines lichaman eall buton þe heafod to .v. hundred punda, 7 þa þe he ongean com, þa offrede hit Crist 7 Sancte Peter.' Irvine, Susan (ed.), *MS E*, ASC, 7 (Cambridge, 2004), 70–1.

[19] See the entry for 963 in Michael Swanton (trans.), *The Anglo-Saxon Chronicles*, rev. edn (London, 2000), 117 n. 16.

Excavating the Cross in Elene

crucified.[20] References to the *inventio crucis*, extant in Latin, Greek and Syrian texts, as well as in various medieval vernaculars, can be traced to the mid-fourth century, that is, less than thirty years after the discovery supposedly took place.[21]

I do not mention this circumstance as an argument for the narrative's authenticity; for the purposes of this study, it is immaterial whether the story goes back to an actual discovery or not. What interests me is the underlying archaeological imagination and the implications the alleged historicity of the event has for the texts' understanding of temporal and historical processes. In this regard, it is noteworthy that the legend was subject to historical development: while the earliest references to an *inventio crucis* merely mention the event without further expanding on the act of discovery, later accounts tend to be much more detailed, thereby enhancing their potential to highlight questions of materiality and temporality. Moreover, these longer accounts usually involve one or more individuals who are credited with the discovery, which adds a component of personal involvement that is absent from the earlier texts.

Possibly the oldest and certainly the most widely disseminated of these more elaborate accounts involves Saint Helena, the mother of Constantine I, the first Roman emperor to convert to Christianity.[22] The story appears to have been especially popular in early medieval Britain: apart from being mentioned in various sources, historiographical and other,[23] the discovery of the True Cross also forms the subject of at least three elaborate

[20] Otter, *Inventiones*, 27. As a matter of fact, the title of the modern standard version of the story, *Acta Cyriaci*, suggests that the *inventio crucis* can be read as part of the deeds of Jerusalem's legendary first bishop, Judas Cyriacus, even though it involves a number of equally or more important *personae*.

[21] On the development of the legends, see Stephan Borgehammar, *How the Holy Cross Was Found: From Event to Medieval Legend* (Stockholm, 1991); Jan Willem Drijvers, *Helena Augusta: The Mother of Constantine the Great and the Legend of Her Finding of the True Cross* (Leiden, 1992), 79–81; Barbara Baert, *A Heritage of Holy Wood: The Legend of the True Cross in Text and Image*, trans. Lee Preedy (Leiden, 2004).

[22] According to Drijvers, even though Helena may have been the first individual to be credited with recovering the cross, the attribution is still relatively late and not corroborated by reliable historical evidence: none of the fourth-century texts in which the True Cross is mentioned associate her with its discovery (*Helena Augusta*, 81).

[23] A point made, among others, by Stacy S. Klein, 'Reading Queenship in Cynewulf's *Elene*', *JMEMS*, 33:1 (2003), 47–89, at 65. The event is mentioned, for instance, in the F recension of the *Anglo-Saxon Chronicle*, which dates the event to the year 200; that is, around three-quarters of a century before Constantine's birth. This is either a mistake (cf. *Elene*'s similar error in lines 1–5) or points to another, altogether different version of the *inventio* story that has not come down to us.

Remains of the Past in Old English Literature

retellings in Old English – the narrative poem *Elene*, preserved in the late tenth-century Vercelli Book and one of four surviving poems to include the name 'Cynewulf' in acrostic runes, Ælfric's homily *Inuentio S. Crucis*, roughly contemporaneous with *Elene*'s manuscript, and an anonymous prose homily titled *In inventione sanctæ crucis*.[24] In addition, *The Dream of the Rood*, a lyric poem with homiletic and at times almost mystical overtones based around a dream vision of the True Cross and transmitted alongside *Elene* in the Vercelli Book, also includes a short reference to the *inventio*, this time told from the perspective of the cross itself.

The story's popularity in Britain may have been due to the early misconception, present already in Aldhelm's prose *De virginitate* (composed around the turn of the seventh to the eighth century), that Constantine was born in Britain. According to Antonina Harbus, this erroneous assumption may have originated in the circumstance that Constantine was first proclaimed emperor in Eboracum (today's York), then the imperial capital of the province of northern Britain. This event, which took place on 25 July 306, is mentioned in several well-known historiographical texts alongside the information that Constantine was the son of his father Constantius's 'concubine' Helena. Harbus surmises that the textual proximity of the two details – Constantine's birth from Helena and his proclamation in Britain – may have given rise to the idea that Constantine was actually *born* in Britain.[25]

---

[24] As Heide Estes notes, *Elene* and Ælfric's considerably shorter homily differ in focus, the latter also being more historically accurate overall; see Heide Estes, 'Colonization and Conversion in Cynewulf's *Elene*', in Catherine E. Karkov and Nicholas Howe (eds), *Conversion and Colonization in Anglo-Saxon England* (Tempe, AZ, 2006), 133–51, at 138–9.

[25] Antonina Harbus, *Helena of Britain in Medieval Legend* (Cambridge, 2002), 14–15. Early texts recording the two events in conjunction include Jerome's translation of Eusebius's *Chronicon* and Eutropius's *Breviarium*. Constantine was proclaimed emperor following the death of his father, Constantius 'Chlorus' (Flavius Valerius Constantius), who died in York after successfully campaigning against the Picts. Jerome writes, 'Constantius XVI imperii anno diem obiit in Brittania Eboraci. Post quem filius eius Constantinus ex concubina Helena procreatus regnum inuadit' [Constantius died in Britain, in York, in the sixteenth year of his reign. After him, his son Constantine, born from his concubine Helena, took over the rule; Latin text quoted from Harbus, *Helena*, 14 n. 26]. Harbus conjectures further that the key to the spread of the 'British' Helena tradition might lie in 'the imperfect grasp of Latin by writers of Old English adaptations', though she concedes that in Aldhelm's case his extensive knowledge of Latin and possibly Greek texts forbids this assumption (*ibid.*, 43, 38). By contrast, the Old English translation of Bede's *Historia ecclesiastica* clearly misinterprets its Latin source when it states: 'Writeð Eutropius þæt Constantinus se casere wære on Breotone acenned, 7 æfter his fæder to rice feng' [Eutropius writes that Emperor Constantine was born in Britain, and suc-

Excavating the Cross in Elene

Some later narratives even go so far as to make Helena the daughter of a spurious British king (named 'Coel' or 'Cole' in two twelfth-century texts). The royal descent established here contrasts with her lowly social background in virtually all early texts,[26] a circumstance that appears to have become increasingly problematic towards the end of the first millennium, when changing attitudes towards royal concubinage and the emergence of a concept of queenship made it desirable to suppress her traditional status as Constantius's concubine.[27] *Elene* does not mention Helena's family background, but portrays her as a commanding figure, using the epithets *cwen* [queen] and, occasionally, *hlæfdige* [lady] where Latin versions of the *inventio crucis* usually refer to her by her proper name. Moreover, *Elene* attributes to Helena a particularly authoritarian demeanour,[28] suggesting that the idea of her royal origin was already in circulation when the text was written.

---

ceeded to his father's rule; Old English text quoted from Thomas Miller (ed.), *The Old English Version of Bede's* Ecclesiastical History of the English People, EETS OS, 95 (London, 1890), 42]. Bede's original text merely notes: 'Scribit autem Eutropius quod Constantinus in Brittania creatus imperator patri in regnum successerit' [Eutropius writes that Constantine was created emperor in Britain and succeeded his father in his rulership; *HE* i.8 (ed. and trans. Colgrave and Mynors, 36–7)]. See further Harbus, *Helena*, 39–44; as well as Cynthia Wittman Zollinger, 'Cynewulf's *Elene* and the Pattern of the Past', *JEGP*, 103:2 (2004), 180–96, at 184 n. 12.

[26] Harbus, *Helena*, 49. According to Ambrose, Helena had worked as a *stabularia* [stable maid, or perhaps innkeeper]. Harbus speculates that the historical Helena may have been no more than the concubine or common-law wife of Constantius. She was 'probably' born in the province of Bithynia in Asia Minor, although Procopius, the earliest witness for this information, may have been misled by the fact that Constantine renamed the city of Drepanum (today's Hersek) Helenopolis after his mother's death. According to Harbus, Constantius's decision to separate from Helena to marry the current emperor Maximian's daughter Flavia Maximiana Theodora may have had less to do with Helena's social background than with the fact that all four members of Diocletian's original tetrarchy were related by marriage: Constantius was subsequently made junior emperor (Caesar) under Maximian and became senior emperor (Augustus) after Diocletian and Maximian had abdicated in 305 (*ibid.*, 12–14).

[27] Klein, 'Reading Queenship', 51–2, 67. As Klein notes, Helena's historical status as concubine also conflicted with her typological status as a symbol for the Holy Church, for which she presented 'a rather unfortunate choice' (*ibid.*, 66–7). The earliest references to Helena's alleged royal British origins can be found in two tenth-century Welsh genealogical lists, one of which was appended to the early ninth-century *Historia Brittonum* (Harbus, *Helena*, 52–3). There is no direct connection between these lists and the text I will discuss in this chapter, the Old English poem *Elene*.

[28] Klein, 'Reading Queenship', 56.

Remains of the Past in Old English Literature

Helena's social position is important to my argument because it forms an integral part of the political narrative that *Elene* interweaves with the hagiographical story of the *inventio crucis*. While the text presents the discovery of the True Cross as a triumph of historical and spiritual 'truth' that authenticates the biblical story of the crucifixion, it simultaneously highlights Helena's privileged position as a representative of the Roman Empire in interpreting the relics and deciding on their provenance – in fact, she even orders a set of highly sacred objects – the nails by which Christ was fastened to the cross – to be transformed into royal insignia embodying Constantine's status as divinely sanctioned ruler. I have already noted the *inventio*'s penchant for narratives of legitimisation, narratives in which the material and spiritual continuities suggested by the relic alleviate the impression of what might easily be perceived as a moment of rupture. In *Elene*, this interplay of continuity and change is turned into a model of supersession along the lines of the classical *topos* of *translatio*, in which divinely sanctioned political and spiritual authority passes on to the representatives of the Roman Empire while Rome acquires Jerusalem's erstwhile status as Christianity's main centre of religious worship. But even as this model of supersession comes to increasingly dominate the narrative, the poem opens up a number of further, alternative temporal perspectives – perspectives it ultimately fails to resolve (or is perhaps not interested in resolving) into a single, overarching temporal scheme, but which, taken together, touch on the very question of why people seek confirmation of historical 'truth' in objects from the past, and whether such historical insight is possible in the first place.

Debating the Past: The Conditions of Historical Transmission

Comprising 1,321 alliterative lines, the poem *Elene* constitutes the longest extant retelling of the *inventio crucis* story in Old English. It is preserved in the tenth-century Vercelli Book (Vercelli, Biblioteca Capitolare CXVII) alongside other poetic texts in the vernacular, including *Andreas*, *The Fates of the Apostles* and *The Dream of the Rood*, as well as a number of prose homilies, commonly known as the Vercelli homilies.[29] As far as the plot is concerned, *Elene* follows its Latin source (a version of the *Inventio sanctae crucis* similar to the one preserved in St Gall, Switzerland, St Gall 225) fairly faithfully, incorporating almost all materials of the Latin version of the legend as it was circulating between the seventh and tenth centuries, but also adding a number of elements, including a homiletic medita-

---

[29] Quotations from *Elene* are from George Philip Krapp (ed.), *The Vercelli Book*, ASPR, 2 (New York, 1932), 66–102; 132–52 (notes).

Excavating the Cross in Elene

tion on the Last Judgement that segues into the similarly eschatological 'Cynewulf' epilogue.[30]

Much of the poem's earliest criticism was devoted to determining its sources, literary background and textual cruces (to say nothing of conjectures about Cynewulf's identity).[31] Scholarship from the 1960s onwards tended to focus on the text's figural and semiotic aspects – an issue I will return to in the last chapter[32] – while more recent studies have attempted to link *Elene* to historical issues, such as engagements with contemporary forms of paganism, processes of nation-building or the rise of a distinct concept of queenship – approaches that have provided

[30] According to Gordon Whatley, the *inventio* legend as it was circulating in Western Christendom had acquired a more or less fixed form with little variation by the ninth century, with changes made between the seventh and tenth centuries being mainly of an editorial nature; Gordon Whatley, 'The Figure of Constantine the Great in Cynewulf's *Elene*', *Traditio*, 37 (1981), 161–202, at 162 n. 2. A composite text of this version, named after the alleged finder of the cross and first bishop of Jerusalem, Saint Judas Cyriacus, is found in the *Acta Sanctorum* for May (not March, as Gradon suggests) 4th, under the title 'Acta Apocrypha [Quiriaci] Pars I', in Godefroid Henschen [Godefridus Henschenius] and Daniel van Papebroche (eds), *Acta Sanctorum: Maius*, rev. edn (7 vols, Paris, 1866), vol. 1, 450–6. According to Pamela O. E. Gradon, who edited *Elene* for Methuen's Old English Library, the closest surviving version of the Latin *Acta* is the one in St Gall manuscript 225, whose readings are given as 'B' in Alfred Holder's edition; see Pamela O. E. Gradon (ed.), *Cynewulf's* Elene (London, 1958), 19, 20; Alfred Holder (ed.), *Inventio sanctae crvcis: Actorum Cyriaci pars I; Latine et Graece; Ymnvs antiqvs de sancta crvce; Testimonia inventae sanctae crvcis* (Leipzig, 1889), 1–29. Gradon maintains that 'there is little in *Elene* which can be shown to be original [...] little which is not to be found in some version of the *Acta Cyriaci*' (*Cynewulf's* Elene, 19, 20 [quotation]). The somewhat shorter Old English prose homily likewise features an independent ending, which narrates the home journey of Elene's earls but omits some material featured in the Latin tradition from which both *Elene* and itself derive; see Mary-Catherine Bodden (ed.), *The Old English Finding of the True Cross* (Cambridge, 1987), 30, 37–45, and 35 (concerning *Elene*).

[31] For an overview of early studies of *Elene*'s language, metre, intellectual background, authorship, sources, etc., see the bibliography provided by Gradon (ed.), *Cynewulf's* Elene, 76–80.

[32] Studies focusing on *Elene*'s figural and semiotic aspects include Thomas D. Hill, 'Sapiential Structure and Figural Narrative in the Old English *Elene*', *Traditio*, 27 (1971), 159–77; Hill, 'Time, Liturgy, and History in the Old English *Elene*', in Samantha Zacher (ed.), *Imagining the Jew in Anglo-Saxon Literature and Culture* (Toronto, 2016), 156–66; Jackson J. Campbell, 'Cynewulf's Multiple Revelations', *Medievalia et Humanistica*, 3 (1972), 257–77; Catharine A. Regan, 'Evangelicism as the Informing Principle of Cynewulf's *Elene*', *Traditio*, 29 (1973), 27–52; Martin Irvine, 'Anglo-Saxon Literary Theory Exemplified in Old English Poems: Interpreting the Cross in *The Dream of the Rood* and *Elene*', *Style*, 20:2 (1986), 157–81.

Remains of the Past in Old English Literature

many new insights, but have also been hampered by the difficulty of establishing a clear date for the poem's composition.[33] In a less historically specific perspective, and thus in greater proximity to the approach embraced by the present study, Cynthia Wittman Zollinger and Christina M. Heckman have focused on *Elene*'s concern with historical knowledge. While Zollinger traces the concurrence of pagan and Christian traditions at work in the poem, Heckman suggests that that the poem depicts a contest between Christian and Jewish learning based on a dialectical process of truth-seeking through the discovery of arguments, in which the cross constitutes 'a figure for the crux of the argument for the truth of Christianity'.[34] I would go even farther, however, and argue that *Elene*'s crucial argument is not so much about the question of different historiographical traditions as about the fundamental epistemological conditions of historical knowledge *tout court*. When Heckman posits that the physical hiding place of the cross represents a literalised *topos* used in the *inventio* of arguments, she not only allegorises the poem's narrative (an approach that she explicitly criticised earlier in her paper), but she also downplays the materiality of the cross and nails, which, as I will argue, is absolutely crucial to their deployment in the political and spiritual *translatio* enacted in the text.[35] It is my contention that *Elene*'s exploration of archaeological objects is not only tied to the pursuit of historical knowledge, but also to the uses to which such knowledge can be put, including the establishment of a form of rulership that allows sacred and imperial history to converge.

---

[33] See, for instance, Klein, 'Reading Queenship' (on *Elene*'s image of queenship); Estes, 'Colonization' (linking *Elene* to early medieval English nation-building and engagement with pagan invaders); Nicholas Howe, 'Rome: Capital of Anglo-Saxon England', *JMEMS*, 34:1 (2004), 147–72 (for a discussion of *Elene*'s depiction of Rome as the imperial and spiritual centre as well as its meaning to the poem's audience); Andrew Scheil, *The Footsteps of Israel: Understanding Jews in Anglo-Saxon England* (Ann Arbor, MI, 2004); Kathy Lavezzo, *The Accommodated Jew: English Antisemitism from Bede to Milton* (Ithaca, NY, 2016), 28–63 (on Christian engagements with Jews). On the question of dating, see Klein, 'Reading Queenship', 50. Klein cites R. D. Fulk, who maintains that the poem is not earlier than 750 if Mercian and not earlier than 850 if Northumbrian, and Patrick Conner, who links the Cynewulfian canon to the late tenth-century Benedictine reform; R. D. Fulk, 'Cynewulf: Canon, Dialect, and Date', in Robert E. Bjork (ed.), *Cynewulf Basic Readings* (New York, 1996), 3–21, at 16; and, in the same volume, Patrick W. Conner, 'On Dating Cynewulf', 23–55.

[34] Zollinger, 'Cynewulf's *Elene*'; Christina M. Heckman, 'Things in Doubt: *Inventio*, Dialectic, and Jewish Secrets in Cynewulf's *Elene*', *JEGP*, 108:4 (2009), 449–80, at 450.

[35] Heckman, 'Things in Doubt', 455.

Excavating the Cross in Elene

That history and the passing of time are central concerns in *Elene* is made clear from the very beginning of the poem, which starts by precisely situating the action within intricately correlated sacred and secular temporalities:

Þa wæs agangen   geara hwyrftum
tu hund ond þreo   geteled rimes,
swylce XXX eac,   þinggemearces,
wintra for worulde,   þæs þe wealdend god
acenned wearð,   [...]
          Þa wæs syxte gear
Constantines   caserdomes,
þæt he Romwara   in rice wearð
ahæfen, hildfruma,   to hereteman.

[When two hundred and three years had passed, reckoned in numbers, and thirty more winters for the world, measured in time, since the ruling God was born [...] then it was the sixth year of Constantine's imperial reign, after he came to the rulership of the Romans, that the prince rose to military leader; lines 1–10.]

The poem here establishes two different temporal reference points to date the events that it describes: the time of the incarnation and the beginning of Constantine's reign. This twofold reference recalls Bede's approach in the *Historia ecclesiastica*, which likewise employs a combination of different dating systems, including the received chronological frameworks provided by the birth of Christ and the foundation of Rome, as well as the more relative regnal dates of various Roman and sub-Roman rulers, thereby establishing a complex framework of chronological and relative dating.[36] From the outset, *Elene* thus models itself in the tradition of Latin historiography. At the same time, the text's double frame of temporal reference is also intimately linked to the rise of Christian rulership, one of *Elene*'s central concerns. By connecting the internal chronology of Constantine's imperial reign to the all-encompassing progress of sacred history, the poem highlights the convergence of two erstwhile separate time schemes at precisely the historical moment when sacred and imperial history came to intersect: that of Constantine's vision of the True Cross, which prompted him to convert to Christianity and led, in the long run, to its becoming the sole official religion of the Roman Empire.

This connection is emphasised by a significant change to the original tradition of the *visio Constantini*, which the emperor's advisor and later

---

[36] For a discussion of Bede's practice, see Donald J. Wilcox, *The Measure of Times Past: Pre-Newtonian Chronologies and the Rhetoric of Relative Time* (Chicago, IL, 1987), 142–4.

biographer, Eusebius of Caesarea, had linked to the Battle of the Milvian Bridge on 28 October 312.[37] Historically, this battle marked the culmination of an internal conflict between various members of the tetrarchy, resulting in Constantine's victory over his rival Maxentius. Both *Elene* and its probable source, the *Acta Cyriaci* (which uses the same double dating), transform and postdate this intra-Roman conflict by turning it into a fight against Germanic and Hunnic invaders on the banks of the Danube, on the Empire's northern border. Nicholas Howe observes that this reinterpretation of the battle as a clash between Germanic-speaking pagans and a Roman civilisation on the verge of converting to Christianity must have had particular resonances for Old English-speaking communities in early medieval Britain, who regarded themselves as the descendants of the Germanic conquerors of a former Roman province, conquerors who were at that point still pagan, but whose descendants would later convert to the Roman Church. According to Howe,

> through this significant rewriting of political geography, the poem takes on a specific religious charge and implicates Constantine's vision of the Cross into the history of Germania – of Huns and Hrethgoths along the Danube – so that it can take on a kindred significance for the Anglo-Saxons in England.[38]

Zollinger, too, regards the poem's depiction of the battle as an attempt to reconcile two different historical traditions prevalent in early medieval Britain: that of an ancestral past associated with the origins of an 'English' identity in Britain, and that of the island's colonial Roman and Christian history, of which Constantine, through his British associations, was an integral part.[39] Zollinger interprets this convergence as a process of cultural supersession, with the unanimous conversion of the poem's Jews implicitly paralleling the collective conversion of the early medieval 'English'.[40] For her, Constantine's battle against Germanic barbarians marks the fault line between two different frames of reference intersecting

---

[37] Eusebius, *Vita Constantini* i.28.
[38] Howe, 'Rome', 162–3; Howe's argument is not invalidated by the fact that he mistakenly regards this as an innovation of the Old English text. An early medieval 'English' identity appears to have developed over an extended period, involving the assimilation of various Celtic- and Germanic-speaking communities in the English-speaking parts of Britain into a single Christian 'English' identity that may have been galvanised by the common struggle against pagan Viking raiders and settlers; see Heinrich Härke, 'Anglo-Saxon Immigration and Ethnogenesis', *Medieval Archaeology*, 55 (2011), 1–28, esp. 20.
[39] Zollinger, 'Cynewulf's *Elene*', 185.
[40] *Ibid.*, 189–90. Zollinger notes that in other versions of the legend Helena persecutes and expels those among the Jews who refuse to convert.

Excavating the Cross in Elene

in the narrative; namely, the pre-conversion past and the Christian sense of history, which acknowledges but ultimately displaces the pre-Christian tradition.[41] The presence of specifically Germanic invaders in a poem otherwise exclusively concerned with 'Romans' and 'Jews' makes a conceptual link to the imagined past of the early medieval 'English' an attractive proposition, but such a reading ignores the fact that *Elene*'s vision of imperial Roman history is not one of straightforward supersession. For one thing, the poem sees imperial rulership and Christian doctrine as fundamentally compatible: Constantine's former paganism is supplanted, but it is never actually described, nor is it set in direct opposition to his later Christian faith. The convergence of Christian spiritual 'truth' and Roman imperial politics takes place on equal terms; structurally, the two paradigms occupy different spheres but are of equal importance, complementing rather than contradicting each other.[42] Second, even in the case of the poem's Jews, *Elene* does not envision a straightforward displacement of an outdated Jewish tradition by a more recent and 'true' Christian knowledge. At least in the figure of Judas Cyriacus, the Christian can be seen to be transmitted within the Judaic, a point I shall revisit below. Perhaps most importantly, although the poem does engage with the truth values of the respective historical traditions, its central concern is not with historical accuracy – *Elene* implicitly accepts the truth of the Scriptural account without discussing it in detail – but with the fundamental epistemological conditions of historical knowledge and its transmission.

Before delving more deeply into the poem itself, it is instructive to take another look at Bede's *Historia ecclesiastica* as one of the central works of early medieval historiography. In his preface, Bede lists his sources, oral and written, affirming their respective trustworthiness but adding the caveat that, in spite of his best efforts to collect the most reliable information, he cannot be held responsible for any inaccuracies that may have found their way into his work: 'Quod uera lex historiae est, simpliciter ea quae fama uulgante collegimus ad instructionem posteritatis litteris mandare studuimus' [For, in accordance with the principles of true history, I have simply sought to commit to writing what I have collected from common report, for the instruction of posterity].[43] Judith McClure and Roger Collins note that Bede borrows the phrase 'principles of true

---

[41] Zollinger sees this notion of supersession reflected in the displacement of Constantine's boar standard with its pagan (Germanic) overtones by the sign of the cross, which the emperor carries into battle (*ibid.*, 185).

[42] Zollinger admits as much when she speaks of 'the fusion of Romanitas and the Christian faith [...] celebrated by this poem', but she nevertheless fails to acknowledge that the relationship between the two historiographical traditions is likewise one of fusion and not of supersession (*ibid.*, 186).

[43] *HE* Praefatio (ed. and trans. Colgrave and Mynors, 6–7).

Remains of the Past in Old English Literature

history' from Jerome to justify 'the inclusion of material based on commonly held belief'.[44] For Bede, the accuracy of his account ultimately rests upon the reliability of his sources. He is not concerned with the availability of information – or lack thereof – other than noting that he learned from Abbot Albinus 'whatever seemed worth remembering' ('quae memoria digna uidebantur') of the history of Kent and its neighbouring kingdoms. For Bede, everything 'worth remembering' had been preserved; it was only a question of choosing the most reliable source.

By contrast, *Elene* negotiates the problems associated with historical transmission as such. A central passage features a dialogue between two of the main characters – Constantine's mother Elene and Judas, a particularly knowledgeable Jew who will later become Jerusalem's first bishop. This dialogue can be read as an extended discussion of the precarious nature of transtemporal transfer in general, and the possibility of archaeological recovery in particular.[45] Here, a brief summary of the plot up to this point in the narrative is in order. Having received a vision of the cross on the eve of battle, the Roman emperor Constantine adopts the symbol of the crucifixion as his standard and emerges victorious. It is only after his return to Rome, however, that he starts enquiring about the sign's meaning. Although information concerning the Christian faith is at first difficult to obtain, Constantine eventually learns about Christ's sacrifice and converts to Christianity. The story behind the sign stirs his desire to recover the original cross upon which the Saviour suffered. Constantine therefore sends his mother Elene to Jerusalem to look for the relic, which he expects to have been hidden under the earth ('under hrusan hyded'; line 218); by studying the written accounts of the Scriptures, he has also been able to deduce its general geographical location. Elene herself appears to be convinced that the cross was hidden on purpose so as to cover up the crime of killing Christ.[46] Upon her arrival, she summons those among Jerusalem's citizens who are most learned in theology in order to interrogate them. But rather than ask directly for information concerning the cross's whereabouts, Elene accuses them of having taken part in a crime – a crime whose actual nature she does not explain, much

---

[44] Bede, The Ecclesiastical History of the English People: *With the* Greater Chronicle *and* Letter to Egbert, ed. Judith McClure and Roger Collins, trans. Bertram Colgrave (Oxford, 2008), 361 n. to page 5.

[45] The debate is closely modelled after the *Acta Cryiaci*; see Henschen and Papebroche (eds), *Acta Sanctorum: Maius*, 451; Holder (ed.), *Inventio sanctae crvcis*, 7–8.

[46] Scheil argues that 'by hiding the location of the cross, the Jews are, in a sense, re-enacting the crucifixion, extending their original crime' (*Footsteps*, 226). However, the poem makes it clear that the Jews Elene is speaking to are unaware of the cross's location and indeed of the crucifixion itself.

Excavating the Cross in Elene

to the confusion of the citizens, who do not appear to have heard of the crucifixion and believe that Elene is accusing them of having transgressed against Constantine. Elene thus turns what initially appears like a kind of proto-archaeological search into a criminal investigation: she does not so much seek information about the biblical event as confirmation and acknowledgement of its spiritual truth. To the queen, the Jews' guilt is already a given – it is only the *corpus delicti* that is still missing.

Elene's attention is eventually directed to Judas, a man presented by his peers as particularly knowledgeable about the past. Judas, who has learned about the crucifixion from his father and grandfather, suspects that Elene is looking for the cross, but decides to keep silent. (In front of the other Jews, he later claims that he kept his knowledge to himself because, were it made known, 'ne bið lang ofer ðæt / þæt Israhela æðelu moten / ofer middangeard ma ricsian' [it would not be long after that that the tribe of Israel would not be able to rule any more over the earth; lines 432b–4].) When Elene commands him to reveal the place where the cross is hidden, Judas not only pleads ignorance, but also explains his alleged lack of knowledge in temporal terms as the result of a gap in historical transmission. Such a loss of information, he argues, is a typical effect of historical distance:

> Hu mæg ic þæt findan   þæt swa fyrn geweard
> wintra gangum?   Is nu worn sceacen,
> CC oððe ma   geteled rime.
> Ic ne mæg areccan,   nu ic þæt rim ne can.
> Is nu feala siðþan   forðgewitenra
> frodra ond godra   þe us fore wæron,
> gleawra gumena.   Ic on geogoðe weard
> on siðdagum   syððan acenned,
> cnihtgeong hæleð.   Ic ne can þæt ic nat,
> findan on fyrhðe   þæt swa fyrn geweard.

[How can I find that which has become so ancient through the passing of years? It is now many that have hastened away, two hundred or more told in number. I cannot recount, since I don't know the number. It is now many who have since departed, intelligent and good ones, wise men who were before us. I entered youth in later days, a young man given birth afterwards. I cannot do what I do not know, find in my mind that which happened so long ago; lines 632–41.]

Judas's reference to the telling of years recalls the opening of the poem, his supposed lack of knowledge contrasting with the precise numbers given in the earlier passage. Judas presents history as a process of forgetting that denies secure historical knowledge to those born later: the more time has passed since an event, he implies, the less likely it is to be

Remains of the Past in Old English Literature

remembered. The past is cut off from the present by the passage of time – a process, he contends, that necessarily entails a loss of knowledge along the way. Judas's argument thus reflects a perception of time that modern scholars frequently deny to premodern societies: an awareness that the past is irrevocably gone and potentially different in ways that can never be fully reconstructed.[47]

Judas's emphasis on the failure of historical transmission and the pessimistic attitude towards the possibility of secure historical knowledge this implies contrast with Elene's assured trust in the potency and accuracy not only of the Scriptures, but of historical records in general. She retorts:

> Hu is þæt geworden   on þysse werþeode
> þæt ge swa monigfeald   on gemynd witon,
> alra tacna gehwylc   swa Troiana
> þurh gefeoht fremedon?   Þæt wæs fyr mycle,
> open ealdgewin,   þonne þeos æðele gewyrd,
> geara gongum.   Ge þæt geare cunnon
> edre gereccan,   hwæt þær eallra wæs
> on manrime   morðorslehtes,
> dareðlacendra   deadra gefeallen
> under bordhagan.   Ge þa byrgenna
> under stanhleoðum,   ond þa stowe swa some,
> ond þa wintergerim   on gewritu setton.

> [How has it come about in this people that you know so much in your mind of all the deeds which the Trojans achieved through fighting? That was much longer ago, the open ancient conflict, than this noble event, in the passing of years. You are immediately capable of recounting clearly all that there was in terms of the number of men in the slaughter, of dead dart-bearers fallen under the shield-defence. Then you must [also] have recorded in writing that tomb under stone-cliffs, and also the place, and the number of winters; lines 643–54.]

Elene is here ridiculing the temporal logic of Judas's argument by imputing to it a strictly linear mechanism, making it appear as if the loss of knowledge occurred at a steady rate. Hence, she reasons, if the Jews possess detailed knowledge of the Trojan War, they must also be aware of the more recent event of the crucifixion.

Judas responds by highlighting the selectiveness of historical transmission:

---

[47]   See Roy M. Liuzza, 'The Tower of Babel: *The Wanderer* and the Ruins of History', *Studies in the Literary Imagination*, 36:1 (2003), 1–35, who argues that such an awareness is displayed by the narrator of the Old English poem *The Wanderer*. For a detailed discussion of this question, see Chapter 2, 118–21.

Excavating the Cross in Elene

We þæs hereweorces,   hlæfdige min,
for nydþearfe   nean myndgiaþ,
ond þa wiggþræce   on gewritu setton,
þeoda gebæru,   ond þis næfre
þurh æniges mannes   muð gehyrdon
hæleðum cyðan,   butan her nu ða.

[We closely keep in mind those deeds of war, my lady, of necessity, and set in writing those violent deeds, the people's conduct, and [yet] have never heard of this being made known to men from any man's mouth, except here and now; lines 656–61.]

Judas admits that the Jews know about the Trojan War and have recorded it in writing, but suggests that there is no way they could not have done so, with the phrase 'for nydþearfe' [by necessity] implying that the deeds of the Greek and Trojan heroes are so famous that it would have been strange had they not heard of them. By contrast, according to Judas, the particular event that Elene is interested in is not common knowledge: unlike the Trojan War, it has not been proclaimed publicly, at least not among the Jewish people. Judas's emphasis on *hereweorc* [deeds of war] and *wigþracu* [violent deeds] suggests that, in his view, it is these specific types of event that are liable to be remembered and committed to writing, whereas other matters are prone to remain unrecorded. In comparing different kinds of historical information and the different grades of probability with which they are remembered, Judas thus directly comments on historiographical practice, and he does so in a much more critical manner than Bede.

In addition, Judas's distinction between recalling (*myndgian*, literally 'bringing to mind'), recording (*on gewritu settan*) and proclaiming (*cyþan*) addresses Elene's earlier emphasis on writing: according to the latter's reasoning, if the Jews are aware in their minds ('on gemynd witon'; line 644b) of the Trojan War, then they must likewise have committed to writing ('on gewritu setton'; line 654b) the particulars of the crucifixion. Here, 'knowing' is inextricably linked to 'writing': what is known of the past is known because it has been learned from written records.[48] Judas complicates this straightforward relationship between knowing and writing by implying that what is recorded in writing has first to be made known orally ('þurh æniges mannes muð'; line 660), presumably by someone with first-hand knowledge of the events or access to some other

---

[48] Irvine notes *Elene*'s textual orientation, evident in the poem's change of the *Acta Cyriaci*'s term 'traditiones' [traditions], which could refer to oral transmission, to 'fyrngewritu' [ancient writings] ('Literary Theory', 169). However, as we will see, the poem's stance towards writing is much more ambiguous than Irvine's discussion implies.

source; consequently, events not made known in speech will not become part of the written record. Judas does not deny the potential historicity of the crucifixion, but he maintains that the Jews have no knowledge of the event, and therefore have not committed it to writing.

Ironically, this reflects quite accurately the situation of Jerusalem's Jews, none of whom appear to possess any knowledge of the crucifixion, except for Judas alone. On the contrary: when Elene first summons the wisest men of Jerusalem and charges them with having denied and executed Christ, they appear to be genuinely puzzled. And when Judas eventually recounts what he has learned about the event from his father and grandfather, they profess to being completely ignorant of the matter:

Næfre we hyrdon   hæleð ænigne
on þysse þeode,   butan þec nu ða,
þegn oðerne   þyslic cyðan
ymb swa dygle wyrd.

[Never have we heard any man in this people, any other thane except you now here, speak in this manner about so obscure an event; lines 538–41a.]

Judas, then, is the only individual in Jerusalem who has any form of knowledge about Christ's death on the cross.[49] Elene's suspicion vis-à-vis the Jews' truthfulness is thus correct only with regard to him;[50] as far as the majority of Jerusalem's inhabitants are concerned, Judas's history of forgetting turns out to be more accurate than Elene's trust in the common availability of historical knowledge through written records. Hence, the passage cited is not so much about the difference between Jewish and Christian traditions, as Robert DiNapoli and Kathy Lavezzo have maintained, as about the forgetfulness of history in general.[51] Nor can it be read as a straightforward expression of the antisemitic stereotype of the 'deceitful' Jew, except in the case of Judas alone.

As a matter of fact, Judas's explanation neatly encapsulates the problems faced by Constantine earlier in the poem, when he first tries to gather information about the sign of the cross: even though Elene will shortly after allude to the crucifixion as if it were common knowledge, at this juncture most people in Rome have apparently never heard of it. The counsellors whom Constantine summons to tell him 'what that God was [...] whose emblem this is' ('hwæt se god wære / [...] þe þis his beacen wæs';

---

[49] This is a point also made by Estes, 'Colonization', 148.
[50] Irvine calls Judas a 'deceitful rhetorician' ('Literary Theory', 169).
[51] See Robert DiNapoli, 'Poesis and Authority: Traces of an Anglo-Saxon Agon in Cynewulf's Elene', Neophilologus, 82 (1998), 619–30, at 623; Lavezzo, Accommodated Jew, 62–3.

Excavating the Cross in Elene

lines 161b–2) have no answer – only the wisest ('þa wisestan'; line 169a) declare it to be 'the sign of the heavenly king' ('heofoncyninges tacen'; lines 170b–1a). On hearing this, the Roman Christians rejoice, because they may now reveal to the emperor the truth of the Gospels ('ðæt hie for þam casere cyðan moston / godspelles gife'; lines 175–6a). The use of the word *cyþan* [reveal, make known, proclaim; line 175] clearly suggests that the Christian doctrine is not common knowledge at this point in the story. Rome's Christians are said to be few ('þeah hira fea wæron'; lines 174b), and their knowledge is presented as arcane, revealed only through the sacrament of baptism ('þa þurh fulwihte lærde wæron'; lines 172b–3a) and through 'spiritual mysteries' ('gastgeryne'; line 189b[52]). All this implies that up to Constantine's conversion, the Christian doctrine was a carefully guarded privilege, and Elene's contention that the people of Jerusalem would surely have committed to writing the site of the burial and the number of years that have passed since the crucifixion (lines 652b–4) remains unsubstantiated.

Elene does not mention the widespread tradition that Helena was already a Christian when Constantine experienced his nightly vision of the cross.[53] Nevertheless, from the moment that she enters the poem, she is portrayed as a zealous and devout Christian. Based on what the text tells us, we must assume that Elene's conversion is recent, having taken place after her son's investigation into the meaning of the cross had proved successful. It is thus possible to read Elene's reference to written records ('gewrit'; line 654) in the light of her own (or, rather, her son's) indebtedness to written information regarding the location of the crucifixion. As mentioned above, it was Constantine's study of the Scriptures that enabled him to identify Jerusalem as the place where Christ's sacrifice took place: 'Þa se æðeling fand, / [...] þurh larsmiðas, / [...] on godes bocum / hwær ahangen wæs heriges beorhtme / on rode treo rodora waldend' [Then the noble man found, through his teachers, in God's books, where the ruler of firmaments was hung by the host's tumult; lines 202–6]. While Constantine's book-learning may at first glance appear to stand in opposition to the Jewish counsellors' description of the crucifixion as 'swa dygle wyrd' [so obscure an event; line 541a], this is only a superficial contrast, since the scriptural account is presented as similarly arcane: Constantine needs the help of *larsmiþas* [teachers, counsellors; line 203] to discover the site of the event, and the fact that these experts kept their knowledge hidden until Constantine sought them out – the majority of his counsellors had never heard of it, despite the fact that they, too,

---

[52] Irvine notes that the term *gastgeryne* is an exegetical term referring to allegory and typology ('Literary Theory', 147).

[53] See, however, Drijvers, *Helena Augusta*, 35–8.

'had learned their wisdom from old writings' ('þa þe snyttro cræft / þurh fyrngewrito gefrigen hrefdon'; lines 154b–5) – implies that, at least as far as spiritual knowledge is concerned, written sources are by no means commonly available.

In light of all this, Elene's insistence on the common availability of written records appears to be deliberately ironic. It makes sense only in the context of her attempt to catch out the Jews, whom she suspects of having known about the crucifixion all along. Elene realises that knowledge of the crucifixion is arcane, but she seems to believe that the Jews – or at least some of them – have kept the memory of their 'crime' alive, which is true only of Judas. Elene's emphasis on written records is also ironic on the plot level: while she rightly suspects that Judas knows about the crucifixion, he does so not through written records, but rather through a direct line of oral transmission via his father and grandfather – just as the Christians of Rome received their knowledge through baptism rather than the study of texts. More intriguingly still, Elene may even be aware of the manner in which Judas came by his knowledge. Her comment a few lines later appears to suggest that she overheard Judas when he was speaking about the crucifixion to the other Jews:

> Wiðsæcest ðu to swiðe   soðe ond rihte
> ymb þæt lifes treow,   ond nu lytle ær
> sægdest soðlice   be þam sigebeame
> leodum þinum,   ond nu on lige cyrrest.

> [You deny too much the truth and right concerning that tree of life, and yet a little ago you spoke truthfully to your people about that victory-tree, and now you revert to a lie; lines 663–6.]

If Elene is indeed aware not only of Judas's knowledge of the crucifixion but also of the specific manner in which it was obtained, this means that her entire response to his problematisation of historical transmission is suffused with deliberate irony – an irony also discernible in her repeated, mocking invocation of the Jewish counsellors' alleged wisdom, which soon 'begin[s] to ring hollow'.[54] Elene has known all along that the whole discussion is pointless because, ultimately, neither Judas's nor her own arguments are relevant to the endeavour of discovering the holy relic – what is needed is Judas's admission of the historical and theological truth of the crucifixion.

---

[54] Scheil, *Footsteps*, 222.

Excavating the Cross in Elene

Recovering the Past: Archaeological Discovery, Conversion and the Epistemic Status of Historical Artefacts

That Elene's interrogation is not meant to bring to light any new historical information becomes clear when Judas finally gives in to the torture that she inflicts on him and admits to his familiarity with the account. As it turns out, Judas's knowledge does not in fact surpass any information that Elene already possesses – after all the effort she has put into her search, even the one person in Jerusalem who has actually heard about the crucifixion does not know where the cross was hidden. In the event, the location is revealed by a divine miracle, as are the cross's authenticity and, later on, the Holy Nails. And although it is Judas whose prayers initiate these miracles, it is not so much his historical knowledge as his latent faith that singles him out as worthy of this deed.

Heckman observes that Judas's conversion constitutes 'the necessary condition for [...] the *inventio crucis*': without it, the cross – the visible proof or, in Heckman's words, the crucial argument for the truth of Christianity – could not have been discovered.[55] But it is not Judas's 'ancestral knowledge' as a member of the Jewish people that enables this discovery, as Heckman maintains, but rather his latent faith as a proto-Christian: it is only by means of miracles that the cross can be discovered and identified, a point that Heckman herself concedes.[56] It is therefore difficult to account for her insistence that 'Elene cannot complete her quest without the revelation of the Jews' wisdom in the law and their knowledge of divine secrets'.[57] Indeed, I would argue that *Elene* highlights the limits not merely of Jewish, but also of Christian learning, as even the information contained in the Scriptures proves insufficient to locate the hidden cross. As far as the poem is concerned, Christian wisdom is based not on a transmission of knowledge, but on revelation. Thus, in contrast to the Jews, whose wisdom is based on *wordgeryno* [secret sayings; lines 289b, 323b], the Roman Christians attained their knowledge of the divine mysteries through *gastgeryno* [secrets of the spirit; line 189b]. In the same fashion, the discovery both of the cross's spiritual significance and the whereabouts of its physical relics relies on revelation.

As pointed out above, the poem's insistence that, in the final instance, historical insight is possible only through divine revelation means that the entire argument between Elene and Judas concerning the availability of

---

[55] Heckman, 'Things in Doubt', 452.
[56] *Ibid.*, 463, 473 (regarding Judas's 'ancestral learning'); 477–8 (regarding the manner in which the cross is found).
[57] *Ibid.*, 463.

historical knowledge is pointless. In fact, Elene herself seems to be aware of this irony: although the rationale behind her course of action is never explained, she appears to know that the ultimate aim of her investigation is not to garner information as to the cross's whereabouts, but to avail herself of the individual capable of performing the miracle required to discover it. From this perspective, the queen's strategy of confronting ever new groups of people with enigmatic allusions to a crime they have supposedly committed (and of demanding an answer to a question that she never actually poses) appears to be directed not at gaining historical knowledge, but at eliciting an acknowledgement of the truthfulness of the biblical account of the crucifixion. Elene pursues this approach until she manages to find the one person whose affirmation not only of the historicity of the event itself but also of its theological implications brings about both the *inventio* and the conversion of Jerusalem's citizens.

In *Elene*, then, historical knowledge – at least as far as it concerns the matter of *historia sacra* – is secret, but will be readily revealed once one is prepared to accept its theological implications. As Thomas D. Hill points out, 'Elene's questions to the assembled Jews presuppose an understanding of Christianity', and since the wise men she has summoned do not possess this knowledge, she 'simply berates the Jews while they stand there noncomprehendingly'.[58] The distinction is thus not between oral and written history, but between knowledge that is commonly available and knowledge that is arcane. In contrast to the former, the latter requires not only familiarity with a historical event, but also an understanding of its significance: knowledge of the crucifixion is tantamount to understanding its meaning and truth. Despite Elene's insistence on the ready availability of a written historical record, her own approach accentuates the spiritual nature of the event of the crucifixion.[59] This, however, does not turn *Elene* into a purely allegorical poem, as Hill would have it.[60] Ironically, the fact that only those who know about the crucifixion as a historical event also understand its spiritual meaning confirms Judas's – rather than Elene's – position in the debate: as time passes by, knowledge of the past is continually lost, either because of a gap in transmission or because an event was not recorded in the first place. This, Judas maintains, is indeed the usual scenario, unless somebody recognises the event's significance and chooses to preserve it for posterity, in writing or by passing on an oral account: such was the case with the Trojan War, and such was the case with the crucifixion, whose theological implications Judas's forebears alone among the Jews were able to grasp. In *Elene*, any unrecorded his-

---

[58] Hill, 'Sapiential Structure', 166.
[59] *Ibid.*
[60] This is not to deny the figural dimension of the poem, which I will discuss in more detail in Chapter 4.

Excavating the Cross in Elene

torical knowledge can only be attained through God, which is precisely what Judas has been arguing all along – although, ironically, with regard to the question at hand, more details were actually known to him than he initially wished to reveal.

This has important implications for our reading of *Elene* as an archaeological narrative, as well as for the epistemic status of the cross as a historical artefact. In the poem, the cross is practically worthless for purposes of historical investigation. In this respect, it differs strikingly from the objects of modern archaeological enquiry, which, even in the absence of any historical records, may still reveal a plethora of details about their age, function and social significance, as well as about their original users and producers. This is hardly surprising, given that modern archaeology is capable of wielding a wide array of methods and technologies from fields as diverse as biochemistry and technical engineering. The characters in *Elene*, by contrast, can rely only on divine revelation once the available historical records have been exhausted. Agency is thus shifted from the human actors to providence: the cross is not found through the characters' own efforts, but because God chooses to reveal it.

This spiritual dimension is particularly prominent in the characters of Constantine and Judas, both of whom accept the Christian truth before formally converting. When the victorious Constantine starts enquiring after the meaning of his nightly vision, he is already aware of the sign's potency and is prepared to believe in the God whose emblem it is. As in the case of the Roman Christians, who were instructed through baptism ('þa þurh fulwihte / lærde wæron'; lines 172b–3a), for Constantine, learning about the crucifixion and converting to Christianity constitutes a single step (lines 189–93). Judas, on the other hand, has known about the crucifixion long before he converts, accepting the account's spiritual truth internally, as had his father and grandfather before him.[61] It is his latent faith, the text suggests, that singles him out as worthy of initiating the miracles required to find and authenticate the cross and nails.[62] From this perspective, Judas

---

[61] Before his formal conversion, Judas is not as explicit in his acceptance of the Christian faith as his father Symon, who states that he and his own father 'believed that the God of all glories suffered horrible torture for mankind's great need' ('Forþan ic soðlice ond min swæs fæder / syðþan gelyfdon / þæt geþrowade eallra þrymma god, / [...] laðlic wite / for oferþearfe ilda cynnes'; lines 517–20). Yet Judas's statement that his father instructed him with 'true sayings' ('mec fæder min [...] septe soðcwidum'; lines 528–30a) implies that he, too, has accepted the truth of the crucifixion in all its implications.

[62] According to Heckman, 'Judas [clearly] believes in Christ, but his lingering doubts must be answered with the arguments and proofs that only the ancient and secret wisdom of the Jews, combined with the miracle requested by Judas, can reveal. Gentile Christians seemingly cannot find these proofs by themselves' ('Things in Doubt', 463).

Remains of the Past in Old English Literature

is necessary not so much as an agent of archaeological discovery, but as a subject of conversion.

Given *Elene*'s elaborate description of the events leading up to the recovery of the cross, the *inventio* itself comes as something of an anti-climax, leaving the excavators unable to discover which of the three crosses they have found is the one upon which Christ was crucified. Another miracle is needed to authenticate the True Cross. When this is achieved, Elene suddenly decides to search for the Holy Nails, a process that requires yet another miracle. The *inventio crucis*, which up to this point had appeared to be the poem's central concern, suddenly seems less important than the events accompanying it, including Judas's appointment as Jerusalem's bishop and the wholesale conversion of the city's population. Like other medieval *inventiones*, *Elene*'s version of the *inventio crucis* can thus be read as a narrative of conversion: opening with a vision of the cross that leads Constantine to adopt the Christian faith, the poem later foregrounds the role of the *inventio* in the conversion of Judas and the Jerusalemites. This, indeed, is what many scholars have long pointed out, with Manish Sharma, for instance, stating that *Elene*'s 'central theme [...] is conversion – through the cross and, by extension, through Christ', and Hill going so far as to argue that 'the whole narrative of the "Inventio crucis" is in effect a metaphor of conversion'.[63] Yet while I do agree that conversion plays a prominent role in the poem, I feel that it is not an end in itself. As I will argue below, conversion in *Elene* is intimately connected to the theme of imperial politics that pervades the entire poem, from the opening battle and its dating to the *translatio* of the nails to Rome. But let us not jump ahead, let us remain, for the time being, with the theme of conversion and its implications for the cross as a historical artefact.

Elene's emphasis on conversion and divine intervention means that the cross is turned into a tool of providence; it loses its value as an object of historical enquiry. This assessment is borne out by the passage describing the actual *inventio*, where it is suggested that the act of finding serves primarily to convince Judas of the power and truth of the Christian faith. Thus, when Judas finally sets eyes on the artefact lying in the earth,

---

[63] Manish Sharma, 'The Reburial of the Cross in the Old English *Elene*', in Samantha Zacher and Andy Orchard (eds), *New Readings in the Vercelli Book* (Toronto, 2009), 280–97, at 280; Hill, 'Sapiential Structure', 165. Intriguingly, as Klein points out, Elene herself is the only (main) character who does not convert – but then, neither is she granted the discovery of the True Cross; rather – and significantly – it is Judas, the character whose conversion is traced in the main part of the poem, who becomes the direct agent of that discovery ('Reading Queenship', 61).

Excavating the Cross in Elene

Þa wæs modgemynd   myclum geblissod,
hige onhyrded,   þurh þæt halige treo,
inbryrded breostsefa,   syððan beacen geseh,
halig under hrusan.

[Then was [his] mind much gladdened, [his] heart strengthened, through that holy tree, [his] heart inspired, when he saw the sign, holy under the earth; lines 839–42a.]

Given that Judas has just excavated a material object, the *halig treow* of line 840b, it may initially seem odd that the text almost immediately designates it as a 'beacen', that is, as a sign, token or emblem, without providing so much as a hint as to *what* it is supposed to signify. Obviously, in Christian discourse, the cross serves as a multivalent sign; its multiple meanings all deriving from its prominent function in the crucifixion as the central event of salvation history.[64] Yet even so, designating a physical object, whose materiality is thrown into sharp relief by the soil upon it, a 'sign' seems counter-intuitive, to say the least. In the present passage, however, the context suggests a very specific meaning for the ambiguous 'beacen': when Judas agrees to look for the cross, he prays to God and asks him to let a fragrant smoke rise over the spot where the artefact lies hidden. He also adds that this sign of God's grace would effect the transformation of his already latent faith into true belief:

'if þin willa sie,   wealdend engla,
þæt ricsie se ðe on rode wæs,
[…]
gedo nu, fæder engla,   forð beacen þin.
[…]
          Forlæt nu, lifes fruma,
of ðam wangstede   wynsumne up
under radores ryne   rec astigan
lyftlacende.   Ic gelyfe þe sel
ond þy fæstlicor   ferhð staðelige,
hyht untweondne,   on þone ahangnan Crist,
þæt he sie soðlice   sawla nergend,
ece ælmihtig,   Israhela cining,
walde widan ferhð   wuldres on heofenum,
a butan ende   ecra gestealda.

[If it be your will, ruler of angels, that he who was on the rood should rule, […] show forth now, father of angels, your sign. […] Let now,

---

[64] Irvine, 'Literary Theory', 171. I will return to this point in the final chapter.

author of life, smoke rise pleasantly from this place under the firmament's orbits, moving hither and thither in the air. I shall the more believe in you and fix even more strongly [my] soul, [my] unwavering hope, on the crucified Christ, that he be truly the saviour of souls, eternally almighty, the Israelite's king, that he shall rule forever the glories in heaven, the eternal dwellings, always without end; lines 772–3; 783; 792b–801.]

The use of the word *beacen* in the description of the *inventio* is thus a repetition of the term employed in the preceding prayer (line 783). Here, however, the word does not refer to the cross, but rather to the smoke that will indicate the location where it is hidden, and hence to the miracle attesting God's power and grace. In his prayer, Judas essentially proposes a bargain: if God provides a 'beacen', this will strengthen his faith and turn him into a fervent believer. The significant repetition of the word 'beacen' in the account of the actual *inventio* implies that its referent is not so much the material object of the cross, but rather the fact that God chose to reveal it: to Judas, the 'token' of God's grace is not the cross itself but being allowed to discover it. Thus, Judas's conversion is not brought about by the relic's material presence, but rather by the miraculous manner in which the relic is revealed: 'Judas is finally convinced of Jesus's divinity by the resulting sign indicating the location of the cross.'[65] Here, the mere presence of the archaeological artefact proves nothing. Without the miracle, there would have been no evidence to confirm that what was found is indeed the True Cross upon which Christ suffered; it could have been just any cross – a point driven home by the fact that yet another miracle (involving the resurrection of a dead person, no less) is required to confirm which of the three crosses recovered is the right one.

Read as a narrative of conversion, the story de-emphasises the materiality of the True Cross and foregrounds the miraculous nature of its discovery, which in turn proves its authenticity and spiritual significance. That said, the object's physicality cannot be fully excised from the equation. Without the presence of an artefact, the *inventio* would be impossible; in other words: there is no act of finding without something to be found. Nor does the poem completely dispense with the notion of the relic's inherent powers: after all, the text implies that the second miracle, which identifies the cross on which Christ suffered, is effected by – or at least channelled through – the artefact itself. For the cross to take on the typical properties of a Christian relic, which operates as a conduit for the divine or saintly

---

[65] Estes, 'Colonization', 148–9. Nevertheless, Judas's comments concerning his quasi-Christian upbringing show that he is already latently Christian.

Excavating the Cross in Elene

power to interact with worshippers and perform miracles, the presence of the material object is indispensable.

What *is* being suppressed, however, is the cross's temporality as a historical artefact. By the end of the poem, it has been raised in a church as an object of adoration, encased in a silver casket and adorned with gold and jewels. Found separately, the nails by which Christ was fastened to it have been transformed into a bit for the bridle of Constantine's horse, their sacred power ensuring his future martial successes. As relics, the cross and the nails possess a synchronic quality, allowing direct interaction with God through prayer and the occurrence of miracles; and it is these qualities that the poem stresses at the expense of their historicity.

Only in the discussion between Elene and Judas is the historical dimension of the cross allowed to surface: it is here that it can be imagined not merely as a hidden object, but as an artefact whose location, identity and historical existence have become obscured and all but forgotten due to the historical distance separating the characters' present from the historical past of the crucifixion. Implicitly, *Elene* thus acknowledges the existence of a second kind of archaeological artefact besides the relic: one that is not possessed of sacred power and revealed by divine intervention; one that requires investigation or the possession of historical information in order to be found and authenticated. In so doing, the poem defines the relic as a special type of archaeological object whose historicity is subsumed by the ahistorical temporality of God's ever-present 'now'. Hence, *Elene* posits a second kind of archaeological narrative besides the miracle-guided, conversion-bringing *inventio* of relics, a narrative that takes centre stage in the lengthy discussion between Judas and Elene about the precariousness of historical transmission and the possibility of archaeological recovery only to subsequently be shown as irrelevant to the specific artefact at hand.

In light of this discussion, and given the manner in which the cross is eventually found, the poem's outlook appears to be rather pessimistic when it comes to the chances and merits of conducting the kind of archaeological investigation originally envisaged by Constantine: we are given to understand that the search for a historical artefact whose whereabouts have become shrouded by the passage of time and that cannot rely on the occurrence of miracles is doomed to fail. As far as Elene's quest is concerned, neither historical records nor any other means of investigation turn out to be much help. While her problems are eventually solved by God's intervention, the narrative's exclusive reliance on divine aid is not exactly encouraging when it comes to archaeological objects more generally. If the location of an artefact as important as the True Cross is not recorded by Scripture, how can we hope to find – and, more importantly, authenticate – more mundane objects? From this perspective, *Elene*'s ostensibly triumphant affirmation of God's ability to salvage material objects from historical wreckage reads like a cautionary tale suggesting that archaeological endeavours not supported by providence are point-less: but for the grace of God, Judas's gloomy view of history – a history of forgetting – would have been vindicated.

Connecting to the Past: People and Artefacts

In the previous section I have argued that, as far as *Elene*'s overarching argument as a narrative of conversion is concerned, the materiality of the cross as a historical artefact – in other words, its status as an archaeological object – plays a subordinate role. In this respect, the plot's development stands in marked contrast to the characters' expectations and, perhaps even more significantly, to their reaction once the relic is found. This is the more surprising because in *Elene*, unlike in many other *inventio* narratives, the initial impulse to search for the instrument of Christ's Passion is not provided by God (or at least not directly). Whereas the more common impetus for *inventiones* is a dream or a vision – involving, for instance, a saint appearing to the dreamer and demanding a worthier funeral – in *Elene* it is the human characters themselves who decide to look for the relics, rather like Schliemann did when he resolved to embark on his search for the remnants of Troy. This circumstance appears to jar with the narrative's general theological thrust:[66] if the cross, as an object of historical enquiry, is practically worthless, if it cannot prove, by itself, the historicity of the crucifixion, then why express such a strong desire to obtain it in the first place? To the characters, I suggest, the cross represents more than a tool of providence, more than a means of effecting the conver-sion of the Jews. As a historical object that connects their own time with the past, it acts as an intermediary, a physical link between the time of Christ's physical presence and their own here and now. This capacity not only to recall, but to physically connect believers with, the past is a quality that the True Cross shares with other relics. It is a quality by which many archaeological objects continue to affect searchers, finders and observers to the present day; it is a quality, moreover, that makes it possible to exploit such objects for political and ideological ends, a point I will discuss in the last part of this chapter.

---

[66] Admittedly, Constantine's decision to send his mother to search for the cross can be linked ultimately to his vision on the eve of battle. Yet here, unlike in similar visions in other *inventiones*, the angelic messenger does not explicitly command him to embark on such a quest; that is a decision Constantine arrives at through studying the Scriptures. I will discuss the issue in more detail below.

Excavating the Cross in Elene

At first sight, *Elene*'s emphasis on conversion and divine intervention may appear thoroughly medieval. And yet it is striking to note the degree to which many much more recent accounts of archaeological finds – especially well-publicised ones that catch the attention of a non-specialist audience – still conform to the pattern of the *inventio* and its reliance on emotions and miracles (or fortuitous coincidence, in the parlance of our times). Indeed, the modern reader may detect an almost Schliemannesque quality about Elene's search – or, perhaps more accurately, come to the realisation that the former's excavation of Troy in some respects bears an uncanny resemblance to *Elene*'s version of the *inventio crucis*. For instance, both Schliemann (or at least his autobiographical *persona*) and *Elene*'s Constantine are inspired by written accounts, accounts that rouse their curiosity but also affect them emotionally: Schliemann professed to having been inspired by his childhood reception of Troy narratives, and later used the *Iliad* as a guide to discover and authenticate the city's remains; in *Elene*, no explicit reason for Constantine's desire to find the cross is given, but the text establishes an implicit connection between the emperor's wish to acquire the artefact and his study of the Scriptures, after which 'the praise of Christ was in the emperor's mind, [who was] from then on mindful of that excellent tree' ('Þa wæs Cristes lof þam casere / on firhðsefan, forð gemyndig / ymb þæt mære treo'; lines 212–14a). Admittedly, providence may always be at work in a medieval narrative, and Constantine's endeavour can ultimately be traced to his nightly vision. Still, this vision does not immediately prompt the search; rather, it provokes the emperor's curiosity about the sign, which first leads to his conversion and study of the Scriptures, and only then elicits his ardent wish to lay his hands on the artefact. Significantly, Constantine is not driven by an urge to appropriate the relic's marvellous properties, of which he seems to be unaware at this point – even though it is precisely such an act of appropriation that the narrative ultimately leads to; rather, the text suggests that the desire for the object has its roots in the affective power of the story of the crucifixion. To Constantine, Christ and the cross are inseparably connected: 'Þa wæs Cristes lof þam casere / on firhðsefan, forð gemyndig / ymb þæt mære treo.' In the grammatical structure of the sentence, Christ's praise and the cross occupy the same position: to praise Christ is to think of the cross; to think of the cross means to praise Christ. It seems as if, in Constantine's mind, being able to see, touch and handle the cross will allow him to praise Christ more directly, to experience more fully the meaning and effect of his sacrifice, which is precisely how relics were perceived by medieval believers. Christ's praiseworthy deed and the redemptive meaning of the crucifixion are inseparably bound up with the physical artefact of the cross.

Stacy S. Klein argues that 'discovering the meaning of the cross is shown to be profoundly dependent upon first actually finding it'.[67] I do not find Klein's argument particularly persuasive when applied to the poem as a whole – as we have seen, the discovery of the physical cross appears more like a by-product of the debates that reveal its theological significance than the other way round – but it does seem to describe quite aptly the expectations Constantine associates with the discovery. Will these expectations be fulfilled? We have no way of knowing, since, somewhat ironically, Constantine is the only named character in the poem *not* present at the *inventio*. Nor do we witness him personally encountering the cross: although he rejoices at the news that it has been found ('þa ðam kininge wearð / þurh þa mæran word mod geblissod, / ferhð gefeonde' [Then through this glorious message the King's heart was gladdened, his spirit exulted; lines 988b–90]) and orders a church to be built on the site of its discovery, he never actually travels to Jerusalem. We do not even learn about his reaction when Elene sends him the bit fashioned from the Holy Nails. His apparent lack of interest is quite puzzling; perhaps the confirmation of the Scriptures' historical veracity afforded by the relics is sufficient, after all. But what follows after the *inventio* tells a different story: the cross's exaltation, its decoration with gold and jewels and encasement in a silver casket, and the assurance of its readiness to support the afflicted: 'þær bið a gearu / wraðu wannhalum wita gehwylces, / sæce ond sorge' [there [it] is an ever-ready support for the infirm, in every punishment, trial and sorrow; lines 1028b–30a]. As one the most sacred of all Christian objects, the cross clearly possesses a strong affective power.

Being affected by the sight or touch of objects is a common motif, not only within literature but also in everyday conversation. Rita Felski notes that scholarly discourse usually associates this kind of 'emotional' response with laypeople, as opposed to a supposedly objective, 'detached' academic point of view.[68] Indeed, both Constantine's (fictional) and Schliemann's (semi-fictionalised) emotional attachment to the objects they pursue can be classified along those lines: the former is not a theologian, and the latter an ambitious amateur rather than a professional archaeologist. However, Felski insists, the distinction is not as clear-cut as it may seem, not only because scholars and scientists do tend to have emotional investments of their own (however much they may disown them in public), but also because emotional attachment is merely one of many possible ways to describe the versatile and multifarious relationships between people and objects. Attachments, she argues, always 'involve

---

[67] Klein, 'Reading Queenship', 55.
[68] Rita Felski, *Hooked: Art and Attachment* (Chicago, IL, 2020), 4. Felski is primarily concerned with non-tangible 'objects' such as TV shows, music or works of literature, but she notes that the same holds true for more 'material' artefacts.

Excavating the Cross in Elene

thought as well as feeling, values and judgments as well as gut response'.[69] This obviously holds true for medieval theology, which cannot afford to lose sight of the affective power of religious narratives and the objects associated with them. But it also applies, Felski claims, to all relationships between people and objects. Drawing on actor-network theory, she argues that these relationships are always multiple, formed by and dependent upon a plethora of connections, only some of which can be rationalised by the human actors involved. The relationships between people and objects are thus never purely emotional or intellectual, aesthetic or political, but rather informed by multiple factors (though not necessarily to the same degree).[70] Attachments, in this sense, are relational rather than causal.[71] If we follow Felski in adopting actor-network theory's vocabulary, we can say that the objects themselves constitute active agents insofar as they trigger, through the characteristics and affordances specific to them, certain responses, including revulsion, enjoyment, emotional or intellectual fulfilment, and so on.

In many instances, the relationships between people and objects have a discernible temporal dimension. Material artefacts may evoke a person's past, recalling moments of enjoyment, absent loved ones, or, conversely, unpleasant memories; they may also be tokens of hope, keepsakes holding out the promise of a future reunion. But not all objects that people invest with significance have an intimate connection to their own lives. Visitors frequently describe the experience of being confronted with historical sites and artefacts as deeply affecting. In some cases, such as Stonehenge, this emotional impact is the result of the object's mysteriousness, its great age or its remarkable ability to withstand the destructive power of time. In other cases, it stems from the fact that a specific item is implicated in a powerful historical narrative – the pistol used by Gavrilo Princip in the assassination of Archduke Franz Ferdinand of Austria, an event widely believed to have triggered World War I, is just one particularly evocative example.[72] What becomes evident here (and, of course, in the narratives of Priam's Treasure and the True Cross with which I am primarily concerned) is the object's capacity to make present, in the observer's imagination, that which is absent, to connect the viewer to a bygone moment and thereby make that moment tangible, to bridge the temporal gap between the past

---

[69] *Ibid.*, ix.

[70] *Ibid.*, 5–6, 13–14.

[71] *Ibid.*, 19–20.

[72] The pistol is on permanent display at the Heeresgeschichtliche Museum (HGM) in Vienna, together with other items from the assassination, including the Archduke's car, his bloodstained uniform and the chaise longue on which he died.

Remains of the Past in Old English Literature

and the here and now – albeit at the price of focusing on just one moment out of that object's long diachronic existence.

In medieval theological discourse, the relic's contribution to salvation is often regarded as being predominantly the product of its affective nature, its power to make present past virtue and suffering, and hence its capacity to lead the worshipper on the path to compassion or contrition. The transtemporal spiritual experience described by Margery Kempe, analysed by Carolyn Dinshaw and rehearsed in the introduction to the present study,[73] is brought about not by a relic, but by a sacred image; however, as Caroline Walker Bynum points out, the distinction between these categories was never unequivocal.[74] A similar connection is made in the metapoetic part of *Elene*'s 'Cynewulf' epilogue, where the narrator contrasts his recognition of the cross's virtue as 'tree of life' with his former worries about his own sinfulness, which he overcame by meditating on the meaning of the crucifixion and by turning his mind to the writing of poetry, an ability he received through God's grace (lines 1236–56a). As with Constantine, grasping the significance of the cross comes about through the study of written texts and divine revelation,[75] but both trajectories are inextricably linked to a desire for the physical artefact that will connect the believer more directly to Christ.

A similar kind of affective power is ascribed to more profane objects and the stories associated with them. Today, instruments played by famous musicians or items of clothing worn by celebrities fetch fantasy prices at auction – especially if their owners are no longer alive.[76] In keeping with this observation, Philip Schwyzer has persuasively argued that the affective power exerted by material traces of the past ultimately derives from a longing for real contact with the dead.[77] In some cases, the finding or handling of such objects may become a quasi-religious, almost transcendental experience. Schliemann, for instance, frequently

---

[73] See, for instance, Dinshaw's discussion of Margery Kempe's mystical experience of the crucifixion ('Temporalities', 17–19).

[74] Bynum, *Christian Materiality*, 29. Relics and other holy objects will be addressed in greater detail in Chapter 4.

[75] Zollinger, 'Cynewulf's *Elene*', 193.

[76] To give a few examples: George Michael bought the piano on which John Lennon composed *Imagine* for £1.45 million in 2000; three years later, the copy of *Double Fantasy* that Lennon signed for his killer Mark David Chapman was put up for sale for $525,000. A scrap of paper signed by Charles Dickens and accompanied by the date and a short quotation from *A Christmas Carol* ('And so, as Tiny Tim observed, God bless us every one!') – described by an American dealer as 'The Holy Grail for all Charles Dickens collectors' – was on sale in 2023 for $75,000; cf. William Baker, Andrew Gasson, Graham Law and Paul Lewis, *The Collected Letters of Wilkie Collins: Addenda and Corrigenda*, vol. 14 (London, 2023), 12 n. 2.

[77] Schwyzer, *Archaeologies*, 20–4.

Excavating the Cross in Elene

stylised his obsession with Homer's texts – not so much as works of literature but as historical accounts linked to a set of physical objects – in terms recalling Christian worship. According to his autobiography, 'the words of Homer were to him a gospel [...]; his belief in them was strong enough to defy from the outset the learned scruples according to which the allusions to location in the verses of the Iliad were no more than the product of unbridled poetic fantasies.'[78] In another passage, Schliemann refers to Troy as 'holy Ilios',[79] and he reputedly insisted on placing a copy of the *Iliad* on his son Agamemnon's head during the baptismal ceremony. Philippa Langley, who played a central role in the excavation of the bones of Richard III, likewise shrouds her account in terms that recall the supernatural:

> My passion for the search was based on personal intuition, which only became stronger and stronger. The moment I walked into that car park in Leicester the hairs on the back of my neck stood up, and something told me this was where we must look. A year later I revisited the same place, not believing what I had first felt. And this time I saw a roughly painted letter 'R' on the ground (for 'reserved parking space', obviously!). Believe it or not, it was almost directly under that 'R' that King Richard was found.[80]

Perhaps these writers consciously or subconsciously echoed the language usually reserved for sacred objects in order to emphasise their passion; perhaps they found it hard to express their experience of the affective power of the artefact in terms other than metaphysical. What these examples suggest, in any case, is that the desire for the object and the access it promises to a bygone past lies at the very heart of many, perhaps all archaeological fantasies, medieval and modern.

Appropriating the Past:
Archaeology, Imperialism and the Concept of translatio

What kinds of connection to the past do archaeological objects afford? We have seen that for many users and observers, ancient artefacts have the capacity to make present bygone moments of virtue and suffering, or the

---

[78] 'Die Worte Homers galten ihm [...] als ein Evangelium, und sein Glaube daran war stark genug, ihn von vornherein über die gelehrten Scrupel hinwegzusetzen, wonach die Andeutungen der Oertlichkeit in den Versen der Ilias nur das Werk frei sie erschaffender dichterischer Phantasien seien.' Schliemann, *Selbstbiographie*, 33.

[79] *Ibid.*, 38.

[80] 'A Personal Message from Philippa Langley', quoted from Schwyzer, 'Return', 84–5.

Remains of the Past in Old English Literature

past more generally – not only in the case of religiously charged relics, but also in that of much more profane items. Today, many archaeological objects are accorded a far higher value than suggested by their material components or their present-day functionality (which, in many cases, will approach nil). The monetary or sentimental value that people ascribe to objects may vary, both between different individuals and historically, but it is clearly informed by the historical associations these objects evoke. The more deeply an object is implicated in a certain personal or historical narrative, the more highly it will usually be valued by those who put their stakes on that narrative.

I have already drawn attention to the important role played by relics (especially their *inventiones* and *translationes*) in narratives intended to bolster the authority and legitimacy of the institutions that owned them. But even in the Middle Ages, it was not only religious objects that could be used in this fashion. The exhumation of what were proclaimed to be the remains of King Arthur and Queen Guinevere at Glastonbury in the 1180s constituted what Philip Schwyzer calls a 'secular' kind of *inventio*. Recorded by Gerald of Wales, the event occurred at a time when the monastery's church was being rebuilt after a disastrous fire in 1184. Schwyzer explains that the exhumation and the accompanying publicity may well have served to generate financial support for the undertaking.[81] At the same time, he argues, the event could also have had a political dimension. Gerald mentions Welsh traditions concerning Arthur's future return, to which, he feels, the incontrovertible evidence of the bones must surely put paid – tellingly, Gerald places the exhumation during the reign of Henry II, who had restored Anglo-Norman hegemony over Wales. Similarly, many archaeological excavations of the nineteenth and early twentieth centuries received their impetus (and, not infrequently, their funding) from nationalist cultural projects dedicated to tracing the origins of the respective nation states to an imagined common past; in some cases, the endeavours were directed explicitly at the 'restoration' of the respective historical sites in order to produce privileged places in the collective imagination that could act as 'historical "memory factories" for the nation'.[82] Today, the sometimes heated debates over the repatriation not only of human remains but also of cultural objects seized during colonial rule draws attention both to the high value that different communities place on these

[81] Schwyzer, 'Return', 91.
[82] Michael Dietler, 'A Tale of Three Sites: The Monumentalization of Celtic *oppida* and the Politics of Collective Memory and Identity', *World Archaeology*, 30:1 (1998), 72–89, at 72–3. See also Bettina Arnold and Henning Hassmann, 'Archaeology in Nazi Germany: The Legacy of the Faustian Bargain', in Philip L. Kohl and Clare Fawcett (eds), *Nationalism, Politics and the Practice of Archaeology* (Cambridge, 1996), 70–81.

Excavating the Cross in Elene

objects, and to the role of colonial archaeology in assembling the collections of Western museums. Schliemann may have acted predominantly out of personal ambition when he started searching for Homeric Troy, but the objects he transported (and, sometimes, smuggled) out of Turkey not only ended up in Western collections, but also became subject to conflicting claims – first, between the Turkish government and Schliemann himself, who felt entitled to keep the objects he had excavated on account of the money and effort that he had invested, and later between Germany, Turkey and Russia, after Priam's Treasure, which had been kept at the Ethnological Museum and the Kunstgewerbemuseum in Berlin, was taken to the USSR as part of the 'restitution in kind' policy agreed on by the Allies after their defeat of Germany in 1945, a transfer that was only officially acknowledged by the Russian government in 1993.[83]

Whatever Schliemann's motives for smuggling Priam's Treasure out of Turkey may have been,[84] the fact that it came into German possession at all can only be understood in the more general context of colonial politics that led to a stream of objects from all over the world pouring into Western collections. Schliemann's defence that the finds would have been inaccessible for further research in Constantinople echoes many similar arguments put forward in defence of the practice of taking objects and even whole architectural structures to Western museums, where, so the story went, they were properly appreciated and stood better chances of being preserved for posterity. Today, the very same claims are once again advanced to counter calls for the repatriation of the very same objects.[85]

The notion that Western societies are more 'advanced' when it comes to the interpretation and preservation of archaeological objects, that they are destined to act as stewards until the countries and cultures that produced said objects have reached a similar level of intellectual and methodological understanding, is based on what might be termed a 'Hegelian' perspective on history.[86] According to this model, which, as Dipesh Chakrabarty has pointed out, lies at the heart of modern Western historicist concepts of history,[87] all cultures or societies undergo a similar development to ever greater complexity and understanding, but not at the same speed.

---

[83] Easton, 'Priam's Gold', 237–40. As Easton notes, it is not clear whether the items now on display in the Pushkin Museum are in fact the ones excavated by Schliemann, 'because before World War I the Berlin Museums had a set of identical copies made and presented them to – guess who – the Pushkin Museum' (*ibid.*, 237).

[84] *Ibid.*, 227, 232–3.

[85] See, for instance, Bénédicte Savoy, *Africa's Struggle for Its Art: History of a Postcolonial Defeat* (Princeton, NJ, 2022).

[86] See Chapter 3, 147 and n. 21 for further discussion of this topic.

[87] Chakrabarty, *Provincializing Europe*, 7–9.

Remains of the Past in Old English Literature

Hence, different societies may have reached different stages of development, even though they coexist at the same moment in linear time. In an extreme, but, for many Westerners, intuitive and hence very powerful sense, this view entails that Western societies will always be one step ahead of all others. Postcolonial critics in the wake of Johannes Fabian's critique of ethnographical practices have emphasised time and again that arguments denying other societies' 'coevalness' with Western civilisation by positing the latter's methodological and technological superiority form the very backbone of modern colonial and neo-colonial practices.[88]

When applied to the societies of antiquity commonly regarded as the 'cradle' of modern Western civilisation, however, the linearity of the model begins to unravel: even though, according to this Western master narrative, all civilisations continue moving forward, an element of retardation enters the scheme. From a historicist perspective, civilisations such as those of ancient Egypt and Mesopotamia constituted the 'most advanced' societies of their time, but their successors somehow lost their historical momentum and were outstripped by others, particularly the inhabitants of modern western Europe and northern America. This process of historical supersession, in which societies lose their status of pre-eminence as others gain it, recalls the classical *topos* of *translatio*, at least in the abstract sense in which it was usually applied in political and historiographical theory from late antiquity to the early modern period. Generally speaking, the term *translatio* denotes a transfer, either of objects such as relics (*translatio reliquiae*), or of abstract concepts such as power (*translatio imperii*), religion (*translatio religionis*) and ideas (*translatio sapientiae*, or later, *translatio studii*). The concept of *translatio imperii* can be traced to the now-lost *Historiae Philippicae*, composed in Latin by the first-century Roman Pompeius Trogus and surviving in condensed form in Justin's *Epitoma historiarum Philippicarum*.[89] Pompeius Trogus used the idea to synchronise historical events from different parts of the world and to integrate them into a single, linear process characterised by the geographic transfer of 'imperium' (understood as the ultimate form of political hegemony) from one people to another. According to the *Historiae Philippicae*, that process was instigated by the Assyrian king Ninus, who was the first to conquer other kingdoms and thereby started a succession of empires that led to the *Imperium Romanum* of Pompeius Trogus's day. As one empire waned or was defeated by another that continued the process, *imperium* moved geographically around the Mediterranean, from Mesopotamia to Italy.

---

[88] Fabian, *Time and the Other*, 31.

[89] The description in this paragraph follows Wilcox, Measure, 108–13. See also Werner Goez, Translatio Imperii: *Ein Beitrag zur Geschichte des Geschichtsdenkens und der politischen Theorien im Mittelalter und in der frühen Neuzeit* (Tübingen, 1958).

Excavating the Cross in Elene

As Donald J. Wilcox notes, the notion of conquest was constitutive of the concept, to the point where the unity of the process 'transcended any particular conquest and consisted in conquest itself, a condition that occurred in time and was transmitted from one polity to another'.[90]

While later historiographers sometimes differed in their identification of the individual peoples who supposedly 'held' *imperium*, the general westward movement of empire provided a certain sense of inevitability and purpose that is discernible far beyond the Middle Ages, most famously perhaps in George Berkeley's poem *On the Prospect of Planting Arts and Learning in America* (1752), whose line 'westward the course of empire takes its way' is cited in George Bancroft's 1834 *History of the United States* and also serves as the title to Emanuel Gottlieb Leutze's 1861 mural in the Capitol. While the painting's imperialist fantasies are concerned primarily with the westward expansion of the United States from the original New England colonies, Berkeley's poem more openly references the element of geographic transfer, as well as the concept's teleological nature:

There shall be sung another golden Age,
The rise of Empire and of Arts,
The Good and Great inspiring epic Rage,
The wisest Heads and noblest Hearts.

Not such as *Europe* breeds in her decay;
Such as she bred when fresh and young,
When heav'nly Flame did animate her Clay,
By future Poets shall be sung.

Westward the Course of Empire takes its Way;
The four first Acts already past,
A fifth shall close the Drama with the Day;
Time's noblest Offspring is the last. [91]

---

[90] Wilcox, *Measure*, 109.

[91] Quoted from George Berkeley, *The Works of George Berkeley, Bishop of Cloyne*, ed. A. A. Luce and T. E. Jessop (9 vols, London, 1955), vol. 7, 373 (1752 version) and 370 (1726 version). These are the last three out of six stanzas (lines 13–24). The poem was written in 1726 but not published until 1742; it was originally titled *America or the Muse's Refuge: A Prophecy* and had a different final line: 'The world's great Effort is the last'. See further Armin Paul Frank, 'Transatlantic Responses: Strategies in the Making of a New World Literature', in Andreas Poltermann (ed.), *Literaturkanon – Medienereignis – Kultureller Text: Formen interkultureller Kommunikation und Übersetzung* (Berlin, 1995), 211–31; Adrian Campbell, 'East, West, Rome's Best? The Imperial Turn', *Global Discourse*, 3:1 (2013), 34–47, at 40.

The last stanza can be read in the context of Christian interpretations of the *translatio imperii*, which tended to associate the concept with the four kingdoms of Daniel's vision in Daniel 7. These would then be followed by God's eternal kingdom on earth ('the fifth').[92] During the Middle Ages and beyond, the last of the four kingdoms was usually identified with the Roman Empire. Incidentally, the eschatological nature of this interpretation of Daniel 7 meant that the Roman Empire could not be understood as having ended at any point; otherwise, the end of the world would already have occurred – hence the medieval and early modern notion of a 'Holy Roman Empire' ('Sacrum Imperium Romanum') that was seen as a continuation of, rather than a successor to, the Roman Empire.[93]

In addition, Berkeley's concern with arts and learning addresses the related concept of *translatio studii*, that is, the transfer of learning from one centre to another. Although this concept is less strictly imperialist in theory, in practice the largely institutionalised nature of study meant (and still means) that what is accepted as academically correct is often tied up with social or political power. The concept was first formulated as *translatio sapientiae* by Otto von Freising in his *Chronica sive historia de duabus civitatibus* (1143–46), apparently as a deliberate parallel to the already current concept of *translatio imperii*,[94] which he was the first to use as a noun phrase: in earlier works, the concepts of *translatio imperii* and *translatio religionis* were expressed by means of verbs, such as *imperium transferre* and *religionem transferre*.[95] Karlheinz Stierle argues that 'Otto seems [...] to have given the formula of *imperium transferre* a new theoretical status

---

[92] In Daniel 2, Daniel interprets Nebuchadnezzar's dream of a statue made of four materials as a reference to four kingdoms; in Daniel 7, he himself has a vision of four beasts that also signify four kingdoms. These kingdoms were interpreted by Christian commentators (including Augustine in *De civitate Dei*) as precursors to God's eternal kingdom on earth, the last being the Roman Empire (although commentators disagreed about whether Rome was to be seen as the fourth kingdom or whether its Christianisation meant that it could be identified with the kingdom of God).

[93] On this issue, see Reinhart Koselleck, *Futures Past: On the Semantics of Historical Time*, trans. Keith Tribe (New York, 2004), 11–17. The denomination 'Holy Roman Empire of the German Nation' ('Sacrum Imperium Romanum Nationis Germanicæ', in German, 'Heiliges Römisches Reich Deutscher Nation') was sometimes used from the late Middle Ages onwards; it never had official status, however; see Peter H. Wilson, 'Bolstering the Prestige of the Habsburgs: The End of the Holy Roman Empire in 1806', *International History Review*, 28:4 (2006), 709–36, at 719.

[94] Goez, *Translatio Imperii*, 118.

[95] Karlheinz Stierle, '*Translatio Studii* and Renaissance: From Vertical to Horizontal Translation', in Sanford Budick and Wolfgang Iser (eds), *The Translatability of Cultures: Figurations of the Space Between* (Stanford, CA, 1996), 55–67, 313–15, at 56–7. For the latter, see Goez, *Translatio Imperii*, 378–81.

Excavating the Cross in Elene

by transforming it into the substantive form of *translatio'*. While that may indeed be the case, the frequency with which the formula *imperium transferre* was used by earlier authors demonstrates the existence of the concept long before it was explicitly formulated as such.[96] The same applies to the term *translatio sapientiae*, which goes back to antiquity – Otto himself names Flavius Josephus as his authority.[97] The later term *translatio studii* was used primarily to denote a transfer of learning from Greece to Rome, and from Rome to Paris.[98] This reflected the idea that Rome's political and cultural superiority had been divided and transferred to different places: while *imperium* had been awarded to the German emperors and *sacerdotium* to Rome, the study of philosophy and the liberal arts had been transferred to Paris.[99]

By the time Berkeley wrote his poem, the idea of a cultural transfer appears to have reverted to the older notion of a general geographical movement from East to West. This is prominently seen in the theory of 'heliotopism', according to which the *translatio imperii* followed the sun, 'moving inexorably from East to West'.[100] Strikingly, a similar notion still seems to haunt Western thinking to the present day; indeed, the very concept of a '*Western* modernity' that is politically and culturally 'more advanced' than the rest of the world is inextricably linked to the idea of a geographical transfer first formulated in the concept of *translatio imperii*. As Adrian Campbell notes, in the twenty-first century, Rome is still 'implicit in the West's identity', notwithstanding the fact that nineteenth-century republican narratives of 'Decline and Fall' appeared to have superseded

---

[96] Stierle, *'Translatio Studii'*, 56. Literary critics dealing with premodern texts frequently face the challenge of writing about texts that seem to display an acute awareness of concepts that were not explicitly theorised at the time. However, as noted in the introduction, literature is capable of opening perspectives that elude more explicit modes of theorisation. Stierle himself discusses Chrétien de Troyes's romance *Cligés* as an example of a text that expresses, in very striking terms, a theory of *translatio* without ever using the word itself (*ibid.*, 57–60).

[97] Goez, *Translatio Imperii*, 118. Goez also mentions Horace and Cicero as authors who speak of a transfer of learning from Greece to Rome. See also Ernst Robert Curtius, *European Literature and the Latin Middle Ages*, trans. Willard R. Trusk (Princeton, NJ, 2013), 29.

[98] Stierle notes that Vincent of Beauvais first uses the expression *sapientiae studium transferre* in his *Speculum historiale* (*c.* 1240–60) to describe a process of transfer by which Charlemagne allegedly brought the study of wisdom, which had formerly been passed on from Greece to Rome, to Paris. Goez and Stierle attribute the formula *translatio studii*, which became current in the late Middle Ages, to Martin of Opava/Martin von Troppau (died after 1278); see Goez, *Translatio Imperii*, 122–3; Stierle, *'Translatio Studii'*, 57.

[99] Stierle, *'Translatio Studii'*, 57.

[100] Campbell, 'East, West', 40.

the 'medieval belief in [...] the eternal survival of a universal Roman empire with supernatural legitimacy'.[101]

Historians and literary scholars alike have long noted the considerable extent to which nationalist narratives of the eighteenth and nineteenth centuries followed the same strategy as the classical and medieval historiographers who used the concept of *translatio* to claim the inheritance of classical antiquity, both in political and in cultural terms.[102] The practice of transporting objects from classical antiquity to collections and museums located in Western Europe and the United States can be seen as part of the same tradition. The notion that Western specialists would bring superior learning and technology to the study, curation and preservation of artefacts produced by cultures regarded not only as the culturally 'most advanced' civilisations of their time, but also as the origins of Western culture in general, involves an operation similar to that at work in the interrelated themes of *translatio imperii* and *translatio sapientiae*. The idea that the Western nation states were in some sense the heirs of a cultural tradition going back to ancient Greece and beyond implies a geographical transfer in which the cultural, military and political centres moved from Mesopotamia via the Mediterranean to north-western Europe and the United States. From this perspective, the appropriation of artefacts can be read as the physical enactment of the spatial movement of power and learning from East to West. In the case of Schliemann's excavation and relocation of Priam's Treasure, the image of *translatio* is especially fitting, since the movement of 'Trojan' objects to pre-World War I Germany – a country with high ambitions of becoming a colonial and world power – directly echoes the medieval foundation narratives of many European proto-states that followed the example provided by Virgil's *Aeneid* in claiming that they had been founded by Trojan princes.

In medieval Britain, such a claim was first formulated in the ninth-century *Historia Brittonum*, attributed to Nennius, and popularised through Geoffrey of Monmouth's early twelfth-century *Historia regum Britanniae*, where it is the Trojan prince Brutus who allegedly 'founded' Britain

---

[101] *Ibid.*, 40–1. Citing Cary J. Nederman, Campbell notes that these political narratives are 'not necessarily mutually opposed' (*ibid.*, 41; Nederman, 'Empire and the Historiography of European Political Thought: Marsiglio of Padua, Nicholas of Cusa, and the Medieval/Modern Divide', *Journal of the History of Ideas*, 66:1 [2005], 1–15).

[102] As well as Campbell's study, see also Elise Bartosik-Vélez, 'Translatio Imperii: Virgil and Peter Martyr's Columbus', *Comparative Literature Studies*, 46:4 (2009), 559–88, at 584–5; Mark Bradley (ed.), *Classics and Imperialism in the British Empire* (Oxford, 2010), especially Chapter 9: Margaret Malamud, 'Translatio Imperii: America as the New Rome *c.* 1900', 249–83.

Excavating the Cross in Elene

and lent the island his name.[103] In the earlier *Elene*, such a connection to Britain is absent, but the poem combines the classical concepts of *translatio imperii, studii et religionis* with a material transfer not at all unlike that involved in the incorporation of objects from classical antiquity into modern Western collections.

Elene's translationes

There are certain affinities between Elene's 'archaeological' project and the above-discussed practices of nineteenth- and twentieth-century imperial archaeology. Regarding the excavation of the True Cross, Elene and Constantine claim interpretative and curatorial authority; they also authorise a physical transfer of relics from Jerusalem to Rome, from East to West. Moreover, if *Elene* is a narrative of conversion, it can be equally termed a narrative of colonisation – not in the sense of Rome's military conquest of Judea, which by the time of the narrative was already a thing of the past, but through the establishing of Rome's ultimate cultural and theological hegemony, which in the poem is the direct corollary of the cross's discovery and the Jews' ensuing conversion: the conversion of Jerusalem's inhabitants may be the result of experiencing at first hand the miracles that reveal the location and identity of the cross, but none of these miracles would have transpired without the military power of the Empire that Elene commands, and that she wields to enforce Judas's compliance.[104]

Elene arrives in Jerusalem, which in the poem appears as a place far from the Empire's political centre, with all the pomp and military strength of an imperial ruler (lines 225–75), and she confronts the city's inhabitants with an imperious attitude and gestures reminiscent of a colonial master approaching the colonised subjects. In this context, it is worth reiterating that Elene is repeatedly referred to as *cwen* [queen], whereas the *Acta Cyriaci* usually employ her proper name and only rarely use the epithet *regina*.[105] Once found, the cross itself remains in Jerusalem (*Elene* makes no mention of the numerous relics produced from its wood that spread all over the world),[106] but its subsequent treatment and whereabouts are

---

[103] Nennius, *Historia Brittonum* 7–10, 16–18; Geoffrey of Monmouth, *Historia regum Britanniae* i.3–18.

[104] For a similar argument concerning the power imbalance that brings about Judas's acknowledgement of the crucifixion, his conversion and, thereby, the *inventio crucis*, see Estes, 'Colonization', 150.

[105] Klein, 'Reading Queenship', 56; see also Estes, 'Colonization', 135–6.

[106] Drijvers quotes a passage from Cyril of Jerusalem's mid-fourth-century *Catechesis* iv.10, where it is said that 'already the whole world is filled with

Remains of the Past in Old English Literature

dictated and monitored by representatives of the Empire: it is Constantine himself who, having learned of his mother's success, orders a church to be built over the spot where the cross was discovered, with Elene directing and supervising the project (lines 998b–1016). It is on Elene's authority, moreover, that the cross is decorated, encased in silver and erected within the building (lines 1017–32a), a physical *translatio reliquiae* of the kind that typically follows the *inventio* of relics, even if in this case it is directed by secular rather than spiritual authorities.

But *Elene* also includes a second instance of *translatio reliquiae* that is much more overtly political in nature. As mentioned above, after the second *inventio* of the Holy Nails, Elene follows the advice of an unnamed 'wise man' and has them reworked into a bit for the bridle-chain of Constantine's horse. This physical transformation changes the relics' semiotic status, turning them from sacred objects into a token of divinely sanctioned imperial power. As the unnamed counsellor observes, 'Bið þæt beacen gode / halig nemned, ond se hwæteadig, / wigge weorðod, se þæt wicg byrð' [That sign shall be named 'Holy to God', and the fortunate one honoured in war, whom that steed bears; lines 1193b–5]. The nails' undiminished status as holy relics ensures Constantine's success in war; at the same time, their use as part of the emperor's combat equipment – arguably the most visible display of his imperial power – signifies to the public that his actions, military and other, reflect the will of God. In *Elene*, the *inventio crucis* and the physical *translationes* that accompany the event signify the beginnings of God's mandation, the religious doctrine of the divine right of kings. The fact that Elene's transformation of the nails is described as the fulfilment of an Old Testament prophecy – the quotation within the anonymous wise man's speech recalls Zechariah 14.20[107] – lends it divine authority, just as the construction of a church to house the cross

---

fragments of the wood of the Cross' (*Helena Augusta*, 82). Gregory of Nyssa's *Vita Macrinae*, composed in *c*. 379, records that a necklace with a small iron crucifix and an iron ring containing a fragment of the cross was found under the clothes of his sister, the abbess Macrina, when her body was laid out after her death (*ibid.*, 90–1).

[107] See Craig Williamson (trans.), *The Complete Old English Poems* (Philadelphia, PA, 2017), 260. Cf. Zechariah 14.20: 'in die illo, erit quod super frenum equi est, sanctum Domino: et erunt lebetes in domo Domini quasi fialae coram altari' [In that day that which is upon the bridle of the horse shall be holy to the Lord: and the caldrons in the house of the Lord shall be as the phials before the altar; all quotations from the Bible are from Weber-Gryson (Latin), with added punctuation, and Douay-Rheims (English)]. In *Elene*, the respective lines are presented as a quotation within a quotation: the unnamed wise man who advises Elene quotes another unnamed 'snottor searuþancum' (line 1189) as having spoken these words ('þæt word gecwæð'; line 1190). Zechariah's prophecy is more usually associated with Christ's entering of Jerusalem.

was earlier described as having been carried out in accordance with God's wishes (lines 1017–22a).

Elene's actions, the poem thus makes clear, are authorised directly by God, but that does not rid them of their colonial and imperial overtones. As Zollinger observes, *Elene* describes the process 'by which the spiritual interests of the Christian faith become identified with the political interests of Constantine and the Roman Empire', a process that starts with the battle against Barbarians at the very beginning of the poem, incidentally the only heathens in the poem not to convert.[108] Once the cross has been installed in the new temple and Elene starts turning her mind to the nails, the poem refers to her as 'cristenra cwen' [queen of the Christians; line 1068a]. Arguably, the poem does so in order to stress her status as queen of the newly converted Jews. But a second reading is possible, one that takes the epithet not as a recently acquired title, but rather as the formulation of an imperial claim: for Elene to become *cristenra cwen*, all the Empire's subjects must convert to Christianity. Against the background of this universal demand, all of Elene's actions are manifestations of both secular and religious authority. As Klein points out in the context of Elene's earlier confrontation with Jerusalem's wise men,

> drawing on the power of the terms *cwen* and *hlæfdige* to signal the Jews' offense against Elene as both secular leader and Holy Church, the poem sanctifies royal authority as it backs Christianity with the power of the state. Resistance to the state and resistance to God are conflated as reciprocal offenses, a point driven home in the poem through Cynewulf's use of the term *þeoden* (prince) as a title for both Constantine and God (267b, 487a).[109]

As a Christian ruler, *cristenra cwen*, Elene claims not only political but also spiritual hegemony over her subjects. In a sense, her approach resembles that of later European colonial endeavours, in which political, military and economic domination went hand in hand with missionary and 'educational' impulses.[110]

Obviously, Constantine himself is a very recent convert to Christianity, and although the poem does not mention any further attempts at proselytisation within Rome itself, the fact that the emperor found it initially difficult to acquire information about his vision of the cross implies that the majority of the Roman populace should be imagined to be pagans at

---

[108] Zollinger, 'Cynewulf's *Elene*', 186.
[109] Klein, 'Reading Queenship', 57.
[110] See, for example, Chakrabarty, *Provincializing Europe*, 10, who draws attention to Homi Bhabha's binary of 'pedagogic' and 'performative' aspects of postcolonial nationalism, with the pedagogic mode continuing to replicate Western narratives and conventions.

this point. Howe observes that in *Elene* 'conversion is an act that forever alters a people and their realm, whether it be Constantine and his fellow heathens in Rome or Judas become Cyriacus and his fellow Jews in Jerusalem'.[111] Ultimately, the poem's central topic is the triumph of Christianity as the sole provider of spiritual, material and historical truth – a complete victory imagined in decidedly imperial terms.[112] Just as the gospels situate Christ's birth during the reign of Augustus, so does *Elene* link conversion to the idea of Empire: it is during the reign of the first Christian emperor that the True Cross is discovered and Jerusalem's Jewish population converted.[113] Moreover, while Constantine himself is eager to change his religious affiliation, the conversion of the Jews 'is represented as a difficult and protracted matter complicated by bad faith and misplaced will';[114] as Estes points out, 'those like Constantine who accept Christianity easily are celebrated; for those who resist Christian faith, the poem legitimises the use of force in accomplishing conversion'.[115] Thus, Elene resorts to torture to bring Judas to acknowledge his latent faith, a measure without which neither the archaeological discovery of the cross nor the subsequent conversion of his compatriots would have been possible.[116] And even after the *inventio*, Jerusalem's citizens have no say in the decision as to what is to be done with the cross; they merely acknowledge the rulers' cultural hegemony by converting to their religion.

The link between Jerusalem's political and spiritual subjection is made explicit early on when Judas quotes his grandfather's prophecy that the Jewish people will lose its secular and religious authority once the cross has been found and the superiority of the Christian faith established:

[111] Howe, 'Rome', 166.

[112] In a way, my own argument thus reverses Estes's contention that 'the clear message in *Elene* [is] that Christian faith itself is sole justification for martial conquest and cultural imperialism' ('Colonization', 137): conversion, in the way imagined in *Elene*, is only possible within an imperialist context.

[113] As Estes points out, the story's dependence on Jerusalem's being peopled by Jews is historically inaccurate: at the time, Jews were prohibited from entering Jerusalem ('Colonization', 147).

[114] *Ibid.*, 149.

[115] *Ibid.*, 147.

[116] Lavezzo sees Judas's refusal to comply with Elene's wishes as part of the 'lithic' mentality ascribed to Jews in the early Middle Ages, a mentality that can be broken only by force (*Accommodated Jew*, 31). By contrast, Heckman argues that Elene's having to take recourse to torture reveals the limits of Christian wisdom ('Things in Doubt', 470). I would argue that whatever ethical judgement we ascribe to the poet or their audience(s), the poem itself portrays the use of force to bring about religious acculturation as an imperial practice.

Excavating the Cross in Elene

> Ne mæg æfre ofer þæt   Ebrea þeod
> rædþeahtende   rice healdan,
> duguðum wealdan,   ac þara dom leofað
> ond hira dryhtscipe,
> in woruld weorulda   willum gefylled,
> ðe þone ahangnan cyning   heriaþ and lofiað.

[The Hebrew people will never after that hold counselling power, rule the multitudes; rather, the fame and lordship will live forever and ever, filled with pleasure, of those who praise and laud the crucified king; lines 448–53.]

Of course, the Jews' stubborn resistance against 'well-meaning' attempts at converting them and their alleged aspirations to world dominion are among the oldest and most persistent anti-Jewish stereotypes.[117] But Elene's imperialist attitude makes it possible to read the passage from a different perspective: not *only* as a Christian poem's reiteration of antisemitic sentiment, but *also* as a colonial subject's reaction against the threat of cultural displacement. Considered in this light, Judas's initial refusal to publicly accept the Christian truth can be interpreted as an act of resistance that defies the colonisers' demand for conformity with their historiographical narrative, a narrative aimed squarely at the assimilation and/or displacement of the subaltern's religion and culture.

The second part of Judas's grandfather's speech, which predicts a pan-Christian future, has obvious eschatological overtones: the conversion of the Jews was frequently held to be the last requirement to be fulfilled before the second *parousia* could take place. Yet converting, and thereby assimilating, the notoriously 'obstinate' Jews (as Christian commentators would have it) can also be read as a manifestation of supreme colonial power, one that far exceeds mere military conquest. As Estes remarks, 'the narrative of *Elene* suggests that if they will not convert, the pagans will disappear, written out of history and legend [...]. The people of Jerusalem become the Other, colonised and converted through force in the imagined universe of the poem [...].'[118] In *Elene*, this colonisation-cum-conversion is inextricably tied up with the figure of the emperor and that of his mother, who acts as his representative and substitute. Neither of the two characters is defined exclusively by their military power, which allows them to compel the colonial subalterns to accept their own version of spiritual truth; rather, Constantine turns into a veritable instrument of grace whose actions bring about the conversion (and thus the salvation)

---

[117] See Lavezzo, *Accommodated Jew*, 37–8.
[118] Estes, 'Colonization', 150.

Remains of the Past in Old English Literature

of his subjects.[119] In the poem, his status as a divinely sanctioned Christian ruler is substantiated by the *inventio* of the cross and further emphasised by the public display of the transformed Holy Nails. Much more than just a poem of conversion, *Elene* describes nothing less than the beginning of a 'Holy Roman Empire' characterised by God-given rulership.

The imperialist narrative pervading *Elene* makes the poem's single reference to Troy all the more meaningful. Elene, as I noted above, challenges Judas's plea of ignorance regarding the crucifixion by drawing attention to the fact that the Trojan War took place much longer ago, but is nevertheless remembered vividly. I have argued above that she uses this parallel in order to ridicule Judas's insistence that historical events are prone to be forgotten the more distant they become by applying a strictly chronological logic: the more recent an event, the more reliably it should be recalled. At the same time, however, Elene's reference to the Trojan War also discreetly reminds Judas of her own status as representative of the Roman Empire, an empire whose power and legitimacy, according to Virgil's *Aeneid*, ultimately derive from Troy.

The *Aeneid* was well-known in early medieval Britain. Helmut Gneuss lists five manuscripts from the ninth to the eleventh centuries containing it, but an intimate knowledge of the text is also suggested in a number of literary works, including some of Aldhelm's, Felix's *Vita Guthlaci* (which includes 'a number of carefully chosen quotations' from the *Aeneid*, according to Joseph Grossi) and, as has been repeatedly argued, even *Beowulf*.[120] According to the *Aeneid*, Rome was founded by Romulus, a

---

[119] This arguably works to the detriment of Elene, whose imperious and unforgiving manner contrasts unfavourably with her son's much more humble and humane demeanour. Although such a reading may be anachronistic in the context of early medieval literature, which seems to value assertive behaviour on the part of queens, one senses the misogynist stereotype of the ambitious mother contrasting with the more restrained (but no less successful) son. As Estes notes, Elene herself does not act as a 'peace-weaver'; rather, the poem stresses her martial role ('Colonization', 141). See, however, Klein, who reads Elene's belligerent attitude as primarily an extension of her function as a representative of royal and religious authority, and stresses her subservience to Constantine ('Reading Queenship', *passim*).

[120] Helmut Gneuss, *Handlist of Anglo-Saxon Manuscripts: A List of Manuscripts and Manuscript Fragments Written or Owned in England up to 1100* (Tempe, AZ, 2001). The five manuscripts listed by Gneuss are items 12e (eleventh century); 477 (eleventh century); 503 (second quarter of the tenth century); 648 (second third of the ninth century); and 919 (second half of the tenth to first quarter of the eleventh century). On Felix's eighth-century *Vita Sancti Guthlaci*, see Joseph Grossi, 'Barrow Exegesis: Quotation, Chorography, and Felix's *Life of St. Guthlac*', *Florilegium*, 30 (2013), 143–65, at 144. On Aldhelm, see Michael Lapidge, 'The Career of Aldhelm', *Anglo-Saxon England*, 36 (2007), 15–69; Lapidge, 'Hypallage

Excavating the Cross in Elene

grandson of the Trojan prince Aeneas, who established his kingdom in Italy after escaping from the burning city of his fathers. Rome's imperial status is thus legitimised by a historical process that, from a medieval perspective, can be described as an instance of *translatio*.[121] This *translatio* operates on several levels. In an abstract sense, Rome's legitimacy stems from the temporal and spatial movement of *imperium* from East to West, from the Assyrians via the Medes, Persians and Macedonians all the way to Rome. This movement is, of course, tied to military achievements, but it transcends, in Wilcox's words quoted earlier, any individual conquest.[122] At the same time, Rome's pre-eminence can also be traced to a physical *translatio* performed by actual human beings who travelled across the Mediterranean to Italy: through the figure of Aeneas, the Roman emperors could quite literally trace their descent to Troy. According to this narrative, the Greek defeat of the Trojans, as recounted in the Homeric epics, was later compensated by Rome's conquest of Greece, whose culture and learning it appropriated – including the textual *translatio* of the story of Troy into Virgil's imperialist narrative. By appropriating the *Iliad*'s legendary subject matter (along with the *Odyssey*'s voyage motif) for the purposes of a legitimising political myth, the *Aeneid* cemented the two Homeric works' status as the foundation of Western literature while simultaneously inscribing itself into a literary history that is likewise tied to a geographical movement from East to West. When *Elene* – a work com-

---

in the Old English *Exodus*', *Leeds Studies in English*, 37 (2006), 31–9. A number of scholars, including Friedrich Klaeber and, more recently, Richard North, have attempted to demonstrate that the *Beowulf* poet was familiar with the *Aeneid*; see Friedrich Klaeber, '*Aeneis* und *Beowulf*', *Archiv für das Studium der Neueren Sprachen und Literaturen*, 126 (1911), 40–8, 339–59; Richard North, *The Origins of Beowulf: From Vergil to Wiglaf* (Oxford, 2006); Andrew James Johnston, '*Beowulf* as Anti-Virgilian World Literature: Archaeology, Ekphrasis, and Epic', in Irina Dumitrescu and Eric Weiskott (eds), *The Shapes of Early English Poetry: Style, Form, History* (Kalamazoo, MI, 2019), 37–58, at 47–8. Johnston argues that *Beowulf* draws on Virgilian ekphrasis to subvert the latter's political significance.

[121] Indeed, the notion of a political transfer from Troy to Rome and on to various European kingdoms was so widespread, especially during the later Middle Ages and the early modern period, that Patrick Poppe proposes the neologism *translatio Troiae* in order to make the phenomenon more tangible, even though such an expression did not exist at the time; see Patrick Poppe, '"Translatio Europae?": Kulturelle Transferdiskurse im Kontext des Falls von Konstantinopel (PhD dissertation, Saarbrücken, 2019), 26; <http://dx.doi.org/10.22028/D291-27907> [accessed 29 February 2024]. Poppe interprets the medieval notion of a *translatio* of the Trojan *gens* from Asia Minor to various European kingdoms as an early attempt to establish a European identity through common filiation ('Filiationsverband') (*ibid.*, 25–6).

[122] Wilcox, *Measure*, 109.

posed in one of the westernmost parts of the then-known world – refers to the Trojan War, it thus perpetuates this very same process.

The poem's treatment of these issues is highly oblique. Apart from the single direct reference, *Elene* never mentions the Homeric and Virgilian epics, nor does it refer overtly to the Trojan foundation myth of the Roman Empire. Even so, I would argue that the expansionist history of the Roman Empire that Virgil's epic was meant to legitimise is implicitly present throughout the poem. Elene's triumphant journey eastward across the Mediterranean symbolically re-enacts the eastward expansion of the Roman Empire, including its defeat of the Greeks that conferred upon it the status of *imperium*. On her journey to Jerusalem, Elene tellingly disembarks her army in Greece ('Creca land'; line 250a), whence her soldiers – whose prowess and military equipment are described at length – march into 'the land of the Jews' ('Iudeas [...] land'; lines 268–70). This passage (which, unlike the queen's reference to the Trojan War, is notably absent from any known version of the *Acta Cyriaci*) emphasises the military legitimisation of *imperium*:

> Wæs seo eadhreðige   Elene gemyndig,
> þriste on geþance,   þeodnes willan
> georn on mode   þæt hio Iudeas
> ofer herefeldas   heape gecoste
> lindwigendra   land gesohte,
> secga þreate.

> [The blessed Elene was mindful, bold in thought, of the prince's will, eager in mood, that she should seek the land of the Jews across battlefields, with the band of tried warriors armed with shields, the troop of men; lines 266–71a.]

Even though the poem claims that Elene was 'mindful' ('gemyndig') of her son's wish that she should make her way to Judea 'across battlefields' ('ofer herefeldas'), nowhere is her army reported to have engaged in any actual battles on its way. Unless we are to imagine Elene as deliberately avoiding military confrontations – and the text in no way endorses such a reading – it is perhaps best to interpret the 'herefeldas' as the sites of *historical* battles: battles fought in the past, whose outcome contributed to the current status quo and thereby directly or indirectly supported Rome's imperial claims. Indeed, no more than a very superficial knowledge of geography is required to see that Elene's eastward movement traces the movement of *translatio imperii* in an inverted direction, from Rome to Asia Minor. Even more intriguingly, taking the land route from Greece (which, from an early medieval perspective, would primarily imply Byzantium) through Anatolia also implies passing through the general region – and

Excavating the Cross in Elene

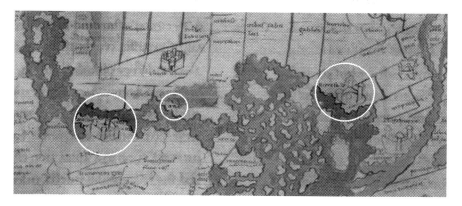

Figure 1   Detail from Cotton Tiberius B.v, fol. 56v, showing Constantinople, Troy and Jerusalem.

possibly even the very site – that had, since antiquity, been associated with the Trojan War.[123]

The name Τρῳάς (γῆ) (Trōiás (gê), [Trojan (land)]) is attested in writing since the fifth century BCE, at which point it was apparently already a destination for pilgrimage. Alexander the Great, who was reputed to have slept with a copy of the *Iliad* under his pillow, allegedly visited the place when he passed into Asia in 334 BCE. Later, it became the site of a Hellenistic settlement ('Ilion') that was built over with a Roman city, 'Ilium', under none other than Julius Caesar himself. The Hellenistic and Roman settlements continued to draw visitors who wished to see the historic site of the Trojan War (and were presumably disappointed when they found souvenir shops rather than soot-blackened walls). The city was only abandoned in the sixth century CE. On the Cotton Tiberius B.v mappa mundi, dated to the mid-eleventh century and the only British mappa mundi to have survived from before the twelfth century,[124] Troy is situated south-east of Constantinople, on the other bank of the Bosphorus, about a quarter of the way to Jerusalem, as the crow flies (Figure 1). While there is no direct connection between this map and the earlier *Elene*, it suggests that, as the early Middle Ages were drawing to a close, Troy figured in the geographical imagination of Britain as a place situated on the coastal route from Byzantium to Jerusalem.

---

[123] The following account follows Latacz, *Troia*, 47–8. Latacz raises the possibility that Homer himself might have visited the site and could have based his descriptions, however loosely, on what he saw. In this hypothetical case, Homer would have been an early 'ruin tourist' (*ibid.*, 230–1).

[124] Catherine E. Karkov, *The Art of Anglo-Saxon England* (Woodbridge, 2011), 289.

As Alexander's visit and the rebuilding programme under Caesar suggest, Troy was associated throughout antiquity with imperial claims and conquests. As the place of origin of Rome's legendary founders, it was moreover inextricably linked to Rome's rise to power, and indeed to the very notion of a 'Roman Empire'. Elene's reference to the Jews' detailed knowledge of the Trojan War – contrasting with their ignorance of sacred history – thus has a decidedly imperialist undertone: knowing his Trojan War, as Elene supposes he does, Judas should also be aware of both the legitimacy and the potency of Rome's imperial power, a power that will allow her to carry out her threats. Even more to the point, he should be aware of the historical determinism implicit in the concept of *translatio* that suggests that Elene will eventually carry the day.

At the same time, *Elene's* juxtaposition of the Trojan War with the crucifixion draws attention to yet another instance of *translatio*, this time involving the cities of Rome and Jerusalem. The *Aeneid's* interpretation of the Trojan War as *the* event through which political and military power passed from Troy to Rome parallels the Christian interpretation of the crucifixion as the event by which spiritual truth is conferred from Jewish to Christian faith, from Old Testament to New Testament. By the same means, Jerusalem is transformed (in a Christian perspective) from the Holy City of the Jews into the Holy City of Christianity. Both transfers are imagined in terms of a direct succession, but also in terms of a genealogical relationship, thereby moving beyond the usually non-genealogical motif of *translatio*. The concept of *translatio imperii*, as already noted, was traditionally regarded as a process whereby *imperium*, understood as universal (or near-universal) political and military dominance, was transferred from one polity to another by means of military conquest. This transfer did not usually involve a genealogical relationship between the two entities involved; indeed, it did not require *any* relationship beyond political or military rivalry. The *Aeneid*, by contrast, posits a genealogical continuity between Troy and Rome, which allowed the Roman rulers to trace their descent directly to the city's ruling elite. In *Elene*, Jerusalem's apparently uniformly Jewish population converts from Judaism to Christianity; the change of status thus affects what is materially and geographically the same city. From this perspective, the earlier transformation of Jerusalem's spiritual significance at the moment of the crucifixion prefigures the later conversion of the city's population.

At the same time, and even more significantly in the context of *Elene's* imperialist narrative, the poem also suggests a spatial *translatio* from Jerusalem to Rome that parallels the geographical relationship between Troy and Rome. Just as the *Aeneid's* Roman foundation myth suggests that political power has passed from Troy to Rome, so does *Elene's* own narrative imply that Rome can now lay claim to the title of 'Holy City' – with the difference that Jerusalem does not lose its own status in the process,

Excavating the Cross in *Elene*

at least not entirely. This *translatio* – in medieval terminology, a *translatio religionis*[125] – is enacted on several levels. On the one hand, Rome's theological authority is presented as surpassing, but also as ultimately originating from, Jerusalem's: the spiritual (and, with regard to the event of the crucifixion, also historical) knowledge that Constantine and Elene attain with the help of their Christian counsellors in Rome is greater than that of the Jerusalemites, whose wisest men are merely versed in Moses' Law ('Moyses æ'; line 283b), as the text takes care to note:

> Heht þa gebeodan   burgsittendum
> þam snoterestum   side ond wide
> geond Iudeas,   gumena gehwylcum,
> meðelhegende,   on gemot cuman,
> þa ðe deoplicost   dryhtnes geryno
> þurh rihte æ   reccan cuðon.
> Ða wæs gesamnod   of sidwegum
> mægen unlytel,   þa ðe Moyses æ
> reccan cuðon.

> [[She] then commanded the wisest citizens far and wide among the Jews, each of the men, deliberating, to come to a meeting, those that could expound the deepest of the Lord's secrets through the right law. Then was gathered from distant parts not a small host, that which could expound Moses' law; lines 276–84a.]

As Estes notes, the discrepancy between the theological competence demanded by Elene – the ability to explain the Lord's secrets through the 'right law' ('rihte æ'; line 281a) – and that possessed by experts in 'Moses' law' ('Moyses æ'; line 283b), a discrepancy emphasised by the parallel construction, underlines the Jews' comparative ignorance in matters of faith.[126] Martin Irvine, too, notes that the Jews lack the proper codes for interpreting the cross's significance, arguing that Elene draws attention to their inferiority – an inferiority that is not merely spiritual but also epistemic – by staging her interrogation as an 'exegetical challenge'.[127] From the outset, then, superior theological authority is associated with Rome; first through the city's (initially invisible) Christians, and then through the characters of Constantine and Elene, who effect the conversion of Jerusalem's Jews.

---

[125] See Goez, *Translatio Imperii*, 378–81. According to Goez, Christian exegetical texts used the expression *religionem transferre* to describe the spread of Christianity from the Jews to other, pagan peoples from the time of Jerome onwards (*ibid.*, 378–9).

[126] Estes, 'Colonization', 145.

[127] Irvine, 'Literary Theory', 168–9.

Remains of the Past in Old English Literature

The fact that the city's population not only failed to acknowledge the crucifixion's spiritual significance, but even, over the course of generations, entirely forgot about it also establishes Rome's greater authority when it comes to the events of the past. This historiographical superiority, too, can be read in terms of a transfer, since, from a Christian perspective, Jewish historiography (in the form of the Old Testament) possessed the highest authority up to the time of the incarnation. Judas's admission of the fragmentary nature of the Jewish historiographical tradition thus implicitly corroborates what Heckman takes to be Elene's implicit accusation against the Jews; namely, that by forgetting about the crucifixion, they have undermined their own learned authority.[128] Elene's 'rihte æ' thus succeeds 'Moyses æ' in more than one sense, surpassing but also originating from it. The transfer of spiritual and historiographical authority from the Old to the New Testament thus goes hand in hand with a geographical movement that can be described by the classical *topoi* of *translatio religionis* and *translatio sapientiae*, signalling Rome's supersession of Jerusalem as the site of superior spiritual and historiographical knowledge.[129] Implicitly, these two *translationes* are linked to Rome's political superiority, which is itself based on the *translatio imperii* alluded to obliquely in Elene's reference to the Trojan War.

Elene enacts and, significantly, materialises this spiritual *translatio* by sending a relic of the crucifixion – the event that established Jerusalem's centrality to salvation history – to Rome: the Holy Nails, transformed into a bit for Constantine's bridle.[130] In so doing, she links the classical *topoi* of *translatio imperii* and *translatio religionis* to the Christian concept of

---

[128] Heckman, 'Things in Doubt', 465–6.

[129] As Estes notes, the impression of Rome's theological superiority is somewhat mitigated by Elene's eventual ceding of authority to the now-converted Judas, renamed Cyriacus and freshly appointed bishop of Jerusalem ('Colonization', 149), but this by no means affects the general operation of *translatio*. Estes argues that Elene's 'deferential manner of addressing him, in direct contrast to her earlier commanding language, shows that Judas has taken his rightful place in the gendered hierarchy of Christianity, and now outranks Helen despite her status as queen. [...] She has remained static, still Christian, still female, while Judas has converted from Jew to Christian and has been elevated to the power of the bishopric'. Nevertheless, as early medieval audiences would have been aware, the highest theological authority appertains to the bishop of Rome.

[130] Bynum points out an intriguing parallel in the tradition, attested from the mid-fifteenth century, that the holy staircase in St John Lateran was not only climbed and descended by Jesus himself on the way to his trial before Pontius Pilate, but also brought to Rome by Constantine's mother as a gift to Pope Sylvester (*Christian Materiality*, 138). There is a similar tradition, also attested from the mid-fifteenth century, relating to the Casa Santa at Loreto, which was allegedly transported to Italy by angels after the fall of Acre in 1291; see Nagel and Wood, *Anachronic Renaissance*, 195–8.

translatio reliquiae: the spatial movement of a relic from an earlier resting place to a shrine where it can be venerated and displayed publicly. The *translatio* of relics likewise involves a transfer of spiritual significance from one place to another, without the former necessarily losing it; at the very least, the relic's contact with the soil where it was found ensures that some of the spiritual power remains at the site of the original *inventio*.[131] In the same manner, Jerusalem did not lose its status as Holy City when the Petrine See was established in Rome, and neither does it lose its spiritual significance in *Elene*. Still, it is a new kind of spiritual significance that characterises Jerusalem, for the city's population has by now converted to Christianity: its spiritual status has been transformed so as to conform to the theological truth of the colonisers.[132] As in the case of the nails, which have been transformed into a symbol of the imperial ruler's divine right, Jerusalem's status has been transformed in a way that transfers the interpretive hegemony to the colonisers. The poem lends this division of spiritual power material emphasis by dividing the relics of the *inventio crucis*: the cross itself remains in Jerusalem, while the nails are sent to Rome. This twofold division, of material relics on the one hand and of spiritual significance on the other, recalls Daniel 2.41, which states that the fourth kingdom – the one usually associated with Rome – will be a divided kingdom. But even here, the spiritual, material and political aspects of *translatio* remain inextricably linked.

Through its various associations, *Elene*'s single reference to Troy evokes a network of different geographical, political, textual and spiritual *translationes* that are not easily divisible, but that all work in tandem to substantiate Rome's political and spiritual power. By juxtaposing the Trojan War and the crucifixion as the two main historical events whose outcome has direct relevance to the present, the poem not only provides two separate points of origin for Rome's secular and religious authority, but also emphasises the material aspect of *translatio*. The spatial *translatio* of the Holy Nails, which are relocated from Jerusalem to Rome, and whose voyage symbolically enacts a transfer of spiritual authority and significance, parallels Aeneas's journey from Troy to Rome, which provides the material basis for the political *translatio* that will eventually result in Rome's rise to political and military hegemony, and historically underlines and justifies the city's imperial claims. In *Elene*, the *inventio crucis*, an archaeological event of the utmost spiritual and political significance, signals the fruition of these imperial claims.

[131] Bynum, *Christian Materiality*, 136.
[132] Estes, 'Colonization', 149.

Conclusion

In *Elene*, I have argued, the archaeological story of the *inventio crucis* is essentially reduced to a spiritual and political narrative in which the physical cross functions primarily as a tool of conversion and a symbol of divinely sanctioned political power. As an object of archaeological investigation, by contrast, it proves practically worthless: it cannot yield any historical insight beyond what the Scriptural accounts of the crucifixion provide; indeed, its very identification as the instrument of Christ's Passion is dependent upon divine revelation. This, one might argue, is hardly surprising, given the different epistemological framework in which medieval investigations into the past usually operated, at least as far as they have come down to us. Contemporary chronicles and historiographical accounts were based on the classical tradition of historiography and Christian theology rather than on scholarly and scientific discourse, which forms the cornerstone of archaeology as a modern discipline. On the other hand, Constantine's wish to gain historical insight from what is by all accounts not only a sacred, but also an archaeological, object, as well as the measures that he takes to find it, including excavation and historiographical research, testify to a desire – and an ability to imagine – a form of archaeological endeavour that is distinct from the miracle-guided religious *inventio* – even if that desire is, in the final analysis, frustrated.

At the same time, the political and social functions performed by the cross in *Elene* are by no means unique to premodern engagements with the material past. As I hope to have shown by discussing the poem alongside modern archaeological undertakings, many practices involving objects from the past, including archaeological excavation, curation and research, are accompanied – and sometimes even driven – by social and political narratives with which they are indissolubly entangled. In *Elene*, these different forms of engagement with the material past converge and culminate in the text's single reference to Troy, arguably one of the most prominent and enduring Western myths of origin, imperial and archaeological, medieval and modern alike.

2

Ruins and Their Multiple Temporalities:
The Wanderer and *The Ruin*

Maxims II, also known as the 'Cotton Maxims' due to its survival in MS London, British Library, Cotton Tiberius B i, opens with a curious reference to stone cities:[1]

> Cyning sceal rice healdan.   Ceastra beoð feorran gesyne,
> orðanc enta geweorc,   þa þe on þysse eorðan syndon,
> wrætlic weallstana geweorc.   Wind byð on lyfte swiftust,
> þunar byð þragum hludast.

> [A king shall rule. Cities will be seen from afar, the skilful work of giants, those that are on this earth, wondrous work of wall-stones. Wind will be swiftest in the air, thunder will be at times loudest; lines 1–4a.][2]

Couched between two fairly banal statements – 'cyning sceal rice healdan' [a king shall rule] and 'wind byð on lyfte swiftest' [wind will be swiftest in the air] – it appears, at first sight, to be no more than a casual observation. Upon closer scrutiny, however, the additional details the text provides suggest that we are not dealing with a mere commonplace here: the poem speaks of 'wrætlic weallstana geweorc' [wondrous work of wall-stones], implying either that the stonework in question has been executed in a particularly skilful manner – a notion further reinforced by the adjective *orðanc* [cunning, ingenious] in the subsequent phrase 'orðanc enta geweorc' [the skilful work of giants] – or that masonry in general is regarded as extraordinary. Citing Peter Ramey and Irina Dumitrescu, Denis Ferhatović points out that the term *wrætlic* [wondrous, awe-inspir-

---

[1] 'City' is the word most commonly used to gloss Old English *ceaster* in modern editions of the text. The exact meaning of the word *ceaster*, derived from Latin *castrum*, is far from clear and may have varied over time and between users. *BT* list 'a fortress; a city, fort, castle, town' (*urbs, civitas, castellum*), *CH* 'castle, fort, town' (s.v. *ceaster*). Whereas Latin *castrum* had a decidedly military connotation, we cannot be sure that its Old English derivative continued to transport the same meaning. Nor need the compound *weallstana* [wall-stones] imply fortifications; the expression might just as well refer to the wall of a particularly impressive building.

[2] Old English text quoted from Elliott Van Kirk Dobbie (ed.), *The Anglo-Saxon Minor Poems*, ASPR, 6 (New York, 1942), 55.

Remains of the Past in Old English Literature

ing], has a distinct aesthetic dimension, conveying the combined senses of materiality, creativity and mystery.[3] In Old English texts, it is frequently used in reference to objects perceived as singularly intricate, impressive (potentially even terrifying) and mysterious. To a certain extent, Ferhatović notes, the latter aspect defines the others: '*Wrætlic* and riddlic go hand in hand.'[4] The artefacts in question often derive their striking quality from a certain incomprehensibility as far as their origin, design and/or meaning are concerned. This is precisely the sort of wonder that seems to be implied in *Maxims II*: there is something awe-inspiring and mysterious about the stone structures mentioned in the poem and the 'giants' who built them. And yet, the ostensibly exceptional status of such structures appears to be belied by the implicit universality of the statement 'ceastra beoð feorran gesyne' [cities are seen from afar], which ties in with the poem's overarching project of compiling pieces of commonplace 'wisdom'; indeed, the qualifying phrase 'þa þe on þysse eorðan syndon' [those which are on this earth] implies that the poem is speaking of (stone) *caestra* in general and not of specific ones.[5]

In purely structural terms, the opening lines of *Maxims II* are hardly unusual for Old English poetry of this kind,[6] which, for want of a better

---

[3] Ferhatović, *Borrowed Objects*, 7, 92; Peter Ramey, 'The Riddle of Beauty: The Aesthetics of *Wrætlic* in Old English Verse', *Modern Philology*, 114 (2017), 457–81. According to Dumitrescu, *wrætlic* 'represents a mixture of horror and admiration that provokes reflection'; Irina Dumitrescu, *The Experience of Education in Anglo-Saxon Literature* (Cambridge, 2018), 128. In *Maxims II* (and, for that matter, *The Ruin*), the aspect of horror appears not to be very pronounced. What the word does convey, however, is a sense of something curious, out of the ordinary. Andrew J. G. Patenall explains that *wrætlic* is related to Old English *wrætt* [jewel, ornament], which might explain its semantic oscillation between wondrousness, beauty and intricacy; Andrew J. G. Patenall, 'The Image of the Worm: Some Literary Implications of Serpentine Decoration', in J. Douglas Woods and David Pelteret (eds), *The Anglo-Saxons: Synthesis and Achievement* (Waterloo, CA, 2006), 105–16, at 111.

[4] Ferhatović, *Borrowed Objects*, 79.

[5] While this is the most plausible reading of the passage, it should be noted that grammatically, the qualifying phrase might also refer to *enta* [giants], thereby providing a tantalising parallel to Genesis 6.4: 'gigantes [...] erant super terram in diebus illis.' I thank the anonymous reviewer for pointing out this alternative possibility.

[6] Regarding the passage under consideration here, P. J. Frankis notes that while in *Maxims II* there does not seem to be a logical connection between one piece of wisdom and the next, the reference to wind that follows the allusion to stone cities matches the wind imagery present in several other Old English texts in which stone structures are mentioned alongside giants. He surmises that 'so strong is the association between the work of giants and wind or storm imagery that one maxim clearly determines the next, just as in *Andreas* 1236b

Ruins and Their Multiple Temporalities

term, has been variously called 'wisdom', 'sapiential' or even 'catalogue' poetry.[7] While many of the observations border on the banal, their presentation suggests an interest in the possible significance and appeal of the mundane, a feature the poems share with the Old English riddles.[8] 'Ceastra beoð feorran gesyne' [cities are (or, perhaps: can be) seen from afar] – the statement may simply reflect the fact that, because of their usually greater size, stone structures can be seen from a greater distance than farmsteads or smaller hamlets. As such, the message is hardly less commonplace than 'a king shall rule' or 'wind will be [i.e., is usually] swiftest in the air' – indeed, the very casualness of the statement suggests that, in spite of the wonder expressed at the quality of the workmanship, the distant sight of stone cities itself constitutes a fairly unremarkable phenomenon. Yet when examining the buildings at close quarters and contemplating their origin – so the syntactic structure of the passage implies – their wonder becomes apparent – as in the Old English riddles, which may reveal, through a change of perspective, 'the great wonder of commonplace things'.[9] In *Maxims II*, such a change in perspective never really occurs, and it is left to the reader to imagine the details of the masonry. The dominant image is that of cities or fortifications seen from afar, part of the overall scenery rather than of the immediate surroundings. The poem's detachment heightens the sense of alterity already evoked by the awe-inspiring stonework, by the builders' designation as 'giants', and perhaps even by the choice of the Latin-derived *ceaster* rather than the native *burh*. These cities are capable of being both at the same time: familiar and strangely Other.

We do not learn whether the cities mentioned in *Maxims II* are abandoned or inhabited, and if so, by whom.[10] Nevertheless, the above-cited passage highlights some of the key qualities that characterise many Old English descriptions of ruins, and especially those in the two other

---

the metaphor of *storm* for "uproar" is determined by *enta ærgeweorc* in the preceding line'; P. J. Frankis, 'The Thematic Significance of *enta geweorc* and Related Imagery in *The Wanderer*', ASE, 2 (1973), 253–69, at 257.

[7] See, for instance, Tom A. Shippey, *Poems of Wisdom and Learning in Old English* (Cambridge, 1976); Nicholas Howe, *The Old English Catalogue Poems* (Copenhagen, 1985); Thomas D. Hill, 'Wise Words: Old English Sapiential Poetry', in David F. Johnson and Elaine Treharne (eds), *Readings in Medieval Texts: Interpreting Old and Middle English Literature* (Oxford, 2005), 166–79.

[8] For a similar argument concerning the riddles, see Patrick J. Murphy, *Unriddling the Exeter Riddles* (University Park, PA, 2011), 7, 26.

[9] *Ibid.*, 7.

[10] Nicholas Howe seems to take the cities to be inhabited; Nicholas Howe, *Writing the Map of Anglo-Saxon England: Essays in Cultural Geography* (New Haven, CT, 2008), 17.

poems discussed in this chapter, *The Wanderer* and *The Ruin*, both found uniquely in the late tenth-century Exeter Book (Exeter Cathedral Library MS 3501): they, too, are imbued with a similar tension between proximity and distance, between personal involvement and detachment, between familiarity and Otherness; and here, too, we encounter ruins referred to as *wrætlic*, the unfathomable 'work of giants'. But there is a further aspect that interests me, one that is not present in *Maxims II*, or at best implicitly: the specific forms of temporality that characterise ruins in general, and the ruins in *The Wanderer* and *The Ruin* in particular.

These forms of temporality are multiple. Most obviously, perhaps, the fragmented condition of ruins recalls and indeed presupposes a moment in which they were whole, or at least more complete than they are now. Ruins thus always draw attention to what is no longer present: a former state that we know must have existed, but that is no longer there. As traces of the past, they constitute what Gayatri Chakravorty Spivak, in para-phrasing Jacques Derrida's concept of the 'trace', has described as 'the mark of the absence of a presence, an always already absent present'.[11] At the same time, however, ruins are also unmistakably a part of the present; they index a present state of the world as much as a past one. The anthro-pologist Tim Ingold remarks that 'for as long as [a] building remains standing in the landscape, it will continue [...] to figure within the envi-ronment not just of human beings but of a myriad of other living kinds, plant and animal, which will incorporate it into their own life-activities and modify it in the process'. Like everything surrounding it, a building is subject to weathering and decomposition; its seemingly fixed, 'finished' state requires regular maintenance and repair: 'Once this human input lapses, leaving it at the mercy of other forms of life and of the weather, it will soon cease to be a building and become a ruin.'[12] Yet even then, the process is not finished: the ruin continues to be subject to the same forces of decay, unless it is repaired, rebuilt or repurposed.

By their very essence, ruins thus signify change, their material state – broken rather than intact, abandoned rather than inhabited – drawing attention to the temporal processes that divide the past from the present. The contemplation of ruins thus always involves at least two points of ref-erence: before and after, then and now. This temporal divide – made up of innumerable moments – calls to be filled with memories, reconstructions or speculations, with the result that 'ruins seem to quite literally speak of the past in the present and bring distinct temporal moments and histories

---

[11] Gayatri Chakravorty Spivak, 'Translator's Preface', in Jacques Derrida, *Of Grammatology*, trans. Gayatri Chakravorty Spivak (Baltimore, MD, 1998), xvii.

[12] Tim Ingold, 'The Temporality of the Landscape', *World Archaeology*, 25:2 (1993), 152–74, at 170.

Ruins and Their Multiple Temporalities

into presence'.[13] Ruins, then, are always inherently polychronic.[14] Their contemplation automatically opens up a multitemporal perspective, and their presence implies a history, even if that history remains untold. One could call their aesthetic effect in literature *chronotopic*, albeit in a sense somewhat different from Bakhtin's, who adopted the term from scientific discourse to describe the specific interplay of space and time in narrative. According to Bakhtin,

> In the literary artistic chronotope, spatial and temporal indicators are fused into one carefully thought-out, concrete whole. Time, as it were, thickens, takes on flesh, becomes artistically visible; likewise, space becomes charged and responsive to the movements of time, plot and history.[15]

For Bakhtin, the chronotope is primarily a tool for assessing the varying treatment of the time-space-complex in different forms of (narrative) literature. To him, the chronotope constitutes the primary point of reference from which the narrative unfolds, the 'glue' that binds together different scenes by integrating them into a spatio-temporal grid: 'The chronotope, functioning as the primary means for materialising time in space, emerges as a center for concretising representation, as a force giving body to the entire novel.'[16] According to Bakhtin, it is the chronotope more than any other feature that 'defines genre and generic distinctions, for in literature the primary category in the chronotope is time'.[17] Although Bakhtin's preoccupation with plot structures results in a very specific – and very limited – application of the chronotope as a literary concept, he maintains that 'any and every literary image is chronotopic' – indeed, his initial definition of the chronotope as 'the intrinsic connectedness of temporal and spatial relationships that are artistically expressed in literature' makes it possible to apply the term in other areas of literature besides narrative.[18] Given that Bakhtin calls the chronotope a 'formally constitutive category of literature' that has 'intrinsic generic significance', one could argue that it is precisely the chronotope that distinguishes narrative in general –

[13] Davies, *Visions*, 29.

[14] See also the introduction to this study, 16.

[15] M. M. Bakhtin, 'Forms of Time and of the Chronotope in the Novel: Notes toward a Historical Poetics', in *The Dialogic Imagination: Four Essays*, ed. Michael Holquist, trans. Caryl Emerson and Michael Holquist (Austin, TX, 1981), 84–258, at 84.

[16] *Ibid.*, 250.

[17] *Ibid.*, 85. Somewhat predictably, Bakhtin takes the interplay of space and time to be at its most complex in nineteenth-century realist novels, especially those of Dostoevsky.

[18] *Ibid.*, 251, 84.

and not only different narrative genres – from other forms of literature, such as the lyrical, plotless and locally restricted depiction of ruins in *The Wanderer* and *The Ruin*. Where narrative always presupposes a temporal movement, even if the characters involved stay in the same place throughout the action,[19] these two poems have at their heart meditations on the very nature of time.

Ruins in Old English Literature

Bakhtin, of course, is more concerned with the aesthetic effect (and ultimately the degree of realism) of the literary representation of time and space than with the actual spatio-temporal perspectives that it helps to establish. But the link between space and time highlighted by the chronotope, and indeed the different speeds at which different material entities may appear to reflect the passage of time (as discussed in the introduction), can help us appreciate just how conducive literary descriptions of ruins can be to the negotiation of complex temporalities.

In light of this, it is all the more striking that the scholarly engagement with references to ruins in Old English poetry (and early medieval texts more generally) has so far yielded a fairly limited number of temporal perspectives, notwithstanding the fact that the existence of a 'ruin motif' in Old English literature was long taken for granted.[20] In earlier discussions, such references were frequently reduced to their perceived function as expressions of worldly ephemerality – for instance, in the introduction to an edited collection that brought together some of the most important essays on the poems commonly referred to as the 'Old English elegies', Martin Green argued that the 'concern with the transitory is a central preoccupation' of many of these texts.[21] It was only from the 1980s onwards

---

[19] *Ibid.*, 84–5.

[20] Kathryn Hume discusses – and dismisses – the possible existence of a 'ruin motif' on the grounds that references to ruins are in fact not quite as widespread in Old English literature as is often assumed. She calls the passages 'that have been considered relevant [...] both disparate and surprisingly limited in number' and posits instead a 'value- and idea-complex associated with the hall', to which the image of ruins is linked; Kathryn Hume, 'The "Ruin Motif" in Old English Poetry', *Anglia*, 94 (1976), 339–60, at 339, 341.

[21] Martin Green, 'Introduction', in Martin Green (ed.), *The Old English Elegies* (Rutherford, NJ, 1983), 1–30, at 12–13. Helena Znojemská similarly suggests that ruins in Old English poetry constitute 'a metaphor of the transitoriness of human life and creation, and of the world in general'; Helena Znojemská, '*The Ruin*: A Reading of the Old English Poem', *Litteraria Pragensia*, 8 (1998), 15–33, at 15. Comparable observations were made, among others, by Alois Brandl, 'Venantius Fortunatus und die ags. Elegien *Wanderer* und *Ruine*', *Archiv für das*

Ruins and Their Multiple Temporalities

that other aspects came into focus, one example being the propensity of Old English literary depictions of ruins – some of which seem to recall Roman building styles – to mark the 'postcolonial' status of early medieval Britain, that is, their capacity to draw attention to Britain's Roman past.[22] Bede himself fosters such a reading in his *Historia ecclesiastica* when he notes:

> Habitabant autem intra uallum, quod Seuerum trans insulam fecisse commemorauimus, ad plagam meridianam, quod ciuitates farus pontes et stratae ibidem factae usque hodie testantur.

> [They [i.e., the Romans] had occupied the whole land south of the rampart already mentioned, set up across the island by Severus, an occupation to which the cities, lighthouses, bridges, and roads which they built there testify to this day.][23]

Howe maintains that stone constructions such as those described in the *Historia ecclesiastica* would have signalled to early medieval observers the former presence of a technologically superior culture. Quoting Richard Muir, he argues that especially the roads built under Roman rule, with their 'straight-line directness', would have drawn attention to 'the inadequacy of indigenous arrangements' and hence to a perceived cultural imbalance recalling the hierarchical power relations between colonising and colonised societies.[24] Early medieval Britain might thus be regarded as 'postcolonial' in more than one sense: geographically and temporally, as a former colony 'after the Roman Empire ceased to function as a political, military, and economic entity in Britain',[25] and psychologically, as a 'landscape filled with the material remains of the colonizing power'.[26] The

---

     Studium der Neueren Sprachen und Literaturen, 73:139 (1919), 84; G. W. Dunleavy, 'A "De Excidio" Tradition in the Old English *Ruin*?', *Philological Quarterly*, 38 (1959), 112–18; Ida L. Gordon (ed.), *The Seafarer* (London, 1960), 19; T. P. Dunning and A. J. Bliss (eds), *The Wanderer* (London, 1969); Christine E. Fell, 'Perceptions of Transience', in Malcolm Godden and Michael Lapidge (eds), *The Cambridge Companion to Old English Literature* (Cambridge, 1991), 172–89, at 180.

[22] See, for instance, Nicholas Howe, *Migration and Mythmaking in Anglo-Saxon England* (New Haven, CT, 1989), 48; Howe, 'Anglo-Saxon England and the Postcolonial Void', in Ananya Jahanara Kabir and Deanne Williams (eds), *Postcolonial Approaches to the European Middle Ages: Translating Cultures* (Cambridge, 2005), 25–47; Fell, 'Perceptions', 179–81.

[23] *HE* i.11 (ed. and trans. Colgrave and Mynors, 40–1).

[24] Howe, *Migration*, 48; *Writing the Map*, 83; 'Postcolonial Void', 29; Richard Muir, *The New Reading the Landscape: Fieldwork in Landscape History* (Exeter, 2000), 148.

[25] Howe 'Postcolonial Void', 25.

[26] Howe, *Writing the Map*, 90. See also Howe 'Postcolonial Void', 35; *Migration*,

Remains of the Past in Old English Literature

ruined state of Roman-period structures – albeit unacknowledged in the *Historia ecclesiastia* – turns them into markers of historical change, their fragmentation reflecting the temporal and cultural distance between the time of Roman Britain and the post-Roman present.

Yet while the importance of Howe's observations cannot be over-stressed, his emphasis on Britain's Roman history, on the one hand, and the early medieval present of the respective writers, on the other, reduces the inherent polychronicity of ruins to a binary opposition between a single past and a single here and now. Moreover, his insistence on feelings of inferiority on the part of post-Roman observers marks a return to the sense of decline that earlier commentators saw as the defining characteristic of early medieval descriptions of ruins.[27] It is not that nostalgic reflections or contemplations of worldly transience do not play a role in Old English texts dealing with ruins, they are simply not as all-pervasive as earlier scholarship made them out to be.

This assertion can be illustrated by a comparison between two passages in the Old English *Orosius* (an adaptation of Paulus Orosius's early fifth-century *Historiae adversus paganos*, a work that nineteenth-century scholars attributed to Alfred the Great) and the Old English poem *Genesis A*, the latter found in the tenth-century Junius Manuscript (Bodleian Library MS Junius 11). The passages in question deal with the Tower of Babel, left to fall into ruin after God had confounded the speech of its builders. In the Old English *Orosius*, the Tower testifies to the greatest building project ever undertaken, but it also serves as a reminder of the ephemerality of even this, the greatest of all human endeavours:[28]

Seo ilce burg Babylonia, seo ðe mæst wæs 7 ærest ealra burga, seo is nu læst 7 westast. Nu seo burg swelc is, þe ær wæs ealra weorca fæstast 7 wunderlecast 7 mærast, gelice 7 heo wære to bisene asteald eallum middangearde, 7 eac swelce heo self sprecende sie to eallum moncynne 7 cweþe: 'Nu ic þuss gehroren eam 7 aweg gewiten, hwæt, ge magan

---

48. In Howe's reading, the situation is complicated further by what Bede describes as the subjugation of the native post-Roman population by conquering Germanic tribes from the continent, the *gens Anglorum* with whom Bede himself identified. According to Howe, the subsequent conversion of this 'English' people, which established a new connection with Rome as the capital of western European Christendom and re-established Latin learning and building styles in the English-speaking parts of Britain, signalled to Bede and his contemporaries 'that the postcolonial void had been bridged' (*Writing the Map*, 92; 'Postcolonial Void', 38).

[27] Fell, 'Perceptions', 180.

[28] On the conflation of Babel and Babylon, which is already found in Augustine's *De civitate Dei*, see Frankis, 'Thematic Significance', 261; Liuzza, 'Tower of Babel', 6 and 25 n. 17.

Ruins and Their Multiple Temporalities

on me ongietan 7 oncnawan þæt ge nanuht mid eow nabbað fæstes ne
stronges þætte þurhwunigean mæge.'

[That same city Babylon, which was the greatest and the foremost of
all cities, is now the least and most desolate. Now the city is such,
which formerly was of all works the strongest and most wonderful
and greatest, as if it were set as a sign for all the world, and also as if it
were speaking to all mankind, and said: 'Now I am thus fallen and gone
away, lo! You may see on me, learn and know, that you have nothing
with you so fast and strong that it can abide forever.']²⁹

The text does not mention that the Tower was unfinished when it
was abandoned; its primary concern is with a much more general lesson;
namely, the message of transitoriness that is here voiced in quasi-prosopo-
poeic speech. The singularity of the bygone moment, and indeed the
uniqueness of the building, are less important than the general applicability of that message: if even the greatest of all buildings has succumbed to
the ravages of time, the same will happen to any lesser work that human
beings might undertake.

By contrast, *Genesis A* sees the Tower primarily as a trace of a particular
historical moment; namely, the point when linguistic change resulted in a
diversification of peoples; a moment of cultural and ethnic disintegration
that resulted in multiple ethnogeneses:

Tofaran þa   on feower wegas
æðelinga bearn   ungeþeode
on landsocne.   Him on laste bu
stiðlic stantorr   and seo steape burh
samod samworht   on Sennar stod.

[Then the offspring of nobles dispersed in four directions, divided, in
search of land. The strong stone tower abided as their trace, and the tall
fortress, uncompleted, stood on [the plain of] Sennar; lines 1697–1701.]³⁰

The migration of the builders, now divided into several distinct peoples
by their inability to communicate, leaves the building site desolate, the
fragmentary edifice abandoned to deterioration and eventual disintegration. Where the Old English *Orosius* attempts to draw a general lesson
from a singular historical event, *Genesis A* focuses on the singularity of
the event and its aftereffects. Here, the desertion of the Tower is not the
result of some universal historical principle, but rather the consequence

---

²⁹ *Old English Orosius* ii.2. Old English text quoted from Janet Bately (ed.), *The Old English Orosius*, EETS SS, 6 (London, 1980), 43–4.
³⁰ Old English text quoted from George Philip Krapp (ed.), *The Junius Manuscript*, ASPR, 1 (New York, 1931).

of the builders' pride, which prompts God to intervene and forestall their endeavour.[31] The event is historically contingent; it is not linked explicitly to a more general scheme of world history.

But even in the Old English *Orosius*, the temporal perspective is more complex than it may initially appear. The project's failure is clearly linked to the notion of the ultimate futility of human aspirations and the impermanence of all manmade things: 'Ge nanuht mid eow nabbað fæstes ne stronges þætte þurhwunigean mæge' [You have nothing with you so fast and strong that it can abide forever]. But even as the imagined voice of Babylon reinforces the message of material and cultural transience, it paradoxically draws attention to the fact that something, at least, still survives amid the rubble – or, rather, *as* rubble. The same is true of *Genesis A*: as Roy M. Liuzza notes, the final image of the abandoned tower suggests that the material remains of the undertaking prove more permanent than the enterprise itself; they will continue to stand, for many years to come, as a sign of past human endeavour.

Both texts project the Tower of Babel as the first of what one might call, echoing Liuzza, the 'ruins of history'; that is, they project a linear historical process in which the vestiges of earlier cultural achievements stand as signs of past events that will never return – and will continue to do so into the future.[32] Renée Trilling observes that

> ruins are particularly well-suited to signify this complex and paradoxical understanding of temporality: their visible and undeniable decay indicates the passage of time, but their equally visible and undeniable existence in spite of their ruinous state asserts the continued presence, as a ruin, of the past. As objects, ruins embody the dialectic of past and present without ever demanding or allowing its reconciliation.[33]

Taken together, Liuzza's reading of *Genesis A* suggests, the ruins of the world present the trace of the 'absent presence' of the human past; they provide the backdrop upon which all human history can be projected. At least in theory, it might thus be possible to conceive of a world history written entirely in ruins – a genuinely archaeological project. Thus, even as ruins may signal the transitoriness of worldly grandeur, their very capacity to act as signifiers demonstrates that the traces of past human construction efforts may survive long after the builders themselves have

---

[31] Liuzza, 'Tower of Babel', 4.

[32] Liuzza actually uses the expression in a very different context; namely, as a metaphor for the loss of an oral culture that is being supplanted by ecclesiastical literary culture and the concomitant loss of the oral and genealogical histories transported by the former; see *ibid.*, 23, and the following section of this chapter.

[33] Trilling, 'Ruins', 160.

perished – in the case at hand, traces that are nothing short of monumental. And as traces of the past, these ruins are necessarily more than just signs of transitoriness: legible or not, they refer back to individual, historically contingent events. Fragmented though the ruins may be, their presence, however battered, amounts to a silent defiance of the general deterioration of the world. They are not merely monuments to the past; through their continued presence, they also project history into the future. And such a sense of futurity – a future that is already foreshadowed in the continued presence of the ruins of the past – is precisely what characterises some of the ruin imagery in *The Wanderer*.

Between Transience and Survival:
The Wanderer's Material Remains

The Wanderer is one of the best-known and most thoroughly studied Old English poems. Even so, discussions of its ruin imagery have tended to concentrate on the aspects of decline and nostalgia that undeniably pervade the poem, whereas attempts to unravel its complex temporal layering have remained few and far between.

The Wanderer revolves around a story of deeply felt personal loss, the philosophical contemplation of which eventually leads to religious consolation.[34] Looking back on the death of his lord and kinsmen, the poem's first-person narrator tells of his ultimately unsuccessful search for a new home, followed by more universal images of death and destruction. Contemplating the transitory nature of earthly life in general, the speaker realises that stability is to be found in God alone. In purely structural terms, the poem's argument thus closely resembles that of *The Seafarer*, another Old English poem from the Exeter Book, alongside which it has often been read.[35] *The Seafarer*'s protagonist likewise progresses from lamenting personal hardship to Christian consolation via a meditation on ephemerality:

---

[34] For a discussion of the text's structure and poetic voices, see Dunning and Bliss (eds), *The Wanderer*, 78–94. The poem's Old English text is quoted from their edition. See also Stanley B. Greenfield, '*The Wanderer*: A Reconsideration of Theme and Structure', *JEGP*, 50:4 (1951), 451–65, at 464.

[35] Dunning and Bliss, for instance, argue that 'the dominant motif of [*The Wanderer*] is not suffering but transience; and it is by his treatment of this motif that the poet creates the mood of the poem' (*The Wanderer*, 98–102, quotation at 98). Studies that discuss the two poems alongside each other include Fell, 'Perceptions', especially 175; Kathleen Davis, 'Old English Lyrics: A Poetics of Experience', in Clare A. Lees (ed.), *The Cambridge History of Early Medieval English Literature* (Cambridge, 2013), 332–56.

Remains of the Past in Old English Literature

> Dagas sind gewitene
> ealle onmedlan   eorþan rices;
> nearon nu cyningas   ne caseras
> ne goldgiefan   swylce iu wæron,
> þonne hi mæst mid him   mærþa gefremedon
> ond on dryhtlicestum   dome lifdon.
> Gedroren is þeos duguð eal,   dreamas sind gewitene;
> wuniað þa wacran   ond þas woruld healdaþ,
> brucað þurh bisgo.

> [The days have passed, all the magnificence of earth's kingdom; there are now no kings nor emperors, nor gold-givers such as there were formerly, when they accomplished between them the greatest martial deeds, and lived in the most distinguished fame. Fallen has all this company, the joys have passed; the weak remain and hold this world, use it through toil; lines 80b–8a.][36]

The passage conveys not merely a message of transitoriness, but is suffused with the notion of a general decline: 'Eorþan indryhto ealdað ond searað, / swa nu monna gehwylc geond middangeard' [The nobility of the earth ages and fades, as now every man does throughout the middle-earth; lines 89–90]. Not only have the kings and emperors of old vanished, but their place is taken by lesser men unable to match their predecessors' achievements; pleasure and deeds of glory have given way to hardship. *The Seafarer*'s vision is one of cultural pessimism, highly sceptical with regard to the potential of a present perceived as deficient and inferior to the past. The image of the weaker using the earth in toil, recalling God's injunction to Adam in Genesis 3.19 ('in sudore vultus tui vesceris pane, donec revertaris in terram de qua sumptus es: quia pulvis es et in pulverem reverteris' [In the sweat of thy face shalt thou eat bread till thou return to the earth, out of which thou wast taken]),[37] conjures up a nostalgic vision of a golden age irretrievably lost. The world, at least in its present state, has nothing to offer, hence *The Seafarer*'s concluding injunction to turn to God for hope and consolation:

> Micel biþ se Meotudes egsa,   for þon hi seo molde oncyrreð;
> se gestaþelade   stiþe grundas,
> eorþan sceatas   ond uprodor.

---

[36] The Old English text is quoted from Gordon (ed.), *The Seafarer*.

[37] *Genesis B* gives the passage as 'þu winnan scealt / and on eorðan þe þine andlifne / selfa geræcan, wegan swatig hleor, / þinne hlaf etan, þendan þu her leofast' [you shall toil and earn your sustenance by yourself on earth, wear a sweaty face, eat your bread, while you live here; lines 932–5; Old English text quoted from Krapp (ed.), *Junius Manuscript*, 3–87].

Ruins and Their Multiple Temporalities

[…]
Uton we hycgan   hwær we ham agen,
ond þonne geþencan   hu we þider cumen;
ond we þonne eac tilien   þæt we to moten
in þa ecan   eadignesse
þær is lif gelong   in lufan Dryhtnes,
hyht in heofonum.

[Great is the terrible power of the Ruler, because it transforms the world; he made steadfast the firm foundations, the expanse of the earth and the heavens above. […] Let us consider where we own a home, then think of how we may get there; and let us also then labour that we may be allowed into that eternal bliss where life belongs in the love of the Lord, high in Heaven; lines 103–5, 117–22a.]

At first glance, the two poems thus seem to have much in common: the outcry of *The Wanderer*'s protagonist, 'Eall is earfoðlic eorþan rice' [full of hardship is all the kingdom of the earth; line 106], seems to echo the above-mentioned biblical image of toilsome labour; and the reminder that 'Her bið feoh læne, her bið freond læne, / her bið mon læne, her bið mæg læne; / eal þis eorþan gesteal idel weorþeð' [Here wealth is ephemeral, here a friend is ephemeral, here man is ephemeral, here kinsman is ephemeral; all the foundation of this earth will become desolate; lines 108–10] expresses a vision of worldly transience quite similar to that of *The Seafarer*.

However, as Davies emphasises, conflating texts like *The Wanderer*, *The Seafarer* and *The Ruin* risks missing the essential differences that exist between them.[38] In one form or another, all three poems meditate on the essential mutability of the world, but they differ significantly in their treatment of the theme – and these differences, I argue, are at least to a certain extent related to the way that the texts discuss material remnants of the past and their ability to survive into the present. In *The Seafarer*, such references are absent. The poem, we have seen, invokes a vision of worldly decline in which the deeds of the present cannot match those of the past. Its central argument, however, is based on the juxtaposition of different ways of living: in the final instance, it is the realisation that all luxury is ephemeral that convinces its protagonist to persist in his ascetic way of life. *The Wanderer*, by contrast, bases its discussion of mutability on images of death and destruction. And yet, paradoxically, these very scenes draw attention to the longevity of material objects, which even in fragmented form continue to refer back, however obliquely, to the past. In

---

[38] Davies, *Visions*, 37.

Remains of the Past in Old English Literature

The Wanderer, a ruin can be a site of memory,[39] but even when all memory of the past has vanished, its presence continues in the surviving rubble, if only in the form of a present absence. The poem's historical vision is thus in many ways more akin to that of the passage in the Old English *Orosius* quoted above, where the transience of cultural achievements is linked to an accumulation of material traces that paradoxically draw attention to those very achievements by testifying to their eventual frustration.

This kinship is particularly noticeable in the image of crumbling walls invoked by *The Wanderer*'s speaker:

Ongietan sceal gleaw hæle   hu gæstlic bið,
þonne ealre þisse worulde wela   weste stondeð,
swa nu missenlice   geond þisne middangeard,
winde biwaune,   weallas stondaþ
hrime bihrorene,   hryðge þa ederas.
Woniað þa winsalo,   waldend licgað
dreame bidrorene,   duguþ eal gecrong
wlonc bi wealle.   Sume wig fornom,
ferede in forðwege: sumne fugel oþbær
ofer heanne holm;   sumne se hara wulf
deaðe gedælde;   sumne dreorighleor
in eorðscræfe   eorl gehydde.
Yþde swa þisne eardgeard   ælda scyppend
oþþæt, burgwara   breahtma lease,
eald enta geweorc   idlu stodon.

[The far-sighted warrior must understand how ghastly it will be when all the riches of this world stand waste, even as now in various places throughout this world walls stand, wind-blown, rime-covered, snow-swept the buildings. The halls crumble, the owner lies, deprived of joy, the company all fallen dead, proud by the wall. One was taken by war, carried away; one a bird carried over the high sea; one the grey wolf dealt his death; one the warrior tearfully hid in the grave. The creator of ages laid waste this middle-earth until, deprived of the noise of the inhabitants, the ancient works of giants stood useless; lines 73–87.]

As in the passage from *Orosius*, the empty buildings stand for a cultural loss that they simultaneously reference. The final image of deserted dwellings, depopulated through the workings of God, certainly recalls the abandonment of Babylon. But whereas in the story of Babel, God's intervention is the direct result of the builders' hubris, in *The Wanderer*

---

[39] 'Sites of memory' (lieux de mémoire) were first theorised by Pierre Nora, for example in 'Between Memory and History: Les lieux de mémoir', *Representations*, 26 (1989), 7–24; see also Davies's discussion of Nora's concept (*Visions*, 5, 9).

the workings of God are incomprehensible, part of a general decline of the world that does not appear to have been brought about by human transgressions. The image of the 'ælda scyppend' [Creator of Ages] laying waste the earthly abode here amounts to little more than a synonym of 'Fate'.[40] Moreover, while the ruins of Babel stand as a monument to its builders' illicit aspirations, a work never to be repeated, *The Wanderer* and *The Seafarer* both make reference to rulers and heroes the likes of whom the world will never see again: in *The Seafarer*, the 'greater men' of the past have been replaced by the lesser ones inhabiting the present; in *The Wanderer*, not even the weaker remain.[41]

What remains, however, are the accumulated traces of their cultural endeavours. *The Wanderer*'s speaker imagines a future without human inhabitants, whose former presence is nonetheless recalled by the crumbling walls that even now can be found 'in various places throughout this world' ('missenlice geond þisne middangeard'; line 75). The vision of deserted ruins is linked to the inevitable advance of the world towards an approaching end. But this 'end' is not the eschatological destruction familiar from conventional apocalyptic imagery; it may not even signify an 'end' at all: the actual poetic image is that of a desolate place, devoid of human life, but filled with incomprehensible remnants whose former meaning is beyond recovery. But even in this capacity, the fragments continue to signify: what they express is the ultimate irreversibility of history and the irrecoverability of the past. *The Wanderer*'s is a vision of history, then, in which the world simultaneously loses its inhabitants while progressively accumulating the debris of the past. In this, it resembles Byron's *Darkness*:

> I had a dream, which was not all a dream.
> The bright sun was extinguish'd, and the stars
> Did wander darkling in the eternal space,
> Rayless, and pathless, and the icy earth
> Swung blind and blackening in the moonless air.[42]

---

[40] Frankis notes that the meaning of *eardgard* (line 85a) is not absolutely clear; it may be synonymous with *middangeard* [the world], or it may refer to the ruins mentioned earlier in the passage and to the cultural milieu(x) of their builders and inhabitants ('Thematic Significance', 254).

[41] The apocalyptical overtones of the passage were noted, among others, by Martin Green, 'Man, Time, and Apocalypse in *The Wanderer, The Seafarer*, and *Beowulf*', *JEGP*, 74:4 (1975), 502–18; Anne Lingard Klinck (ed.), *The Old English Elegies: A Critical Edition and Genre Study* (Montreal, 1992), 62.

[42] *Darkness*, lines 1–5, quoted from George Gordon Byron, *The Complete Poetical Works*, ed. Jerome J. McGann (7 vols, Oxford, 1986), vol. 4, 40. I owe the association of Byron's poem with the absolute stasis of maximum entropy (an implication of the second law of thermodynamics) to the discussion between

Like Byron's poem, *The Wanderer* imagines a world in which the inanimate outlasts the living; its showcasing of the material jumble of history stands in stark contrast to more conventional Christian descriptions of the soul's afterlife, in which the material, while continuing to exist, plays a secondary role.

The Wanderer's post-apocalyptic vision of a desolate earth lends the poem an altogether darker atmosphere than *The Seafarer's* juxtaposition of the protagonist's austere asceticism and the hollow pleasures of the city dweller. Although *The Wanderer* professes to be concerned with the future, the speaker's comment that 'swa nu missenlice geond þisne middan-geard, / winde biwaune, weallas stondaþ' [even as now in various places throughout this world walls stand, wind-blown; lines 75–6], followed by images of general destruction, implies that this specific future has already arrived: ultimately, his search for companionship fails because there is no one left to turn to. The passage's universalising references to generic ruins and unspecified dead rulers and retainers thus stand emblematically for the destruction of society as a whole. *The Seafarer's* protagonist deliberately shuns the company of other human beings; *The Wanderer's* speaker, by contrast, imagines himself as the sole survivor of an all-encompassing catastrophe that has left him bereft not only of his friends and kinfolk, but of human company altogether. The prevailing image is that of a desolate endtime in which present and future collapse into one as the protagonist wanders aimlessly amid the rubble of a past that is irrevocably gone – in a sense very different from that intended by Francis Fukuyama, *The Wanderer's* speaker imagines himself as having arrived at the 'end of history'.[43]

Even more obviously than in the Old English *Orosius*, *The Wanderer's* image of a depopulated world filled with the 'ruins of history' thus signifies not only cultural loss, but also, paradoxically, the material longevity that draws attention to that very loss. P. J. Frankis made a similar observation regarding the paradoxical nature of ruins as symbols both of the durability of matter and of the opposing principle of mutability and transience: 'Imagery of wind and storm emphasises on the one hand the capacity of ancient buildings to survive these forces (as in *The Wanderer* 76, *The Ruin* 11 and *Andreas* 1494), and on the other the failure of ruined buildings to serve their primary function of giving shelter from

---

    Hannah and Valentine in Tom Stoppard's *Arcadia*, Scene 7. *Darkness*, written in July 1816, was at least partly inspired by the pall of darkness caused by the eruption of Mount Tambora in 1815.

43 Francis Fukuyama, *The End of History and the Last Man* (New York, 1992). In this much-criticised book, Fukuyama argued that with the fall of the Iron Curtain, all future events had been rendered historically meaningless unless they pertained to the ultimate *telos* of human history, liberal democracy.

the weather.'[44] Thus, even as the failure to provide shelter means that the structure can longer serve the basic function required of a building, it is nonetheless capable of invoking the former presence of the building that it once was, despite its fragmented state: it forms a trace of that which is no longer there. In the same way, the sense of loss that accompanies *The Wanderer*'s description of ruins draws attention to the multiple but irrecoverable histories connected to these structures.

Eald enta geweorc: *Ancient Structures and the Alterity of the Past*

In *The Wanderer*, the description of material remains invokes a veritable temporal panorama, from remote history to an eschatological future. For even as architectural remnants are left standing throughout the earth in the poem's present and will continue to do so in all eternity, the origin of these structures harks back to a distant past: in a phrase almost identical to the one used in *Maxims II* to describe stone cities seen from afar, *The Wanderer*'s ruins are identified as 'eald enta geweorc' [ancient work of giants; line 87a].

In the historiographical literature of early medieval Britain, stone constructions usually feature as recognisable remnants of the region's Roman past. Many scholars have therefore seen the relevant passages in *The Wanderer* and *The Ruin* as direct reflections of the respective poets' living environments, where the ruins of Roman-period structures would have been a relatively common sight, as testified, for instance, by the large number of Old English place names referencing Roman remains whose Latin elements (such as -*ceaster*, modern '-chester') demonstrate that their provenance was well known.[45] In *The Wanderer* and *The Ruin*, by contrast, there is no comparable ascription of a Roman origin – rather, as in *Maxims II*, the stone buildings in question are referred to as the 'work of giants'.

As noted in the introduction to this study, the expression *eald enta geweorc* [old work of giants] and its variants *enta ærgeweorc* and *giganta geweorc* occur a number of times throughout the Old English poetic corpus, and much ink has been spilled over the question of how to interpret them.[46] Old English *ent* glosses Latin *gigas* [giant], together with the

---

[44] Frankis, 'Thematic Significance', 257–8, the quotation is on 257.

[45] On place names referencing Roman sites, see Semple, *Perceptions*, 40; on the visibility of Roman material remains, see Michael Hunter, 'Germanic and Roman Antiquity and the Sense of the Past in Anglo-Saxon England', *ASE*, 3 (1974), 29–50; Howe, *Writing the Map*, 84–5.

[46] See, for instance, Oliver F. Emerson, 'Legends of Cain, especially in Old and Middle English', *PMLA*, 21:4 (1906), 831–929; Robert E. Kaske, 'The *eotenas* in *Beowulf*', in Robert P. Creed (ed.), *Old English Poetry: Fifteen Essays* (Providence,

words *eten, eoten, gigans/gigant* and *þurs*. Somewhat surprisingly, the first four terms appear not to have been subject to semantic narrowing (with the possible exception of *gigans/gigant*, which occurs almost exclusively in biblical contexts),[47] nor is it entirely clear how beings denoted by them were envisioned. According to Chris Bishop, 'for some commentators these "giants" were physically large, but for the most part they seem to have been imagined as being gigantic in their strength, in their accomplishments and in their wickedness, rather than in their physique'.[48] Bishop argues that the distribution of these terms in the Old English corpus reflects a fundamental division between the non-human and monstrous, on the one side, and the skilful and admirable, on the other: while *ent, eoten* and *gigans* stood for the potentially proud and impious, but skilful (and grudgingly respected) giants of biblical tradition, the Norse loanword *þurs* was used in reference to monstrous marshland creatures, lonely dwellers in exile beyond the pale of human civilisation.[49] Bishop speculates that *entas, eotenas* and *gigantes* might have been seen as one category and mentions the possibility that *ent* – by far the most common among these terms[50] – might itself be derived from Latin *gigans*, meaning that the three types of giant would have been interrelated not only ontologically, but also etymologically.[51] Regardless of whether one accepts

---

RI, 1967), 285–310; Frankis, 'Thematic Significance'; Alexandra Hennessey Olsen, '"Thurs" and "Thyrs": Giants and the Date of *Beowulf*', *In Geardagum: Essays on Old and Middle English Language and Literature*, 6 (1984), 35–42; Jeffrey Jerome Cohen, 'Old English Literature and the Work of Giants', *Comitatus: A Journal of Medieval and Renaissance Studies*, 24 (1993), 1–32; John Miles Foley, *The Singer of Tales in Performance* (Bloomington, IN, 1995); Jacqueline Stuhmiller, 'On the Identity of the *Eotenas*', *NM*, 100:1 (1999), 7–14; Liuzza, 'Tower of Babel'; Lori Ann Garner, *Structuring Spaces: Oral Poetics and Architecture in Early Medieval England* (Notre Dame, IN, 2011).

[47] Cohen, 'Work of Giants', 3.
[48] Chris Bishop, '"Þyrs, Ent, Eoten, Gigans": Anglo-Saxon Ontologies of "Giant"', *NM*, 107:3 (2006), 259–70, at 270.
[49] *Ibid.*, 267. According to Cohen, *þurs* could denote any large monster in Old English ('Work of Giants', 3).
[50] Frankis, meanwhile, argues that the term *ent* cannot have been widely current in colloquial speech as it does not seem to have survived into Middle English – in contrast to *eoten*, which continued to be used for several centuries ('Thematic Significance', 259).
[51] 'It is significant to note, also, that in the *Epinal Glossary* the word *gigans* is written as *ȝiȝæns* with each Latin *g* transcribed as an Anglo-Saxon *yogh*. The palatalised *yogh* would have rendered the spoken form of *gigans* as "yiyans" and *gigantes* as "yiyantes". A softening of the *yogh* towards voicelessness would also render *gigantes* as "iantes", a near phoneme for the Anglo-Saxon plural *entas*' (Bishop, 'Þyrs', 268, 270).

Ruins and Their Multiple Temporalities

Bishop's theory or not, such an interchangeability is also suggested by the variation of the phrases *enta geweorc*, *giganta geweorc*, etc., noted above.

The expression occurs – in one of its various forms – in *Maxims II* (line 2), *The Wanderer* (line 87), *The Ruin* (line 2), *Beowulf* (lines 1562, 1679, 2717, 2774) and *Andreas* (lines 1235, 1495). *Elene* contains a possible variation in 'burg enta' (line 31), but the reference is obscure and has been subject to emendation in some editions.[52] With the exception of one passage in *Beowulf*, none of these occurrences can be unequivocally associated with actual giants. On the contrary, in *Andreas*, the phrase is used in reference to an old paved road (*stræt stanfah*) and a stone edifice with pillars ('stapulas'; line 1494) used as a prison; both of them are situated within a city (*ceaster*) in the land of the Mermedonians, that is, in a Roman province.[53] Although the reference to 'giants' may have been prompted by the Mermedonians' cannibalistic and hence monstrous behaviour, the presence of Latin loanwords (*stræt*, *ceaster*, *stapulas*) suggests that the phrase is here associated primarily with Roman building skills. As Frankis remarks,

> the poet may have thought in historical terms of St Andrew evangelizing the Roman empire, or he may have thought in terms of his own environment, seeing St Andrew as a Christian missionary in a pagan country, like St Augustine among the Anglo-Saxons, and describing the land of the Mermedonians in terms of England of the missionary period, with the Roman roads and other buildings that must have been so conspicuous there.[54]

Frankis's second explanation arguably applies also to *Maxims II*, *The Wanderer* and *The Ruin*: the cultural context in which these poems were produced and presumably read suggests that the stone structures in ques-

---

[52] In the manuscript, *burgenta* is spelt in one word and occurs in a passage describing the advancing Hunnish and Germanic forces about to engage Constantine and his Roman army on the banks of the Danube: 'lungre scynde ofer burgenta beaduþreata mest' [forthwith hastened over the giants' castle the greatest battle-force; line 31]. Krapp remarks that '[a] noun *burgent* seems highly improbable, and unless the MS. is emended, it seems best to take as two words, though written as one in the MS' (*Vercelli Book*, 133, n. to line 31); see also the emendations proposed by other scholars cited in the same note.

[53] 'Drogon deormodne [...] efne swa wide swa wegas lagon, / enta ærgeweorc, innan burgum, / stræte stanfage' [They dragged the bold-minded one [...] as far as roads stretched, the ancient work of giants, from within the city, the paved roads; lines 1232–8a]. The term *ceaster* occurs in various inflected forms and compounds, for example, in lines 1125, 1174, 1237; Old English text quoted from Krapp (ed.), *Vercelli Book*, 3–51.

[54] Frankis, 'Thematic Significance', 256. Garner concurs by noting that 'the variation of the "enta geweorc" formula suggests an ancient worth predating the occupation of the cannibalistic Mermedonians' (*Structuring Spaces*, 108).

Remains of the Past in Old English Literature

tion – walls, buildings or even entire cities (these latter again denoted by the Latin-derived *ceastra* in *Maxims II*) – can be interpreted as the remains of building projects undertaken in Britain under Roman rule. *The Ruin* uses the native *burgstede* instead of *ceaster*, but it nevertheless seems to depict the ruins of a Roman settlement; in fact, the seeming specificity of the visual details has led many modern readers to identify the city described as the ruins of Roman Bath or, alternatively, Chester.[55] As in the case of *Maxims II* and *The Wanderer*, *The Ruin*'s language – Old English – might suggests that the ruined city can be understood as a remnant of Roman Britain. On the other hand, unlike the former two, the poem does not invoke a specifically insular scenario, and could thus be taken to describe any ruined city of Roman provenance.

Given this apparent invocation of *romanitas*, it is striking that none of the three poems explicitly names Romans as the respective builders; indeed, there is no attempt to identify the builders at all, beyond the epithet 'the work of giants'. Cohen is inclined to ascribe this absence of an explicit identification to a lack of historical knowledge, arguing that 'after the Romans disappeared and the memory of their occupation retreated into scholarly histories, it is no wonder that their already ancient monuments, along with pre-Celtic stone rings and dolmens, should be considered *enta geweorc*'.[56] This seems unlikely, however – at least for the environment in which Old English texts were read, copied and, arguably, produced: after all, as Howe has remarked, thanks to the existence of textual records, Roman-period stonework 'would [not] have posed any great mysteries' to most early medieval writers; moreover, 'even if such accounts had not been available to Bede and others, they could have learned who built these structures, and when they did so, from the inscriptions on many of them'.[57]

That said, it is by no means necessary to identify a stone structure in a historically unspecific and by all accounts fictional text such as *The Wanderer* or *The Ruin* as Roman merely because it appears to resemble real-world Roman remains and because the poem containing it was composed in a former Roman province: such a structure could just as well be thought of as the product of an imaginary people whose works the poet envisioned in a way similar to Roman ones. It is thus quite possible to take the phrase literally and to identify the craftspeople as actual giants. For instance, as mentioned above, *Beowulf* includes a passage where the expression *enta geweorc* occurs – twice – in reference to an item made by

---

[55] For further details of this debate, see nn. 149 and 150 below.
[56] Cohen, 'Work of Giants', 11.
[57] Howe, 'Postcolonial Void', at 29. See also Howe, *Writing the Map*, 83.

Ruins and Their Multiple Temporalities

actual giants, namely the antediluvian producers of the sword that the poem's protagonist uses to slay Grendel's mother.[58]

There is a biblical tradition that associates giants with craft and technology. The race of giants, who, according to Genesis 6.4–7, emanated from the union of 'the sons of God' and 'the daughters of men', is described as possessing superior knowledge and skills: in the apocryphal Book of Enoch, which appears to have been well-known in early medieval Britain,[59] the fallen Angels who fathered the Nephilim or giants taught humanity the production of weapons and jewellery, as well as augury, astrology and the manufacture and application of make-up. Genesis 6.4 is less explicit but speaks of them in a tone of admiration: 'gigantes autem erant super terram in diebus illis: postquam enim ingressi sunt filii Dei ad filias hominum, illaeque genuerunt, isti sunt potentes a saeculo viri famosi' [Now giants were upon the earth in those days. For after the sons of God went in to the daughters of men, and they brought forth children, these are the mighty men of old, men of renown]. In medieval literature, the Babylonian king Nimrod, responsible for the building of the Tower of Babel in extra-biblical traditions, was also often regarded as a giant: the Old English *Orosius* speaks of 'Membras se et' [Nimrod the giant], and the Old English homily *De falsis deis* notes that 'Nembroð and ða entas worhton þone wundorlican stypel æfter Nohs flod' [Nimrod and the giants constructed a marvellous tower after Noah's Flood].[60] Again, these giants are credited with extraordinary building skills.

Given the biblical giants' association with craft and technology, it is thus entirely possible to read the expression *enta geweorc* in *Maxims II*, *Andreas*, *The Wanderer* and *The Ruin* (and possibly also in *Elene*) as a reference to antediluvian giants, the poems' apparent invocation of *romanitas* notwithstanding. On the other hand, none of these texts include any

---

[58] It is in lines 1562 and 1679 that the expression explicitly refers to giants; in line 2774, at least (and probably also in 2717b), the craftspeople are clearly human beings.

[59] See Robert E. Kaske, '*Beowulf* and the Book of Enoch', *Speculum*, 46:3 (1971), 421–31; Ruth Mellinkoff, 'Cain's Monstrous Progeny in *Beowulf*: Part I, Noachic Tradition', *ASE*, 8 (1979), 143–62; Mellinkoff, 'Cain's Monstrous Progeny in *Beowulf*: Part II, Postdiluvian Survival', *ASE*, 9 (1980), 183–97; as well as the discussion in the next chapter. Bishop notes that Ælfric traced the *entas*' ancestry to Enoch ('Þyrs', 262).

[60] See Frankis, 'Thematic Significance', 264; Liuzza, 'Tower of Babel', 7. Nimrod was already identified as a giant by Augustine and Isidore and, even earlier, in ancient Jewish tradition, as the builder of Babel, due to a conflation of Babel and Babylon (Frankis, 'Thematic Significance', 261; Cohen, 'Work of Giants', 20). Frankis notes that there are at least five references to the story in the surviving corpus of Ælfric's writings, besides others in Old English and Latin texts ('Thematic Significance', 261).

103

additional clues that would support such a reading. On the contrary, as Cohen observes, 'neither *The Wanderer* nor *The Ruin* necessarily presuppose that [actual] giants were historically responsible for the fragmented architecture that spurs the elegy; the former inhabitants are envisioned as departed men in both poems'.[61] Here, as in *Andreas* and *Maxims II*, the phrase does not appear to be referring to literal giants at all, but to human builders only conventionally denominated as giants, possibly due to their technological prowess.

Against this backdrop, it has been argued that the phrase *enta geweorc* might be no more than a formulaic expression denoting superiority in skill, strength or workmanship.[62] This, however, does not mean that it is semantically empty: from what we can see in the existing corpus of Old English verse, the term would immediately have conjured up a sense of wonder – just like the word *wrætlic* discussed at the beginning of the chapter. Moreover, even if the phrase did indeed form a stock item of oral-formulaic composition, it might still have been associated in the mind of the reader or listener with a specific cultural background or identity – be it Roman, biblical or otherwise. As Frankis notes, even in cases where *enta geweorc* appears to be used primarily for metrical purposes, the possibility of a specific connotation – such as an implicit Roman context – adds a further dimension to the passage in question.[63] On the other hand, one might well wonder why the texts did not choose to make this dimension explicit. Or, to put it differently, if the expression were indeed formulaic in the sense that it had become grammaticalised to such an extent that its literal meaning was not normally activated, if *enta geweorc* were not to be understood as a reference to giants – literally or metaphorically

---

[61]   Cohen, 'Work of Giants', 11.

[62]   To the masonry that the *enta* are associated with in most passages, *Beowulf* adds products of metalwork, another craft requiring highly specialised skills. Bishop suggests that 'the *entas, eotenas* and *gigantes* were universally credited with an arcane knowledge that included blacksmithing, construction and sorcery' ('Þyrs', 270). This fits Ferhatović's observation that imagery involving weather, sound and architecture – a combination that, as Frankis has noted, characterises several of the *enta geweorc* passages – is frequently part of metapoetic reflection in Old English poetry (Ferhatović, *Borrowed Objects*, 98; Frankis, 'Thematic Significance', 256–7). The strong association of giants with superior skill and craftsmanship thus suggests a pronounced aesthetic component, one that also characterises the respective passages in *The Wanderer* and *The Ruin*, as we will see below.

[63]   Frankis, 'Thematic Significance', 257. Johann Köberl similarly notes with regard to the literary technique of variation: 'Variation is not always mere formal embellishment, let alone meaningless padding. Where it does not contribute to semantic content it may still add emphasis.' Johann Köberl, 'The Magic Sword in *Beowulf*', *Neophilologus*, 71 (1987), 120–8, at 121.

Ruins and Their Multiple Temporalities

(as in 'dwarfs on the shoulders of giants') – but rather to some unnamed human beings, then why are these human beings not identified elsewhere in the text? Why make *enta geweorc* the only reference to the otherwise unmentioned builders?

One possible explanation, and the one favoured here, is offered by the two instances in *Beowulf* where the expression does *not* denote actual giants. For if *Beowulf* contains the only passage in the existing corpus where the phrase indeed refers, beyond doubt, to actual giants, it also contains the one passage where it unambiguously describes the products of human beings. In line 2774, the phrase is used in reference to items of treasure found in the dragon's hoard, one of which seems to resemble a Roman standard.[64] This hoard is earlier associated with a people from a distant past whose name the narrator claims not to know:

> Þær wæs swylcra fela
> […] ærgestreona,
> swa hy on geardagum gumena nathwylc,
> eormenlafe æþelan cynnes,
> þanchycgende þær gehydde.
>
> [There were many such, in that earth-hall, of ancient treasures, which in days of yore an unknown man carefully hid there, the great legacy of a noble people; lines 2231a–35.][65]

A little later on, both the hoard and its hiding place are described as 'enta geweorc' (lines 2717b and 2774a), despite the fact that the sole survivor who hid the treasure is clearly human. Here, then, we have conclusive evidence of the phrase being used in reference to the material culture of human beings – albeit from a past so remote that their names and ethnic background have been forgotten.

Anthropologists and folklorists have argued that the figure of the giant stands for the ultimate Other, whose cultural alterity is usually combined with a notion of temporal anteriority.[66] Accordingly, Walter Stephens stresses the inhuman, threateningly antagonistic aspect of giants as representatives of 'the non-culture, non-"Us" by means of whose death or domestication [the respective culture] constituted and defined itself'.[67]

---

[64] See Emily V. Thornbury, '*Eald enta geweorc* and the Relics of Empire: Revisiting the Dragon's Lair in *Beowulf*', *Quaestio*, 1 (2000), 82–92.

[65] The Old English text of *Beowulf* is quoted from R. D. Fulk, Robert E. Bjork and John D. Niles (eds), *Klaeber's* Beowulf *and* The Fight at Finnsburg, 4th edn (Toronto, 2014), omitting length marks and diacritics.

[66] See Walter Stephens, *Giants in Those Days: Folklore, Ancient History, and Nationalism* (Lincoln, NE, 1989), 31–61; Cohen, 'Work of Giants', 7.

[67] Stephens, *Giants*, 52.

Remains of the Past in Old English Literature

By contrast, Cohen also draws attention to their 'explanatory function as creators of landscape, ruins and architecture' and thus to their more general applicability as a means of representing past cultures as 'that which predates contemporary man and has vanished long before the poet's epoch': 'Anthropologically speaking, [...] the passing of giants is the displacement of anterior culture; giants represent the unconquered remnant of a past which eludes the complete historical memory of the recorder.'[68]

Applied to *Beowulf*, this means that, in the absence of any secure information on the basis of which the narrator can identify the unknown people, either culturally or historically, their work becomes 'the work of giants'. I use the term 'narrator' because I wish to make it quite clear that I am not speaking about the same kind of historical ignorance by which Cohen tries to explain the lack of a Roman identification in *Maxims II, The Wanderer* and *The Ruin*. In a fictional setting like that of the passage in question, the absence of any form of further identification – an absence to which the narrator in fact draws attention ('gumena nathwylc') – is clearly not to be explained by any lack of historical knowledge on the author's part. Even Tom Shippey, who has recently argued very effectively for reading the Danish and Geatish-Swedish sections of the poem as a reflection of – really quite accurate – traditions surrounding actual historical events, regards the character of Beowulf and his fights against supernatural beings as purely fictional.[69] In *Beowulf*, the phrase *enta geweorc* becomes a strategy by which the poem deliberately veils the identity of the former owners and producers of the hoard. The term *ent* is thus used as a means of defamiliarisation that allows the text to invoke a sense of historical distance.

It is my contention that the same holds true for the other poems that employ the phrase. In this, I follow the lead of scholars such as Lori Ann Garner and John Miles Foley, who have suggested (somewhat more abstractly than I have done here) that employing the term *enta geweorc* is first and foremost a strategy of temporal Othering. Foley remarks that 'what these usages [of *enta geweorc*] share [...] is not the particular circumstances in which they appear, or any literal relationship to giants and their works, but rather the idiomatic value of retrojection into the deep

---

[68] Cohen makes a direct connection to *The Ruin*, arguing that in that poem the reference to giants stands for 'that which predates contemporary man and has vanished long before the poet's epoch' ('Work of Giants', 11).

[69] Tom Shippey, Beowulf *and the North before the Vikings* (Leeds, 2022). Shippey speaks of the '*pure fantasy of the fights*' (*ibid.*, 13, emphasis in the original), and observes that 'everything to do with the character Beowulf looks like fiction' (*ibid.*, 8).

past'.[70] Based on Foley's perceptive observation, one could argue that it is ultimately irrelevant whether the cultural environments in which these texts were produced, read or listened to were in fact ignorant of the actual historical circumstances that produced works of stone like those described: in either case, the phrase *enta geweorc* opens up a semantic space that allows the respective builders to be identified as giants, Romans or members of any other people whose name has been forgotten, while at the same time projecting their existence into a deep past that is beyond the grasp of the present. To put it succinctly, irrespective of whether the poets in question were aware of Britain's Roman past, the phrase *enta geweorc* draws attention to a lacuna, a gap in information, feigned or real. Through the surrogate figure of the mythical 'giant', it produces an impression of insurmountable temporal distance, a sense that this 'deep' past is accessible only by means of its incomprehensible traces. The giant thus stands in for a piece of historical information that has been lost along the way, while simultaneously projecting onto the past an image of cultural Otherness. Rather than constituting an instance of 'primitive', pre-scientific and pre-historiographical aetiology, the stock phrase *enta geweorc* draws attention to the processes of distortion and forgetting that accompany the passing of knowledge from living memory into historical transmission, even to the point where the latter is cut off and its subject consigned to oblivion.

The Wanderer: 'Recent' and 'Deep Past'

Andrew Shryock and Daniel Lord Smail have pointed out the inherent difference between a past conceived of as 'simply a repository of the "natural"' (whether in terms of geology or biology) and a 'deep history' characterised by behavioural and cultural practices that are subject to change and variation, even if these practices remained unrecorded at the time and are thus difficult or even impossible to reconstruct.[71] Prehistory,

---

[70] Foley, *Singer of Tales*, 99. Garner, too, suggests that the phrase, whatever its further connotations within a specific literary context, is employed first and foremost as a means of cultural Othering: 'The material legacies of this "deep past", poetically marked as "enta geweorc", are awe-inspiring, to be sure, but in a way that is at the same time removed from distinctly Germanic traditions' (*Structuring Spaces*, 54). In a similar vein, Howe has perceptively noted that *Maxims II*'s statement that stone cities can be seen from a distance might not only refer to their visual prominence in the landscape, 'but also opens the possibility for a more temporal vantage: these cities can be seen as having their own distant history' (Howe, *Writing the Map*, 85). See also Howe, 'Postcolonial Void', 31.

[71] Andrew Shryock and Daniel Lord Smail, 'Introduction', in Andrew Shryock

Remains of the Past in Old English Literature

Shryock and Smail note, is often regarded as 'marked by long periods of behavioral fixity and cultural stasis', as well as by a lack of certain cultural forms, such as a notion of ethnicity; moreover, it is frequently assumed that the deep past 'is best understood in relation to a fixed human nature or universal behavioral tendencies'.[72] Such a conception of prehistory, which tends to favour behavioural explanations at the expense of cultural ones, 'has no room for contingency, no room for change, no way to understand the path-dependent nature of variation within systems'.[73] Their own concept of 'deep history', by contrast, attempts to 'reconceive the human condition as a hominin one – that is, one that includes all the species in the genus *Homo* that are ancestrally as well as collaterally related to *Homo sapiens*'.[74]

Even though Shryock and Smail primarily engage with prehistory, they argue that the division between 'history' and 'deep history' cannot be understood simply as a single rupture marked by the advent of historical records (or writing more generally). As written records are always selective, and tend to favour certain parts of the population and their cultural practices, the methodological problems faced by researchers of prehistory and, say, early medieval rural life are in many respects comparable: 'The logic that makes Neanderthals and other early hominins visible to a deep history is the same logic that has made subalterns everywhere visible to modern historical praxis.'[75] From this perspective, 'deep history' differs from 'history' not in terms of its subject matter (hominin history), but in terms of its sources and methods (archaeological and anthropological investigation rather than the study of texts) as well as the degree to which it allows changes or developments to be reconstructed and dated. Prehistory is just as full of events as history, but of these events no records exist, except in the form of archaeological traces.

This distinction between a 'history' that can be known and studied and a 'deep history' before the beginning of secure historical knowledge, a history whose existence can only be inferred, draws attention to a boundary line between a 'recent' past within the grasp of human historiography and a more distant one lying beyond it, thereby producing a sense

---

and Daniel Lord Smail (eds), *Deep History: The Architecture of Past and Present* (Berkeley, CA, 2011), 3–20, at 12–13. Shryock and Smail ultimately aim to integrate the 'short' and 'long chronologies' (in other terms, 'prehistory' and 'history' with its emphasis on the centuries after about 1750) into a single historical narrative (*ibid.*, 11–12).

[72] *Ibid.*, 13.

[73] *Ibid.*, 12.

[74] *Ibid.*, 15.

[75] *Ibid.*

Ruins and Their Multiple Temporalities

of temporal layering. But unlike in modern grids of periodisation, this boundary line is not static: not necessarily defined by a specific, allegedly all-changing event, it may be moving forward as personal memory and transmitted knowledge pass into oblivion.

It is precisely such a distinction between a knowable, even familiar recent past and an incomprehensible 'deep past' that *The Wanderer* invokes. Roy M. Liuzza has suggested that the poem's ruins draw attention to material culture's potential to outlast human memory. In the poem, Liuzza argues, ruins stand emblematically for a 'loss of the past', a loss understood not merely in a physical sense – that is, as the progressive fragmentation of the respective structures or the disappearance of their human builders – but also in terms of the memories attached to them. Like everything else in this world, the histories of those who built and lived within the former buildings are ultimately doomed to be forgotten:

> Ruins represent the obliteration of memory, the end of the arc of civilization in a rumbling pile of forgotten rubble. They are a figure of the anxiety of history itself, of being forever perched on the mute lip of oblivion. Underwritten by a profound recognition of belatedness, they place before the speaker the vision of a past that is both glorious and thoroughly vanished, absent but deeply desired.[76]

Like the structures' erstwhile builders, whom *The Wanderer*'s speaker, in the absence of more specific knowledge, can only describe as 'giants', all events in human history will eventually fade from memory – including the speaker's own. The latter's grief, Liuzza argues, derives not only from the loss of his companions, but also from the realisation that their very memory will vanish from the world – as will, in due course, his own.[77]

In *The Wanderer*, then, the separation between personal and universalised loss is not always easy to maintain. Even within passages that seem to be concerned with generalised reflections on worldly transience, such as the description of ruined buildings discussed above or the famous *ubi sunt* catalogue immediately following it, there are details that imply a more personal involvement on the speaker's part. The *ubi sunt* passage is introduced as the speech of a hypothetical 'wise' man, someone (or, rather, anyone) who has reflected deeply on the ephemerality of human life:[78]

---

[76] Liuzza, 'Tower of Babel', 14.
[77] *Ibid.*, 12–14. The speaker's namelessness can be interpreted as a foreshadowing of his own inevitable disappearance.
[78] For a discussion of the passage and its possible sources and analogues, see J. E. Cross, 'Ubi Sunt Passages in Old English: Sources and Relationships', *Årsbok: Yearbook of the New Society of Letters at Lund* (1958–59), 21–44.

Se þonne þisne wealsteal   wise geþohte,
ond þis deorce lif   deope geondþenceð,
frod in ferðe,   feor oft gemon
wælsleahta worn,   ond þas word acwið:
Hwær cwom mearg?   Hwær cwom mago? Hwær cwom
    maþþumgyfa?
Hwær cwom symbla gesetu?   Hwær sindon seledreamas?
Eala beorht bune!   Eala byrnwiga!
Eala þeodnes þrym!

[Then he who has wisely reflected upon this foundation and has deeply contemplated this dark life will often remember from afar, wise in mind, the large number of battles, and speak these words: Where has gone the steed? Where has gone the man? Where has gone the treasure-giver? Where has gone the pleasure of the feast? Where are the joys of the hall? Alas, bright chalice! Alas, armoured warrior! Alas, majesty of the prince! Lines 88–95a.]

Introduced as the words of one who has 'deeply contemplated this dark life' ('þis deorce lif deope geondþenceð'; lines 88–9), the catalogue of losses must by necessity appear generic, a universalisation of the more personal losses the speaker lamented earlier in the poem: anyone who has gone through the same experience, the speaker implies, will ask these same, rhetorical questions.

But then, surprisingly, a much more specific reference is introduced:

Hu seo þrag gewat,
genap under nihthelm,   swa heo no wære.

[How that time has passed away, grown dark under the helm of night, as though it did not exist; lines 95b–6].

'Seo þrag' [that time] implies that the speaker is here thinking of a specific moment, namely the time when 'the armoured warrior' ('byrnwiga'; line 94b) and 'the prince' ('þeodnes þrym'; line 95a) still existed. While Liuzza reads these lines as a reference to a vanished heroic age, a pagan past the passing of which is mourned by the speaker, I would venture that their particular phrasing indicates that what is being envisioned here are very particular individuals whose memory the foregoing catalogue has conjured up:

Stondeð nu on laste   leofre duguþe
weal wundrum heah,   wyrmlicum fah.

[Now there stands as a vestige of the dear company a wall wondrously high, coloured in a serpentine manner; lines 97–8.]

Ruins and Their Multiple Temporalities

The adjective *leof* [dear] implies that this 'company' (*duguþ*) is no longer the cast of generic princes and warriors of the preceding lines, but rather a group of specific people known personally to the speaker. Put differently, over the course of the speech, the generic warriors retroactively become specific ones, as, in the speaker's mind, the contemplation of universalised losses mixes with personal memories. Thus, in retrospect, the *þeoden* [prince] of line 95a is no longer quite as generic as he initially appeared – and, one suspects, was originally intended by the speaker: here, we witness the sudden collapse of the distinction between the speaker and the hypothetical 'everyman' whose more general reflection on transience the catalogue supposedly reproduces. Intended as a means for overcoming the speaker's personal grief through a reflection on the universal nature of human loss, the passage falls back on images from his own personal experience, thereby becoming historically and biographically specific. The lines performatively illustrate the speaker's failure to universalise his inward pain as his enumeration of generic losses evokes personal memories that awaken fresh grief.

My reading of this passage as progressing from universalised to personal images is supported by the wall's description as 'wundrum heah, wyrmlicum fah' [wondrously (or: remarkably) high, coloured in a serpentine manner]. The visual details suggest that what the speaker has in mind is not just any kind of historical rubble, but a specific wall that stands in some sort of relation to the *leofe duguþ* [dear company; line 97b] whose loss he is mourning. Hume argues that the speaker 'is not seeing a wall but imagining one'.[79] This may well be true, but even so, this imagined wall is clearly not a completely generic one, but modelled after a specific type of wall the speaker is familiar with, one that is particularly high and decorated in a specific way.[80] For the speaker, this wall is associated with certain memories; namely, those of the otherwise unspecified 'dear company', probably his former lord and his fellow retainers. It is this combination of sudden visual specificity and the speaker's apparent familiarity with that particular detail that singles out the image from among the

---

[79] Hume, 'Ruin Motif', 354.

[80] The former is also noted by Christopher Dean, who observes that 'the singular form of the word suggests a particular wall' and draws attention to the pains the speaker takes to describe its decoration, something he does not do with the other walls he mentions. Still, Dean's contention that the speaker's insistence on the continuing existence of the wall ('stondeð nu'; line 97) means that it is a recent construction (and indeed one built by the speaker himself, as Dean argues) is not convincing: the fact that the wall is still standing does not preclude its being part of a ruin; indeed, as my foregoing discussion shows, it even supports such a reading; see Christopher Dean, '*Weal wundrum heah, wyrmlicum fah* and the Narrative Background of *The Wanderer*', *Modern Philology*, 63:2 (1965), 141–3, at 143.

Remains of the Past in Old English Literature

other items of the *ubi sunt* catalogue: here is a detail too specific to permit universalisation. The image of the decorated wall works like a visual mnemonic, reminding the speaker of his fallen companions – perhaps against his will.

But even as the expression *leofe duguþ* suggests that the people referred to were known to the speaker personally, the description of the wall as 'wundrum heah, wyrmlicum fah' implies that the visual details, albeit familiar, are still in some way perceived as exceptional or even strange: the wall's height is unusual, even awe-inspiring, and its decoration is alluded to in a way that suggests that the speaker is aware of a deeper significance he is unable to grasp. Like the stone structures in *Maxims II*, the wall is both familiar and Other. The phrase 'wyrmlicum fah' is difficult to interpret. As T. P. Dunning and A. J. Bliss note in their edition of *The Wanderer*, it occurs nowhere else in the Old English corpus. They argue, moreover, that 'the phrase *wyrmlicum fah* can hardly be dissociated from the *wreoþenhilt and wyrmfah* of *Beowulf* 1698', and that 'there can be little doubt that the phrase means "decorated with serpentine patterns"'.[81] The adjective *wyrmlic* literally means 'worm-like', with *wyrm* signifying a wide range of meanings, from 'serpent' or 'reptile' to 'insect' or 'worm', as Ferhatović observes.[82] Dunning and Bliss gloss *fah* as 'decorated', arguing that 'it is perhaps pointless to discuss whether the patterns were carved or painted'.[83] Still, *fah* usually means 'coloured' – neither Clark Hall nor Bosworth-Toller include any translation implying ornamentation or decoration, but only list entries related to colour, with the additional implication that this colour is especially bright or variegated.[84] Literally, then, the adverbial phrase translates as 'coloured in a wormlike manner', although it is difficult to say what exactly is meant by that. The phrase might allude to the serpentine ornamentation found on many early medieval stone monuments from north-western Europe and in insular manuscripts such as the Book of Kells, but then again it might not.[85] What is clear, however,

---

[81] Dunning and Bliss (eds), *The Wanderer*, 74.

[82] Ferhatović, *Borrowed Objects*, 51. Frankis discusses a possible relationship between the serpent-like decoration and references in Isaiah 13.19–22 and Jeremiah 50–1 to ruins inhabited by wild animals and monsters; in the latter passage, these are specified as *dracones*. To Frankis, the biblical reference provides a possible explanation for the poem's mentioning of worms in the context of desolation, although he concedes that the exact reasons – not least for changing the living monsters of the Bible into a depiction – remain unclear ('Thematic Significance', 268 n. 2).

[83] Dunning and Bliss (eds), *The Wanderer*, 131, 74.

[84] 'Coloured, stained, dyed, tinged, shining, variegated; tinctus, cŏlōrātus, vărius, versicŏlor, discŏlor' (*BT*, s.v. 'fag'); 'variegated, spotted, dappled, stained, dyed, [...] shining, gleaming' (*CH*, s.v. 'fag').

[85] Andrew James Johnston draws attention to the possibility of making such a

112

Ruins and Their Multiple Temporalities

is that similar constructions with *fah* – such as 'atertanum fah' [(perhaps) lined with poisoned twigs; *Beowulf*, line 1459]; 'bleobrygdum fah' [shining with bright (or: variegated) colour; *The Phoenix*, line 292]; 'fyrmælum fag' [variegated with marks of fire; *Andreas*, line 1134] – suggest a striking visual appearance. The same appears to be true of *The Wanderer*, where the speaker's admiration of the wall's construction as 'wundrum heah' [wonderfully high; line 98a] is combined with a reference to its extraordinary decoration.

It is, of course, perfectly possible to admire the achievements of one's own colleagues, friends or family. But given the poem's earlier acknowledgement of the ruins of a more distant past, the 'eald enta geweorc' of lines 85–7, it seems more plausible to assume that the remarkable wall and its serpentine patterns were not, in fact, made by the *leofe duguþ* themselves, but became associated with them as part of their living environment, perhaps through inheritance or spoliation. Such a scenario has been imagined, for instance, by Tony Millns, who argues that the wall 'is not conceived of as contemporary Anglo-Saxon work at all' and associates the serpentine pattern with Roman herring-bone masonry – although again I must point out that the poem's description is too unspecific to allow for identification with any specific building style, but instead emphasises the alterity of both the structure and its decorations.[86]

---

connection in his discussion of the sword hilt in *Beowulf* described as 'wreoþen-hilt ond wyrmfah' (line 1698); Andrew James Johnston, 'Global *Beowulf* and the Poetics of Entanglement', in Jan-Peer Hartmann and Andrew James Johnston (eds), *Material Remains: Reading the Past in Medieval and Early Modern Literature* (Columbus, OH, 2021), 103–19, at 110–11.

[86] Tony Millns, '*The Wanderer* 98: "Weal wundrum heah wyrmlicum fah",' *RES* NS, 28:112 (1977), 431–8, at 432, 434–8. Most critics appear to share Millns's feeling that the patterns are in some form or another related to Roman material culture, although this conviction seems to stem mainly from the poem's historical context, that is, its being a product of post-Roman early medieval Britain. Thus, Anne Lingard Klinck argues that 'in all probability [the worms] refer to some kind of decoration on a Roman structure', the exact nature of which 'is impossible to determine' (*Old English Elegies*, 125). Garner, following Millns, sees a connection to Roman herringbone masonry, but opts to interpret the image with Donald Fry as a traditional motif invoking death and destruction (*Structuring Spaces*, 165–6). See also R. F. Leslie (ed.), *The Wanderer* (Manchester, 1966), 86–7 and the literature cited by Klinck and Millns ('*The Wanderer*', 433). Other explanations have been put forward: R. O. Bowen proposed that the wall 'can be explained according to the maggot pattern decoration of Neolithic burial monuments common throughout Britain and Bretagne'; R. O. Bowen, '*The Wanderer*, 98', *Explicator*, 13 (1955), 60–1. Dean similarly associated the wall with a burial monument, but regarded it as an early medieval one: 'The serpent shapes carved on the rocks then become Anglo-Saxon work and may very well be those intertwining ribbon-like animals that appear so frequently in all

Remains of the Past in Old English Literature

The reuse and modification of ancient monuments is well-attested throughout human history. In early medieval Britain, a wide range of different monument types were reused, including Roman forts, temples and villas; prehistoric ditches and earthworks; hillforts, henge monuments and burial sites. According to Sarah Semple, author of the most comprehensive study of monument reuse in early medieval Britain to date, these sites served a variety of purposes, acting, for example, as places of assembly, settlement or burial, as boundary markers or execution sites.[87] Practices involving monument reuse were also frequently part of strategies aimed at establishing or substantiating political or territorial claims; for instance, through the appropriation of ancestors.[88] Many prehistoric sites were subject to multiple phases of use and reuse, interrupted by periods of abandonment. Showing traces of human activity as early as the Mesolithic Period, the site of Yeavering, close to what is now the English-Scottish border, is a case in point: it became the site of a permanent settlement during the Bronze Age; the location of an Iron Age hillfort; and, after an apparent hiatus, an elaborate early medieval settlement and ceremonial complex, boasting one of the largest timber halls known from this period, which archaeologists have identified as an early Northumbrian royal site.[89]

Another common scenario was for ruined structures to be quarried for building materials. A number of early medieval stone churches, for example, incorporate fragments from Roman-period buildings, some of

---

forms of Anglo-Saxon art' (Dean, 'Narrative Background', 143). W. H. French even suggested that 'wyrmlicum fah' does not refer to ornamentation at all, but rather represents 'the channels and passages cut by engraver beetles and their larvae' on the outer surface of the timbers of an early medieval hall; W. H. French, '*The Wanderer* 98: *Wyrmlīcum fāh*', *Modern Language Notes*, 67:8 (1952), 526–9. The apparent strangeness of the patterns, discussed above, would seem to speak against French's explanation and would also disqualify Dean's, if taken at face value. However, as I have noted above, it is not necessary to read *The Wanderer* mimetically in a specific historical context; in other words, it does not matter what historical context fits the poem's description best as long as we recognise that the worm-like ornamentation represents something strange and wondrous from the perspective of the poem's speaker.

[87] Semple, *Perceptions*.

[88] Estella Weiss-Krejci, 'The Plot Against the Past: Reuse and Modification of Ancient Mortuary Monuments as Persuasive Efforts of Appropriation', in Marta Díaz-Guardamino, Leonardo García Sanjuán and David Wheatley (eds), *The Lives of Prehistoric Monuments in Iron Age, Roman, and Medieval Europe* (Oxford, 2015), 307–24.

[89] Pam J. Crabtree, *Early Medieval Britain: The Rebirth of Towns in the Post-Roman West* (Cambridge, 2018), 71; Semple, *Perceptions*, 256; Brian Hope-Taylor, *Yeavering: An Anglo-Saxon Centre of Early Northumbria* (London, 1977); Richard Bradley, 'Time Regained: The Creation of Continuity', *Journal of the British Archaeological Association*, 140:1 (1987), 1–17.

Ruins and Their Multiple Temporalities

them still bearing legible inscriptions.[90] Even more than reused monuments, such *spolia* incorporated into new buildings draw attention to the polychronicity of material objects, that is, to their inherent capacity to develop new associations in the course of their potentially long existence. As Ferhatović observes, *spolia* complicate the relations between past and present in belonging 'neither fully to the new context nor to the older one' from which they have been taken, combining the two 'to yield something else'.[91] Metonymically invoking different times and places, such self-consciously recycled objects simultaneously index continuity and rupture; they 'become coherent when fixed in a larger, new context, but at the same time gesture towards something outside of it, temporally, spatially and existentially. [...] *Spolia* interconnect while remaining distinct'.[92] Both reused monuments and structures incorporating *spolia* can thus be simultaneously imbued with connotations of cultural alterity and traces of the more recent past, while frequently being integrated into everyday life to such an extent that their primary focus has shifted from the past to the present.

The two practices of monument reuse and spoliation intersect in a particularly striking manner in the late Roman theatre at Canterbury, as Paul Bennett's recent discussion of the site's long-term use over nearly one millennium impressively demonstrates. Built towards the end of the late second century CE in the location of an earlier and somewhat smaller theatre, it appears to have survived 'as a conspicuous and important monument at the heart of the ruined town well into and possibly throughout the Anglo-Saxon Period', together with the city wall and rampart, sections of which can still be seen today.[93] When Canterbury began to be re-occupied in the late fifth century after a period of abandonment, the early medieval town seems to have developed around the site of the theatre, due partly to the presence of open ground, but also, Bennett suggests, in consequence of the theatre's role 'as an important, visible nodal point and place of congregation'.[94] Although it was partially spoliated for the construction of churches after the conversion of the Kentish king Æthelberht in 597, it continued as a spectacular ruin at the intersection of major thoroughfares

---

[90] See, for example, Howe, *Writing the Map*, 91–6; Garner, *Structuring Spaces*, 67; and especially Tim Eaton, *Plundering the Past: Roman Stonework in Medieval Britain* (Stroud, 2000), 58–93.

[91] Ferhatović, *Borrowed Objects*, 63, 21, 35.

[92] *Ibid.*, 21, 35 (quotation).

[93] Paul Bennett, 'Canterbury in Transition: The Role of the Roman Theatre', in Andrew Richardson, Michael Bintley, John Hines and Andy Seamen (eds), *Transitions and Relationships over Land and Sea in the Early Middle Ages of Northern Europe* (Canterbury, 2023), 1–26, at 7–8.

[94] *Ibid.*, 13.

Remains of the Past in Old English Literature

and *en route* a processional way to the inner *burgh* well into the ninth century and beyond, when it became an enormous quarry for building materials used, among other places, in the construction of the churches of St Mildred and St Dunstan, until, by the late eleventh century, it had vanished completely.[95] Especially in the settlement's early days, however, it would have provided a conspicuous point of reference, a landmark familiar to its inhabitants and visitors in all its temporal and cultural alterity: 'Those entering the walled circuit through old Roman gates in the early sixth century would have seen the ruined theatre at the centre of a small community, living within the decaying vestiges of the past.'[96]

The Wanderer's references to ruined structures whose aspect is at once familiar and strikingly Other invoke a similar situation of a latter-day people living within the remains of an earlier civilisation. These ruins have a layered material history: on the one hand, they are called 'eald enta geweorc' (line 87), implying that their historical origins are so distant that they can only be referred to in mythical terms. On the other hand, they have been used and reused by later, historically less distant inhabitants: the – presumably – human rulers and their retinues whose passing the speaker mentions in the same passage (lines 78b–84), and who seem to be culturally distinct from the original builders referred to as 'giants'. The two temporalities coalesce in the image of the remarkably high and strikingly decorated wall, which reminds the speaker of a known and familiar past, the recent past of the *leofe duguþ* still present in his mind, while at the same time gesturing, through its unusual and perhaps incomprehensible details, to an earlier and apparently inscrutable past. This past is perhaps identical with the mythical 'deep past' associated with the 'giants' who constructed the now-ruined buildings mentioned earlier in the text (lines 75–87), buildings of which the decorated wall may well have been part. The combination of familiarity and alterity, expressed through the visual specificity of the image and its association with familiar people, on the one hand, and the allusion to superior construction skills and the unusualness of the decoration, on the other, suggests two different sets of temporal relations: like the *spolia* in Ferhatović's discussion, the wall complicates the relationship between past and present in that it is associated with more than one temporal context without fully belonging to either: even when taken as an integral and coherent part of its present context, the remarkable ornamentation still gestures towards something outside of it.[97]

---

[95] *Ibid.*, 21, 23–4.
[96] *Ibid.*, 15.
[97] Ferhatović, *Borrowed Objects*, 63, 35.

Ruins and Their Multiple Temporalities

The wall's capacity to invoke both a remote and a more recent, familiar past recalls the argument advanced by archaeologists Chris Gosden and Gary Lock that prehistoric perceptions of temporality might have operated on two levels, one 'historical' and one 'mythical':

> History [...] operates in a time continuous with the present, even if change is acknowledged, whereas mythical structures refer back to a previous state of the world, where human beings either did not exist, or had no power, and where processes of cause and effect manifest themselves differently.[98]

These two perceptions of time, they maintain, 'are not mutually exclusive, but [...] are linked means of dealing with the past, which can easily coexist'.[99] Drawing on anthropological studies undertaken by Chris Ballard in the Tari Basin of the southern Highlands of Papua New Guinea, Gosden and Lock suggest that in preliterate societies, history is remembered and recounted through the device of genealogy: the succession of individuals genealogically linked to the present (whether real or imagined) becomes the basis for stories about the past as well as for measuring the temporal distance between a specific point in the past and the present. Such genealogical histories, they argue, do not rely on human memory alone, but also utilise mnemonic markers in the form of burial mounds, drainage ditches or other features of the landscape named after or associated with specific individuals. Mythical time, by contrast, concerns events linked to forces or beings that may still have an effect on the present, but are themselves cut off from it.

Gosden and Lock's comparison between aboriginal groups in Papua New Guinea and prehistoric peoples is problematic both historically and ethically, as it implies that the former are denied coevalness with contemporary 'civilised' (in other words, Western) societies: as Johannes Fabian has famously pointed out, the tacit implication of such equations is that present-day aboriginal groups still share in the 'deep time' of prehistoric people, as if they inhabited a temporal continuum different from that of modern Western culture.[100] There is, moreover, no evidence that perceptions of time in prehistoric Britain operated in the way imagined by Gosden and Lock, but that is not the point that I wish to make here. Intriguingly, it is *The Wanderer* itself that imagines its protagonist's per-

---

[98] Chris Gosden and Gary Lock, 'Prehistoric Histories', *World Archaeology*, 30:1 (1998), 2–12, 5. They adopt this distinction from Alan Rumsey's discussion of aboriginal groups' perceptions of the land; see Gosden and Lock, 'Prehistoric', 4–5; Rumsey, 'The Dreaming, Human Agency and Inscriptive Practice', *Oceania*, 65 (1994), 116–30.

[99] Gosden and Lock, 'Prehistoric', 5.

[100] Fabian, *Time and the Other*, 31.

Remains of the Past in Old English Literature

ception of the decorated wall in terms of just such a duality, invoking at once a sense of unsurmountable temporal distance and memories of a fairly recent past, a past whose memory is still vivid in the speaker's mind and can be passed on to the poem's audience before it, too, falls into historical oblivion.

Could the wall's capacity to signify two sets of temporal relations suggest a scenario in which the speaker's former associates reused or spoliated the material remains of earlier cultural activity, remains whose historical provenance and meaning they were unable to fully understand? The poem does not elaborate the point, but the unexplained details and their paradoxical characterisation as both familiar and Other certainly invites its audience to contemplate a layered past of which the decorated wall forms an enduring trace.

The Wanderer's ruins, then, elicit two apparently contradictory responses to temporality: on the one hand, they highlight the general transitoriness of the world, metonymically signifying the disappearance of personal memories and past cultures; on the other, they exemplify the durability of matter and hence the ability of ruins to continue to exist long after their builders have vanished from the face of the earth and from human memory. In addition, even as the image of the decorated wall evokes familiar memories in the speaker's mind, it also draws attention to the difficulty of interpreting its specific design. This difficulty, of course, arises precisely because the wall's durability means that it can continue to be used long after the original meaning of the decorations has been forgotten: matter outlasts meaning. And yet, the very same matter still continues to signify, as the wall's capacity to remind the speaker of his own past succinctly demonstrates. The two responses to temporality here outlined are thus intimately linked.

Ultimately, the poem's historical vision is one in which the past does not vanish in its entirety but leaves material traces; these traces, however, are fragmented, and their meaning is beyond recovery. As Liuzza notes:

> The ruins in *The Wanderer* are monuments not to the legibility but to the inscrutability of history, [...] they reveal the past not as a stable place from which the present takes its legitimate origin but as a place of loss, decay, silence, rupture, and brokenness, ultimately a warning to the present that our story will be told by the fragments we leave behind.[101]

The Wanderer's image of the decorated wall emphasises precisely this inscrutability. Liuzza does not discuss the passage directly, but he interprets the poem's references to warriors and treasures in the lines directly

---

[101] Liuzza, 'Tower of Babel', 13–14.

Ruins and Their Multiple Temporalities

preceding the description of the wall as allusions to a heroic pagan past known to the speaker from orally transmitted songs. In an ingenious move, he then reads the poem's ruin imagery in conjunction with the protagonist's apparent inability to communicate his feelings – an inability only superficially glossed over by the speaker's assertion that stoic silence is a noble virtue (lines 11–18). That inability is evident, however, in the speaker's lament for the loss of his lord's counsel (line 38) and his realisation that the cries of seabirds cannot substitute for human speech (line 55).[102] To Liuzza, *The Wanderer* presents 'a nostalgic poem about nostalgia itself, a lament for the comfortable feeling that the past was knowable and worth knowing, an elegy for the possibility of speaking truly about what has gone before and will never return'.[103] This unfulfillable longing for a knowable and comprehensible past appears to be reflected in the speaker's inability both to speak about his own past and to recover the origins and meaning of the ruins around him, which for him have become inscrutable *enta geweorc*. To Liuzza, the speaker's dilemma expresses a feeling of disconnectedness with the past, which he links to a perceived 'devaluation of a shared cultural memory and a living oral tradition in favour of a textualised past':[104]

> The *topos* of ruins deployed in *The Wanderer* is one way an Anglo-Saxon poet thought about the transition from memory to written record and the many acts of silencing and forgetting it entailed. The ruins stand in for the perception that the social memory of the heroic world itself was under the threat of subversion – the ties that bound the storied past to the lived present were stressed to the breaking point by the transition from oral remembrance to textual record.[105]

For Liuzza, *The Wanderer* thus recalls a very specific moment of cultural transformation: the replacement of a (pagan) oral culture by a (Christian) literary one. Historically speaking, such a moment of replacement never happened, of course, as many historians of oral theory have pointed out: the oral continues to live along with and amid the written. But that does not impinge on Liuzza's argument that *The Wanderer* imagines just such a moment of cultural transformation and the emotional response of someone who experiences it. Viewed from this perspective, *The Wanderer* might be interpreted as an early example of medievalism, that is, a text

---

[102] *Ibid.*, 12–13.

[103] *Ibid.*, 17.

[104] *Ibid.*, 19. Liuzza reads the speaker's inability to speak about his own past against the confusion of languages in the aftermath of Babel (*ibid.*, 13); the poem's ruins thus stand in a literary tradition that links the image of ruins to an inability to recreate the past even in words.

[105] *Ibid.*, 22.

nostalgically envisioning a more simple, comprehensible past on the verge of disappearing.[106]

But we do not have to follow Liuzza's linking of *The Wanderer*'s intimation of cultural loss to a specific historical configuration (that is, the transition from an oral pagan culture to a literary Christian one) in order to appreciate that the image of the adorned wall signifies a fragmented temporality: on the one hand, it reminds the speaker of his own, recent experiences; on the other, it points back to a more distant past, the significance of which has been lost. There is a difference between the speaker's nostalgia for his own remembered past and his regret of the loss of information about a more remote one. The only way that the speaker can connect to this remote past is through his appreciation of the wondrous masonry and the strange patterns adorning the stone. But his inability to fully fathom the ruins' origin and historical meaning makes him aware of the precariousness of the memory of his own past, which cannot be fully verbalised and survives only in fragments that, with the passing of time, will become both fewer and increasingly difficult to comprehend. The speaker's contemplation of the wall, richly decorated but potentially broken, familiar yet strangely Other, draws attention to the difference between nostalgia and historical oblivion – the loss of knowledge pertaining to the past – but also to their inherent relatedness: the former is personal, drawing upon memory, whereas the latter marks historical alterity, relating to that which can no longer be remembered; and yet the one will eventually turn into the other. The boundary between a past that is still recalled and one that is irrevocably lost, between 'history' and 'deep history', is continually moving forward; every individual death means the loss of an individual memory, of the history that came before and was still remembered until that death. No account, oral or written, can fully substitute for the vivid memory of past experiences, *The Wanderer* suggests – and that, I argue, is the reason for the protagonist's inability to verbalise his grief.

Ruins, Davies remarks, 'illustrate the territory between preservation and oblivion'.[107] In *The Wanderer*, the sight of the ruins awakens in the protagonist an existential terror of the obliteration of the past and, in consequence, of the future obliteration of his own present; in Liuzza's words, 'ruins are the broken mirror of the present'.[108] The speaker's contemplation of ruins, then, leads not only to the Christian message that stability

---

[106] In her introduction to *The Cambridge Companion to Medievalism*, Louise D'Arcens defines medievalism as 'the reception, interpretation or recreation of the European Middle Ages in post-medieval cultures'; Louise D'Arcens (ed), *The Cambridge Companion to Medievalism* (Cambridge, 2016), 1–13, at 1.

[107] Davies, *Visions*, 30.

[108] Liuzza, 'Tower of Babel', 12.

is only found in heaven (lines 114–15), but also to the discovery both of a historical consciousness – a sense of the irrevocable pastness of the past – and its 'terrible burden'.[109] This discovery, I would argue, is not merely tied to the realisation that all cultural endeavours must eventually end in inexplicable rubble – a variation on the traditional theme of worldly transience; it derives in equal measure from the recognition of different layers of pastness, and hence of different stages of historical forgetting, emblematised in the image of the decorated wall. The ruins described by *The Wanderer*'s speaker are both strange and familiar, universal and associated with personal memories. As such, they invoke a complex temporal panorama, a *longue durée* that still leaves room for personal micro-histories. History is full of such micro-histories, *The Wanderer* suggests, but they cannot be recovered, even though ruins and other material objects continue to act as traces of their former presence. It is the speaker's realisation of the continued presence of these traces, traces that bear witness to the multi-layered, macro-historical scheme of which the speaker's own experiences form only a minute part, that makes the discovery of historical obliteration all the harder to bear.

The Ruin: *Material Resilience and Recreation*

Even more prominently than in *The Wanderer*, *The Ruin*'s description of a deteriorating city stages the fundamental inaccessibility of the past. It does so, however, with an emotional detachment that suggests the appreciative gaze of the Romantic tourist rather than the existential terror displayed by *The Wanderer*'s speaker. Where the latter appears to be on the verge of despair in the face of the inexorable workings of time, *The Ruin* sets against the finality of historical oblivion the cyclical nature of successive generations and polities, and the capacity of the human mind to imaginatively recreate past lives and histories. These recreations, however, must necessarily be the product of the present. In the case at hand, this is emphasised by the lack of cultural specificity that characterises the historical pageants conjured up by the narrator, a lack heightened further by the striking contrast between the conventionality of the imagined past and the poem's detailed and highly visualised description of the present aspect of the ruined buildings.

Like *The Wanderer*, *The Ruin* has often been read as a 'meditation on [...] the transitoriness of worldly glory'.[110] Yet as Lawrence Beaston observes,

---

[109] *Ibid.*, 17.
[110] The quotation is from Abram, 'In Search', 23. See also the literature cited in n. 21 above.

despite the fact that the ruined city 'has been relentlessly pounded by the powerful forces of nature [...] as a physical object [it] is not so very ephemeral after all'.[111] Like *The Wanderer*'s ruins, then, the deteriorating city described in *The Ruin* draws attention to the longevity and resilience of matter. According to Beaston, the poem's central message therefore 'concerns not the mutability of the world but the fleeting nature of human life'.[112] What militates against this by no means untypical verdict, however, is the fact that the poem's speaker does not appear to be overly affected by the demise of the city's former inhabitants: there is none of the anguish and despair displayed by *The Wanderer*'s speaker at the realisation of the transitoriness of human existence. As I will argue in the following pages, it is not the ephemerality of human lives and achievements that lies at the centre of the poem's meditations, but the very durability of those achievements and their potential to outlast not only the lives of their human architects, but also the span of human recollection. *The Ruin* suggests that even when all memory of the past has been irretrievably lost, the material traces of that past can still evoke an emotional response that connects the observer with the forgotten builders and inhabitants: wonder, appreciation, fascination, perhaps even elation at the resilience of matter amid the mutability of the world.

Given *The Ruin*'s partial survival within a sole textual witness, the manuscript conventionally referred to as the 'Exeter Book' – incidentally, the same manuscript that also contains the only surviving versions of *The Wanderer* and *The Seafarer* – it is hardly surprising that it has become a widespread *topos* among critics to refer to the poem itself as 'a ruin'.[113] The

---

[111] Lawrence Beaston, '*The Ruin* and the Brevity of Human Life', *Neophilologus*, 95 (2011), 477–89, at 482.

[112] *Ibid.*, 482. I concur with Beaston's judgement that 'the poem's point is that the things that people make out of the substances of this world have the capacity to outlast their makers', a point also made by Edward B. Irving, Jr, 'Image and Meaning in the Elegies', in Robert P. Creed (ed.), *Old English Poetry: Fifteen Essays* (Providence, RI, 1967), 153–66, at 156. Nevertheless, Beaston appears unable to move beyond the *ubi sunt*-paradigm long associated with the Old English elegies in general, which reappears in an 'ars longa vita brevis'-form. Thus, he goes on to argue that since the capacity of things to outlast their makers also draws attention to the brevity of human life, 'we might expect that the speaker must have sensed that his own life was somehow diminished by his having come across the ruin' ('*The Ruin*', 486), despite the clear absence of any expression of such sentiment on part of the speaker.

[113] See, for example, Abram, 'In Search', 23. Michael Swanton speaks of *The Ruin* as 'a poem of re-enactment, in which not merely the imagery but its broken syntactic structure endorses its theme and deepens its present significance. The ruined state of the poem, far from obstructing our appreciation of it, only cor-

poem's fragmentary nature – the text is truncated at the end and contains numerous lacunae of varying length – makes it difficult in places to assess its original form and content. With respect to its present state, however, it is safe to say that *The Ruin* is altogether different in tone from *The Wanderer*. As Christine Fell notes, there is 'no overt Christian comment' in the surviving text: 'We are not formally invited to look at the transient in the light of the eternal.'[114] Thus, whereas *The Wanderer* has its speaker experience the fears and regrets that go with the recognition that the past is irretrievably gone, *The Ruin*, while acknowledging the fundamental irrecoverability of the past, is evidently fascinated with the monumental traces of bygone cultural activity and the awe-inspiring skills of their makers. Even the inscrutable workings of *wyrd* [fate], which have turned mighty buildings into piles of rubble, are less a cause for horror than a source of fascination:

> Wrætlic is þes wealstan,   wyrde gebræcon;
> burgstede burston,   brosnað enta geweorc.

> [Wondrous is this wall-stone, broken by Fate; the city-places broke asunder, the work of giants crumbles; lines 1–2.][115]

In my discussion of the word *wrætlic* at the beginning of this chapter, I quoted Ferhatović's observation that the word appears to denote a quality that combines the impressive with the mysterious.[116] It is just such a quality that seems to be suggested here: from the perspective of the implied narrator, there is something both awe-inspiring and incomprehensible about the way that the foundations have been broken by 'Fate', but also, perhaps, about the way they were first constructed.

My choice of the term 'implied narrator' is deliberate: unlike *The Wanderer*'s speaker, who uses a personal narrative to convey a more general point, *The Ruin*'s narrator does not feature as a character in their own right, but only as a passive observer – in Patricia Dailey's words, 'although the descriptive narrative of this poem appears to be a subject's meditation on a past, no subject appears as an authorial voice'.[117] Alain Renoir diagnoses the presence of 'a speaking voice but no speaker', and

---

roborates the truth it imports'. Michael Swanton, *English Poetry before Chaucer* (Exeter, 2002), 132–3.

[114] Fell, 'Perceptions', 180.

[115] The Old English text is quoted from George Philip Krapp and Elliott Van Kirk Dobbie (eds), *The Exeter Book*, ASPR, 3 (New York, 1936), 227–9, 364–6 (notes).

[116] See n. 3 above.

[117] Patricia Dailey, 'Questions of Dwelling in Anglo-Saxon Poetry and Medieval Mysticism: Inhabiting Landscape, Body, and Mind', *New Medieval Literatures*, 8 (2006), 175–214, at 183.

notes that the poem foregrounds 'a series of tableaux rather a narrative or philosophical monologue'.[118] Nevertheless, these tableaux are clearly the product of an implied observer's perception and imagination. Many scholars have noticed that the speaker's emotional involvement is minimal and confined mainly to expressions of admiration and awe, as in the opening lines quoted above.[119] Yet while it is true that no direct interaction takes place between the speaking voice and the ruins described – Howe calls the poem 'static'[120] – there is emotional as well as imaginative involvement, a point that will become important to my argument.

The narrator does not specify whether it is the skilfulness of the work or the destructive power of time that they are chiefly impressed by; perhaps it is a combination of both that leads them to experience a sensation similar to the Romantics' Sublime.[121] Elsewhere in the poem, it is the ingeniousness of the builders that is praised (for instance, the way the foundations of a wall are reinforced with metal – 'hwætred in hringas, hygerof gebond / weallwalan wirum wundrum togædre' [someone knowledgeable about rings, strong in purpose, wonderfully bound together the wall-foundations with wires; lines 19–20]), but also the beauty of the city in its prime, as the narrator imagines it: 'Beorht wæron burgræced, burnsele monige, / heah horngestreon' [Bright were the city-halls, many the bath-houses, high the wealth of gables; lines 21–2a]. Even references to the destructive power of 'Fate' – for instance in line 1b (cited above) and line 24b ('oþþæt

---

[118] Alain Renoir, 'The Old English *Ruin*: Contrastive Structure and Affective Impact', in Martin Green (ed.), *The Old English Elegies* (Rutherford, NJ, 1983), 148–73, at 149–50.

[119] See, for example, Stanley B. Greenfield, 'The Old English Elegies', in E. G. Stanley (ed.), *Continuations and Beginnings: Studies in Old English Literature* (London, 1966), 142–75, at 146: '*The Ruin* is completely impersonal and objective, with never a word to suggest the state of mind induced in the observer (other than awe), while *The Wanderer* uses an ethopoeic speaker who laments his personal fate as well as the evanescence of all worldly things.' This is obviously an exaggeration, as is evidenced by the admiration expressed at several points in the poem. Christine Fell goes so far as to suggest that '*The Ruin* is unique among [the Old English elegies] in having no persona, no "I" whose anonymous experiences are presented. It is a poem about a place not a person, and we have no voice between us and the poet's direct observation' ('Perceptions', 179). Fell does not properly distinguish between the author ('poet') and the narrator, however. Crucially, the 'observations' are those of the narrator and not of the poet: even if the poem constructs a scenario in which a speaker is standing amid the ruins of a city, it is perfectly imaginable that the text was composed in entirely different circumstances, and that the emotions sometimes expressed by the speaking voice do not (or not exclusively) match those of the composer.

[120] Howe, *Writing the Map*, 89.

[121] See Cohen, 'Work of Giants', 9–10.

Ruins and Their Multiple Temporalities

þæt onwende wyrd seo swiþe' [until that was changed by Fate the mighty]) – appear to give utterance not so much to horror as to awe at the sight of the corrosiveness of time. The lack of personal involvement allows the narrator to maintain a detached view of the demise of earlier societies: the former inhabitants' disappearance is not read as a foreshadowing of the narrator's own identical fate, but merely as the singular historical event responsible for the city's abandonment. As an archaeological site, the ruined city described in the poem is less a memorial to the material achievements of a specific culture than a testament to the persistence of matter and its ability to preserve fragments of the past across different cultural layers and beyond the limits of historical knowledge.

The *longue durée* stretching between the time when the structures were first erected and the here and now of the narrator is the subject of a passage that describes the demise of the original builders:

> Eorðgrap hafað
> waldend wyrhtan   forweorone, geleorene,
> heardgripe hrusan,   oþ hund cnea
> werþeoda gewitan.   Oft þæs wag gebad
> ræghar ond readfah   rice æfter oþrum,
> ofstonden under stormum;   steap geap gedreas.

> [The grip of the earth has the deceased, departed ruling wrights, the hard grip of the ground, until a hundred generations of peoples have passed away. Often this wall bided one kingdom after the other, lichen-grey and red-coloured, steadfast during storms; the lofty gable fell; lines 6b–11.]

The passage emphasises the long duration of the city's existence through its invocation both of the original builders and a hundred later genera-tions – again without ever becoming culturally specific, the poem's only cultural/ethnical ascription being the generic 'enta geweorc' of line 2. The passage's temporal perspective, we will see, is remarkably complex and full of ambiguities, with identities and sequentialities particularly difficult to tie down.

The appellation *waldend wyrhtan* (line 7a), presumably a reference to the city's builders previously referred to as 'enta' [giants; line 2b], has occasioned some debate. Most editors and translators read the two words as a compound noun (an interpretation followed here); in this case, the literal meaning would be something like 'ruling wrights' (S. A. J. Bradley translates 'lordly builders'),[122] with the possible implication that these 'wrights' were particularly vigorous and skilful craftspeople. Beaston

---

[122] S. A. J. Bradley (trans.), *Anglo-Saxon Poetry: An Anthology of Old English Poems in Prose Translation with Introduction and Headnotes* (London, 1982), 402.

125

seems to follow this interpretation when he speaks of the *waldend wyrhtan* as 'the master builders, whose craftsmanship could inspire such awe'.[123] However, Krapp and Dobbie remark that 'such a compound would be highly unusual', suggesting instead to emend the line to 'waldend and wyrhtan' or else to read the two words 'as two nouns in asyndetic parataxis'.[124] In either case, the phrase would lose some of its flavour of extraordinariness – with the words 'waldend' and 'wyrhtan' merely referring to 'rulers' and 'builders', not to 'ruling (or, perhaps, mighty) builders' – but the overall meaning would not be substantially different, so that the question is of minor importance to my purpose here: regardless of how we interpret the phrase, those who built and ruled the city (envisioned either as a single group or two distinct ones) are now deceased.

The phrase 'hund cnea werþeoda' [a hundred generations of peoples; lines 8b–9a] conveys a sense both of duration and of temporal distance, the double plural implying that we are dealing not only with successive generations, but also with different ethnic groups or 'nations' that followed one upon the other. A similar impression is created by the image of the wall that has outlasted a number of successive rulers or kingdoms: 'Oft þæs wag gebad / ræghar ond readfah rice æfter oþrum' [often this wall bided one kingdom after the other, lichen-grey and red-coloured; lines 9b–10]. Bradley translates the phrase 'oþ hund cnea werþeoda gewitan' as 'while a hundred generations of humanity have passed away',[125] which would suggest that the temporal point of vantage is that of the narrator: since the death of the builders, a hundred (or perhaps simply 'many') generations have come and gone. Usually, however, *oþ* means 'until', 'up to', 'as far as', giving the passage an eschatological ring: the builders will remain in the grip of the earth until the end of time, that is, until the rising of the dead on Judgement Day.[126]

---

[123] Beaston, '*The Ruin*', 483. The phrase could, of course, also imply that the narrator is speaking of rulers who were themselves builders or vice versa, a reading that would fit a literal interpretation of the 'enta' in line 2b as actual giants.

[124] Krapp and Dobbie (eds), *Exeter Book*, 365, n. to line 7. The latter suggestion is less convincing, since in this case, the second phrase would lack a predicate: 'The grip of the earth has the rulers (literally, 'ruling ones'); the builders, deceased, departed; the hard grip of the ground.' Semantically, however, this reading would be somewhat closer to an interpretation of *waldend wyrhtan* as a compound, since the two phrases could be interpreted as an instance of variation: 'The rulers are in the ground; the builders [are] under the earth.'

[125] Bradley (trans.), *Anglo-Saxon Poetry*, 402.

[126] See also Dailey, who notes that the use of the preterite indicative 'serve[s] to indicate the implied futurity of a perfect tense' ('Questions of Dwelling', 187). The manuscript form *gewitan* is, strictly speaking, not the preterite indicative (which would be *gewiton*), but rather the infinitive. Rory Critten argues that the presence of the 'timeless, untranslatable infinitive' instead of the expected

Ruins and Their Multiple Temporalities

If we take the phrase as an eschatological reference, this might well imply that after the demise of the original builders, the city remained deserted while the generations of people and the sequence of kingdoms mentioned in the following line succeeded – or are still in the processes of succeeding – each other. This seems also to be suggested by the wall's description as 'ræghar ond readfah' [lichen-grey and red-coloured; line 10a]: presumably, the owners of the building would have kept their walls clear of lichen, had they still been there. On the other hand, given that the wall is said to have outlasted not only the onslaught of storms (line 11a) but also a succession of kingdoms (line 10b) before it succumbed, and that, at a later point, the wall's collapse is explicitly linked to the downfall of the last inhabitants, which prevented them from maintaining the city in a state of repair (lines 28b–31a), lines 9b–11 might also be read in the sense that the citizens of the successive kingdoms mentioned in line 10b were in fact inhabitants of the now-ruined city, meaning that the settlement continued to be populated after the original builders had perished.

Given the temporal ambiguities arising from the fact that Old English has only two grammatical tenses to express a complex system of temporal levels, perhaps one should not put too much weight on the poem's poetic (and at times lamentably garbled) syntax. If we assume, however, that the poem envisages the city as having been inhabited throughout many generations and successive kingdoms, this would mean that its history consists of a sequence of cultural layers whose representatives successively used and reused it. Davies remarks that the 'central passage' from lines 25 to 37 'appears to distinguish between multiple historical moments and describe the inhabitation of the buildings by different groups', while also noting that 'it is difficult to ascertain the exact chronological order of these scenes and the precise degree of overlap between the communities'.[127] He goes on to argue that the poem draws a distinction between 'Anglo-Saxon'

---

present or past indicative (or, one might add, subjunctive) could be interpreted as a deliberate device to unbalance the poem's temporality: 'At this point in the poem, it is unclear where the speaker stands in history vis-à-vis the ruin. Have one hundred generations since the departure of the king's builders already passed? Are they in process? Or are they still to come?' Rory G. Critten, 'Via Rome: Medieval Medievalisms in the Old English *Ruin*', *JMEMS*, 49:2 (2019), 209–31, at 213. Syntactically, however, the infinite *gewitan* is not merely 'untranslatable' but in fact meaningless. Intriguing as Critten's suggestion is, given the phonological closeness of *gewitan* to the third person preterite indicative *gewiton* (especially in spoken language), and given the fact that the convergence of the two forms must already have been underway in spoken Old English at the time the poem was copied, it seems more sensible to follow most scholars in regarding *gewitan* as a preterite form.

[127] Davies, *Visions*, 26–7. Ferhatović similarly speaks of different temporal and spatial layers (*Borrowed Objects*, 2).

and 'non-Anglo-Saxon' (that is, Roman or Celtic) communities, a distinction that he suggests is reflected in what he regards as the contrastive use of the terms *beorn* with its 'clear Germanic overtones' and the more neutral *wer* (related to Latin *vir*), both denoting 'man' in its gender-specific sense.[128] It is difficult to ascertain whether these terms really did transport the distinctive connotations that Davies ascribes to them; in any case, the rather general quality of the descriptions and, more importantly, their lack of any form of direct identification make it difficult to support such culturally specific ascriptions.

Following a similar line of argument, Critten has posited that the 'overlaying [*sic*] projections from the Roman and legendary Germanic past', discernible in the architectural details of the poem's ruins and the 'familiar stereotypes' of a heroic past that pervade the images of former city life, would have invited the poem's audience to imagine a process of 'superposition' in which the Roman builders of the city were supplanted by culturally 'Germanic' inhabitants.[129] Such a process, Critten contends, could be understood in terms of a *translatio imperii* and would have enabled the early medieval communities in Britain to regard themselves as the 'inheritors of Rome'.[130] In my view, the fact alone that no ethnic or cultural identification is ever made throughout the text (with the exception of the generic *enta*) would seem to argue against such a culturally specific subtext. Moreover, the temporal and emotional distance existing between the speaker and the communities of the past makes such an unequivocal identification unlikely: from the narrator's perspective, these 'Germanic' communities (if we wish to identify them as such) are no more present than the 'Roman' builders, as they, too, have long vanished from the face of the earth.[131]

---

[128] Davies, *Visions*, 28. Trilling argues that while the speaker seems to associate the city's past with 'Germanic' heroes, modern readers 'recognize' that the inhabitants must have been Romans – an argument that rests upon historical 'facts' whose application to an essentially fictional text must surely be taken with a pinch of salt ('Ruins', 164).

[129] Critten, 'Via Rome', 210.

[130] *Ibid.*, 218–19.

[131] Critten attempts to solve this problem by ingeniously suggesting that the poem takes on the perspective of a future that can regard both Britain's Roman past and the medieval present in which the poem was produced as things of the past. To Critten, *The Ruin* constitutes an instance of 'medieval medievalism' that imagines its own time of production as it might be understood from the perspective of the future (*ibid.*, especially 210, 214, 219, 224). While this is a fascinating and not at all implausible idea, Critten's suggestion that the poem imagines a future when native achievements have come to equal those of the Roman period and the city will be restored (*ibid.*, 215) once again ignores the fact that the city's supposedly 'Germanic' past is presented to be just as

Ruins and Their Multiple Temporalities

Specific ascriptions of identity aside, however, I agree with Davies and Critten that the references to different 'cnea werþeoda' [generations of peoples; line 8a] and the phrase 'rice æfter oþrum' [one kingdom after another; line 10b] suggest that the ruined city bears the imprint of many different cultures. In its present condition, the city presents an accumulation of multiple historical traces that do not allow for a reconstruction of the various pasts associated with them: the generations of inhabitants remain nameless and faceless, as do the kingdoms whose collapse the wall witnessed.

The image of the wall outlasting the passing of generations and kingdoms highlights the longevity of stone and its capacity to impress even in a ruined state. As Edward B. Irving, Jr, notes, 'The wall – and whatever it may suggest about man's heroic and doomed effort to hold things together, to hold self together, to resist change and death – is crumbling and battered by storm, but it endures, somewhat in the way that the hero's fame endures.'[132] Even more explicitly than *The Wanderer*, *The Ruin* emphasises – one is tempted to say, even celebrates – the durability of material culture, and it does so by showcasing the multiple temporalities of the city's stonework and the lives of its builders and inhabitants. Against the backdrop of the linear *longue durée* of the city's existence, the lives of human beings appear cyclic: generations and kingdoms follow each other in seemingly endless succession – until the end of time, if the *oþ* of line 8b is read in an eschatological sense.[133]

But apart from this single potentially eschatological reference, *The Ruin* lacks *The Wanderer*'s apocalyptic outlook.[134] The city's ruins are situated firmly in the present, signalling perhaps the destructive power of time – line 6a names old age rather than fate as the reason for the buildings' collapse ('ældo undereotone' [underminded by age]) – but not an approaching eschaton. Time progresses in linear fashion – one generation, one kingdom follows the other; the city was built at some point and is now slowly decaying. Yet the progression is aimless: with the single above-mentioned exception, nothing in the poem suggests a teleological

---

irrecoverably gone as its 'Roman' one. If a future restoration of the city is indeed alluded to in the poem – a reading I find much less plausible than the hypothesis that the poem imagines its own present's future – this future must be culturally different from previous phases of inhabitation.

[132] Irving, 'Image and Meaning', 156.

[133] Davies suggests that the ruins' progressive deterioration is marked by the repetition of alliterating b-sounds and final n-sounds during the first couple of lines (*Visions*, 25); see also Dailey, 'Questions of Dwelling', 187.

[134] As Klinck notes, 'unlike the pattern in *The Wanderer* and *The Seafarer*, the movement towards the close of *The Ruin* is not eschatological but retrospective' (*Old English Elegies*, 63).

Remains of the Past in Old English Literature

narrative. Against this implicit linearity *The Ruin* sets an alternative model of temporality: the cyclical rhythm of ever-new but ultimately indistinguishable epochs. Nor is there any sense of a cultural decline, as we find it in *The Wanderer* and *The Seafarer*: the narrator's admiration for the builders' skill need not imply, as it does in *The Wanderer*, any sense of inferiority on part of the observer – rather, it resembles the curiosity displayed by a visitor of an exceptionally spectacular historic site. Admiration of this kind is described, for instance, in the story of Saint Cuthbert being shown a Roman fountain in Carlisle, as told in the anonymous *Vita Cuthberti* and Bede's prose *Life of Saint Cuthbert*.[135] In purely structural terms, Cuthbert's experience resembles that of a modern tourist gazing at an archaeological object: the fountain is interesting, the architectural achievement admirable, but it does not signify superiority over the present – and hence a sense of cultural decline – nor an approaching end of the world.[136] *The Ruin*'s narrator, too, does not play off the past's achievements against those of the present. The passing of generations and kingdoms is merely a sign of the passing of time, and as such does not imply cultural progress or devaluation. In other words, it is sequentiality, not progression that is being stressed.

Similarly, the city's ruinous state, rather than being attributed to a present lack of technical skill, is linked to a specific historical event; namely, a plague that killed the inhabitants and prevented them from repairing whatever damage occurred with the passing of time:

Crungon walo wide,   cwoman woldagas,
swylt eall fornom   secgrofra wera;
wurdon hyra wigsteal   westen staþolas,
brosnade burgsteall.   Betend crungon
hergas to hrusan.   Forþon þas hofu dreorgiað,
ond þæs teaforgeapa   tigelum sceadeð
hrostbeages rof.

[The slaughtered fell, days of pestilence came, death took all the host of men; their bulwarks became deserted places, the city-site disintegrated. The repairers fell dead, the sanctuaries to the ground. Because of that the

---

[135] *Life of Cuthbert* vi.8; Bede, *Prose Life of Cuthbert* 27.

[136] The passage is linked to the military defeat and death of Cuthbert's king Ecgfrith, whom he advised against his ill-fated campaign against the Picts: in a non-causal way, the bishop's visit to the Roman ruins is thus connected to the end of Northumbria's imperialist aspirations. The passage's implications are clearly political, however, and have no bearing on questions of multiple temporalities.

courtyards deteriorate and the strong roof-frame sheds the red crooked tiles; lines 25–31a.][137]

The adjectival noun *betend*, deriving from the weak verb *betan* [to make better, to improve, amend, repair, restore],[138] apparently means 'those who repair'; the online edition of Bosworth-Toller translates the phrase 'betend crungon' (line 28b) as 'those who should have repaired them (that is, the *burgsteall* [city-site] of line 28a) were dead', which suggests that it is less the constant wear that material objects are subject to than the absence of people who might have mended them that is responsible for the city's deterioration. Such restoration work would have been commonplace during the time that the city was still inhabited. According to James E. Anderson, 'the mention of restorers implies that the walls have toppled more than once, an unusual observation for a poet thinking merely of a literal ruin'.[139] *Ex negativo*, even the destructive power of time is put into a non-linear perspective: damage occurs, but it may be repaired as long as there is someone to carry out the work. The city only starts to age noticeably once it ceases to be inhabited. In *The Ruin*, linear and cyclical time are thus not mutually exclusive theories of history, but rather different perspectives on the same sequence of events: on the one hand, the city experiences a seemingly endless succession of generations and kingdoms, as well as the inevitable cycles of damage and repair that come with all forms of material culture; on the other hand, once it has been deserted, it starts to deteriorate and eventually falls into ruin, just as the entire world will eventually come to its destruction.

This multitemporal angle is enhanced by the poem's shifting perspective from line 21 onwards, when the text starts to move to and fro between the present of the narrator's contemplation of the ruined city

---

[137] The phrase 'þæs teaforgeapa tigelum' (line 30) is difficult to translate; I take the phrase as a genitive construction referring to 'rof' (line 31a). The elements of the compound *teaforgeap* mean 'red' and 'high, crooked' individually; Clark Hall notes that the meaning of the compound is 'doubtful' (*CH*, s.v. 'teafor'). See also the discussion in Krapp and Dobbie (eds), *Exeter Book*, 365 n. to line 30; Klinck (ed.), *Old English Elegies*, 216–17.

[138] *BT*, s.v. 'bétan', (I) to make better, to improve, amend, repair, restore; emendare, reparare, reficere, mederi, expiare.

[139] James E. Anderson (ed. and trans.), *Two Literary Riddles in the Exeter Book*: Riddle I *and* The Easter Riddle; *A Critical Edition with Full Translations* (Norman, OK, 1986), 170. Dailey discerns in the poem '[a] circularity and cyclical temporality [...] that could even be described as a recycling', but does not discuss the form *betend* as an actual reference to the process of recycling that forms the basis for the circularity that seems to have characterised much of the city's existence ('Questions of Dwelling', 187).

Remains of the Past in Old English Literature

and its imagined past. After the opening description of the ruins and the references to the builders' skilfulness and eventual demise, the narrator begins to actively imagine what life in the city might have been like:

Beorht wæron burgræced,   burnsele monige,
heah horngestreon,   heresweg micel,
meodoheall monig   mondreama full,[140]
oþþæt þæt onwende   wyrd seo swiþe.

[Bright were the halls of the city, many the bathhouses, high the wealth of gables, great the army's clamour, many the mead-halls full of human revelry, until that was changed by Fate the mighty; lines 21–4.]

This description of urban hustle and bustle is followed by the afore-mentioned passage recounting the downfall of the last inhabitants (lines 25–31a), wherein the details of the deteriorating structures again prompt the narrator to envision the deserted city as a place that was once filled with life: in the very same place that is now a ruin, the narrator claims, 'many a man' ('beorn monig') used to see wonderful treasures ('hryre wong gecrong / gebrocen to beorgum, þær iu beorn monig [...] seah on sinc'; lines 31b–5a); the stone buildings were still standing, and a hot stream 'sent up a great fountain' in the bathhouses ('stanhofu stodan, stream hate wearp / widan wylme [...] þær þa baþu wæron'; lines 38–40). The poem continues to describe the pleasures of the hot baths, but rapidly deteriorates from this point onwards due to increasing manuscript damage. Much of these final lines was obliterated by a hole burned into the folio, leaving legible only a few words. It is clear from what remains, however, that the poem stays in the present, depicting further architectural details. Since the next line on the same folio (124v) opens a new poem (Riddle 61 in the numbering proposed by Krapp and Dobbie), it is also clear that not a great deal of text has been lost.

Throughout much of the second half of the poem, then, the observer's gaze, wavering between past and present, works like a double vision: crumbling structures evoke scenes of former splendour that accentuate, and hence must again give way to, descriptions of the present desolation. The shifting images imply that, in the narrator's mind, the two visions are inseparably bound up with each other: past and present intertwine, thereby making visible the city's inherent polychronicity. As Trilling observes, *The Ruin* emphasises simultaneity – coevalness – rather than linearity: 'The past may be something separate and foreign, but it is some-thing that constitutes a part of the present as well.'[141] If, moreover, we

---

[140] I have expanded the M-rune to the now traditional reading of 'mondreama', as suggested by Krapp and Dobbie (eds), *The Exeter Book*, 365 n. to line 23.

[141] Trilling, 'Ruins', 160.

Ruins and Their Multiple Temporalities

read the historical pageants as references not to one specific point in time, but to different times within the city's long existence (as suggested by the poem's distinction between the past of the builders and that of the city's last inhabitants), the vision becomes multiple rather than double, juxtaposing not only past and present, but multiple pasts that converge in the present of the observer's contemplation.

In *The Ruin*, Davies points out, 'time does not unfold in a strictly linear manner. Instead, moments are woven together to create a rich sense of the recursive patterns of time and memory. [...] *The Ruin* [...] is polychronic and multitemporal'.[142] Given the poem's insistence on the multiplicity of temporalities that characterise the ruined city, it is intriguing to note that while technical details that can still be seen or easily inferred by the narrator (such as the city's architecture or the hot baths) are described with such a degree of precision as to imply first-hand observation – thereby creating a fictional situation in which the narrator is rendering into words what they are seeing at this exact moment – the descriptions of past life are, for the most part, conventional, employing stock phrases about men 'happy and clothed in golden splendour' ('glædmod ond goldbeorht gleoma gefrætwed'; line 33) or 'proud and intoxicated with wine' ('wlonc ond wingal'; line 34a) – familiar stereotypes in Old English poetry.[143] The colourful depictions of former city life are thus in fact no more specific than the poem's earlier identification of the builders as 'enta' [giants; line 2b] or 'waldend wyrhtan' [mighty builders (or, perhaps, even less specifically, 'rulers and builders')], a phrase conveniently non-committal with regard to the question of whether we are to imagine the builders as actual giants or not. Apart from the information that the inhabitants were killed by a plague rather than in battle, they remain both nameless and surprisingly non-descript. The poem thus sets a present that can be experienced and described in minute detail against a past that can only be imagined: an 'imaginary time', as Anderson puts it,[144] whose poetic recreation all too easily becomes a collection of conventional images of a clichéd heroic

---

[142] Davies, *Visions*, 25.

[143] Similar images are used, for instance, in *The Seafarer*'s description of the life of the city-dweller (which likewise uses the expression 'wlonc ond wingal' in line 29) and in *Vainglory* (lines 13–21a, esp. line 14: 'wlonce wigsmiþas winburgum in' [proud war-mongers in wine-cities]); Old English text quoted from Krapp and Dobbie (eds), *Exeter Book*, 147–9 and 298–300 (notes). Against Ferhatović's contention that the speaker transforms the people who formerly inhabited the city 'into figures from a literary convention closer to him in time' (*Borrowed Objects*, 2), I would argue that it is precisely the conventionality of the images that makes them culturally unspecific, universal.

[144] Anderson, *Two Literary Riddles*, 178.

age. The narrator fills the ruins with images of past cultural life, but the result lacks historical specificity: the past, this use of conventional imagery suggests, cannot be recovered, and, in the absence of any specific historical information, is only to be reconstructed poetically. If the speaker of *The Wanderer* – deliberately but ultimately unsuccessfully – tries to use conventional images to universalise his emotions, the narrator of *The Ruin* seems unable to move beyond stock phrases, to give the city's various pasts their own specific language and imagery. Ironically, whereas in *The Wanderer* it is the specificity of the visual details that draws attention to the irrecoverability of the past, in *The Ruin* it is the conventionality of the narrator's recreation.

According to Davies, *The Ruin* 'is less interested in creating a detailed image of the building than investigating what meanings it holds in the present and held in the past and how those meanings are and were generated'.[145] He argues that by creatively filling in the gaps produced by the forgetfulness of historical transmission, the poem demonstrates that the past is not the only moment that defines a place's meaning. The work of the present – that is, the narrator's engagement with the city's ruins that gives rise to their imaginary recreation of the past – is just as integral to the present's interpretation of the past and its traces as the past itself.[146] Even in the face of historical oblivion, the material past thus continues to generate meaning. In the view of new materialist thinkers like Karen Barad, meaning is produced through the 'intra-action' of human cognition with the material world.[147] *The Ruin* illustrates this point rather nicely: throughout the poem, the narrative voice tries to make sense of the ruins it observes by imagining how their present state might have been shaped by past events. This is what Patricia Dailey seems to have in mind when she argues that '*The Ruin* offers itself as an allegory for the relatedness of [the] poem to its own present and to its own interpretive act, drawing upon fragmented pasts reassembled for other ends':[148] in the narrator's mind, the ruined structures become the product as well as the subject of past cultural activity, their present state the result of various processes involving human and non-human forces. Arguably, it is the recognition that such processes must have taken place, that they are in fact still taking place, that evokes the sense of awe expressed by the narrative voice at the powers of 'time' (in the guise of *yldu* [age]) and 'fate' (*wyrd*): for the

---

[145] Davies, *Visions*, 25.

[146] *Ibid.*, 20, 23.

[147] For the term 'intra-action', which stresses the interdependence of human cognition and the world's materiality in the emergence of meaning, see Karen Barad, 'Posthumanist Performativity: Toward an Understanding of How Matter Comes to Matter', *Signs*, 28:3 (2003), 801–31, esp. 814.

[148] Dailey, 'Questions of Dwelling', 192.

narrator, it is these processes as much as the structures themselves that are *wrætlic* [wondrous].

Given the narrator's fascination with architectural details, it is surprising that no attempt is made in the surviving poem to identify the city's builders, except for the stock phrase 'enta geweorc' (line 2b) and the even less committal 'waldend wyrhtan' (line 7a) – all the more surprising, in fact, since some of the features described, including the use of stonework and the presence of baths, have suggested to many scholars that the poem provides a more or less faithful description of a Roman city within Britain, usually identified as Bath or, alternatively, Chester;[149] even those who have argued in favour of a more generic representation of a ruined city usually assume a Roman provenance.[150] Frankis calls the 'possibility of a Roman connotation in this imagery of ancient stone buildings, evidently thought of as the work of a technologically superior past [...] indisputable'; for him, as for Michael Hunter and many others, the sense of awe voiced by the speaker reflects a similar astonishment on part of Britain's early medieval population when confronted with the architectural traces of Roman Britain.[151] The fact that the poem itself fails to make such an ascription has usually been ignored or else explained away as a product of its poet's ignorance. I have already quoted Cohen's contention that a general knowledge of the Roman provenance of such buildings had disappeared by the early medieval period.[152] Howe has similarly argued that

[149] Chester was proposed by Dunleavy, '"De Excidio" Tradition'. The identification with Bath, resting chiefly on the references to hot streams in lines 43 and 46, was first made by Heinrich Leo, *Carmen Anglo-Saxonicum in Codice Exoniensi servatum, quod vulgo inscribitur 'Ruinae'* (Halle, 1865) and then by John Earle, 'An Ancient Saxon Poem of a City in Ruins, supposed to be Bath', *Proceedings of the Bath Natural History and Antiquities Field Club*, 2 (1870–73), 259–70. For a short bibliography of studies either identifying the ruined city with a particular place or arguing against such an identification, see Abram, 'In Search', 24 n. 2.

[150] There is, however, one prominent hypothesis suggesting that *The Ruin* might actually refer to Babylon. This theory rests on the poem's use of the phrase *enta geweorc* (line 2) in conjunction with the aforementioned fact that the biblical king Nimrod was sometimes identified as a giant in medieval texts while also being thought responsible for the building of the Tower of Babel. See H. T. Keenan, '*The Ruin* as Babylon', *Tennessee Studies in Literature*, 11 (1966), 109–17; A. T. Lee, '*The Ruin*: Bath or Babylon? A Non-Archaeological Investigation', *NM*, 74 (1973), 443–55; Frankis, 'Thematic Significance', 266–7.

[151] Frankis, 'Thematic Significance', 257; Hunter, 'Germanic and Roman Antiquity'. Raymond I. Page notes that early medieval buildings could themselves be imposing; however, this does not seem to have provoked similar poetic responses; see Raymond I. Page, *Anglo-Saxon Aptitudes: An Inaugural Lecture Delivered before the University of Cambridge on 6 March 1985* (Cambridge, 1985), 22–4, quoted from Abram, 'In Search', 29.

[152] Cohen, 'Work of Giants', 11.

Remains of the Past in Old English Literature

writing long after the Germanic migrations, [*The Ruin's*] poet could have no direct knowledge of urban life in a Christian and Roman Britain. He could only express his wonder at the mute remains of a mysteriously and infinitely richer civilization. For him, as for other OE poets, the city is *enta geweorc*, 'the work of giants'.[153]

Howe appears later to have modified his views when he argued that Roman stonework did not pose any mysteries to early medieval writers such as Bede;[154] or perhaps he wished to make a distinction between Latinate ecclesiastics like Bede and vernacular writers such as the anonymous poet of *The Ruin* – although, as Christopher Abram reminds us, much early medieval poetry, whether Latin or in the vernacular, was produced by the same cultural milieux and was thus part of a bilingual tradition that saw, for instance, Aldhelm compose what was regarded as first-class poetry both in Latin and in the vernacular (although sadly no examples of the latter appear to have survived).[155] Given the pervasiveness of Latin learning in early medieval Britain already centuries before the earliest surviving Old English poetry was written down, and given the prominence of Britain's Roman past in much of the period's historiographical writing, a scenario in which the *Ruin* poet was actually unaware of the provenance of Roman-period structures seems highly implausible. Hines suggests that, given the date of its copying into the Exeter Book late in the tenth century, *The Ruin* is likely to 'embody some of the ideological attitudes' that also influenced King Eadgar's decision to stage his dramatic coronation ceremonies in 973 in the former Roman centres of Bath and Chester, the two sites' still visible imperial grandeur serving to underscore his own political aspirations.[156] To assume a complete lack of knowledge of Britain's Roman past on part of the poet would, in effect, make it necessary to assign the poem an exceptionally early date or to regard it as the product of a milieu far removed from educated circles.

Instead, I would argue that the expression *enta geweorc* and the similarly unspecific *waldend wyrhtan* form part of the same strategy of marking the historical processes of forgetting and obliteration as does the narrator's use of stock images to describe the city's past. My interpretation thus resembles Howe's insofar as I read the expression *enta geweorc* as marking a gap in historical knowledge. But whereas Howe explains this knowledge gap with ignorance on part of the poet, I argue that the poem's use of these

---

[153] Howe, *Migration*, 48.
[154] Howe, 'Postcolonial Void', 29; Howe, *Writing the Map*, 83.
[155] Abram, 'In Search', 42–3.
[156] John Hines, 'Literary Sources and Archaeology', in Helena Hamerow, David A. Hinton and Sally Crawford (eds), *The Oxford Handbook of Anglo-Saxon Archaeology* (Oxford, 2011), 968–85, at 973.

Ruins and Their Multiple Temporalities

expressions is part of a literary strategy that allows the poem to construct temporal alterity.[157] In other words, the builders' designation as *enta* and *waldend wyrhtan* suggests the narrator's ignorance, but not necessarily the poet's. In my reading, the city's obvious Roman provenance becomes significant precisely because it draws attention to the fact that the narrator is avoiding the question of the builders' real identity. What might look like an instance of the stereotypical medieval inability to discern historical difference thus turns out to be a literary ploy by which the poem constructs historical difference between the present and an unknown, inaccessible 'deep past' that can only be imagined in the most conventional of terms.[158]

It is, of course, ultimately immaterial whether we assume the poet, the narrator or the original audience associated the poem's ruins with Roman Britain. In *The Ruin*, at least in its fragmentary state, the identity of the builders has been suppressed, consciously or not, and comparison with other texts employing expressions such as *enta geweorc* suggests that the same would have been true of the poem in its complete form. The invocation of *enta*, 'giants', marks a lacuna in historical knowledge, as it does in *The Wanderer*; it draws attention to the fact that the real identity

---

[157] Beaston similarly argues that the use of the term *enta* reflects the speaker's awareness that the buildings stem from a distant past that was culturally different from the present ('*The Ruin*', 477–8).

[158] Intriguingly, Beaston does consider the possibility that the lack of a cultural ascription in the poem constitutes a literary strategy. After noting the different positions occupied by the medieval poet who, on encountering the ruins, mistakes them as the 'work of giants', and that of the modern reader who recognises in them the work of Roman Britain, he continues: 'Parenthetically, I cannot help wondering whether the speaker's puzzling ignorance of the Romans' involvement in Britain is not a deliberate device of the poet to create in the minds of his contemporary readers something of the same sense of superiority that modern readers tend to have with respect to the speaker. [...] Perhaps, then, the poet was setting his reader up to see the obvious limitations of the speaker's perspective, to see the narrowness of the horizons within which the speaker lived' (*ibid.*, 487). For Beaston, then, the narrator deliberately takes on the limited perspective of an epistemologically inferior past to create in their audience an effect of being part of a more enlightened present – a literary strategy not so very different from that found in many works of modern literature (and, for that matter, in *Beowulf*, as discussed in the following chapter). Beaston's reading of *The Ruin* differs from my own in that he sees the feigned cultural alterity of the past as manifesting itself in a narrative of development in which the past is perceived as less enlightened than the present, whereas in my own interpretation, the cultural alterity ascribed to the past serves to highlight the processes of historical forgetting – an interpretation that does not rest on a hierarchical relationship between the past and the present, which is arguably at odds with the speaker's admiration of the achievements of his precursors.

Remains of the Past in Old English Literature

of the builders is not known or, at any rate, not disclosed;[159] and as in *The Wanderer*, this lacuna, glossed over as a reference to a primordial, mythical past, invokes an inaccessible 'deep past' beyond the grasp of the present. But at the same time, the speaker's imagination fills this deep past with scenes of splendid urbanity, a form of life whose traces still persist in the form of the city's impressive ruins. According to Cohen, the notion of 'deep history' as proposed by Shryock and Smail 'opens historiography to the "realm of the imagination"' by drawing attention to what lies outside the frame of directly transmitted historical knowledge.[160] This, I would argue, is precisely *The Ruin*'s point: impossible to reconstruct historically, the past life in the city can only be recreated by means of the poet's imagination. In *The Ruin*, the deep past becomes a deep history that the narrator imagines as layered; it is part of the *longue durée* of the city's existence that stretches from its construction to the narrator's present, and, for all the narrator can say, far beyond into a potentially infinite future. Evoking multiple pasts whose various traces survive to a certain extent, the ruined city imagined in the poem is polychronic; in the narrator's imagination, which juxtaposes these different layers in quick succession, the vision becomes multitemporal.

The poem's construction of different time frames, representing snapshots of different historical moments in a series of successive generations and kingdoms, can be read as an effort to produce a non-teleological history. This history is marked by almost cyclical and ultimately aimless succession rather than by any form of historical development. In *The Ruin*, the unspecific and ultimately conventional pageants suggest that what counts is not so much the specific details of historical events, but rather their result – and this result, despite or perhaps even because of its fragmented state, is in itself fascinating and awe-inspiring. Ultimately, however, it is the present, not the past, that lies at the heart of the poem's fascination; and in this present, the city's ruined state is not so much a cause for regret as a matter of wonder and amazement.

[159] Dailey makes a similar point when she argues that the word *westen* (in line 27b, 'wurdon hyra wigsteal westen staþolas' [their bulwarks became deserted places]) 'implies a time before time, or behind time, to use Howe's words, in its implications of a prehistory that conditions the constitution of the living' ('Questions of Dwelling', 187).

[160] Jeffrey Jerome Cohen, *Stone: An Ecology of the Inhuman* (Minneapolis, MN, 2015), 289 n. 29, using quotations from Shryock and Smail (eds), *Deep History*, 15. I am not sure whether this is the intended meaning of the paragraph cited by Cohen, although Shryock and Smail do acknowledge the extent to which all historiography must rely on certain master narratives in order to make its story imaginable. Cohen's insightful observation goes one step further in acknowledging the human imagination as a necessary ingredient of historiography.

Ruins and Their Multiple Temporalities

A number of scholars have observed the remarkably optimistic, perhaps even joyful note of the poem's ending.[161] Davies links this positive tone – which pervades much of the poem but manifests itself not so much in a tangible sense of optimism as in the striking absence of any statement directly implying regret at the loss of the past – to the creative potential that even an absent past can afford to the present: in his highly compelling meta-poetic reading, *The Ruin* self-reflexively enacts the process of creatively turning a little-understood past into a literary achievement. For Davies, the poem expresses a sense of 'hope amidst the ruins': '*The Ruin* insists that the past is present: a source of cultural potential and hope for the future.'[162] This cultural potential of imaginative recreation aside, I would argue that the past is always 'present' in the present inasmuch as the present is always the direct result of the past – a 'trace' in Derrida's sense of the term. In Trilling's words, the poem's ruined structures 'embody the paradox of historical temporality – the continuing presence of the absent past'.[163] But even as the past is still present in the way it shaped the ruins observed and experienced by the narrator in the here and now, it nevertheless remains inaccessible in its historical specificity. Unlike the protagonist of *The Wanderer*, however, *The Ruin*'s narrator does not appear to be troubled by the past's inaccessibility. Rather than deploring the general transitoriness of earthly life and its cultural achievements, *The Ruin* celebrates the resilience of material artefacts and their ability to be meaningful in the present, even as that present is unable to discover – and perhaps not even interested in discovering – the actual histories attached to the object in question.

---

[161] Dailey speaks of 'the strangely uplifting tone that persists throughout the poem and dominates the second half' ('Questions of Dwelling', 185), while for Trilling, the 'final image is not one of destruction, decay, or ruin, but rather of the very full lives of the people who once inhabited this spot: it ends, not in nostalgia, but redemption' ('Ruins', 164). Anderson strikes a similar note when he argues that the last surviving lines 'probably' refer to 'the joyful and "convenient" pouring of life-giving waters in heaven' (*Two Literary Riddles*, 178). However, religious interpretations must contend with the conspicuous absence throughout the poem of any sort of Christian commentary, as Howe notes: '*The Ruin* finds its subject in the need to interpret a visible feature of the landscape that does nothing, yet troubles the eye because it cannot be evaded. And from this fact, that the site must be observed, comes an acutely rendered description of the world here and now that should make one all the more hesitant to offer an allegorical reading of the poem.' Nicholas Howe, 'The Landscape of Anglo-Saxon England: Inherited, Invented, Imagined', in John Howe and Michael Wolfe (eds), *Inventing Medieval Landscapes: Senses of Place in Western Europe* (Tallahassee, FL, 2002), 91–112, at 96–7.

[162] Davies, *Visions*, 29. Dailey similarly notes that the poem's uplifting tone 'literally revives the past into a celebratory moment of praise' ('Questions of Dwelling', 185).

[163] Trilling, 'Ruins', 161.

Conclusion

The poems discussed in this chapter present more than conventional ruminations on the theme of human transience: they examine how different temporal processes are perceived or constructed by human observers. Ruins, being subject to what may appear an irreversible process of decay, may be taken to symbolise the general decline of the world, but they simultaneously signal the enduring presence of the material traces of a bygone past, while also being capable of marking local and temporally restricted changes. Opening up a panorama of temporal responses, the texts discussed here ultimately address the relation between linear time – the continuous passing of years – and 'history', the meaning ascribed to successive events that may or may not be seen as directly sequential within linear time.

I have already quoted Davies's observation that ruins 'bring distinct temporal moments and histories into presence'; it is for this reason, he argues, that the image of the ruin acts as such a powerful vehicle of cultural – and, one might add in the context of *The Wanderer*, personal – memory.[164] In the texts under consideration here, some of the temporal moments invoked by the sight of ruins are remembered personally, some are inferred, and others still are open to the imagination. The spectrum of responses suggests that ruins, perceived as markers of time and history, draw attention not only to the ways in which memory works – including its limitations – but also to the fundamental problem of historiographical knowledge and indeed of historical reconstruction altogether.

Davies points out that modern narratives of progress frequently posit that premodern societies felt directly connected to the past, citing Pierre Nora's notion of the 'collective memory' of peasant societies as an example of this attitude. According to Nora, such a 'collective memory' established a kind of 'natural connection between people and their past' that the 'hopelessly forgetful modern societies' have lost.[165] As Davies notes, despite its seemingly positive valuation, the alleged 'connectedness' with the past so favourably appraised by Nora is in effect just another version of premodernity's supposed inability to discern historical alterity, and hence a sign of a lack of 'proper' historical consciousness, depending as it does 'on a nostalgic vision of the Middle Ages as a simpler "before" that does not yet know the alienation and complexity of modernity'.[166] By contrast, as I hope to have shown in this chapter, the texts examined here exhibit precisely such an ability to understand and articulate a sense of historical alterity – be it through expressions such as *eald enta geweorc*, which I have

---

[164] Davies, *Visions*, 29.
[165] *Ibid.*, 5; Nora, 'Between Memory and History', 7.
[166] *Ibid.*

Ruins and Their Multiple Temporalities

argued signifies a deep history whose existence can be inferred from its material traces even though it eludes historical reconstruction, through the existential terror displayed by *The Wanderer*'s speaker in the face of historical oblivion, or through the imaginative reconstructions of the past undertaken by the implied speaker of *The Ruin*. What becomes evident here is an awareness of historical rupture and forgetting far more complex than that implied by the conventional transience *topos* so often invoked in scholarly discussions of these texts. The loss of historical memory is always delayed; it occurs at different speeds, as some memories continue to persist while others are lost. Yet as *The Ruin* in particular suggests, the fact that all personal memories are ultimately doomed to oblivion need not be a cause of despair: the city's ruins, as material traces of forgotten histories, demonstrate that human achievements may continue to create meaning long after specific historical details have been forgotten.

Where *The Wanderer*'s multitemporal vision is always on the verge of collapsing into painful commemoration of the speaker's personal past, in *The Ruin* the narrator's gaze is dispassionate, their emotions directed at the aesthetic pleasure of observing and imagining the technologically remarkable historical site, even more impressive in its state of dereliction. Unlike the protagonist of *The Wanderer*, who is horrified by the prospect of a future without a meaningful past, *The Ruin*'s narrator compensates the lost knowledge epitomised by the ruins with a radical celebration of the present, a present in which the aspect of the ancient city inspires admiration and awe despite – or perhaps even because of – of its ruined state. The city's material remains, coupled with the observer's imagination, can still generate meaning in the present even as their earlier significance has been lost. They draw attention both to the destructive power of time and to the ability of material objects to survive and continue to impress even as fragments: from the narrator's perspective, both of these aspects are equally remarkable and impressive – or, in the poem's own words, 'wrætlic'.

3

The Perils of Anachronism:
Beowulf and the *Legend of the Seven Sleepers*

At least since Jacob Burckhardt's *Civilization of the Renaissance in Italy* (1860), historians have frequently argued that the Middle Ages lacked historical consciousness; that is, a proper sense of the 'pastness' of the past and its fundamental alterity from the present.[1] Medieval people, the argument runs, 'thought that the world had always been the way they saw it'.[2] By contrast, the representatives of later ages are credited not only with a notion of progression from one event to the next, but also with an understanding of the singularity and uniqueness of these events, and hence their difference from those preceding and following them. The historical past, Zachary Sayre Schiffman stresses, 'is not simply *prior* to the present but *different* from it':[3]

> The distinction between past and present that constitutes 'the founding principle of history' rests on something other than mere priority in time; it reflects an abiding awareness that different historical entities exist in different historical contexts.[4]

Schiffman links the development of historical consciousness to an awareness of anachronism, 'the clash of period styles [understood in the widest possible sense] or mentalities', according to Thomas M. Greene's definition.[5] Anachronism, Jacques Rancière emphasises, is not the confusion of dates – putting Caesar after Nero, for example, constitutes a simple chronological error and not an instance of anachronism – but rather the confusion of epochs, the latter being 'not simply cut out from the continuity of successions', but marking 'specific regimes of truth, relations of

---

[1]   For an in-depth discussion of this issue, see Andrew James Johnston, *Performing the Middle Ages from* Beowulf *to* Othello (Turnhout, 2008), 1–20.
[2]   Burke, 'Sense of Anachronism', at 158; Burke attributes this particular notion of medieval alterity to Gaston Paris.
[3]   Schiffman, *Birth of the Past*, 2, emphasis in the original.
[4]   *Ibid.*, 3.
[5]   Thomas M. Greene, 'History and Anachronism', in Gary Saul Morson (ed.), *Literature and History: Theoretical Problems and Russian Case Studies* (Stanford, CA, 1986), 205–20, at 205.

the order of time to order that is not in time'.[6] The recognition that certain features are specific to certain historical contexts and hence may not fit others presupposes an awareness of historical change, of innovation and supersession, but also of erasure and loss.[7] Thus, it is only through the knowledge that mechanical clocks were invented at a specific point in time that the idea of their presence at an earlier moment of history appears anachronistic.[8] Conversely, things may become dated or disappear altogether: picturing dinosaurs in a temporal setting that postdates their extinction would equally constitute a case of anachronism.

Anachronism is not always imagined in such absolute terms, however: a recognition of historical contingency can also express itself in the notion that things may appear *as if* 'before' or 'after' their time. Schiffman discusses the example of the Rock N Roll McDonald's in downtown Chicago, which, from its construction in 1983 until 2005, featured two sections furnished in 1950s and 1960s style, respectively. According to Schiffman, the restaurant's interior was deliberately designed to look dated; its division into sections supposedly representing the very essence of a specific decade's sense of fashion and design, Schiffman argues:

> epitomizes the intimate connection between our sense of history and our sense of context. The former manifests itself in our perception of the past as an objective space lying 'back there' in time; the latter manifests itself in our idea of anachronism, in a sensitivity to context so acute that we can routinely distinguish a 50s from a 60s aesthetic. [...] The pervasive awareness of anachronism at every level of our culture – from McDonald's to academe – confirms the intersection between our historicizing and contextualizing habits of mind.[9]

In linking the presence of a historical consciousness to an awareness of anachronism, Schiffman is hardly innovative, nor is his thesis that 'a sustained awareness of anachronism emerged only with the Renaissance'[10] – the same conclusion was already reached by Erwin Panofsky in his

---

[6] Jacques Rancière, 'The Concept of Anachronism and the Historian's Truth', trans. Noel Fitzpatrick and Tim Stott, *InPrint*, 3:1 (2015), 21–52.

[7] Burke, 'Sense of Anachronism', 157.

[8] Schiffman, *Birth of the Past*, 3.

[9] Zachary Sayre Schiffman, 'Historicizing History/Contextualizing Context', *New Literary History*, 42:3 (2011), 477–98, at 477.

[10] Schiffman, *Birth of the Past*, 144. Schiffman says as much when he notes that 'the novelty of this thesis lies merely in the starkness with which I have presented it and the conclusions I've drawn from it' (*ibid.*) – though even this is somewhat overstated.

Renaissance and Renascences in Western Art (1960),[11] and it has been echoed time and again by scholars from a wide range of fields. Peter Burke, for instance, claims that 'during the whole millennium 400–1400, there was no "sense of history" even among the educated'.[12] In the same vein as Panofsky, Burke argues that this is because the Middle Ages lacked a clear sense of anachronism, as evidenced by the many instances of anachronistic detail observable in medieval literature. Renaissance humanists, by contrast, allegedly possessed a far more developed sense of anachronism and hence of historicity, if not yet as acute as that of modern scholars.[13] Greene concedes that some earlier thinkers, for instance of the Alexandrian school, were sensitive to anachronistic errors, but maintains that such cases were few and far between. Like Burke, he contends that among Renaissance writers, the 'sensitivity to the risk of anachronism [was] far more developed' than among the people of earlier epochs.[14]

Implicit in statements such as these is an understanding of history as a history of progress in which relative naïveté gradually gives way to more complex understanding. One of the defining moments for this kind of narrative is Lorenzo Valla's treatise *De falso credita et ementita Constantini donatione declamatio* (1440), in which Valla claims to expose as a forgery a document allegedly written by Emperor Constantine. According to many modern accounts, Valla does so by pointing out chronological discrepancies and the anachronistic use of language. However, as Margreta de Grazia has pointed out, Valla is not actually concerned with the dating of events or linguistic forms; rather, she notes, Valla discusses the likelihood of certain events and of certain persons using the particular style employed in the document: 'It is not the forger's anachronisms that incense Valla, but his barbarisms. He denies Constantine's authorship of the document not because it refers to phenomena that postdate Constantine but because he would never have written such bad Latin.'[15] De Grazia argues that sensi-

---

[11] Erwin Panofsky, *Renaissance and Renascences in Western Art* (2 vols, Stockholm, 1960).

[12] Peter Burke, *The Renaissance Sense of the Past* (London, 1969), 1.

[13] Burke, 'Sense of Anachronism', 161.

[14] Greene, 'History and Anachronism', 206.

[15] Margreta de Grazia, 'Anachronism', in James Simpson and Brian Cummings (eds), *Cultural Reformations: Medieval and Renaissance in Literary History* (Oxford, 2010), 13–32, at 22–3. De Grazia quotes Valla's discussion of the word *satrapa*, which modern scholarship has demonstrated to have not been used of Roman officials before the mid-eighth century: 'Why do you want to bring in *satraps*? You blockhead, you dolt! Do emperors talk that way? Are Roman decrees normally drafted like that? Who ever heard of satraps being named in the deliberations of the Romans? I cannot recall reading that anyone, either in Rome or even in the provinces of the Romans, was ever named a satrap' (*ibid.*, 23).

The Perils of Anachronism

tivity to anachronism is a later phenomenon, roughly coinciding with the appearance of the term itself in the first half of the seventeenth century, and hence more or less coeval with the Newtonian idea of an absolute, linear timeline.[16] Indeed, it has been pointed out that Renaissance writers mingle elements from different periods just as happily as their medieval predecessors – only that in the case of the Renaissance, this practice is called 'creative' and taken as a sign of an awareness of anachronism, whereas in the case of the Middle Ages it is called 'naïve'.[17] Yet in exposing this incongruity in modern scholars' reasoning, de Grazia merely postdates the supposed break between a premodernity distinguished by its lack of a sense of anachronism and hence of proper historical understanding, on the one hand, and a more enlightened modernity, on the other.

Jeremy Tambling has rightly observed that this kind of narrative is tied to a 'history of ideas' and hence duplicates its own argumentation: 'The Renaissance became aware of historical change, and so of anachronism; and so built itself on a "history of ideas".'[18] In such an account, human history is conceived of as a history of progress in which the later moment is superior to the earlier in terms of learning and know-how: as history progresses, new discoveries and inventions produce new knowledge, which thus accumulates with the passing of time. Even though this *grand récit* concedes that some information is lost along the way, it tends to portray the present as possessing superior skills and knowledge as compared to the past.

At the same time, the accumulation of knowledge is usually not regarded as a gradual process, but rather as one marked by sudden and radical shifts. As Latour observes:

---

[16] *Ibid.*, 20, 32.

[17] The terminology is Greene's. Greene distinguishes five different categories of anachronism: naïve (produced by a culture lacking a strong historical sense); abusive (used crudely without attention to context); serendipitous (the incorrect identification with a certain date; both abusive and serendipitous anachronisms are the product of a culture struggling for historical awareness); creative (used self-consciously and as a means of dramatization); and pathetic or tragic (the awareness that oneself is destined to become outdated); Greene, 'History and Anachronism', 207–9. Alexander Nagel and Christopher S. Wood have coined the image of an 'anachronic Renaissance' that creatively engages with anachronism and different concepts of temporality. While Nagel and Wood's argument is not specifically directed at establishing the historical novelty of the Renaissance's engagement with time and history, they, too, are convinced that the anachronic can be connected to the humanist occupation with history, and the emergence of new systems for storing and retrieving information (*Anachronic Renaissance*, 10).

[18] Jeremy Tambling, *On Anachronism* (Manchester, 2010), 7.

the moderns [...] do not feel that they are removed from the Middle Ages by a certain number of centuries, but that they are separated by Copernican revolutions, epistemological breaks, epistemic ruptures so radical that nothing of that past survives in them – nothing of that past ought to survive in them.[19]

It is perhaps no coincidence that the Middle Ages' supposed lack of an awareness of historical change was first formulated during the nineteenth century, an age that appears thoroughly preoccupied with ideologies of progress, revolution and radical change. Indeed, one might argue that a sense of anachronism always presupposes some notion of historical rupture, since the concept draws attention to that which violates the strict succession of events in a history perceived as linear and steadily progressing. In other words, a sense of anachronism is contingent upon a temporal grid where there is a clearly defined 'before' and 'after': whatever is being perceived as anachronistic does not fit the historical context because it is either supposed to have disappeared or else presupposes certain innovations or developments that have not yet taken place.

A sense of anachronism, then, is closely tied to a concept of periodisation. Periodisation formulates a norm and censures as anachronistic that which does not conform to this norm. It operates on a temporal scheme based on the notion of a succession of styles, modes, mentalities, etc. An instance of anachronism always constitutes a violation of what is taken to be the current norm – the regime of truth – determined by the respective period. Hence, periodisation is prone to deny the possibility of a synchronicity of several styles or mentalities, ignoring – or labelling as anomalous – instances of archaism, antiquarianism and 'late survival'; or, conversely, innovations that do not gain immediate acceptance and thus have the appearance of existing 'before their time' (such as the various steam-powered devices invented in late antiquity and the early modern period).

The concept of anachronism can thus be linked to the 'denial of coevalness' observed and criticised by Johannes Fabian in modern anthropology – the anthropological practice of assigning non-Western cultures a different 'time' by identifying them with past periods in the prehistory of Western cultures. As Fabian explains:

Physical Time is seldom used in its naked, chronological form. More often than not, chronologies shade into *Mundane* or *Typological Time*. As distancing devices, categorizations of this kind are used, for instance, when we are told that certain elements in our culture are 'neolithic' or 'archaic'; or when certain living societies are said to practice 'stone age

---

[19] Latour, *We Have Never Been Modern*, 68.

The Perils of Anachronism

economics'; or when certain styles of thought are identified as 'savage' or 'primitive'. [20]

Identifying contemporaneous practices with the past implies a historical determinism centred on the idea that different cultures must inevitably undergo the same stages of historical development (for example, Stone Age, Bronze Age, Iron Age, industrialisation, globalised capitalism). According to this concept, influentially expressed by Georg Wilhelm Friedrich Hegel in his *Lectures on the Philosophy of History*,[21] all cultures (if they 'survive') eventually reach the same level of modernity, but they do not necessarily do so at the same time. Elements in other cultures that are perceived as 'archaic' by Western observers supposedly persist because these cultures have 'not yet' reached the same stage of development as the West; and since Western modernity provides the vantage point from which other cultures are described (and hence the norm by which they are judged), other cultures are by necessity placed 'in the past' and considered anachronistic. Non-Western cultures and the European past thus share a common fate as Western modernity's temporal Other: both are not only distinguished, but indeed defined by 'not yet' having reached the stage of Western modernity; they exist in a state of perpetual 'premodernity'.

Alexander Nagel and Christopher S. Wood link the emergence of such ascriptions of 'cultural anachronism' to the concurrence of Renaissance engagements with the past, which they argue were frequently directed at enabling direct comparison with the present, and increasing contact with cultural Otherness via new commercial and colonial networks:

> The two remotenesses, temporal and spatial, were confused, and from that moment onwards non-Europeans were condemned as non-synchronic, out of sync, trapped in states of incomplete development. The hypothesis of cultural anachronism made it possible for Europeans to deny the synchronicity of other people they shared the world with, and so to refuse to engage with them in political terms.[22]

We have seen that in the case of Western modernity's own past, this 'not yet' is frequently said to include a sense of anachronism; indeed, the

---

[20] Fabian, *Time and the Other*, 30–1. Fabian defines the 'denial of coevalness' as 'a persistent and systematic tendency to place the referent(s) of anthropology in a Time other than the present of the producer of anthropological discourse' (*ibid.*, 31). For reasons of readability, I do not set the term culture in inverted commas, although I am aware of the problems involved in its use; for example, the fact that cultures neither exist in isolation nor are internally uniform.

[21] See Georg Wilhelm Friedrich Hegel, *Vorlesungen über die Philosophie der Weltgeschichte* (4 vols, Hamburg, 1988–93), esp. vol. 1, *Die Vernunft in der Geschichte*, ed. Johann Hoffmeister (Hamburg, 1994 [1993]), 50–78.

[22] Nagel and Wood, *Anachronic Renaissance*, 10.

alleged absence of a fully developed historical consciousness constitutes one of the criteria by which modernity distances itself from its own past and sets it up as its Other. Premodernity's supposed inability to understand historical time as a succession of periods differentiated by historical change thus ironically allows modernity to construct just such a radical rupture; and since the criteria are of modernity's own making, the resulting narrative is necessarily self-fulfilling.

In this chapter, I will discuss two Old English texts that draw attention to the implications and perils of the kind of radical periodisation discussed above, one that renders anachronistic anything that does not conform to the current cultural norm. Both *Beowulf* and the anonymous Old English prose version of the Legend of the Seven Sleepers feature living beings whose continued existence – either brought about by or in direct defiance of divine interventions into history – constitutes a violation of the principles of periodisation: these beings have become, in all but name, living anachronisms. Moreover, the two works highlight not only these beings' anachronic mode of existence, but also the ensuing chronological problems – and they do so despite the fact that they both predate the supposed emergence of an awareness of anachronism (as most modern accounts will have it) by several centuries.

Following Greene's argument of a gradual development of ever more complex forms of anachronism, one might class the two texts' engagements with questions of periodisation as instances of 'creative anachronism' – that is, the second highest of his five categories, which posits the self-conscious use of anachronism as a means of dramatisation.[23] As such, they might prove simply to be exceptions to the rule – in other words, they would themselves qualify as anachronistic, occurring as they do 'before their time' in terms of the mentality prevailing in the period of their production. On the other hand, the fact that many modern scholars continue to deny premodern societies a sense of anachronism despite evidence to the contrary can also be explained by pointing out that said scholars are often guilty of employing the term 'anachronism' in a very restricted sense. Schiffman, for instance, subsumes under it two opposed, if related, operations without explicitly distinguishing between the two. In one case, the phenomenon labelled as anachronistic is judged to be too early, in the other, too late for its historical context: for instance, the 'Rock N Roll McDonald's' with its styling reminiscent of the 1950s and 1960s appears anachronistic in the context of the 1980s to early 2000s, but would likewise have done so in the 1940s. Limiting his understanding of anachronism to a binary of anteriority or posteriority within an absolute,

---

[23] Greene, 'History and Anachronism', 207–9; cf. n. 17 above.

The Perils of Anachronism

linear timeline[24] without even distinguishing between the two conditions, Schiffman fails to take into account the temporal complexities involved in any kind of operation that categorises something as 'out of sync' with a certain present.

Indeed, 'untimeliness' – the state of being out of joint with one's historical context, as Jonathan Gil Harris put it – is a much more multifaceted phenomenon.[25] Historically, the term anachronism likewise encompasses a far greater range of relationships with time than modern everyday usage suggests: derived from Middle Greek ἀναχϱονισμός, which, according to Srinivas Aravamudan, originally meant 'late in time', the word entered the European vernaculars via the Italian *anacronismo*, denoting a 'chronological misplacement'.[26] It is first attested in the context of humanist endeavours to harmonise the various dates and chronologies found in historical sources from antiquity. In his *Opus novum de emendatione temporum* (1583), Joseph Justus Scaliger uses the term synonymously with *atopema* [incorrect] to identify the chronological errors of other chronologies, while employing the term *prochronismos* to denote instances of antedating.[27] Anachronism, understood as a concept signifying chronological misplacement, can thus subsume a number of different phenomena; Giambattista Vico's *Principi di Scienza Nuova d'intorno alla Comune Natura delle Nazioni* (1725), for instance, describe four types of anachronistic error:

> The first error regards as *uneventful* periods which were actually full of events. [...] Conversely, a second error regards as *eventful* those periods which were actually uneventful. [...] A third error *unites* periods which should be separated [...]. Conversely, a fourth error *divides* periods which should be united.[28]

Tambling, employing an even broader notion of the term without any claim to exhaustiveness, identifies no fewer than seven types of anachronism in Proust's *À la recherche du temps perdu*, which he then proceeds to

---

[24] For a critique of the notion of absolute, linear time as the basis of historiography, see Wilcox, *Measure*, 16–50.

[25] See Harris, *Untimely Matter*, esp. 11.

[26] Srinivas Aravamudan, 'The Return of Anachronism', *MLQ*, 62:4 (2001), 331–53, at 331.

[27] Wilhelm Schmidt-Biggemann, 'Geschichte, Ereignis, Erzählung: Über Schwierigkeiten und Besonderheiten von Geschichtsphilosophie', in Andreas Speer (ed.), *Anachronismen: Tagung des Engeren Kreises der Allgemeinen Gesellschaft für Philosophie in Deutschland (AGPD) vom 3. bis 6. Oktober 2001 in der Würzburger Residenz* (Würzburg, 2003), 25–50, at 25–6.

[28] Giambattista Vico, *New Science: Principles of the New Science Concerning the Common Nature of Nations*, trans. David Marsh, 3rd edn (London, 1999), 333, quoted from Aravamudan, 'Return', 331.

map onto the works of Shakespeare. For both authors, Tambling claims, 'love is an anachronic force, and their principal subject'.[29] In his reading, anachronism 'undermines questions of historical inscription, memory, and fashion, and love and homosexuality and secrecy, trauma and obsessionalism; old age and being out of date'; it draws attention to that which is, at a given moment in time, socially unacceptable.[30]

Tambling's capacious concept of anachronism reminds us that there are many ways in which a person or thing may appear 'out of sync' with their historical context. The recent proliferation of studies highlighting the manifold forms of 'untimeliness' in medieval and Renaissance texts demonstrates that the absence of a proper term to describe these phenomena and a lack of explicit theorisation do not necessarily mean that anachronism as a concept was not understood in premodern cultures; indeed, it might even be taken as a sign that the narrow definition of anachronism usually employed in modern supersessionist chronologies should perhaps itself be viewed as historically contingent, as only one of a variety of alternative perceptions that has been granted temporary hegemony, but may already be in the process of being supplanted by others. From this perspective, modern scholarship's penchant for restricting and narrowing down notions of anachronism can be seen as part of Western modernity's tendency to confine multiplicity (a process Latour describes as 'purification') and its 'enormous intellectual commitment to the promotion of its supposed singularity', as Amitav Ghosh aptly put it.[31] And this tendency, Joshua Davies notes, stands in marked contrast to an implicit premodern acknowledgement that 'relationships between and among epochs must be understood as multiple, with many temporalities at work in a single age'.[32]

It would certainly be overly simplistic to assume that premodern societies lacked the kind of chronological thinking necessary to point out errors of historical sequence, and hence a system of periodisation based on a perception of historical difference. On the contrary, when one traces the development of Western historiography from antiquity to postmodernity, the sheer number of surviving annals and chronicles seems to suggest that premodern historians were obsessed with chronology – even though, as Wilcox has argued, the majority of these texts did not choose to chart his-

---

[29] Tambling, *On Anachronism*, 21.

[30] Tambling, *On Anachronism*, 21.

[31] Latour, *We Have Never Been Modern*, 10–11 (on the role of purification); Amitav Ghosh, *The Great Derangement: Climate Change and the Unthinkable* (Chicago, IL, 2016), 103, quoted from Davies, *Visions*, 4.

[32] Davies, *Visions*, 4. The quotation is from Maura Nolan, 'Historicism after Historicism', in Elizabeth Scala and Sylvia Federico (eds), *The Post-Historical Middle Ages* (Basingstoke, 2009), 63–85, at 67.

The Perils of Anachronism

torical events on a single, forward-moving arrow, but rather saw them in relation to each other.[33] On the other hand, as Dinshaw in particular has demonstrated, many premodern texts appear to be especially interested in forms of temporal experience that conflict with more common perceptions of time,[34] exhibiting a profound fascination with instances of 'untimeliness', that is, forms of or encounters with temporality that are markedly different from those discussed in modern historicist accounts of history.

One could argue that a similar discrepancy characterises premodern and modern conceptions of anachronism – at least in the form still prevalent in more conservative accounts.[35] From a medieval perspective, a depiction of Aeneas as a medieval knight may well be less disturbing than the existence of a postdiluvian giant, that is, a member of a race described as having been wiped out in the Flood in Genesis 6.4–7; indeed, the biblical Deluge, one of the most pervasive and universal myths found in premodern societies, poses perhaps the most rigid period boundary imaginable. Nevertheless, the existence of postdiluvian giants was not unheard of in medieval and post-medieval texts – both classical antiquity and Germanic legend were full of them, in fact – and Christian writers had to find ways to come to terms with their presence, not least since the Bible itself seemed to imply that some of their number had survived.[36]

As noted in the introduction, many premodern texts address questions of temporal asynchrony by taking recourse to material objects and the traces of the past they have acquired throughout their existence. In cases where these traces are ignored, the object in question is usually perceived as 'timeless', but there are other instances – especially those referred to in this study as 'archaeological' – in which objects are defined precisely by their historicity. Drawing attention to their own survival, their persistence into or reappearance in the present, such archaeological objects are, in a certain sense, themselves 'anachronic', capable of cutting through and binding together multiple times, as Johnston argues in his discussion of Nagel and Wood's concept;[37] and it is this ability to transgress temporal

---

[33] Wilcox, *Measure*.

[34] Dinshaw, *How Soon*. I will return to the simultaneity of different temporalities in my discussion of figural and historical time in the next chapter.

[35] In the case of more recent literary criticism, at least, there has been a proliferation of studies that emphasise 'anachronic' conditions of existence as those outlined above; see, for instance, Aravamudan, 'Return'; Tambling, *On Anachronism*.

[36] As, for instance, in Numbers 13.34. For even more explicit references to postdiluvian giants in apocryphal texts that were widely read or even considered canonical during the early Middle Ages, see Mellinkoff, 'Cain's Monstrous Progeny, II'.

[37] Andrew James Johnston, 'Anachronic Entanglements: Archaeological Traces in *Beowulf*', in Estella Weiss-Krejci, Sebastian Becker and Philip Schwyzer (eds),

Remains of the Past in Old English Literature

boundaries that affords objects of this type the potential to question the internal coherence of historical models based on a concept of periodisation.

In the two texts discussed in this chapter, the respective archaeological artefacts highlight the equally anachronistic survival of particular living beings, to whose eventual fate they in turn contribute, either directly or indirectly: in the Legend of the Seven Sleepers, the saints' possession of dated gold coins betrays their survival of Decius's persecution and exposes the supernatural nature of their 200-year-long sleep, thereby ironically hastening their miraculously deferred death; in *Beowulf*, it is the hilt of the giants' sword that calls attention to the fact that Grendel and his mother should not have survived into the present, associated as they are with the antediluvian giants supposedly annihilated in the biblical Flood.

Becoming Anachronic in the Legend of the Seven Sleepers

One of the most widely disseminated of medieval saints' legends (and, in Dinshaw's words, 'the most popular asynchrony tale in the Western Middle Ages'), the Legend of the Seven Sleepers tells the story of seven Christian youths from Ephesus, who, fleeing from persecution at the hands of the third-century Roman emperor Decius, hide in a cave, where they fall into a God-sent sleep.[38] When Decius's men discover their place of refuge, the emperor commands the Sleepers to be immured alive; miraculously, they survive and awake during the reign of Theodosius II (408–50), only to expire soon after.

The earliest surviving versions of the Legend are a poetic homily by the Syrian bishop James of Sarug (*c.* 450–521) apparently based on a lost precursor in Greek, and a Syriac prose text that may date back to as early as the late fifth century.[39] Popularised in western Europe through Gregory of Tours' summary in *De gloria martyrum*, it was further disseminated in several other Latin versions, including Gregory's own *Passio septem dormientium*, which he claimed had been translated with the assistance of a certain Syrian: 'siro quodam interpretante'.[40] The story eventually made

---

Interdisciplinary Explorations of Postmortem Interaction: Dead Bodies, Funerary Objects, and Burial Spaces Through Texts and Time (Cham, 2022), 97–112, at 100.

[38] Dinshaw, *How Soon*, 44. Dinshaw notes that the manuscript tradition of the Legend spans 'fifteen centuries in genres ranging from saint's life to charms' (*ibid.*, 55).

[39] For a more detailed discussion of the Legend's transmission, see Hugh Magennis (ed.), *The Anonymous Old English Legend of the Seven Sleepers* (Durham, 1994), 3–6. The Old English text is quoted by line from Magennis's edition.

[40] *Ibid.*, 4.

The Perils of Anachronism

its way into Jacobus de Voragine's mid-thirteenth-century *Legenda aurea*, whence it was translated into the various vernaculars.

Earlier than the *Legenda aurea*'s rendition of the narrative, the anonymous Old English version, preserved in two manuscripts from the early eleventh century,[41] was based on the other major Latin text of the Legend during the early Middle Ages besides Gregory's *Passio*. This text, thought to derive from a Greek version of the Legend but also displaying knowledge of the *Passio*, is usually referred to in scholarship as L_1.[42] In spite of its demonstrable indebtedness to this Latin text, the anonymous Old English version is, according to its most recent editor Hugh Magennis, a 'free and considerably expanded rendering' of the Latin source, with its 'assured and confident' approach suggesting to Magennis 'a milieu [...] of considerable literary sensibility'.[43] Although the Old English text follows closely the plot of its Latin source, it lends special emphasis to certain elements of the story; in particular, it is very much concerned with the psychological state of the Sleepers, both during their persecution and after their awakening.[44] Even more strikingly, however, the Old English text highlights the way that material details may reflect – or, in some cases, do not reflect – the passage of time.

Of course, the temporal chasm between the moment the saints fall asleep and their awakening is not only revealed by items of material culture: during their 200-year sleep, the seven youths have missed nothing less than the Roman Empire's conversion to Christianity; as Dinshaw observes, the story 'is very much about world-historical change'.[45] By the time of the saints' awakening, the Christian faith has become fully embedded into the everyday lives of the Ephesians, who 'did not conduct any speech there except in the name of Christ' ('nane spæce þær ne drifon butan æfre on Cristes naman'; lines 483–4). The awakening occurs, the text explains, when a 'very intelligent man' ('ænne swa geradne mann'; lines 378–9) – the owner of Celian Hill ('Celian dune'; line 379), the piece of land where the Sleepers' cave is situated – allows his shepherds to build cots all about the hill as shelter against the cold. During their search for suitable

---

[41] These are BL Cotton Julius E.vii and the fragmentary BL Cotton Otho B.x. Incidentally, both manuscripts also contain Ælfric's Old English *Lives of Saints* (Cotton Julius E.vii in fact constitutes the principal source for the collection), among which is another – much shorter – retelling of the Legend of the Seven Sleepers. The anonymous version has sometimes been attributed to Ælfric, too. The story of the Sleepers is also mentioned in the *Life of St Willibald*, written *c.* 780 by the English nun Huneberc on the continent, and in the anonymous *Life of King Edward*; see further Magennis, *Anonymous Legend*, 4–5.

[42] *Ibid.,* 4.

[43] *Ibid.,* 11, 7.

[44] *Ibid.,* 24.

[45] Dinshaw, *How Soon*, 55.

Remains of the Past in Old English Literature

material, the shepherds eventually demolish the wall erected by Decius's men to seal the cave, thereby accidentally re-opening it. Once the wall has been breached, God lifts the miraculous sleep and causes the Sleepers to wake, an act that the text explicitly links to his capacity to kindle new life in the unborn and to resurrect the dead.[46]

Significantly, the Sleepers' awakening stands in direct relation to the reuse of the hewn stones that sealed the cave: just as the Sleepers are granted a 'new life' in order to testify to God's capacity to resurrect the dead, so are the stones given a new context and meaning, no longer imprisoning but providing shelter. What the text describes, then, is not a random instance of the reuse of building materials, a practice as wide-spread in the Mediterranean of late antiquity as it was in early medieval Britain; in terms of the plot, the divinely ordained act of spoliation is the very prerequisite for the awakening of the Sleepers.[47]

Spoliation operates as a potent metaphor for the reuse of narrative material in new contexts (in later medieval usage, at least, *materia* can denote both physical matter and the subject matter for narrative discourse),[48] as Tolkien's allegory of the tower at the beginning of his seminal 'Beowulf' essay suggests.[49] Yet in the anonymous Old English version, the act of spoliation also has the potential to summon an anachronic presence, to literally bring the past back to life. The appearance of the Sleepers in post-conversion Ephesus constitutes a case of anachronism, both literally and metaphorically: their miraculous re-emergence from the cave after an interval of two centuries is literally anachronistic, since it would be

---

[46] For a discussion of how the asynchronous image of the baby in the womb likened to the resurrected body undermines the patriarchal temporal line, see *ibid.*, 58–9.

[47] Both the act of spoliation and the awakening of the Sleepers are portrayed as the direct consequence of God's intervention: 'God ælmihtig gescifte ænne swa geradne mann [...] And he ða se ilca goda let ðær aræran ealle abutan ða dune his hyrdecnapan cytan' [God almighty arranged for a very intelligent man [...] and he, that same good (man), let raise there, all about that hill, his shepherds' huts; lines 378–81]; 'and he ða ure Hæland, [...] he sylf synderlice mid his agenre dæde þas seofon halgan þe on ðam scræfe slepon he hi awehte ða of ðam slæpe' [and he then, our Saviour, [...] he himself singularly by his own deed awakened the seven saints, who slept in that cave, from their sleep; lines 391–6].

[48] This is the case in a number of twelfth-century works, including Matthew of Vendôme's *Ars versificatoria* (*c.* 1175), Geoffrey of Vinsauf's *Documentum de modo et arte dictandi et versificandi* (*c.* 1215) and John of Garland's *Parisiana poetria* (1230s). See Rita Copeland and Ineke Sluiter (eds), *Medieval Grammar and Rhetoric: Language Arts and Literary Theory, AD 300–1475* (Oxford, 2009), 551–6.

[49] John Ronald Reuel Tolkien, 'Beowulf: The Monsters and the Critics', in *The Monsters and the Critics and Other Essays*, ed. Christopher Tolkien (London, 1997), 5–48, at 7–8.

The Perils of Anachronism

impossible in linear time without divine intervention; and the saints with their third-century outlook are also hopelessly out of joint with fifth-century Ephesus, despite the fact that the city's turn to Christianity should actually have facilitated their social integration.

As Dinshaw points out with an eye to 'sleeper' stories more generally, the sleepers' sense of asynchrony is first of all the result of their not having sequentially experienced the changes that occurred between the beginning and the end of their long dormition.[50] In that sense, of course, all sleepers can testify to the fact 'that our *lived* sense of time can differ from the measured time of successive linear intervals', if on a much smaller scale – and indeed, it is ultimately the commonness of experiences of temporal asynchrony that Dinshaw wishes to point out: sleep, like sorrow and drunken partying, exemplifies our disrupted relationship with 'the metrical clocking of time that measures a succession of moments one after the other'.[51] In the Legend, however, the Sleepers' feeling of asynchrony is increased considerably by the unusual – in fact supranatural – duration of their sleep and hence by the extended temporal gap in their waking consciousness, as well as by the miraculous suspension of temporal processes that resulted in the perfect preservation of their bodies and possessions, making it appear as if no time had passed at all:

> And hi sæton ealle upp gesunde æfter heora agenum gewunan, and heora sealmas sungon, for ði him næs nan deaðes mearc on gesewen, ne heora reaf næron nan þingc moðfretene, ac ægðer ge þa ilcan reaf þe heom onuppan lagon wæron ealle gesunde, and heora halgan lichaman hi gesawon eall blowende.

> [And they all sat up sound after their own custom, and sung their psalms, because there was no mark of death upon them, nor were their clothes in any way moth-eaten, but the same clothes that they had on were all sound, and likewise their holy bodies they saw all in bloom; lines 396–401.]

Yet whereas the Sleepers' bodies and clothes have been preserved as in a time capsule, the land around their cave has not. Assuming that they have slept only one night, the Sleepers send one of their midst, Malchus, to Ephesus to buy bread. Malchus is somewhat puzzled ('healfunga þæs wundrode'; line 448) by the cut stones strewn all about the hill; having fallen asleep before Decius's men arrived, he cannot know that they had been used by the latter to seal the cave. Still fearing Decius's persecution, Malchus does not pursue the matter further ('þeah na swiðe embe þæt ne smeade'; lines 448–9), and is all the more astonished to find the city of

---

[50] Dinshaw, *How Soon*, 10.
[51] *Ibid.*, 9.

155

Remains of the Past in Old English Literature

Ephesus quite different from how he remembered it: indeed, so extensive is the city's transformation that Malchus has to enquire whether he has come to the right place. Most of all, Malchus is surprised by the inhabitants' conversion to Christianity, which, from his perspective, appears to have happened overnight. The profound change of mentality has even affected the Ephesians' manner of speaking: 'And þa he com ful neah into cypinge þær gehwilce men heora ceap beceapodan, þa gehyrde he hu þa menn him betwynan spræcon and oft and gelome Cristes helda sworon, and hi nane spæce þær ne drifon butan æfre on Cristes naman' [And when he came close to the market-place where all men conducted their purchasing, he heard how these men spoke among themselves and often and continually swore Christ's allegiance, and they did not conduct any speech there except in the name of Christ; lines 481–4]. The text's concession to changes in language use notwithstanding, Walter William Skeat noted that 'it is curious that the writer never thought of the *philological* difficulty involved in the story; for he assumes that Malchus was readily understood, i. e. that the language of the Ephesians suffered *no change* during nearly four centuries'.[52] In my university library's copy, an anonymous mid-twentieth century (to judge by the handwriting) annotator replied: 'Ha Ha – unfortunately the writer was not acquainted with Prof. Skeat. How should he know?' Yet Skeat's mild astonishment is surely less out of place than the anonymous reader's witty reference to the early medieval author's presumed ignorance of philological rules (a commentary, by the way, that betrays a firm belief in historical progress) – after all, the degree to which the Old English text constructs temporal difference between the time that the Sleepers fell asleep and the time they awoke is truly striking.

That said, the text's high degree of historical consciousness most clearly manifests itself in archaeological rather than in linguistic terms: while Malchus does register the idiomatic changes in the spoken language of the Ephesians, he is more immediately struck by the physical transformation of the city. Upon his arrival, he is astonished to see a cross fastened above all the gates of Ephesus, but as it turns out, the city's cultural transformation is not restricted to the addition of Christian symbols. In fact, the very aspect of the buildings is different:

> and eac þa byrig he geseah eall on oþre wisan gewend on oþre heo ær wæs, and þa gebotla geond þa byrig eall getimbrode on oþre wisan on oþre hi ær wæron; and he nan þincg þære byrig ne cuþe gecnawan þe ma þe se man þe hi næfre ne geseah mid his eagan.

---

[52] Walter Skeat (ed.), *Aelfric's Lives of Saints: Being a Set of Sermons on Saints' Days formerly Observed by the English Church; Edited from Manuscript Julius E.VII in the Cottonian Collection, with Various Readings from other Manuscripts*, EETS OS, 76 (2 vols, London, 1881), vol. 1, 553 (emphases in original).

The Perils of Anachronism

[And likewise the town he saw all changed to a form different to what it was before, and the buildings throughout that town all built in a different fashion from what they used to be before; and he could not recognise any thing of the town, like a man who never saw it with his eyes; lines 464–8.]

If the text does not imagine the Ephesians' language to have changed enough as to impinge upon Malchus's ability to communicate with them, it certainly envisions a radical transformation of their city's outward appearance.

The physical and cultural transformation of Ephesus does not end with the city's buildings, however – it also involves much smaller objects. The text's attention to numismatic variance and the awareness of the process this implies on part of the people who first produced and read the text is perhaps its most frequently discussed aspect in modern scholarship.[53] The Old English text notes that coinage changed four times during Decius's reign, and that the money Malchus carried with him was shown by its inscription to have been minted during the first year of the emperor's reign, which means that it would have contained more silver than subsequent mintings in a real-world setting, a circumstance that seems not to have escaped the story's fifth-century Ephesians:

And wæs þæs feos ofergewrit þæs ylcan mynetsleges þe man feoh on sloh sona þæs forman geares þa Decius feng to rice. Feower siðon man awende mynetisena on his dagum þe ðas halgan ðagyt wunodon onmang oþrum mannum; and on þam frummynetslæge wæron twa and sixtig penega gewihte seolfres on anum penege, and on þæm æftran em sixtig, and on þæm þryddan feower and feowertig, and on þam feorþan git læsse, swa hi þær heoldon. Ða wæs þæt feoh þæt Malchus hæfde þæs forman mynetslæges on Decies naman.

[And the money's inscription was of the very minting that had been struck in the first year when Decius received the rule. Four times the minting was changed in his days when the saints still dwelt amongst other men; and in that first minting were sixty-two pence weight of silver in one coin, and in the next about sixty, and in the third forty-four, and in the fourth even less, as they held it there. The money that Malchus had was of the first minting in Decius's name; lines 432–40.]

[53] See, for instance, Dorothy Whitelock, 'The Numismatic Interest of the Old English Version of the Legend of the Seven Sleepers', in R. H. M. Dolley (ed), *Anglo-Saxon Coins: Studies Presented to F. M. Stenton on the Occasion of his 80th Birthday, 17 May, 1960* (London, 1961), 188–94; Catherine R. E. Cubitt, '"As the Lawbook Teaches": Reeves, Lawbooks and Urban Life in the Anonymous Old English Legend of the Seven Sleepers', *English Historical Review*, 124 (2009), 1021–49.

Remains of the Past in Old English Literature

The material details here described – the inscription, the proportion of silver – all have their bearing on the story, for it is the coins that lead to the eventual discovery of the Seven Sleepers' anachronic state. Initially, however, the Ephesians presume a more mundane archaeological act to have taken place. When Malchus attempts to buy bread, the merchants first study the coins and hand them around as a curiosity, then declare that they must stem from a hidden treasure trove:

> 'Butan tweon hit is soð þæt we ealle her geseoð, þæt þæs uncuþa geonga cniht swiðe ealdne goldhord wel gefyrn funde, and hine nu manega gear dearnunga behydde.'

> ['Without doubt it is true what we all see here, that this foreign young man formerly found a gold hoard of very old age, and has hidden it now for many years'; lines 520–2.]

This archaeological explanation – that the gold coins originate from a hidden hoard – is not only the most natural explanation from the perspective of the Ephesians, who cannot know of the miraculous survival of the Seven Sleepers, it is also quite literally true: like the Sleepers themselves, the coins had been hidden in a sealed cave, cut off from the surrounding world as in a time capsule.[54] Thanks to God's miraculous act of preservation, they even look new, a characteristic not usually shared by other archaeological objects (compare, for instance, the rusty objects in *Beowulf*'s dragon's hoard discussed later in this chapter). The unusual preservation of the Sleepers and their possessions thus draws attention to their anachronic state.

What neither the Ephesians nor indeed the Sleepers themselves are able to fathom at this point is that Malchus and his companions have likewise been turned into relics from the past; no less archaeological, in fact, than mummies or bog bodies, but with the undeniable difference that they are still alive. To understand this miracle, another form of archaeological proof is required – one that has been provided by two of Decius's men, Þeodorus and Gaius, two secret Christians who were present when the

---

[54] As Cartlidge remarks, the citizens' contention that the young man had been hiding the treasure for many years does not make sense from their own perspective, although he does not observe that, ironically, the statement is in fact literally true. Cartlidge explains the apparent incongruence as 'probably the result of a mistranslation of the Latin (the Old English apparently taking the suggestion in the Latin that the treasure had been hidden for many years to mean that it had been hidden for many years by the "young man")'; Neil Cartlidge, 'Evidence of the Past in the Legend of the Seven Sleepers', in Jan-Peer Hartmann and Andrew James Johnston (eds), *Material Remains: Reading the Past in Medieval and Early Modern British Literature* (Columbus, OH, 2021), 57–77, at 64.

The Perils of Anachronism

Sleepers were walled in. Anticipating the Sleepers' rediscovery, these two men foresightedly engraved a leaden tablet with the saints' martyrology and put it into a casket, which they then sealed and secretly laid beside the Sleepers:

> þæt hit mid him þærinne læge to swutelunge oð ðone byre þe hi God ælmihtig awehte and hi mancynne swutelian wolde, þæt ealle men ðurh ðæt gewritt eft ongytan mihton hwæt þa halgan wæron þe man ðærinne funde, þonne þæt Godes wylla wære.

> [so that it might lie therein with them as a testimony until that time that God almighty would wake them and reveal them to humankind; that all human beings through that writing might then perceive who those saints were that one should find therein, when it should be God's will; lines 306–10.]

Sending a message to the future in order to explain an act of the present is by no means uncommon – we find monumental inscriptions on tomb walls in Pharaonic Egypt, public buildings in ancient Rome and rune stones in pre-Viking Age Scandinavia, among others. Neither is the motif of the ancient text as the only surviving witness of saintly martyrdom unique to the Legend of the Seven Sleepers: William of St Albans's twelfth-century *Passio Sancti Albani* and Matthew Paris's *Gesta abbatum*, for example, both use the same narrative device.[55] In the field of literary texts, the sudden discovery of such unique textual witnesses is common enough to have gained the label *Schriftauffindung* ('discovery of writings') in scholarly discourse.[56] Yet if the motif of *Schriftauffindung* holds out the promise of an unexpected re-emergence of forgotten information, it also, and more fundamentally, draws attention to the precariousness of knowledge and the inevitability of historical loss – 'the anxiety of history', as Liuzza terms it; that is, the realisation that the past is always under threat of obliteration unless it is recorded (and often even then).[57]

---

[55] See Monika Otter, '"New Werke": *St. Erkenwald*, St. Albans, and the Medieval Sense of the Past', *Journal of Medieval and Renaissance Studies*, 24 (1994), 387–414, at 397–404; Naomi Howell, 'Saracens at St Albans: The Heart-Case of Roger de Norton', in Jan-Peer Hartmann and Andrew James Johnston (eds), *Material Remains: Reading the Past in Medieval and Early Modern British Literature* (Columbus, OH, 2021), 145–71, at 168. Translations of the two texts are found in Matthew Paris, *The Life of Saint Alban*, trans. Jocelyn Wogan-Browne and Thelma S. Fenster (Tempe, AZ, 2010).

[56] Otter, 'New Werke', 402; Otter traces the term to Friedrich Wilhelm, 'Über fabulistische Quellenangaben', *Beiträge zur Geschichte der deutschen Sprache und Literatur*, 33 (1908), 286–339.

[57] Liuzza, 'Tower of Babel', 14.

Remains of the Past in Old English Literature

Communicating with the future by means of a written message is thus a thoroughly archaeological motif: it constitutes a deliberate attempt to produce a material trace that will outlive historical changes that would otherwise erase its meaning, in the hope that the trace will be found and correctly interpreted at some future time. Moreover, while the senders of these messages must needs be optimistic with regard to the legibility of the trace they are producing, many of the narratives that take up this motif highlight the fundamental precariousness of such 'messages' by having them reappear in an illegible state, either due to corrosion or fragmentation, or because of a lack of ability to decipher them.[58] Imagining this latter kind of loss – equivalent to a loss of knowledge – obviously entails the notion that languages and writing systems may change so radically that they cannot be understood by later generations – the inscription on the hilt of the giants' sword in *Beowulf*, to be discussed later in this chapter, is a case in point.

In the Legend of the Seven Sleepers, no such obstacles impair communication between past and present, even without the saints as asynchronic inhabitants of both time frames acting as interpreters. Nevertheless, the narrative does imagine a radical cultural change to have taken place between the time the Sleepers' martyrology was written down and the time it was found; namely, the Empire's conversion to Christianity. The text even projects an awareness of historical change into the past: within the logic of the narrative, the producers of the tablet must have believed, or at least hoped, that such a change would take place in the future, since both the usefulness of the martyrology and the capacity to correctly interpret it, dependent as they are on a particular theological understanding, are tied directly to the survival of Christianity itself.

If the text suggests that in addition to Malchus's coins, written evidence is needed to confirm the Sleepers' story, the introduction of writing nevertheless does not constitute a reversal to the kind of documentary 'proof' so often favoured in medieval charters and historiography – proof rendered hopelessly susceptible to forgery by its exclusive reliance on textual authority. Rather, the leaden tablet constitutes a piece of writing whose authority and potency derive directly from the archaeological circumstances of its transmission: the tablet's double sealing – first, in a casket secured by two silver seals, and second, together with the Sleepers, in the cave – confirms that the message must indeed stem from the time of Decius.

---

[58] Andrew James Johnston, '*St. Erkenwald* und die Verfügbarmachung des Unverfügbaren', *Paragrana: Internationale Zeitschrift für Historische Anthropologie*, 21:2 (2012), 60–76, at 74–5.

The Perils of Anachronism

At the same time, the material context of the tablet's transmission draws attention to the archaeological, and hence anachronic, nature of the Saints themselves: after the passing of two centuries, their re-emergence would not have been possible except by God's grace. The text highlights their asynchronous state not only through the lack of physical change in their possessions or their own bodily appearance, but also through the fact that even though their new historical context should be expected to be much less hostile than the one they left behind, the Saints do not seem to fit into the world into which they have been transported. At the end of the story, they return to their cave where they are marvelled at by a crowd of visitors, indistinguishable from the similarly potent relics of deceased saints, which are likewise, in a sense, 'alive' but nevertheless no longer taking part in the more mundane aspects of everyday life. Having been cut off from the surrounding world through Decius's persecution, they remain, even after their return to life, incongruous, incapable of being integrated into their new historical context, except as curiosities from the distant past that testify to God's ability to grant new life to what by all accounts should be dead and gone.

It is in this capacity to serve as living proof of the resurrection of the body that the spiritual meaning of the miracle must be sought; it is, indeed, the sole purpose of the Saints' survival, as the Old English text makes clear: in a lengthy passage that bridges the temporal interval of their sleep, the text explains that their miraculous reawakening was staged by God as a means of dispelling heretical beliefs current during Theodosius's reign, which denied bodily resurrection (lines 323–74).[59] Dinshaw affirms that the Seven Sleepers' anachronic re-emergence in the time of Theodosius is 'firmly and safely embedded' within a Christian framework; in the Legend, 'the unfolding of alternate temporalities is part of their Christian mission'.[60] Indeed, Ernst Honigmann has suggested that the origins of the Legend may be connected to a short-lived revival of Origenism during the rule of Theodosius, and thus to a rejection of the doctrine of the resurrection of the body, a heresy that the Legend was meant to refute.[61]

The exegetical theme is taken up at the end of the narrative. Once the Ephesians have accepted the truth of Malchus's account, the local bishop, Marínus, sends a letter to emperor Theodosius in which he interprets the miracle accordingly:

---

[59] The text is most explicit in linking the Sleepers' awakening to the emergence of heresy in lines 364–79.
[60] Dinshaw, *How Soon*, 44.
[61] Cited from Magennis (ed.), *Anonymous Legend*, 2–3.

Remains of the Past in Old English Literature

And us seo towearde ærist ealra manna nu gecyðed þurh opene tacna, and Godes halige martyras syndon arisene, and embe þæt spæce habbað to mancynne.

[And the future resurrection of all human beings is now proclaimed to us through open signs, and God's holy martyrs have risen, and are speaking about it to humankind; lines 733–5.]

The story ends with the Sleepers' receiving Theodosius in their cave, promising to remain there for him and to pray for his welfare (lines 766–9). Although the text seems to suggest that the Saints continue to be directly accessible to the living, they are nevertheless separated from them by remaining within their cave, in the manner of anchorites tied to their cells, or, indeed, the enshrined relics of literally deceased saints: these, too, were often seen as in some sense alive and capable of intervening on behalf of the believer, yet nevertheless removed from the world of the living – Jerome, for instance, noted that the saints are 'not called dead but sleeping', even if their bodies have dissolved to ashes.[62] Jerome's choice of words is particularly resonant with the Legend's overarching theme: from this perspective, the Seven Sleepers remain in essentially the same state of existence before and after their awakening.[63]

Other versions of the Legend, including Ælfric's short summary in the second series of the Catholic homilies, are even more explicit in suggesting that the Saints cannot regain their place in the world of the living: surviving just long enough to be presented to Emperor Theodosius as proof of the resurrection of the flesh, they expire soon after their awakening. Once their purpose is accomplished, the Saints' anachronic presence is no longer required. As Neil Cartlidge notes, from their own perspective, the Sleepers' lives appear not, in effect, very much longer than they would have been had Decius found and martyred them:

What the legend essentially celebrates is this amazing journey in time – not their escape from the emperor Decius. Indeed, in a sense, they do not escape at all, for they still die young as a result of his persecution. [...] The effect of the miracle is not to bring about their rescue from

---

[62] Quoted from Bynum, *Christian Materiality*, 178–9.
[63] Bynum discusses the ambiguity of medieval attitudes towards the level of 'life-ness' characterising relics; Aquinas, for instance, argued that relics were not identical with the living bodies of the saints because of the difference of form (the soul having departed the corpse for heaven), but nevertheless *were* the saints by virtue of their identical matter 'which is destined to be reunited with its form' (*Christian Materiality*, 154–5, quotation at 155; see also 177–214).

martyrdom, but to alter the terms in which their deaths might be understood – to make it possible to read the ideal of martyrdom in new ways.[64]

The Saints' unnaturally prolonged lives are thus not a divine gift to the men themselves; rather, their purpose is to testify to God's capacity to bend to his will the natural course of time. But once the evidence has been properly understood, normal temporality reasserts itself: out of joint with their new historical context, the Sleepers must die for linear time to resume its course.

The antiquated coins, too, cannot be put to their original use after they have reappeared in the future: unsuitable for buying bread, they even prove potentially dangerous to Malchus when the Ephesians threaten to torture him should he not willingly reveal the treasure they suspect him of hiding. In the Legend of the Seven Sleepers, then, anachronic objects turn out to be useless or even dangerous to possess; and worse yet, the Legend suggests, no one can be out of sync with their historical context and expect to live for long. As we shall see, *Beowulf* takes a very similar stance.

Anachronic Objects in Beowulf

Beowulf is strewn with archaeological objects that are also anachronic in more than one sense. Ancient heirlooms like Unferth's sword Hrunting; the necklace presented to Beowulf by the Danish queen Wealhtheow, which recalls to the narrator the mythical *Brosinga men*; the cups and pieces of rusty armour that Wiglaf recovers from the dragon's barrow; the sword that Beowulf brings back from the Grendelkin's underwater cave – they all derive their meaning and their (usually questionable) value from the fact that while they do appear in the poem's fictional present, they are simultaneously represented as things from an ancient past. Their age is clearly apparent to the characters and prompts digressions from the narrator, yet the objects' antiquity also frequently interferes with their continuing practical utility: Hrunting breaks when Beowulf uses it against Grendel's mother; the necklace, as the narrator's digression on the *Brosinga men* and its subsequent appearances in the story suggest, brings doom to its bearers; the rusty objects from the dragon's hoard provide neither wealth nor comfort to the Geats, as the dying Beowulf had hoped, but are for the most part burned and buried with him; and the giants' sword remains intact only long enough to kill the last survivors of the Flood before it is damaged in such a way as to become useless for any

---

[64] Cartlidge, 'Evidence', 59.

Remains of the Past in Old English Literature

practical purpose except to serve as a memorial to the events associated with it, rather like a museum exhibit.

Some of these artefacts are literally anachronistic, not merely anachronic in the sense that their proper time seems to be that of the past. The giants' sword, for instance, draws attention to a 'chronological misplacement': albeit produced by the giants supposedly wiped out by the Flood, it not only anachronistically depicts the very event in which its producers – again supposedly – perished, but is in the possession of beings that to all appearances belong to the same race of giants, and must therefore themselves be seen as anachronistic survivors. This is by no means the only instance of such 'misplacement' in *Beowulf*: as Seth Lerer has pointed out, some details in the poem recall features more properly associated with former Roman provinces than migration-age Denmark; for example, the paved or tessellated floor ('fagne flor'; line 725) of King Hrothgar's hall Heorot, which, according to Lerer, conjures up the image of mosaics in Roman-period villas. He also draws attention to the road leading up to Heorot, whose description as 'stræt wæs stanfah' (line 320a) he interprets as a potential reference to a paved Roman road.[65] Meanwhile, Emily Thornbury has suggested that the poem's description of the dragon's lair, which scholars since the Victorian era had usually linked to the Neolithic tombs commonly found throughout northern Europe, might be inspired by architectural features found in Roman buildings ('stanbogan'; line 2545), a hypothesis supported by the presence in the lair of another object with Roman overtones, a golden standard ('segn eallgylden'; line 2767).[66] Thornbury's reading was taken up by Gale Owen-Crocker and more recently by the archaeologist Howard Williams, who argued that while it cannot be ruled out that a megalithic tomb inspired the poem, such structures were significantly less visible before their reconstruction during the later nineteenth and twentieth centuries, whereas other subterranean and semi-subterranean spaces such as Iron Age souterrains, Roman-period temples, mausolea, bathhouses, underfloor heating systems, aqueducts and drains were demonstrably reused by early medieval populations.[67]

---

[65] Seth Lerer, '"On fagne flor": The Postcolonial *Beowulf*', in Ananya Jahanara Kabir and Deanne Williams (eds), *Postcolonial Approaches to the European Middle Ages: Translating Cultures* (Cambridge, 2005), 77–102.

[66] Thornbury, 'Relics'.

[67] Gale R. Owen-Crocker, *The Four Funerals in Beowulf and the Structure of the Poem* (Manchester, 2000), 62; Howard Williams, '*Beowulf* and Archaeology: Megaliths Imagined and Encountered in Early Medieval Europe', in Marta Díaz-Guardamino, Leonardo García Sanjuán and David Wheatley (eds), *The Lives of Prehistoric Monuments in Iron Age, Roman, and Medieval Europe* (Oxford, 2015), 77–97, at 83. Williams does not settle for one type of explanation, arguing instead that the description of the dragon's lair may have been inspired by multiple sources, including geological features. Similarly, Ferhatović states that

The Perils of Anachronism

All these features could be found in early medieval Britain, but they would have been out of place in *Beowulf*'s Scandinavian setting.

Obviously, other explanations for these apparent 'misplacements' could be found: Heorot's *fagne flor* might simply refer to painted wood; the *stanfah stræt* can be imagined as a road lined with standing stones; the dragon's lair can be equated with a prehistoric barrow. We do not know what was on the poet's mind, and any reader or listener could and still can envision these features differently, depending on their own experience and environment. In the case of the giants' sword, on the other hand, it becomes more difficult to find a satisfactory explanation. Postdiluvian giants do appear in medieval texts on a fairly regular basis, as already pointed out in the previous chapter – the Babylonian king Nimrod was frequently taken to be a giant, as was Saint Christopher – but the passage suggests that *Beowulf* is deliberately drawing attention to a lapse in chronology: the writing on the hilt alludes to the wholesale destruction of the very race that produced the sword, and, what is more, it is kept by two creatures that belong to the same race. The image is too self-contradictory, too obviously chronologically improbable, to go unnoticed – unless we revert to the old knockout argument that premodern people were indifferent to questions of chronology and historical difference. Such an assessment does not, however, fit at all well with *Beowulf*'s depiction of a complex and layered history; indeed, the poem's careful handling of matters of chronology, a feature that has often been commended by scholars of history and literature alike, militates strongly against interpreting the text along these lines. The fact that the poem repeatedly associates the sword with the race of giants suggests that, in this case at least, the supposed chronological blunder is by no means accidental. Rather, I argue, *Beowulf* foregrounds the sword's history in order to highlight the problematic nature of the concept of anachronism itself, which denies the legitimacy of certain modes of existence by classifying them as 'out of sync' with their temporal context. I will start my discussion by examining what one might call *Beowulf*'s obsessive engagement with history and chronology before turning to the giants' sword itself, whose presentation in the poem, I suggest, raises the question of anachronic survival, with far-reaching implications for those associated with it.

'the dragon's barrow does not likely correspond to any recoverable Anglo-Saxon structure, but it does bring to mind several types of buildings present in early medieval England. It is a composite space, "layered and textured," much like the literary work that contains it' (*Borrowed Objects*, 153).

165

Layering the Past

It has long been recognised that *Beowulf* displays an acute sense of history. Roberta Frank calls *Beowulf*'s 'reconstruction of a northern heroic age [...] chronologically sophisticated, rich in local color and fitting speeches'.[68] Indeed, the poem's vision of the past is so persuasive that earlier generations of scholars believed they were dealing with a straight-forward account of historical facts – which explains their irritation with the 'fairytale-like' nature of the main plot: Beowulf's fights against giants, hags and dragons. It may be a little unfair to quote Grímur Jónsson Thorkelin, the poem's first editor, who did not, after all, have the benefit of being able to draw on previous scholarship, not to mention his struggle with the poem's language. Yet in his 1815 edition, he concluded that the *Beowulf*-poet was obviously 'an eye-witness of the deeds of the kings Hrodgar, Beowulf and Higelac, and present as encomiast at Beowulf's funeral', and placed Beowulf's death 'in Jutland in A.D. 340'.[69] Indeed, as late as 1948, Kemp Malone was still commending the poem's 'historical accuracy'.[70] In his famous 1936 essay 'The Monsters and the Critics', possibly 'the most-quoted and most-cited academic article ever written in the field of English literature', J. R. R. Tolkien cautioned against such views, arguing that 'the illusion of historical truth and perspective [...] is largely a product of art'.[71] Tolkien's words were meant to warn historians of treating the poem's historical setting as a straightforward reflection of historical facts, but his more immediate goal was to challenge the then-prevailing practice of mining the poem for historical information while neglecting its merits as a literary text: in Tolkien's view, the overall internal coherence and self-consistency of *Beowulf*'s construction of a past primarily serves poetic purposes, chief among which is the creation of an illusion of historical depth.[72]

---

[68] Roberta Frank, 'The *Beowulf* Poet's Sense of History', in Larry D. Benson and Siegfried Wenzel (eds), *The Wisdom of Poetry: Essays in Early English Literature in Honor of Morton W. Bloomfield* (Kalamazoo, MI, 1982), 53–65, at 54.

[69] Quoted from Tom A. Shippey and Andreas Haarder (eds), Beowulf: *The Critical Heritage* (London, 1998), 92.

[70] Quoted from Frank, 'Sense of History', 271.

[71] Shippey, Beowulf *and the North*, 3 (on the article's lasting influence); Tolkien, 'Monsters', 7. Craig R. Davis echoes Tolkien's statement that the sense of antiquity evoked by *Beowulf* 'is part of the *Beowulf* poet's own traditional art, opening up dizzying prospects of pluperfect antiquity in a kind of mise en abîme [...] an endlessly recursive hall of mirrors pulling us inexorably from our present world into fold after fold of an ever-deepening abyss of time'; Craig R. Davis, 'Recovering Germans: Teutonic Origins and *Beowulf*', *Kritikon Litterarum*, 44:1 (2016), 125–42, at 142.

[72] Tolkien, 'Monsters', 27; Frank, 'Sense of History', 54.

The Perils of Anachronism

While Tolkien's essay had an immense influence on subsequent criticism, it did not completely stifle scholarly interest in the relationship between the poem's depiction of 'dark age' history and the actual historical and archaeological background of the story. In his recent reappraisal of the question, Tom A. Shippey has drawn attention to the surprising degree to which the poem's depiction of Danish and Geatish-Swedish wars corroborates what is historically and archaeologically known about fifth-century south-eastern Scandinavia. He also emphasises the poem's compatibility with later Scandinavian accounts of the same events, while simultaneously noting that the former is generally closer and more historically plausible than the latter.[73] Yet when Shippey argues that, ever since and largely because of Tolkien's essay, scholarship on *Beowulf* has tended to treat the entire poem as mere fiction, it seems to me that this is largely a fight against strawmen of his own making: few scholars today would deny the historicity of a character like Hygelac, while, conversely, Shippey himself concedes that 'everything to do with [the character] Beowulf is admittedly fiction (thirty suits of armour, fifty-year reign etc.), including his feat on a historical battle-field'.[74] Enlightening and even ground-breaking as many of Shippey's most recent observations are, it seems to me that in his zeal to rehabilitate the poem's historical accuracy, he is making the poem appear more 'primitive' than is warranted by his own argument. Thus, even as he censures critics who deny Old English literature the subtlety and allusiveness (as well as the use of significant silence) commonly found in modern literary works,[75] he maintains that the inclusion of details unrelated to the main narrative to produce what Roland Barthes calls a 'reality effect' is a typical feature of modern Western literature, and hence 'strikingly anachronistic in an ancient epic'.[76] In other words: for Shippey, *Beowulf*'s many historical digressions were included almost by accident, simply because they were part of the same body of narrative material, and have no aesthetic relevance in themselves.

However, historical accuracy and literary effect are by no means opposing principles, nor does historical accuracy by itself produce an effect of 'reality' or 'depth'. As Joachim Latacz points out, historiographical writing is incapable of producing the same degree of historical depth and immediateness as literature; it is through the use of literary techniques that such a reality effect is created.[77] *Beowulf*'s 'illusion of historical truth and perspective', to quote Tolkien's words, really *is* the product of literary

[73] Shippey, Beowulf *and the North*.
[74] *Ibid.*, 93.
[75] *Ibid.*, 44.
[76] *Ibid.*, 66–7; Roland Barthes, 'The Reality Effect', in *The Rustle of Language*, ed. François Wahl, trans. Richard Howard (Berkeley, CA, 1989), 141–48.
[77] Latacz, *Troia*, 238.

art, regardless of whether the materials used are 'historical'[78] – were it not so, the poem might still be historically accurate, but we should not find in it the same degree of 'reality', the same sense of depth. The way in which the many digressions, flashbacks and prolepses work together in *Beowulf* – interwoven and overlapping with the main story, rather than being presented as a large chunk of background information – exhibits such a high degree of subtlety and consistency that it cannot be the result of a purely mechanical insertion of bits and pieces of historical material.[79] *Beowulf* does indeed display a deep interest in the story's historical background, but in the background is where the historical material remains – as far as the poem's plot is concerned, the main story is that of Beowulf, and the snippets of history (factual or invented) intertwine in such a way as to support rather than eclipse it.

Moreover, *Beowulf*'s sense of historical depth is not merely the product of its use of historical background material. The effect is also due to the subtly interwoven temporal layers created by the poem's digressions, short episodes looking back to events that lie in the main narrative's past or foreshadowing incidents that have yet to transpire. One such digression concerns the building of Heorot, the Danish royal hall, which is followed immediately by an allusion to its destruction in the not-so-remote future:

> Sele hlifade
> heah ond horngeap;   heaðowylma bad,
> laðan liges –   ne wæs hit lenge þa gen
> þæt se ecghete   aþumsweoran
> æfter wælniðe   wæcnan scolde.

[The hall towered high and horn-gabled – it awaited war-flames, the hostile flame; it was not long until the sword-hate of kinsmen by oath after mortal enmity should awake; lines 81b–5.]

Almost immediately after Heorot has been introduced, we are informed that it is soon to be destroyed. Much later in the poem, we learn that, in spite of its imposing aspect, the hall is destined to exist for less than a generation. Piecing together these different bits of information, readers can deduce that the hall was built by King Hrothgar, the very ruler who figures prominently in the Danish part of the story and whom Beowulf rids of the monster Grendel, and that it will be destroyed in a battle between Hrothgar and his son-in-law Ingeld, a conflict that Beowulf

---

[78] Tolkien, 'Monsters', 7.

[79] Tolkien specifically mentions the 'avoidance of obvious anachronisms' (alongside the 'absence of all definitely *Christian* names and terms', emphasis in original) as signs of an intentional effort on part of the poet (*ibid.*, 45 n. 20). See also Frank, 'Sense of History', 54.

The Perils of Anachronism

himself predicts in lines 2024–69. At this early point in the poem, however, we are merely treated to a tantalisingly vague glimpse into the future. The piecemeal distribution of information pertaining to the same historical object – famously criticised by Friedrich Klaeber as the poem's 'lack of steady advance'[80] – not only means that the audience has to constantly revise its picture of the history that the poem apparently seeks to convey; it also creates the sense of a wealth of historical information that, if one makes the right connections, contributes to the creation of a complex and multidimensional internal history.

This impression is intensified by a discrepancy in the degree of historical knowledge possessed by the narrator, the characters and the audience. It is quite evident that the former is removed from the events told in the story not only by a lapse of time, but also by a completely different theological and philosophical outlook: the narrator's perspective – or so it initially appears – is that of the poem's author and its original audience. As Tolkien points out, drawing on an earlier essay by Chambers, the text's setting is that of 'a northern heroic age imagined by a Christian', who, looking back from his more enlightened vantage point with antiquarian admiration and regret, perceives that era as noble but ultimately doomed: doomed not only because of its ignorance of the Christian faith, which consigns the characters to hell, but even within its own ideology of courage without hope, which knows only eternal defeat.[81] The past as portrayed in *Beowulf* is conceived not simply as the present's anterior, but as altogether different, separated from the poem's contemporaries by fundamental changes in religion and mentality. Craig R. Davis remarks that 'there is no poem [...] where the pastness of the past is quite so deep, so old and so utterly irrevocable'.[82] The aim, arguably, is not so much to achieve historical accuracy as temporal difference.

In many respects, the narrator's historical perspective is fuller than that of the poem's characters. The events surrounding Heorot's building and destruction occur within a single generation, well within the temporal

---

[80]   Friedrich Klaeber (ed.), Beowulf *and* The Fight at Finnsburg, 3rd edn (Boston, 1941), lvii.

[81]   Tolkien, 'Monsters', 45. Tolkien is here drawing on R. W. Chambers, '*Beowulf* and the Heroic Age', in Archibald Strong (trans.), Beowulf: *Translated into Modern English Rhyming Verse, with Introduction and Notes* (London, 1925), vii–xlix. Tolkien's identification of *Beowulf*'s tragic heroism with the mythical Ragnarök from the Eddaic poems is, of course, problematic. Tolkien seems to be aware of this: '*With due reserve* we may turn to the tradition of pagan imagination as it survived in Icelandic. Of English pre-Christian mythology we know practically nothing. But the fundamentally similar heroic temper of ancient England and Scandinavia cannot have been founded on (or perhaps rather, have generated) mythologies divergent on this essential point' ('Monsters', 22, my emphasis).

[82]   Davis, 'Recovering Germans', 142.

horizon of personal memory or the predictable future, and are thus not perceived as historically different from the narrative's present. Other episodes, by contrast, include details that are known to the characters only vaguely, if at all. At Grendel's first appearance, for example, the narrator provides the audience with the monster's name and some details of his history, information that the poem's characters do not possess:

wæs se grimma gæst   Grendel haten,
mære mearcstapa,   se þe moras heold,
fen ond fæsten;   fifelcynnes eard
wonsæli wer   weardode hwile,
siþðan him scyppen   forscrifen hæfde
in Caines cynne –   þone cwealm gewræc
ece drihten,   þæs þe he Abel slog.

[This grim spirit was called Grendel, a notorious haunter of the marches, who held the moors, fen and stronghold; the unfortunate man dwelled for a while in the land of giants [or: monsters], after the Creator had condemned him among Cain's kin – the eternal Lord avenged that death, that one when he slew Abel; lines 102–8.]

The Christian narrator and audience, with their knowledge of biblical history, can classify Grendel and his mother as 'Caines cyn' [Cain's kin; line 107a], whereas the heathen Danes are unaware of their adversaries' lineage: Hrothgar is compelled to admit that the monsters' origins are unknown to him (1355b–7b). Later, when he is presented with the sword hilt that Beowulf has retrieved from the underwater cave after his fight with Grendel's mother, the narrator explains that the writing on the artefact describes the destruction of the race of giants in the Flood; the king, however, contemplates the hilt in silence and then speaks of entirely different matters, admonishing Beowulf to adhere to the moral principles of the warrior society to which they both belong.

The connection between Hrothgar's contemplation of the hilt and his subsequent speech – often termed 'Hrothgar's sermon' by modern critics due to its exhortatory character – has been the object of much scholarly debate. Marijane Osborn, for instance, has argued that, being a pagan, Hrothgar cannot make sense of the biblical allusions on the artefact in the same way that the poem's post-conversion audience can: although he is granted some degree of 'cosmic' understanding that leads him to accept, 'if not precisely to imagine', the existence of a Creator God, he does not 'himself [...] recognize that [theological] level in the words he speaks'.[83] In other words: Hrothgar is able to *read* the inscription, but he does not

---

[83] Marijane Osborn, 'The Great Feud: Scriptural History and Strife in *Beowulf*', *PMLA*, 93:5 (1978), 973–81, at 973, 977–8, quotations at 978.

The Perils of Anachronism

understand its theological implications. Lerer pursues a similar direction when he argues that the pagan Danish king's response to script is less immediate than that of the narrator and their audience; having noticed the signs on the hilt, it takes Hrothgar some time to decipher and understand what is written.[84] Meanwhile, Johann Köberl hypothesises that Hrothgar identifies the name on the sword as that of Heremod (which in turn sets off a chain of associations linking Beowulf's and Heremod's fates, and thereby prompts the king's sermonising speech), but he also notes the possibility (already voiced by Robert W. Hanning) that Hrothgar simply cannot read what is written on the hilt.[85] Although Köberl dismisses this possibility as unconvincing within the literary framework of the poem, the fact that Hrothgar does not in any way allude to the content of the inscription and had earlier admitted to his ignorance concerning the origins of Grendel and his mother – two details that the narrator, unlike the king, is able to supply – actually speaks for this possibility.[86]

That said, whether Hrothgar's ignorance is to be explained by his inability to read the writing on the hilt (or even to read at all) or whether it is due to his ignorance of Christian salvation history (as Osborn suggests) is ultimately less material than the fact that his knowledge is depicted as significantly limited when compared to the narrator's. As Michael R. Near argues, the discrepancy between the levels of knowledge possessed by the narrator and the poem's characters makes it possible for the former to 'disclose the details of the narrative suggested by the sword hilt and by an incomplete paraphrase of the hilt's runic inscription without implicating Hrothgar in the act of reading, without even hinting that Hrothgar had any idea of the implications of the matter that lay engraved in his hands'.[87] The king's specific position in historical chronology places him at a distinct disadvantage regarding access to historical knowledge.[88]

But there are also instances where the poem implies that certain historical details are no longer accessible to the poem's Christian narrator and audience. One such instance occurs in direct conjunction with the scene just described. Apart from depicting the giants' fate, the narrator tells us, the hilt also records for whom the sword was first made:

---

[84] Seth Lerer, *Literacy and Power in Anglo-Saxon Literature* (Lincoln, NE, 1991), 166.

[85] Köberl, 'Magic Sword', 121, 125; Robert W. Hanning, '*Beowulf* as Heroic History', *Mediaevalia et Humanistica* NS, 5 (1974), 77–102.

[86] Andrew James Johnston, '*Beowulf* and the Remains of Imperial Rome: Archaeology, Legendary History and the Problems of Periodisation', in Lars Eckstein and Christoph Reinfandt (eds), *Anglistentag 2008 Tübingen* (Trier, 2009), 127–36, at 130.

[87] Michael R. Near, 'Anticipating Alienation: *Beowulf* and the Intrusion of Literacy', *PMLA*, 108:2 (1993), 320–32, at 324.

[88] Johnston, 'Imperial Rome', 130.

Swa wæs on ðæm scennum   sciran goldes
þurh runstafas   rihte gemearcod,
geseted ond gesæd,   hwam þæt sweord geworht,
irena cyst   ærest wære
wreoþenhilt ond wyrmfah.

[And in the same wise was correctly marked through rune-letters on the sword-guard of bright gold, set and told, for whom that sword was first wrought, the choicest of irons, with twisted and serpentine ornamentation; lines 1694–8a.]

Strangely, however, the narrator fails to produce the name recorded on the hilt, which, as Johnston argues, raises the alluring possibility that they have no idea who forged the weapon – a carefully contrived effect by which the poem creates an impression of darkness, of historical oblivion.[89]

The plausibility of this reading is enhanced by a similar situation later in the poem, when the narrator describes the hoard guarded by the dragon that Beowulf dies killing. The treasure, we learn, was buried by the last surviving member of an ancient people, but neither the man nor the people are identified by name:

Þær wæs swylcra fela
in ðam eorðse(le)   ærgestreona,
swa hy on geardagum   gumena nathwylc,
eormenlafe   æþelan cynnes,
þanchycgende   þær gehydde,
deore maðmas.

[There were many such, in that earth-hall, of ancient treasures, which in days of yore an unknown man carefully hid there, the great legacy of a noble people, the precious treasure; lines 2231a–6a.]

The man is explicitly referred to as *guma nathwylc* [an unknown man], while the people to which he belongs is merely described as *æþel cynn* [a noble people] – again, the narrator appears not to have at his disposal the information that they vaguely gesture towards.

This ignorance is all the more striking given the narrator's usual air of omniscience: it is precisely by way of the many digressions, flashbacks and prolepses that they present themselves as possessing a degree of historical knowledge far exceeding that of the poem's characters or audience – in fact, the very passage describing the treasure's origins demonstrates the narrator's superiority in that regard: in contrast to the poem's characters,

---

[89] Andrew James Johnston, 'Medialität in *Beowulf*', *Germanisch-Romanische Monatsschrift*, 59:1 (2009), 129–47, at 143.

The narrator at least has some idea of the hoard's earlier history and is able to pass it on to the audience. But at the same time, the incompleteness of the account (which the narrator draws attention to) creates an impression of lacunae within the body of historical knowledge. It is through instances such as these that *Beowulf* suggests gaps in transmission that make it impossible to fully reconstruct the past. By creating an impression of historical obscurity, the poem effectively communicates that it is harking back to a past so remote that even the narrator is ignorant of the exact details. Johnston speaks of 'an archaeological surface, i.e. a surface that is damaged and hence disappoints any longing for textual wholeness':

> The effect is one of darkness, of a past full of unknown territory. Aesthetically, the effect contrasts markedly with that usually associated with the epic's digressions. Whereas the digressions tend to create the sense of a huge wealth of history gestured towards but never fully revealed, what is here being gestured towards is the exact opposite: a whole world of inaccessible history that will never be revealed. The name of the sword's original owner has entered a vast and remote realm of absolute alterity.[90]

Like an archaeological object, the understanding of which is always in some way fragmented, a mere piece in the puzzle of the past, *Beowulf* offers the audience no more than glimpses – and while these glimpses do suggest historical depth, they prove incapable of reducing the remoteness associated with temporally distant events.

Beowulf thus depicts a past that it is not only radically different from the present, but that itself looks back on an even more different past; in Frank's words, the poem shows an 'awareness of historical change, of the pastness of a past that itself has depth'.[91] For the narrator and their audience, the heroic age is irrevocably over, separated from their own present by fundamental changes in religion and mentality, but that heroic age reflects upon an even remoter past, a past neither the poem's characters nor the narrator are capable of fully reconstructing.

The characters' historical perspective is indeed extremely limited – to the Danes, for instance, their own known history appears to begin with the 'mythical' origin of the Scylding dynasty – the arrival by boat of the infant Scyld Scefing, a foundling of unknown ancestry – but that foundational moment occurred no more than three generations ago. The narrator, by contrast, is able to look both further back and forward, beyond the characters' lives; but as we have seen, even that horizon is limited. By introducing these different historical layers, *Beowulf* constructs an implicit

---

[90] Johnston, 'Imperial Rome', 133.
[91] Frank, 'Sense of History', 53.

Remains of the Past in Old English Literature

scheme of periodisation: the Christian present of the narrator looks back upon a heroic age with its own chronology based around the building of Heorot and the fortunes of the Scylding dynasty, and confronts it with an even earlier, even darker past, a 'deep history' that includes the antediluvian age of the biblical giants, but also the burying of the treasure by the nameless 'last survivor' and the hoard's later appropriation by the dragon. The lack of relative dating between these episodes suggests that for this historical period, no reliable sequence of events can be established; we are given only vague glimpses of what went on before Scyld's arrival in Denmark. Known history, the poem suggests, extends no further back than that; knowledge of what happened before is fragmentary and cannot be integrated into the same kind of absolute chronology as the events remembered, witnessed or predicted by Beowulf and his contemporaries. Even the narrator with their Christian learning possesses only a vague and incomplete knowledge of that 'deep history'.

So far, I have treated the narrator and their audience as if they existed on the same historical plane, despite my earlier intimation that this might not be the case. Strictly speaking, the very first reading, the very first recital of a poem postdates the moment of its production, although it might establish a sense of simultaneity by feigning direct contact between the narrator and the audience; for instance, by staging it as an oral performance. *Beowulf* does not fall into that category. According to Frank, the poem's choice of words reflects different registers and degrees of datedness,[92] distancing the narrator linguistically from the audience. Tolkien, too, noted that *Beowulf* is suffused with a language that would have appeared antiquated even to an audience of the eighth century, the time Tolkien assumed for the poem's production: 'The diction of *Beowulf* was poetical, archaic, artificial (if you will), in the day that the poem was made. Many words used by the ancient English poets had, even in the eighth century, already passed out of colloquial use for anything from a lifetime to hundreds of years.'[93] He cites as examples archaic words

---

[92] Roberta Frank, 'Sharing Words with *Beowulf*', in Virginia Blanton and Helene Scheck (eds), *Intertexts: Studies in Anglo-Saxon Culture Presented to Paul E. Szarmach* (Tempe, AZ, 2008), 3–16. Frank discusses, among other things, different words for 'cups' employed in the poem, including the unusual *full* [goblet] and *fæted wæge* [ornamented vessel], which she contends are part of the inventory of the poem's reconstructed Scandinavian heroic age. By contrast, *orca* and *bune* do occur in other Old English poetic texts, but they appear in contexts that suggest archaic scenes. Frank addresses a number of further items, including *fær* [ship, vessel], *heoru* [sword], *umbor* [infant], *gombe* [tribute], *þengel* [prince, lord, king], before concluding that '[w]hatever his century, when the *Beowulf* poet put words such as *bune*, *fær*, and *heoru* to work, he engaged powerful and significant cultural "others" [...]' (*ibid.*, 15).

[93] John Ronald Reuel Tolkien, 'On Translating *Beowulf*', in *The Monsters and the*

The Perils of Anachronism

such as *guma* [man], *ongeador* [together], *gamol* [old] and *sin* [his], noting that the ancestors of their modern equivalents – *mann, togædere, old* and *his* – were already more common at the time that the poem was written. Tolkien's contention that *Beowulf* sounded archaic even at the time of its composition is the more striking given that his attribution of the poem to 'the age of Bede' (noted *en passant*) can be considered early by the standards of current scholarship (if not by those of his predecessors and contemporaries).[94] And yet, despite its deliberately archaic air, Tolkien argues, *Beowulf* is 'late' in the sense that it draws attention to changing values, codes and manners of presentation:

> *Beowulf* is not a 'primitive' poem; it is a late one, using the materials (then still plentiful) preserved from a day already changing and passing, a time that has now forever vanished, swallowed in oblivion; using them for a new purpose, with a wider sweep of imagination, if with a less bitter and concentrated force.[95]

Distinctly poetic and/or antiquated diction is, of course, characteristic of much of Old English poetry, but if we accept Tolkien's argument that *Beowulf* styles itself as archaic by employing a deliberately archaic language,[96] this introduces a further historical layer that distances the narrator from the audience, even as the narrator is distanced from the events in the story: a triple distancing move, as it were, in which the audience listens to an (allegedly) old tale concerning even older events, whose par-

---

    Critics and Other Essays, ed. Christopher Tolkien (London, 1997), 49–71, at 54.

[94] 'I accept without argument throughout the attribution of *Beowulf* to the "age of Bede" – one of the firmer conclusions of a department of research most clearly serviceable to criticism' (Tolkien, 'Monsters', 20). In the notes to his lecture that formed the basis of the famous essay, Tolkien goes into further detail: 'The poem fits well into the period (eighth century) to which it can be assigned on dry and logical and unsubjective grounds, and is so illuminated by that placing that it cannot any longer be doubted that so set it is seen against its natural background.' John Ronald Reuel Tolkien, Beowulf *and the Critics*, ed. Michael D. C. Drout (Tempe, AZ, 2002), 88. As the controversies around two sizable volumes of essays devoted to the dating of *Beowulf* attest, Tolkien's certitude is no longer uncontested; see Colin Chase (ed.), *The Dating of* Beowulf (Toronto, 1981); Leonard Neidorf (ed.), *The Dating of* Beowulf: *A Reassessment* (Cambridge, 2014).

[95] Tolkien, 'Monsters', 33.

[96] A similar point concerning *Beowulf*'s 'lateness' is made, with different emphasis, by Johnston, who argues that, far from displaying the innocence or naiveté often attributed to early vernacular literature, *Beowulf* deliberately obscures its keen grasp of the complexities of dynastic politics with the help of the 'mask of archaism' provided by the ostensible display of nostalgic longing for a simpler warrior society (*Performing the Middle Ages*, 23–90).

Remains of the Past in Old English Literature

ticipants again look back to an even remoter time. In using dated language to present its even more ancient subject, *Beowulf* thus anticipates its own effect on posterity, its future datedness:

> When new *Beowulf* was already antiquarian, in a good sense, and it now produces a singular effect. For it is now to us itself ancient; and yet its maker was telling of things already old and weighted with regret, and he expended his art in making keen that touch upon the heart which sorrows have that are both poignant and remote.[97]

Beowulf, one can argue with Tolkien, styles itself as old, and thereby renders its audience – even its original, contemporary audience – 'modern' by comparison. The poem thus pre-empts its inevitable destiny of becoming dated, of becoming an object of curiosity to later generations, the ultimate fate of all art. In Greene's terminology, a literary text's awareness of becoming dated forms the fifth and most complex form of engagement with anachronism, one he refers to as 'pathetic' or 'tragic' anachronism:

> All of us and all the things we wear and make and build and write [...] are condemned to anachronism insofar as we and they endure into an estranging future. [...] Pathetic anachronism derives from the destiny of all enduring human products, including texts, since all products come into being bearing the marks of their historical moment and then, if they last, are regarded as alien during a later moment because of these marks. Things that survive are 'dated', and in the negative implications of that term lies the potentiality for pathos.[98]

Greene identifies a literary awareness, if not theorisation, of this kind of anachronism in the literature of classical antiquity, arguing that the respective texts deal with the threat of superannuation through their presentation of characters perceived as superannuated.[99] *Beowulf*, I will argue next, is replete with such characters; indeed, compared to the poem's narrator and audience, the entire cast of heroic-age warriors appears outdated in their archaic customs, conduct and expressions. If the argument outlined here is accepted, *Beowulf*'s way of dealing with its own future reception is even more sophisticated than the approach described by Greene: here, the vulnerability of the text becomes manifest not only in the 'visible vulnerability of the superannuated character',[100] but is linked to its own poetic language, pre-empting its future superannuation.

---

[97] Tolkien, 'Monsters', 33.
[98] Greene, 'History and Anachronism', 209.
[99] *Ibid.*, 210–11.
[100] *Ibid.*, 213.

The Perils of Anachronism

Objects, Periodisation and Anachronism

If *Beowulf* is obsessed with history, it is perhaps even more obsessed with material objects. Ancient artefacts, we have seen, provide the point of departure for many of the poem's digressions; they form an integral part of the strategy by which it achieves its effect of historical layering, and they also prompt shorter allusions to past or future events, as, for instance, in the description of the neck-collar that Beowulf receives after his defeat of Grendel. The torque not only motivates the story of Hama's stealing of the Brosinga necklace, but also prompts the narrator to mention Hygelac's death, an event that at this point in the narrative still lies in the future. *Beowulf*'s interest in material artefacts is thus intimately connected to its concern with history.

Most artefacts mentioned in *Beowulf* are described as *eald* [ancient], as *ealdgestreon, ærgestreon, longestreon* [old treasures] or as *laf* [heirlooms], suggesting a longevity that endows them with the potential to participate in other past or future events.[101] The description of Unferth's sword Hrunting, for instance, sounds as though it might prompt any number of digressions, even if, at this particular juncture, the narrator chooses to resist that temptation:

> þæt wæs an foran   ealdgestreona;
> ecg wæs iren,   atertanum fah,
> ahyrded heaþoswate;   næfre hit æt hilde ne swac
> manna ængum   þara þe hit mid mundum bewand,
> se ðe gryresiðas   gegan dorste,
> folcstede fara;   næs þæt forma sið
> þæt hit ellenweorc   æfnan scolde.

> [That was unique among ancient treasures; the edge was of iron, decorated with poisoned twigs, hardened with battle-blood; never had it failed any of those men who grasped it in hands in battle, who dared to go the terrible way to hostile dwelling-places; it was not the first time that it should perform deeds of valour; lines 1458–64.]

The tantalising claim 'næs þæt forma sið / þæt hit ellenweorc æfnan scolde' [it was not the first time that it should perform deeds of valour] implies that the sword was involved in a number of heroic deeds, some of which the narrator might be capable of reciting.

---

[101] For *eald*, see, for instance, lines 472a, 2415a, 2760a, 2774a; the term also occurs in compounds such as *ealdsweord* (lines 1558a, 2979a). For *ealdgestreon*, see lines 1381a, 1458b; *ærgestreon* line 1757a; *longestreon* line 2240b. *Laf* occurs in lines 454b, 2191b, 2611b, as well as in compounds denoting ancientness, such as *ealde laf* (lines 1488b, 1688a), *yrfelaf* (lines 1053a, 1903a) or *gomelra laf* (lines 2036b, 2563b).

Remains of the Past in Old English Literature

Heirlooms like Hrunting are handed down from generation to generation, suggesting temporal as well as cultural continuity: as the artefacts pass through different hands, they accumulate traces of the past, traces that could, at least in theory, tell a micro-history of the cultural world they are part of. Yet there are also other items of material culture whose presence pierces this illusion of unbroken historical connectivity. The artefacts in question constitute traces of a 'deep past', a layer of history that is entirely cut off from the present, an era perceived as fundamentally different in terms of culture and mentality. The image of cultural alterity evoked by these objects renders them not merely old, but 'archaeological'. Heorot's *fagne flor* and the *stanfah stræt*, which Lerer argued may denote Roman-type structures,[102] can be imagined along such lines, even though the poem mentions them only in passing without discussing their origin: read as remnants of a pre-Danish material culture, that is, as anatopic parallels to Roman mosaics and stone roads in early medieval Britain, they would operate as signposts pointing towards a layer of history that differs radically from the poem's present.

Less controversially, the dragon's hoard, buried by the last survivor whose name and provenance have been lost to history, is characterised by an even more powerful form of rupture. Buried after the survivor's people and culture have become extinct, the treasure has lain untouched for centuries before being appropriated by the dragon. The fact that it does not re-enter circulation but is buried together with Beowulf indicates that the alterity produced by its long sojourn in the barrow has transformed it beyond human recovery: the reference to an 'ealde riht' [ancient law; line 2330a] that Beowulf believes he has trespassed against may indicate that the treasure is cursed; perhaps we are meant to assume that ancient valuables, once their continuous use has been disrupted, cannot re-enter into circulation. When the gold is reburied, the narrator comments that it is again 'swa unnyt swa hyt (æro)r wæs' [as useless as it was before; line 3168]. At this specific point in the narrative, the phrase suggests that the gold is beyond the reach of human beings, just as it had been before it was 'excavated' by Wiglaf. On the other hand, many of the objects Wiglaf carried into daylight are said to be rusty and damaged.[103] This is not true of all them: the gold-plated cup ('sincfæt'; line 2231a; 'fæted wæge'; line 2282a) that an unnamed slave steals when he accidentally stumbles across the hoard, thereby rousing the dragon, must have appeared sufficiently valuable to buy his ransom (lines 2281a–3a). Nonetheless, the negative

---

[102] Lerer, 'On fagne flor'.
[103] 'Geseah ða [...] / orcase stondan, / fyrnmanna fatu, feormendlease, / hyrstum behrorene; þær wæas helm monig / eald ond omig' [He saw there [...] flagons standing, the vessels of ancient men, without a polisher; there was many a helmet, old and rusty; lines 2756–63a].

consequences of the theft clearly outweigh any monetary value that the cup might have possessed; one of the more immediate consequences of the cup's re-emergence is Beowulf's death. Maybe it is because neither Beowulf nor his people survive long enough to enjoy the treasure that the narrator designates it as 'useless': as the herald who announces Beowulf's demise to his people predicts, their king's death renders them defenceless against their enemies. As a people, the Geats are destined to disappear as their feud with the Swedes approaches its bitter conclusion.

Whichever explanation we prefer, the treasure's history repeats itself: buried by the surviving Geats before they, too, vanish from history, it returns to the same earth, in almost the same spot where the last survivor had placed it centuries before. The treasure's sudden reappearance, followed almost immediately by its return into historical oblivion, heralds the end of a people, their culture and, ultimately, their historical period. Its burial signals the dusk of an age: in this case, the heroic age peopled by Geats and Scyldings, which is, from the perspective of the poem's audience, the matter of history and legend.[104] The treasure thus connects different historical layers, interrupted by long periods of subterranean existence. It creates a scheme of periodisation based on the notion of historical breaks: indeed, its very mode of existence is intimately connected to the notion of rupture. Moreover, the dragon's hoard establishes a connection between time and history, here understood as concepts diametrically opposed to each other: even as its longevity suggests a continuous timeline stretching far back into the past and forward into the future, its temporality is fractured, broken into more or less self-contained episodes, a seemingly endless existence in continuous time punctured by short intervals that can be linked to specific periods within human history.

A second, even more pertinent example of a material object introducing a scheme of periodisation is the aforementioned sword that Beowulf brings back in fragmentary form from the underwater cave. The sword's presence, I suggest, renders visible an element of anachronism that, albeit implicitly, pervades the poem's engagement with items of material culture in general, including those that recall, however obliquely or unintentionally, an anatopical Roman influence. But where those latter cases are characterised by an ambiguity that leaves open the possibility of alternative explanations, the sword's history as presented in the poem constitutes an instance of internal incoherence that cannot be reconciled with the poem's scheme of periodisation: even as the sword depicts the demise of its own producers, it is nevertheless in the possession of members of the same race

---

[104] See further Roberta Frank, 'Germanic Legend in Old English Literature', in Malcolm Godden and Michael Lapidge (eds), *The Cambridge Companion to Old English Literature* (Cambridge, 2013), 82–100.

Remains of the Past in Old English Literature

which the Deluge ought to have eradicated (as the narrator points out in lines 1688b–93).

According to the narrator, the sword is 'giganta geweorc' [the work of giants; line 1562b] and 'enta ærgeweorc' [the ancient work of giants; line 1679a]. As discussed in the previous chapter, these more or less synonymous terms need not necessarily denote actual 'giants', but are often used to evoke a sense of great age and uncertainty of origin. In *Beowulf*, however, there can be no doubt that the sword's producers were actual giants. For one, the weapon is described as being of enormous size: 'hit wæs mare ðonne ænig mon oðer / to beadulace ætberan meahte' [it was greater than any other man might bear into the play of battle; lines 1560–1]; and to make doubly sure there can be no misunderstanding, the narrator employs not one but two unequivocal designations, *eotenisc* [of giant-provenance; line 1558a] and *gigant* [giant; line 1562b], at the sword's first appearance:

> Geseah ða on searwum sigeeadig bil,
> ealdsweord eotenisc ecgum þyhtig,
> wigena weorðmynd; þæt [wæs] wæpna cyst, –
> buton hit wæs mare ðonne ænig mon oðer
> to beadulace ætberan meahte,
> god ond geatolic, giganta geweorc.

> [He saw then among the war-gear a victory-blessed blade, an ancient giant-sword with strong edges, an honour in battle; that was a desirable blade, but it was greater than any other man might carry to battle-play, good and adorned, the work of giants; 1557–62.]

In contrast to the term *ent*, which the narrator uses later when referring to the sword as the 'work of giants' for the second time (line 1679a), the word *eoten*, cognate with Old Norse *jötunn*, refers unambiguously to literal giants, not metaphorical ones, at least as far as the surviving evidence can be trusted. The Latin-derived *gigant* is used predominantly in the Old English corpus to gloss giants in scriptural settings, which fits the biblical context of the Flood that the poem goes on to invoke. What the use of these more specific terms instead of the common formula *enta geweorc* suggests, then, is that the narrator wants to make absolutely clear that the reference is to giants in the literal sense.

As already noted in the previous chapter, giants occurred in widely divergent textual traditions: classical literature, Germanic legend and biblical sources. In the case of the sword, the narrator leaves no doubt that it is the latter tradition that is being referred to:

> On ðæm wæs or writen
> fyrngewinnes; syðþan flod ofsloh,

The Perils of Anachronism

gifen geotende   giganta cyn,
frecne geferdon;   þæt wæs fremde þeod
ecean dryhtne;   him þæs endelean
þurh wæteres wylm   waldend sealde.

[On this [hilt] was carved the beginning of ancient strife, when the Flood
killed, the pouring ocean, the giant-kin; they fared terribly. That was a
people foreign to the eternal Lord; the ruler gave them this final reward
through the waters' surging; lines 1688b–93.]

In the pertinent passage in Genesis 6.4–7, the Flood is only implicitly
connected to the existence of giants:

4 gigantes autem erant super terram in diebus illis: postquam enim
ingressi sunt filii Dei ad filias hominum, illaeque genuerunt, isti sunt
potentes a saeculo viri famosi. 5 videns autem Deus quod multa malitia
hominum esset in terra, et cuncta cogitatio cordis intenta esset ad malum
omni tempore, 6 paenituit eum quod hominem fecisset in terra, et tactus
dolore cordis intrinsecus. 7 delebo, inquit, hominem, quem creavi, a
facie terrae, ab homine usque ad animantia, a reptili usque ad volucres
Caeli: paenitet enim me fecisse eos.

[4 Now giants were upon the earth in those days. For after the sons of
God went in to the daughters of men, and they brought forth children,
these are the mighty men of old, men of renown. 5 And God seeing that
the wickedness of men was great on the earth, and that all the thought
of their heart was bent upon evil at all times, 6 It repented him that he
had made man on the earth. And being touched inwardly with sorrow
of heart, 7 He said: I will destroy man, whom I have created, from the
face of the earth, from man even to beasts, from the creeping thing even
to the fowls of the air, for it repenteth me that I have made them.]

Yet the apocryphal Book of Enoch, which appears to have been widely
available in early medieval Britain, is more explicit in this regard: here,
the Flood is a direct consequence of the evil deeds committed by the fallen
angels and their giant progeny.[105] Robert E. Kaske and Ruth Mellinkoff
have pointed out that this account seems to have had a particularly strong
influence on *Beowulf*'s depiction of giants in general, and of Grendel in
particular.[106]

The term *giganta cyn* [giant-kin; line 1690b], which occurs in the
description of the biblical Flood, can be read as a deliberate echo not only
of the above-cited passage from the Vulgate, but also of the compound
giganta geweorc, which the narrator employs when first introducing the

[105] Kaske, 'Book of Enoch', 422–3; Mellinkoff, 'Cain's Monstrous Progeny, I', 145–6.
[106] Kaske, 'Book of Enoch'; Mellinkoff, 'Cain's Monstrous Progeny'.

sword (line 1562b) – a similarity suggesting that the *giganta* drowned in the great Deluge are identical with the weapon's producers. If the giants who made the sword were killed by the Flood, the sword must predate their demise – but how, then, can their violent end be depicted on its hilt? Unless that depiction was made by somebody else or the giants possessed the foresight to accurately foretell the manner of their own destruction – and neither possibility is mentioned in *Beowulf* – then the poem's account of the sword's origins must be anachronistic in a very literal sense: a 'chronological misplacement', an 'error in chronology'.

That the story of the giants' sword revolves around precisely such an 'error in chronology' is suggested by the poem's description of the creatures it is associated with; namely, Grendel and his mother. Although the narrator does not explicitly identify them as the sword's owners, Beowulf sees it hanging on the wall in their underwater cave. It is also the only weapon capable of killing Grendel's mother, Unferth's apparently man-made sword Hrunting having failed at the task. This latter circumstance, in particular, suggests a certain affinity between the Grendelkin and the sword: presumably, it is only through a weapon made by giants (and arguably to *kill* giants) that Grendel's mother can be overcome. Moreover, although neither Grendel nor his mother are actually referred to as giants, Grendel at least is implicitly connected to them: he is said to have dwelt for some time in 'fifelcynnes eard' [the land of monsters/giants; line 104; Bosworth and Toller gloss *fifel* 'monstrum marinum, gigas'], and, like the giants, he has been condemned by God as a member of Cain's progeny (lines 106–7a; 1258b–68), a race from whom all sorts of monsters are descended, including 'eotenas' [giants], 'ylfe' [elves], 'orcneas' [evil spirits] and 'gigantas' [giants; lines 112–13a]. In effect, then, the references to 'eotenas' (line 112a) and 'gigantas' (line 113a) foreshadow the description of the sword's hilt, thereby linking Grendel's lineage to the race of giants who drowned in the Flood.

As if this were not enough, Grendel is portrayed by Hrothgar as a creature of colossal stature:

Ic þæt londbuend, leode mine,
selerædende secgan hyrde
þæt hie gesawon swylce twegen
micle mearcstapan moras healdan,
ellorgæstas. Ðæra oðer wæs,
þæs þe hie gewislicost gewitan meahton,
idese onlicnæs; oðer earmsceapen
on weres wæstmum wræclastas træd,
næfne he wæs mara þonne ænig man oðer.

The Perils of Anachronism

[I heard the country-dwellers, my people, hall-counsellors say that they saw two such great march-stalkers, alien spirits, hold the moors. One of these was, as far as they could know with certainty, in the likeness of a woman; the other walked the paths of exile misshapen, in the form of a man, except that he was greater than any other man; lines 1345–53.]

The passage unambiguously calls Grendel 'mara þonne ænig man oðer' [greater than any other man]. It does not mention his mother's size – she is merely described as 'idese onlinæs' [having the likeness of a woman; line 1343a] – but the reference to 'twegen micle mearcstapan' [two great march-stalkers; line 1348a] implies strongly that both are significantly taller than Hrothgar's retainers. The narrator and the characters certainly regard her as monstrous; in another passage, she is referred to as 'aglæc-wif' [she-monster; line 1159].

Yet if Grendel and his mother can be classed among the giants, they are subject to the same chronological lapse as the sword with which they are killed: both have survived the Deluge that was supposed to have spelled their doom.[107] Cohen sums up Grendel's position very pithily: 'Grendel [...] seems to exist in a narrative temporality which is simultaneously before the Deluge (in its biblical time frame) and after it (in its historical / Germanic setting).'[108] The potential explanation afforded by their existence – the giants' destruction could be depicted on the sword hilt because the Grendelkin or their ancestors survived to record it – thus merely perpetuates the error: as giants, Grendel and his forebears ought to have perished in the Flood. Their anachronic survival thus represents not only an error in chronology, but also a theological problem: how could some giants be alive after the Flood if the Bible expressly states that all of them were killed in it? If we take the Bible (and *Beowulf*'s paraphrase of it) at face value, then Grendel's appearance at the Danish court constitutes an anachronistic blunder of the first order – after all, it is difficult to imagine a more radical rupture than the biblical Deluge, which supposedly wiped out all living beings except for those saved on Noah's Ark. To put it differently, Grendel and his mother simply *cannot* have existed after the Flood.

Scholars have come up with a number of solutions to the chronological problem, none of which are totally satisfying within the context of the poem. Mellinkoff, for instance, has drawn attention to the fact that even though the universality and effectiveness of the Flood were never contested by orthodox medieval exegetes, 'there is interesting evidence that in less conservative quarters not all were persuaded that the deluge was

---

[107] At least Grendel's mother is killed with the sword. The poem is not clear about whether Grendel is already dead or in the process of dying when Beowulf severs his head.

[108] Cohen, 'Work of Giants', 22.

total'.[109] She cites a number of Jewish and Christian texts that suggest that some giants may have survived the Deluge – the Babylonian king Nimrod is identified as a giant in the Old English *Orosius* ('Membras se ent') and that the Old English homily *De falsis deis* explicitly speaks of giants after the Flood ('Nembroð and ða entas worhton þone wundorlican stypel æfter Nohs flod').[110] But if *Beowulf* took such a postdiluvian survival of giants for granted, we would expect the narrator to be less sweeping in the claim that 'giganta cyn [...] þæs endelean / þurh wæteres wylm waldend sealed' [the giant-kin was given a last reward through the raging waters; lines 1690b–3]. As it were, the incompatibility of the narrator's two claims regarding the sword – it was fashioned by giants, and the writing on the hilt mentions the Flood that annihilated the race of giants – is too obvious not to deserve some sort of comment, particularly in a poem that otherwise succeeds so admirably in the 'avoidance of obvious anachronisms', as Tolkien notes.[111]

Allen J. Frantzen proposes that the hilt depicts only the Flood, not the giants' death – in other words, the giant swordsmiths recorded the beginnings of the Deluge that they still witnessed, but the reference to their eventual demise is added by the narrator, whose knowledge of biblical history enables them to complete the inchoate story on the artefact. This scenario would explain *one* seeming incongruity, but the biblical narrative would still be at odds with the realities within the poem, where at least two giants are still on the loose long after the Flood. Frantzen admits as much when he observes:

> The sword hilt is not necessarily a story of endings; it may quite possibly be a story of beginnings. It may tell of the beginning of an evil line, rather than its end, and in *Beowulf* it may serve to establish continuity between the curse of Cain, the descendants of creatures who escaped the flood, and the evil that has escaped Beowulf's own retribution and that will destroy him.[112]

---

[109] Mellinkoff, 'Cain's Monstrous Progeny, II', 185 (quotation). Stephens notes that the chronological problems raised by traditions attesting to the postdiluvian existence of giants seem to have troubled Christian commentators early on: 'Indeed, although no writer I have encountered explicitly voices his concern over the problem, a number of them are noticeably worried by its implications. Augustine, in particular, recognized that the whole narrative of antediluvian Giants created a potential stumbling block for the faithful, when treated as a literal story of cause and effect' (*Giants*, 65, 84–5).

[110] Cf. Chapter 2 above; Frankis, 'Thematic Significance', 264; Liuzza, 'Tower of Babel', 7.

[111] Tolkien, 'Monsters', 45 n.20.

[112] Frantzen, *Desire for Origins*, 188.

The Perils of Anachronism

If we follow Frantzen's reasoning, then the hilt provides an alternative account to the orthodox biblical narrative rehearsed by the narrator. This suggests two possible explanations: either the poem wants us to think that the narrator has completely misunderstood what is depicted on the hilt, or it makes a point of juxtaposing two different, and contradictory, stories about giants. In either case, its repeated insinuations that the Grendelkin are to be associated with the biblical giants and the narrator's simultaneous insistence that all giants perished in the Flood seem to be part of *Beowulf*'s overarching narrative strategy. Given the poem's usual care in matters of chronology, I suggest that it deliberately stages what seems like a chronological blunder in order to draw attention to the incompatibility of the two diverging historical accounts, while also admitting to their simultaneous existence. The fact that the two narratives are mutually exclusive introduces the idea of alternative histories, histories existing side by side, overlapping but also partly contradicting each other.

Chakrabarty has pointed out that in present-day India, the received historical accounts imposed by Western normativity frequently exist side by side with alternative subaltern histories.[113] In *Beowulf*, too, we find such alternative histories in the form of two contradictory renditions of the giants' fate: the orthodox biblical account, unknown to the as yet unchristianised Danes, and *Beowulf*'s story, where at least two such monsters have survived. Given the supersessional logic of conversion, this might mean that the poem – and perhaps even the narrator – wishes us to understand that the story of Beowulf's fights against monsters is fiction, a legend that has come down to the present from a distant past, but lacks any actual historical foundation. On the other hand, the narrator does not treat the 'monstrous' elements of the story differently from the 'historical' Danish and Geatish materials, which Shippey has convincingly shown to have at least some historical basis, and is therefore likely to have been perceived as historically accurate by the poet and their audience. Hence, from the perspective of the poem, either both or neither ought to be understood as historical. But if the poem does not expose the fictionality of the Beowulf story, is it then criticising the account of Genesis 6:4–7 – which, after all, other biblical narratives (such as the then-canonical Book of Enoch) contradict?

Radical periodisation of the kind undertaken by the biblical story of the Flood denies the legitimacy of other, incompatible accounts; it creates a single regime of temporal truth that seeks to impose its norms upon all other historical narratives. In setting up a scenario in which the biblical account is presented as true and yet is contradicted on the level of plot, *Beowulf* does not so much challenge the truthfulness of Scripture

---

[113] Chakrabarty, *Provincializing Europe*, 40.

as the impermeability of the period boundaries it attempts to enforce. Historical narratives based on radical periodisation, the poem suggests, will always engender anachronism, because they set up norms that do not reflect the temporal complexity of historical events. In other words, *Beowulf* invokes the most rigid period boundary imaginable – the biblical Flood – in order to question the concept of periodisation by highlighting the permeability of period boundaries and the potential of the past to survive into the present.

Ending the Heroic Age

If *Beowulf* draws attention to the existence of alternative histories that challenge strictly enforced period boundaries, the poem also addresses the cost of adhering to a model of periodisation in the first place, the price that must be paid by those who fall outside the chronological norm, but also, in the long run, by the propagators of historical progress themselves. The biblical account denies Grendel and his mother the right to exist, and so do the human actors in the story, notwithstanding the fact that the pagan Danes and their equally pagan Geatish guests have no knowledge of biblical history and are thus unaware of the chronological problems posed by the presence of the two giants. Admittedly, the enmity is mutual; it is Grendel who, annoyed by the joyful noise emerging from the newly built hall of Heorot, initiates hostilities by killing Hrothgar's retainers.

In temporal terms, the feud between the Danes on the one side and Grendel and his mother on the other can be conceptualised as a collision of cultural norms, one of which is about to supersede the other. Grendel and his mother are perceived – and perceive themselves – as alien to the culture currently striving for dominance, the Danish warrior society under Scylding kingship. As such, they feature as the Danes' cultural and temporal Other: as Adam Miyashiro has observed, the Grendelkin can be described as an indigenous culture engaged in a desperate struggle to resist displacement or assimilation, and like all colonial peoples, they cannot but appear anachronistic – it is the colonisers' culture that provides the norm and denies coevalness to those not adhering to it.[114]

Grendel and his mother can thus be read as superannuated characters whose physiognomy and way of life, indeed whose very existence, is perceived as monstrous by the Danes. Grendel's severed arm, proudly

---

[114] Adam Miyashiro, 'Homeland Insecurity: Biopolitics and Sovereign Violence in *Beowulf*', *Postmedieval*, 11 (2020), 384–95, esp. 385–7. See also Stephens, *Giants*, 31–2 and 72–3 for the role of giants in Western literature as a hostile or at least unmanageable force outside human society and the way their Otherness is conceived of not only in anthropological but also in temporal terms.

The Perils of Anachronism

displayed under Heorot's roof (lines 835–6), and his head, held up for inspection in lines 1637–50, are presented as tokens of the archaic culture's horrific Otherness, morbid curiosities whose mode of presentation is reminiscent of modern museums of natural history, where visitors marvel at the size of the fossilised bones of dinosaurs or mastodons. Perhaps even more pertinently, the Danes' treatment of Grendel's body parts bears an uncanny resemblance to the way that Western collectors dealt with the human remains of colonised peoples well into the twentieth century (and sometimes beyond). *Beowulf*'s monsters function as tangible vestiges of a soon-to-be-displaced past, a savage, pre-civilisatory stage in human history that the Danes, like the nineteenth- and twentieth-century visitors of Western anthropological collections and curiosity shows, look upon with a mixture of horror and fascination. To the Danes, Grendel and his mother constitute relics from an earlier stage of history whose very survival runs counter to the trajectory of historical progress; they are living anachronisms whose existence ought to have ended long ago.

The hostilities between Grendel and the Danes can thus be interpreted as expressing an underlying conflict between the old and the new: the primordial giants, whose genealogy reaches back to Cain and the antediluvian period, attempt to the resist the introduction of the cultural practices of the much more recently arrived Danes, whose royal lineage reaches back no further than three generations, and whose banqueting hall has only just been completed, but whose proto-Christian religion, which finds expression in the scop's 'Song of Creation', is more akin to the cultural practices of the poem's audience and hence, from their perspective, more 'modern'. On the other hand, the fact that the Danish warrior society would itself have appeared outdated to the poem's original audience introduces a sense of irony that necessarily has a major impact on its portrayal of progress in general. As the poem's vocabulary of feuding and revenge makes clear, the violent retribution exacted by Grendel's mother for her mortally wounded son is entirely in tune with the ethical norms of the Danish and Geatish cultures. In conversation with Beowulf, Hrothgar leaves no doubt that he is fully aware why the killing has not stopped with Grendel's death: 'Heo þa fæhðe wræc / þe þu gystran niht Grendel cwealdest' [She avenged that feud in which you killed Grendel last night; lines 1333a–4]. Perhaps, then, for the narrator and their audience, the ethical gulf between the Danes and the Grendelkin would not have appeared so enormous, after all.

Beowulf's historical narrative is one of progress, one of the primordial being superseded by the modern, even if that supersession allows for late survival and sudden re-emergence, as in the case of the dragon: an apparition from the past suddenly 'exploding' into the present, as Harris

Remains of the Past in Old English Literature

memorably describes his concept of a 'temporality of explosion'.[115] The dragon, too, is killed, and although it is nowhere stated in the poem that it is the last of its kind (nor, indeed, that Grendel and his mother are the last of theirs), the poem does invoke a sense that Beowulf's fight against monsters is a fight to end all monsters.[116] Even as the poem permits various forms of continuity and re-emergence, its central character does all in his might to check these manifestations of anachronic survival. To put it differently: *Beowulf* seems obsessed with bringing closure to a history that refuses to be past. Eventually, it succeeds, but only at the cost of the life of its protagonist and the downfall of the warrior society that it so lovingly describes.

Beowulf's life-long battle against monsters exposes the violent mechanisms of a historical determinism that can conceive of change only in terms of supersession. Within the narrative, Grendel and his mother, the anachronistic survivors of the Deluge, are killed off, and so is the dragon; the chronological blunder is corrected, albeit belatedly. As Frantzen observes, the poem 'invites us to assume that when Beowulf kills the monsters, the doom of their race, forecast on the hilt, has been fulfilled'.[117] Johnston concurs, arguing that Beowulf becomes God's unwitting agent in setting history right, in producing a coherent vision of supersessional history where only that which ought to survives.[118]

Ironically, however, it is the very acts by which the protagonist brings closure to the past that also separate him from the poem's present. From the audience's perspective, the monster-slaying hero is himself an anachronism, a superannuated character who would have no place in their contemporary world. Beowulf's death after fighting the dragon heralds another radical change: the end of the heroic age peopled by Geats and Scyldings, and by heroes like Ingeld and Beowulf. Having ridded Denmark and Geatland from its atavistic monsters, it is time for the heroic, pagan Beowulf to bow out of history and make space for the potentially lesser, but nonetheless more 'timely', Christian audience of the poem.[119] Looking back from their Christian vantage point, both the narrator and

[115] Harris, *Untimely Matter*, 15.

[116] Thus, in the case of the sea monsters Beowulf boasts of having killed during his swimming contest with Breca, he even claims that 'syðþan na / ymb. brontne ford brimliðende / lade ne letton' [they have not hindered any seafarer from passing about the deep sea-way since; lines 567b–9a].

[117] Frantzen, *Desire for Origins*, 188.

[118] Johnston, 'Anachronic Entanglements', 105.

[119] As Cohen observes, the heroic world of *Beowulf*, itself a complex and layered past, 'is quietly defined against the Christian present of the poet throughout the work; its point of vanishing is the interlocked deaths of Beowulf and the dragon at the close of the poem' ('Work of Giants', 22–3).

The Perils of Anachronism

their audience must regard Beowulf and his world as the embodiment of a pre-Christian past, a heroic culture that has long since vanished. Beowulf's tomb, intended as a monument for his people to remember him by (lines 2802–8) and as a repository for the treasure that he died winning, testifies to the greatness of the heroic age, but also to its pastness. In a supersessionist model of history, progress inevitably turns back upon its proponents, because that which is considered 'timely' is always about to be replaced by something even more 'modern'. Like Schiffman's Rock N Roll McDonald's, *Beowulf*'s heroic world looks anachronistic to its audience, but the poem proffers a reminder that their own culture is bound for the same fate. By situating the narrator, the audience and the characters on different historical planes that signify different stages of enlightenment, the epic exposes the mechanism by which modernity distances itself from its own past, thereby drawing attention to its own destiny of eventually becoming dated.

Beowulf expresses its own relative modernity through the narrator's privileged vantage point, which contrasts with the ignorance of its heroic characters; for instance, regarding their knowledge of the Grendelkin's origins. The chronological contradiction created by the two above-discussed alternative accounts of the giants' fate can be detected only by the poem's audience, not by the characters: the pagan Danes are ignorant of biblical history, and hence cannot know that their monstrous adversaries ought to have been destroyed long ago; even when directly confronted with the story of the Flood, as in the carvings or letters on the sword hilt, they are unable to understand it.

Structurally, the poem's monsters and its human characters are thus placed on the same temporal level. Both are denied coevalness with the narrator and the audience; they are sealed off in a less enlightened past. The structural parallel is made visible by the poem's two moves of temporal and cultural Othering: on the one hand, we have the narrator's audience, looking back upon the noble but pagan warrior society of the heroic age; on the other, we find that same warrior society encountering the monstrous remnants of an even earlier, even darker past. This double move parallels the mechanism by which Western modernity distances itself from its own past, as well as from other, contemporary but allegedly non-coeval cultures. If Beowulf asserts his own 'modernity' by killing the superannuated monsters, he does so at the cost of his own eventual superannuation – in a sense, then, the future loss of one's own present's historical relevance is the price to be paid for subscribing to a model of historical progress. *Beowulf*'s historical outlook, as Tolkien has observed, is antiquarian: the poem looks back to a noble but essentially doomed past

Remains of the Past in Old English Literature

with admiration and regret,[120] but it does not set up the warrior society of the heroic age as a role model for the present. In exposing the mechanisms by which a present that regards itself as 'modern' distances itself from the past, the poem anticipates its own datedness; indeed, as I have argued earlier in this chapter, it does so quite deliberately, pre-empting its own future reception through the use of antiquated language.

Conclusion

Premodern literature, it has often been argued, lacks a proper sense of history, that is, a concept not only of the pastness of the past but also of anachronism, the latter being the implicit corollary of historical change conceived in terms of periods or 'regimes of truth'. *Beowulf* and the anonymous Old English version of the Legend of the Seven Sleepers, I have proposed in this chapter, display just such a sense of historical ruptures on which periodisation depends. At the same time, the two texts also draw attention to the consequences of this kind of historical thinking. Both are ultimately concerned with the problematic nature of a history of progress that censures as anachronistic that which does not comply with the current norm. As pointed out in the first part of the chapter, postcolonial theorists have observed that within the framework of a history of progress, cultural difference is likewise expressed in terms of periodisation. Contemporaneous practices that deviate from the model prescribed by Western modernity are associated with the past, and hence denied coevalness. *Beowulf* exposes the same mechanism: it presents historical change in terms of superannuation, with the present being afforded a privileged historical vantage point that enables it to draw historical connections that the less enlightened past is incapable of perceiving. More problematically still, in *Beowulf*, superannuation entails the loss of one's right to exist.

I have already quoted Latour's dictum that modernity imagines periodisation in such absolute terms that 'nothing of the past survives in them – nothing of the past *ought* to survive in them' (my emphasis).[121] The introduction of the word 'ought' suggests that Latour is well aware that the extinction of the past is less a factual than an ideological proposition. The same, I suggest, is true of *Beowulf*: within the poem's model of historical progress, the past must end for the present to take its place – but this, the text's action demonstrates, is not how history usually works, not even in the case of an ostensibly strict period boundary such as the Deluge.

[120] Tolkien, 'Monsters', 33.
[121] Latour, *We Have Never Been Modern*, 68 (my emphasis).

The Perils of Anachronism

Both *Beowulf* and the Legend use archaeological objects to index historical difference, but also to highlight the chronological problems produced by a strict model of periodisation. The Seven Sleepers' survival into the present is not merely historically problematic; their unchanged aspect throws into sharp relief the chronological problems involved. Unlike more conventional archaeological objects, whose age is betrayed by their state of corrosion, the saints' clothes and coins still look new; the Sleepers themselves have not aged during their sleep (unlike their non-saintly counterparts in C. S. Lewis's *The Voyage of the Dawn Treader*, the Narnian explorers Lord Revilian, Lord Argoz and Lord Mavramorn, who have grown long beards during their magical seven-year-long sleep).[122] In the Legend, the fact that the seven youths and their possessions have been preserved as in a time capsule highlights their anachronic existence, an existence that must be ended in order for history to resume its linear course. In *Beowulf*, meanwhile, it is the apparent chronological blunder associated with the giants' sword that draws attention to the anachronistic presence of the Grendelkin after the Deluge. In both texts, the anachronic survivors are eventually excluded from the present. Nevertheless, objects such as the Sleepers' coins, the giants' sword or the dragon's hoard suggest that the past is not always dead and gone, but has the potential for re-emerging in the present and threatening its established order.[123] Under these circumstances, burying the dragon's hoard together with Beowulf seems like a wise act, if ultimately futile.[124] Although Beowulf manages to check the past's tendency to return and thus 'sets history right', he does so at the cost of the artefacts' integrity and, eventually, his own life. Of the ancient sword, only the hilt survives; the hoard is burned and buried together with Beowulf. Even Grendel, once defeated, is fragmented: of his monstrous body, only the arm and the head are brought back and exhibited in Heorot. The past, these objects suggest, must be fragmented, rendered irrecoverable, in order to be fully past, and thus to pave the way for the present. As *Beowulf* at least seems to be aware, the same fate awaits the two texts themselves.

[122] C. S. Lewis, *The Voyage of the Dawn Treader* (1952), Chapters 13–14.

[123] As Ferhatović points out in the context of the poem's description of a sword spoliated by one of Hrothgar's warriors, whose presence will rekindle the hostilities between Danes and Frisians: 'If one object can wreak such havoc, what could a hoard full of them do? The *Beowulf*-poet demonstrates in these scenes his understanding of the threat inherent in precious artefacts that circulate in the world of his heroes. They encourage violence, standing in for perils of pathological memory and even idolatry' (*Borrowed Objects*, 152).

[124] Note, by the way, the similar logic of Hagen's deposing of the Nibelung treasure in the Rhine in the Nibelungenlied.

4

Visions of the Holy Cross: *Elene,*
The Dream of the Rood and the *Ruthwell Poem*

For much of Christianity's history, the cross has stood as its most recognisable emblem, symbolising a plethora of different things, events and concepts – from the crucifixion and the hope for resurrection to the entire communion of the faithful. The notion of an *inventio crucis*, that is, of the discovery and excavation of the specific cross upon which Christ suffered – a sacred object hallowed by the touch of his body and blood – brings into focus the cross's materiality and temporality as a physical object. No longer only a symbol, it can be imagined as a unique, tangible artefact that has been shaped by its existence in and through time. Yet imagining the cross as such a unique object simultaneously highlights the representational character of other crosses – artefacts shaped to resemble the True Cross, but not physically identical with it. If a 'true' cross is out there, then works of art representing that Cross, including paintings, sculptures and liturgical implements, may be simply that: items standing in for something else.

Obviously, the distinction between the unique, holy artefact, on the one hand, and its representation, on the other, that is, between the material-historical and the symbolic-representational, does not quite work in the way just described. For a start, representations symbolising the True Cross are just as material, from the gesture of the hand when making the sign of the cross to ornate crucifixes furnished from wood, gold and gemstones. These material entities have their own temporalities, their own forms of existence within historical time, parallel to but separate from that of the True Cross they are meant to represent. Moreover, as Calvin B. Kendall points out, from the perspective of medieval typology, the True Cross itself could be a sign: on the literal, historical level, it was an instrument of torture, the means by which Christ was put to death; in a typological sense, it signified Christ and particularly his incarnation; and on the anagogical level, as the tree of life, it was a sign of salvation. Kendall calls the cross a 'sacred sign', because its meaning – so he argues – was regarded as fixed, preordained by God, whereas other signs might be interpreted differently, depending on the viewer and context.[1]

---

[1]   Calvin B. Kendall, 'From Sign to Vision: The Ruthwell Cross and *The Dream of the Rood*', in Catherine E. Karkov, Sarah Larratt Keefer and Karen Louise Jolly

Visions of the Holy Cross

To complicate things further, Caroline Walker Bynum has demonstrated in her discussion of the perception of materiality in late medieval Christianity that the distinctions between different kinds of sacred objects – bodily, contact and effluvial relics, sacramentals such as the Eucharist, holy images and devotional objects – were never clear-cut, despite an increasing wish to authenticate relics and to document their provenance, and despite the propensity of late medieval liturgical artworks to highlight their 'made-ness' by foregrounding the materials and techniques used in their production.[2] Bynum notes that 'devotional objects were not just decorative embellishments of church and chapel or devices to direct attention to the invisible. People behaved as if images *were* what they represented'.[3] Even a representation of the True Cross could thus be treated as a holy object.

Bynum is, of course, referring to the later Middle Ages, and hence to a time frame different from that in which the texts under consideration here were produced. Evidently, Christian beliefs and practices changed over the course of centuries, and Bynum may well be right in arguing that a special emphasis on materiality developed in medieval Christianity only from the twelfth century onwards. But a fundamental ambivalence surrounding matter in general, and holy matter in particular, characterised Christian spirituality from quite early on; an ambivalence that also lies at the heart of the three Old English texts I will discuss in this chapter, all of which deal, in one form or another, with the idea of the True Cross: the narrative poem *Elene*, already considered in the first chapter; *The Dream of the Rood*, an introspective, lyrical poem centring on a dream vision of the True Cross; and the runic text on the Ruthwell Cross, a stone monument with Latin and Old English inscriptions, the latter comprising a poem with verbal and phrasal parallels to *The Dream of the Rood*. All three texts stand in a complex intertextual relationship with each other, the exact nature of which is impossible to reconstruct. All three, moreover, engage with the double nature of the cross as both a thing and a sign – a double nature that, according to Augustine, characterises all signs.

In a seminal essay exploring the presentation of the True Cross in *Elene* and *The Dream of the Rood*, Martin Irvine argued that

---

(eds), *The Place of the Cross in Anglo-Saxon England* (Woodbridge, 2006), 129–44, at 138–9, 142–3.

[2]   Bynum, *Christian Materiality*. On the difficulty of distinguishing clearly between different categories of holy objects, see 29. Bynum mentions the increasing wish to authenticate relics on 329 n. 3. On the tendency of late medieval objects to highlight their material make-up, see 28–9.

[3]   *Ibid.*, 125.

193

in these poems, the Cross functions as a typological sign, a referent in the narrative of sacred history capable of shifting from the level of a signified object to that of signifier, whose interpretation depends on the intertextual codes and overlapping discourses of exegesis, hagiography, and *grammatica*.[4]

Irvine traces this twofold presentation to medieval semiotic theory as expounded in Augustine's *De dialectica* and *De doctrina christiana*, pointing out that the two poems can be seen as 'exegetical extensions of, or supplements to' Latin texts dealing with the crucifixion and the *inventio crucis*, and hence as 'commentaries' that self-consciously reflect on the practices of interpretation and semiotic exegesis they are themselves engaged in.[5] In Irvine's perceptive reading, the retrieval of the cross in *Elene*, linked as it is to Constantine's discovery of the true meaning of the cross as a symbol, can be seen as emblematic of the activity of interpretation *per se*: 'As the Jews hid the Cross, not having the proper codes for interpreting its significance, so the reader must have the meaning of the Cross revealed, uncovered, through correct interpretation which takes the form of a text – the poem itself.'[6] Irvine is ultimately more interested in the manner in which the poems interact with their contemporaneous 'literary' theory than in their presentation of the material and temporal aspects of the cross as an artefact, but he does note its material contingency as a relic and also addresses the temporal aspect of typological interpretation – and as we shall see below, the latter, in linking entities positioned at different points in time, has the potential to collapse the essential linearity of sacred history.

I would like to take Irvine's proposition one step further by arguing that it is precisely the historically distinct materiality of artefacts – including their being subject to material change – that opens up alternative temporal models besides the typological, which in turn complicates the figural interpretation of devotional objects meant to represent holy artefacts. What is at stake, then, is not only the tension-ridden relationship between relics and their representations, but also the temporalities that characterise these objects, as well as the various referents they signify. I have already drawn on Bynum's observation that works of art representing holy objects and used in devotional practices could, from a medieval perspective, be regarded as holy objects themselves.[7] One explanation for this phenomenon is that due to the mechanisms of medieval typological

---

[4]   Irvine, 'Literary Theory', 157.
[5]   *Ibid.*, 157, 175 (quotations).
[6]   *Ibid.*, 168.
[7]   Bynum, *Christian Materiality*, 125.

interpretation, devotional objects were capable of assuming a figural identity with the entities they represented, even while remaining materially and historically distinct from them. That this distinction between a figural and a material dimension was widely recognised in the later Middle Ages at least is shown, for instance, by the fact that works of art from that time often draw attention to the techniques and materials used in their production. Highlighting the material contingency of an artefact places a special emphasis on the *sensus literalis*, differentiating it from the three spiritual senses of allegorical interpretation – and this is the case even though, at least in theory, all four senses are at work simultaneously, with none given priority over the others.[8] Artworks that foreground their historical distinctiveness by highlighting their made-ness, and hence their material difference from that which they represent, all while simultaneously claiming figural identity with it, thus acknowledge an inherent tension between literal and figural interpretations, without necessarily insisting that this tension must be resolved. This distinguishes them from relics, which – although they, too, can be interpreted typologically – usually stand metonymically for the saint from whom they originate: unlike representations, whose capacity to channel miracles derives from their *figural* identity with what they represent, relics owe their special power to their *material* identity with the saint. The distinction is blurred, however, by the practice of enclosing relics in reliquaries or monstrances that take the shape of visual representations, such as figurines, liturgical crosses or containers formed like body parts. In the notion of the True Cross, we find both of these aspects inseparably intertwined: a contact relic hallowed by the touch of Christ's blood, the True Cross is also the source and origin of what is arguably Christianity's most potent and most polyvalent sign, and it is this very circumstance that renders the tension between the semiotic and the literal-historical aspects of the cross especially productive.

Things, Signs and Figural History

Today, the cross as a Christian symbol is hardly surpassed in its polyvalence. This, however, appears to have been a gradual development in

---

[8]   If anything, exegetical practice would be expected to give precedence to the three spiritual senses, as suggested in 2 Corinthians 3.5–6: 'sed sufficientia nostra ex Deo est: 6 qui et idoneos nos fecit ministros novi testament: non litterae, sed Spiritus: littera enim occidit, Spiritus autem vivificat' [But our sufficiency is from God. 6 Who also hath made us fit ministers of the new testament, not in the letter, but in the spirit. For the letter killeth, but the spirit quickeneth].

Remains of the Past in Old English Literature

the history of Christianity, and it is perhaps significant that the cross as a Christian iconographic symbol came to be used extensively only from the fourth century onward, that is, from about the time of its supposed discovery.[9] As Jan Willem Drijvers notes, the origins and early development of the *inventio crucis* legend coincided with a growing interest in the cross both as an object of veneration and as a symbol of the Christian faith: while, during the first three centuries of the Christian era, it had been only of minor importance, 'from Constantine's reign onwards, the Cross became increasingly prominent as a symbol until it eventually became the Christian symbol par excellence'.[10] The material presence of the cross as an 'archaeological' artefact that could be touched and venerated, and whose relics were distributed all over the Roman Empire, thus paradoxically coincided – and possibly even triggered (or was triggered by) – the use of the cross as a symbol that came to stand for a variety of things, not merely for the True Cross itself.

The distinction between the symbolic and material aspects of the cross is implicitly referenced in one version of the *inventio crucis* legend that came to be highly influential during the Middle Ages, and that also forms the basis for the *Acta Cyriaci* and its derivatives, including the surviving Old English retellings.[11] As mentioned in the first chapter, this version combines the *inventio* account proper with two other stories; namely, that of a Jew who helps Helena discover the cross, is baptised and becomes bishop of Jerusalem, and that of the *hoptasia* or *visio Constantini*.[12] The *hoptasia* itself goes back to Eusebius's *Vita Constantini* (i.28–9) and focuses on the cross as sign or symbol: first, Eusebius describes Constantine and his army experiencing a vision of a cross of light in the sky, before a second vision – this time in a dream in which

---

[9] James F. Strange, 'Archeological Evidence of Jewish Believers?' in Oskar Skarsaune and Reidar Hvalvik (eds), *Jewish Believers in Jesus: The Early Centuries* (Ada, MI, 2007), 710–41, at 715. However, already in the early third century, writers such as Tertullian and Clement of Alexandria referred to the cross as 'the sign of the Lord' (Clement, *Stromata* vi.11) and to the body of believers as 'devotees of the Cross' ('crucis religiosi', Tertullian, *Apology* 16); Tertullian also mentions the Christian practice of tracing the sign of the cross on their foreheads (*De corona* 3). The crucifix – a representation of Christ on the cross – is not known before the fifth century; see Drijvers, *Helena Augusta*, 81 n. 3.

[10] *Ibid.*, 81.

[11] This is Borgehammar's 'A' version; see Borgehammar, *How the Holy Cross Was Found*, 201–78. I use the term 'legend' to refer to a tradition of related texts that contain the same core elements and may go back to a single event or source, or a smaller number of sources.

[12] See Bodden (ed.), *Old English Finding*, 32 on Greek and Syriac texts containing Constantine's vision and 24–7 on the combination of the three narratives.

Christ appears to the emperor alone with the same sign and demands that he copy and use it against his enemies – prompts Constantine to adopt the cross as his emblem and later, after he has made enquiries into its meaning, to convert to Christianity.

The *Vita Constantini*, which appears not to have been known in early medieval Britain, does not refer to the *inventio crucis*. In the *Acta Cyriaci*, on the other hand, which simplify the vision to the form in which we have already encountered it in *Elene*, it takes a central role.[13] The combination of the *inventio* and *hoptasia* stories, I will argue in the first part of this chapter, highlights the two different aspects of the cross by making each the central theme of a separate episode: (1) the material-historical dimension that lies at the heart of the crucifixion and *inventio* accounts, and forms the basis for the veneration of the True Cross and its relics as material presences; and (2) the semiotic dimension that allows the cross to act as a symbol representing a broad variety of things, including the crucifixion, the resurrection and, by extension, the Christian faith and Church. But before we move on to the representation of these aspects in the *Acta Cyriaci* and *Elene*, it is helpful to take a short detour to medieval semiotic and typological theory in order to understand how the relationship between the historically contingent nature of artefacts and their capacity to signify other things was conceptualised at the time the texts were composed.

In Augustinian semiotic theory, the material presence of the thing and the semiotic value of the sign do not necessarily contradict each other. Although Augustine divides the world into things (*res*) and signs (*signa*), he regards the distinction as functional and relative rather than ontological.[14] According to Augustine, signs, too, are things: 'Signum est enim res praeter speciem quam ingerit sensibus aluid aliquid ex se faciens in cogitationem venire' [For a sign is a thing which of itself makes some other thing come to mind, besides the impression that it presents to the senses].[15] Things, meanwhile, can also be taken as signs even if they did not previously hold that status:

> Proprie autem nunc res appelavi, quae non ad significandum aliquid adhibentur, sicuti est lignum, lapsis, pecus atque huiusmodi cetera; sed

---

[13] Kendall, 'Sign to Vision', 134–5.

[14] Giovanni Manetti, *Theories of the Sign in Classical Antiquity*, trans. Christine Richardson (Bloomington, IN, 1993), 164.

[15] Augustine, *De doctrina christiana* II.1.i; text and translation quoted from Augustine, *De doctrina christiana*, ed. and trans. R. P. H. Green (Oxford, 1995), 56–7.

Remains of the Past in Old English Literature

non illud lignum quod in aquas amaras Moysen misisse legimus, ut amaritudine carerent, neque ille lapsis quem Iacob sibi ad caput posuerat, neque illud pecus quod pro filio immolavit Abraham. Hae namque ita res sunt, ut aliarum etiam signa sint rerum.

[What I now call things in the strict sense are things such as logs, stones, sheep, and so on, which are not employed to signify something; but I do not include the log which we read that Moses threw into the bitter waters to make them lose their bitter taste [Exodus 15.25], or the stone which Jacob placed under his head [Genesis 28.11], or the sheep which Abraham sacrificed in place of his son [Genesis 22.13]. These are things, but they are at the same time signs of other things.][16]

There are thus two kinds of 'thing': on the one hand, there are things that are not used as signs but can be signified by means of signs – these Augustine calls *significabilia*; on the other hand, there are *signa* – they, too, are things, but, unlike *significabilia*, they have the capacity to signify something else.[17] In other words: all signs (*signa*) are things (*res*), but not all things are signs.[18] However, as Augustine's qualification shows, nothing prevents *significabilia* from becoming *signa* (and this applies not only to religious contexts).

Augustine divides *signa* further into 'natural signs' (*signa naturalia*) and 'intentional' or 'given signs' (*signa data*):[19] the former convey knowledge or information independent of whether they are used intentionally or not,

[16] Augustine, *De doctrina christiana* I.2.ii (ed. and trans. Green, 12–15).

[17] 'Sunt autem alia signa quorum omnis usus in significando est, sicuti verba. Nemo enim utitur verbis nisi aliquid significandi gratia' [There are other signs whose whole function consists in signifying. Words, for example: nobody uses words except in order to signify something; Augustine, *De doctrina christiana* I.2.ii (ed. and trans. Green, 14–15)]. See also Manetti, *Theories*, 165.

[18] Thus Kendall, 'Sign to Vision', 129.

[19] 'Signorum igitur alia sunt naturalia, alia data' [Some signs are natural, others given; Augustine, *De doctrina christiana* II.1.ii (ed. and trans. Green, 56–7)]. Manetti notes that the designation 'conventional signs' for Augustine's *signa data*, frequently used in modern translations, is based on the misconception that Augustine's theory mirrors Aristotle's distinction between 'natural' and 'conventional' signs. However, according to Manetti, Augustine's *signa data* correspond to a very clear communicative intention: 'It is indeed the intentional nature of animal noises which causes Augustine to include them among *signa data*, even though he does not make any precise comments on the nature of animal intentionality' (*Theories*, 166–7).

as in the case of smoke indicating fire;[20] the latter are employed by living beings in order to express their thoughts and perceptions.[21]

From the perspective of Augustinian semiotics, then, the cross can be understood as a *res* that has become a *signum* signifying something else. In this respect, it is comparable to the wood that Moses threw into the waters and the stone used by Jacob to rest his head: it, too, is a thing that attained special significance through association with a specific event. Even so, the cross *qua* symbol has a far greater semiotic range than is usually accorded to the objects named by Augustine, just as its powers considerably exceed theirs – it is not for nothing that Eusebius refers to it as a 'saving sign'.[22] Moreover, the True Cross is also a relic, albeit of a kind different from those produced from the saintly body and metonymically standing in for the person, allowing the saint to intercede on behalf of the believer: it is a

[20] 'Naturalia sunt quae sine voluntate atque ullo appetitu significandi praeter se aliquid aliud ex se cognosci faciunt, sicuti est fumus significans ignem. Non enim volens significare id facit, sed rerum expertarum animadversione et notatione cognoscitur ignem subesse, etiam si fumus solus appareat' [Natural signs are those which without a wish or any urge to signify cause something else besides themselves to be known from them, like smoke, which signifies fire. It does not signify fire because it wishes to do so; but because of our observation and attention to things that we have experienced it is realized that there is fire beneath it, even if nothing but smoke appears; Augustine, *De doctrina christiana* II.1.ii (ed. and trans. Green, 56–7)]. Augustine lists the footprint of a passing animal and the facial expression of an angry or depressed person as belonging to the same category (*ibid.*).

[21] 'Data vero signa sunt quae sibi quaeque viventia invicem dant ad demonstrandos quantum possunt motus animi sui vel sensa aut intellecta quaelibet. Nec ulla causa est nobis significandi, id est signi dandi, nisi ad depromendum et traiciendum in alterius animum id quod animo gerit qui signum dat' [Given signs are those which living things give to each other, in order to show, to the best of their ability, the emotions of their minds, or anything that they have felt or learnt. There is no reason for us to signify something (that is, to give a sign) except to express and transmit to another's mind what is in the mind of the person who gives the sign; Augustine, *De doctrina christiana* II.2.iii (ed. and trans. Green, 56–9)].

[22] As Drijvers notes, Eusebius often uses the expression in reference to the symbol, but in some instances, it seems to refer to the actual relic (*Helena Augusta*, 85–6). As Eusebius's usage demonstrates, the sign of the cross was thus regarded as possessing powers of signification beyond direct reference to the crucifixion even before the *inventio crucis* legend came into being. There is, however, a clear associative chain from the sign of the cross, which signifies the object that in turn signifies the event, to the outcome or meaning of the event, that is, the salvation effected through Christ's sacrifice.

Remains of the Past in Old English Literature

contact relic;[23] that is, an object that has acquired similar status and power through direct bodily touch.

Historically speaking, the diversification of the cross's applicability as a sign is thus paralleled by a development of its material characteristics as a tangible object: just as the semantic range of the cross, originally a *res* signifying the event of the crucifixion, grew to incorporate more and more aspects of that event's spiritual significance (without, however, losing its connection to the original artefact), so the cross as a material entity developed from the chance instrument of Christ's death to a relic, and hence to an object that not only can be venerated, but that also has the power to cause physical effects in the material world. This diversification is already implemented in the theological framework expounded by Augustine: like Jacob's stone in the latter's example, the cross is initially a *significabilium* that acquires the status of *signum* through participation in the biblical event of the crucifixion; and through the touch of Christ's body and blood, it simultaneously becomes a relic worthy of adoration as well as a medium through which divine grace is distributed and intercession is channelled.

Irvine observes that the capacity of things to signify other things is the basis of typology, 'one of the primary exegetical codes, in which an actual historical event or object indicated by verbal signs [...] becomes a sign of something else'.[24] Indeed, the whole system of *allēgoria* – that is, the exposition of Holy Scripture according to four meanings or types of interpretation – rests on the idea that not merely words, but 'all visible objects, [...] people, numbers, places and times, as well as the facts of history' have a spiritual meaning beyond the literal.[25] As Friedrich Ohly explains:

> Every individual thing evoked in language by the sound of a word, every creature created by God which is named by a word, points toward a higher meaning, is the sign of something spiritual, has a *significatio* [...]. Hence we distinguish a twofold meaning, one relating the sound of the word to the thing, the *vox* to the *res*, and a higher meaning connected to the thing, which points from the thing to something higher.[26]

From this perspective, the aforementioned dictum that 'all signs are things but not all things are signs' is no longer valid: all things are in fact *signa* signifying a higher meaning. Kendall observes that Augustine 'tellingly' refrains from explaining what exactly the specific 'things' he

---

23 On contact relics, see the corresponding entry in Frank Leslie Cross and Elizabeth Anne Livingstone (eds), *The Oxford Dictionary of the Christian Church*, 3rd edn (Oxford, 1997), 1379; and Bynum, *Christian Materiality*, 136–9.

24 Irvine, 'Literary Theory', 163.

25 Friedrich Ohly, 'The Spiritual Sense of Words in the Middle Ages', trans. David A. Wells, *Forum for Modern Language Studies*, 41:1 (2005), 18–42, at 22.

26 *Ibid.*, 20–1.

mentions (Moses's tree, Jacob's stone, Abraham's sheep) signify. Noting that all three foreshadow events in the New Testament, he argues that, from the perspective of medieval typology, their meaning was fixed: Bede called these special *signa* 'allegories', and Kendall himself refers to them as 'sacred signs'.[27] The operation that turns these 'things' into signs of future events distinguishes the historical or literal sense of a word from the three allegorical interpretations, with the former constituting the basis for a 'superstructure' of the latter.[28] These three levels of spiritual meaning are: (1) the allegorical or typological sense, relating the scriptural passage to events within sacred history; (2) the tropological or moral sense, interpreting it as a moral exemplum for the individual believer in the present; and (3) the anagogical or eschatological sense, which reads it as a reference to events beyond the world's history. All four senses have a strong temporal component in that they interpret Scripture in relation to events that lie in the past, present or future: the literal sense refers to the biblical passage in its historical setting and thus views it within the linear sequence of events that make up historical time; the typological sense connects events within sacred history, usually between the Old and New Testaments, with an Old Testament type superseded by a New Testament antitype (Jonah, for instance, can be seen as a type of Christ, because his emergence from the belly of the whale can be interpreted as prefiguring Christ's rising from the dead); the tropological sense compares the past event to the believer's present, providing moral instruction and thereby indicating a way to individual salvation; and the anagogical sense establishes a link to the eschatological future, the fate of the souls after the end of the world. However, it is not only the anagogical sense that refers to events beyond the scope of human history – as Ohly notes, all three allegorical meanings can be seen as transcending earthly history in that they extend the historically contingent into the sublime, 'making what is created intelligible with regard to its relation to eternity'.[29]

Although medieval theology taught that the spiritual interpretation of words was appropriate only when it came to the Bible, 'in practice [...] the principle could not be upheld, since in the Middle Ages – as already

---

[27] Kendall, 'Sign to Vision', 129. Kendall notes that Bede does not use the term, but maintains that such a distinction between 'sacred signs', which have a fixed meaning, and other signs open to interpretation was what Bede 'was groping towards' in his *Commentary on Genesis*. For Kendall, the cross, too, constitutes a 'sacred sign' whose meaning was fixed. While this may be true in the context of typology, we have already seen that the cross as a sign could be applied in a much wider variety of contexts from very early on.

[28] Ohly, 'Spiritual Sense', 25. Ohly notes that the term 'superstructure' in this sense is itself medieval.

[29] *Ibid.*, 26.

in classical antiquity – the allegorical method of textual interpretation was applied also to extrabiblical and pagan texts such as Homer, Virgil and Ovid, and even at the level of the vernacular languages as in the *Ovide moralisé*.[30] In order to conceptualise such extra-biblical employment, Erich Auerbach adopted the term *figura* (already employed in patristic writing, albeit in a sense that was less restricted than that of 'typology') to describe the special material-semiotic relationship between type and antitype that integrates both into sacred history and aligns them with an extratemporal, eternal truth. According to Auerbach's famous definition, *figura* denotes a nexus between two concrete historical entities or events that stand in a relationship of promise and fulfilment: 'Figural interpretation establishes a connection between two events or persons, the first of which signifies not only itself but also the second, while the second encompasses or fulfils the first.'[31] This connection is predicated upon an outward similarity or accord that exists between the two poles independent of their actual historical situation.[32] And yet, Auerbach claims, the poles are to be understood first and foremost as concrete historical realities; it is only through their interpretation that they come to be perceived as spiritually linked. On the other hand, the spiritual relationship can itself be regarded as a historical reality, since it is based on an actual accord that is part of God's vision, in which all times exist simultaneously. The two poles – figure and fulfilment – are not identical, but persist as singular, historical entities, while also participating in each other through the spiritual accord that exists between them:[33] as Heike Schlie points out, 'in *figura*, "sign" and "presence" are no contradiction but constitute a dual principle that is constitutive of the whole concept'.[34] Even so, as I have already noted, the resulting duality generates a tension that makes the concept highly productive for the interpretation of liturgical art.

Figural interpretation can thus be seen as the basis of typology, which was first used in patristic literature as a means of integrating the Old and New Testaments into a single coherent vision of history. In such a figural

---

[30] *Ibid.*, 30–1.
[31] Erich Auerbach, 'Figura', trans. Ralph Manheim, in *Scenes from the Drama of European Literature* (New York, 1959), 11–76, at 53.
[32] *Ibid.*, 29.
[33] Christian Kiening, 'Einleitung', in Christian Kiening and Katharina Mertens Fleury (eds), *Figura: Dynamiken der Zeiten und Zeichen im Mittelalter* (Würzburg, 2013), 7–20, at 16.
[34] '"Zeichen" und "Präsenz" sind in der *figura* kein Widerspruch, sondern als duales Prinzip bereits als Grundeigenschaften angelegt.' Heike Schlie, 'Der Klosterneuburger Ambo des Nikolaus von Verdun: Das Kunstwerk als *figura* zwischen Inkarnation und Wiederkunft des Logos', in Christian Kiening and Katharina Mertens Fleury (eds), *Figura: Dynamiken der Zeiten und Zeichen im Mittelalter* (Würzburg, 2013), 205–47, at 205.

vision of history, both parts maintain their concrete historical reality, but
are also linked within the wider scheme of providential history in which
they signify a third, still absent, reality – a reality that they reveal partly,
but that will only become fully manifest in the second *parousia*. *Figura*
thus establishes a model of history based on three points of reference:
(1) promise; (2) first fulfilment and second promise; and (3) ultimate fulfilment. Paradoxically, while the vision is ultimately teleological in that
it looks forward to a transcendental truth at the end of history, it is also
non-linear, since it privileges spiritual significance over cause and effect.

Pheng Cheah has argued that all teleology is ultimately 'circular and
self-returning', since 'in a teleological history, the end or final cause is not
external but originally immanent in its effect'.[35] In other words: the result
is already inherent in the cause and thus inscribed into the process, which
it in turn shapes in order to arrive at the preconceived outcome. This
is obviously true of sacred history, which is the unfolding of a process
towards an end predetermined by God. Yet within the teleological circularity described by Cheah, events still follow each other in a linear
fashion. In a figural understanding of history, by contrast, the events are
not necessarily sequentially connected (or at least do not follow directly
upon each other), but can rather be regarded as cross-referencing each
other across the entire panorama of historical time. Thus, whereas the
teleological circularity outlined by Cheah is still compatible in its linearity with a perception that regards time as a mechanical succession of
events governed by cause and effect (even when it is not oriented towards
a specific *telos*), figural history posits a second temporality besides the
sequential unfolding of historical time: a temporality that interconnects
different historical events while disregarding their actual position within
the linear succession of historical time. Indeed, as Schlie points out, in a
certain sense, *figura* is even a-temporal, since it suggests that the events,
in participating in each other, are contemporaneous: 'In God, there is no
differentia temporis.'[36]

As a consequence, the pan-historical nature of *figura*'s three-stage
model opens up the possibility for post-biblical events to participate in
providential history, since any event can be perceived, simultaneously, as
figure and fulfilment and hence as referring back to an event in the past
and as looking forward to something that has yet to transpire. Moreover,
unlike typology in the strict sense, figural interpretation is not restricted
to Scripture, but can also be applied to secular events, persons and objects.
With respect to medieval liturgical art, Schlie points out, this means that

---

[35] Pheng Cheah, *What is a World? On Postcolonial Literature as World Literature*
(Durham, NC, 2016), 6–7 (all quotations are from 7).

[36] 'Bei Gott gibt es keine *differentia temporis*.' Schlie, 'Klosterneuburger Ambo',
205.

Remains of the Past in Old English Literature

the artwork refers back to the New Testament antitypes of Old Testament events, but also has the potential of prefiguring the Second Coming of Christ[37] – the work of art, she states, 'constitutes a membrane on which is projected and captured that which only becomes representable postfigurally after the incarnation of the Logos and which can only be indicated prefigurally before the Second Coming, because it is unfathomable'. As a material and hence historical reality that simultaneously references something else, the artefact is itself a *figura*.[38] The medieval work of art can thus be regarded as a historical entity that stands in for – and, as Christian Kiening points out, also participates in – something even more valid than itself: it becomes a medium, as Aquinas defines it, that mediates between the two poles it represents.[39]

Kiening's notion of *figura* goes beyond Auerbach's, but it draws attention to a tension already present in the latter's conception of the term: if the two poles of *figura* can represent each other, as well as a transcendental third, there must exist some measure of spiritual identity between them, in spite of their historical – and hence also their material – distinctness. From this perspective, then, *figura* can be said to derive its significance from the special tension that exists between the historical and the spiritual dimensions of the two poles of reference.

This tension between the historical and figural dimensions of an entity also characterises Augustinian semiotics, and hence the interpretation of practices that draw attention to the material and semiotic aspects of the cross. In spite of Augustine's theological exploration of the material-semiotic double nature of signs and things, these two aspects of the cross – a sign that is also a thing and a singular relic hallowed by Christ's touch – are not fully reconciled, because the sign, too, partakes in the salvatory nature of the artefact. According to Reinhard Hempelmann, this is a characteristic shared by all sacraments (in the wide sense of the term as applied by Augustine):

---

[37] *Ibid.*, 242.
[38] '[Das Kunstwerk] bildet eine Membran, an der sich durch die Zeiten hindurch das abbildet und anschaulich einfängt, was postfigurativ nach der Inkarnation des Logos darstellbar wird und präfigurativ vor der Wiederkunft nur angedeutet werden kann, weil es unauslotbar ist. Auch das Bild ist als materielles, verweisendes Ereignis in einem innergeschichtlichen Zusammenhang *figura*.' *Ibid.*, 246.
[39] 'Sie repräsentiert ein Anderes, Gültig(er)es, partizipiert aber auch an diesem – das wäre die Definition des *medium*, das nach Thomas von Aquin etwas von den Extremen, zwischen denen es vermittelt, haben muss.' Kiening, 'Einleitung', 16.

Visions of the Holy Cross

In Augustine, there is a tension, not always resolved, between his neo-platonically-oriented semiotic theory, for which the scheme of archetype and image is constitutive, and the biblical and ecclesiastical orientation of his thought. His sacramental theory is characterised by his hovering between a significational-spiritualistic and an effective-realistic conception, an ambivalence that had a considerable impact on later developments [in the field of sign theory].[40]

The ambiguity between the material and semiotic dimensions of objects was often explored, most productively in exegetical writing, but some authors appear to have felt uncomfortable with it, or at least chose to privilege one aspect over the other. Eusebius's *Vita Constantini* may be one example of a certain tendency in early patristic literature to downplay the material-historical dimension of sacred objects.[41] In spite of the fact that Eusebius provides the earliest reference to Constantine's vision, he is utterly silent on the discovery of the True Cross that supposedly took place during the emperor's reign. Given that Eusebius was Constantine's contemporary and enjoyed the emperor's favour, this could be taken as evidence that the legend was a later invention. On the other hand, Cyril of Jerusalem's *Catecheses*, composed in the 340s (and thus within thirty years of the alleged discovery), already describes the *lignum crucis*, 'the wood of the cross', as being distributed and venerated 'all over the world'; moreover, in a letter to Emperor Constantius II, written in 351, Cyril refers explicitly to the *inventio* as having taken place during Constantine's reign.[42] In addition, Drijvers has argued that a reference in Constantine's letter to Macarius, quoted in Eusebius's *Vita Constantini*, to a 'token of that holiest Passion' (a phrase that Eusebius uses elsewhere in the *Vita* in reference to the cross) that had long been hidden in the earth could well

---

[40] 'Augustins neuplatonisch orientierte Zeichentheorie, für die das Urbild-Abbild-Schema konstitutiv ist, steht bei ihm in nicht immer gelöster Spannung zur biblischen und kirchlichen Orientierung seines Denkens. Durch seine Sakramentenlehre zieht sich eine schwebende Doppeldeutigkeit von signifikativ-spiritualistischer und effektiv-realistischer Auffassung, die für die weitere Entwicklung bedeutsam wurde.' Reinhard Hempelmann, *Sakrament als Ort der Vermittlung des Heils: Sakramententheologie im evangelisch-katholischen Dialog* (Göttingen, 1992), 50. Today's Roman Catholic limitation to seven sacraments was only instituted by the Council of Trent (1545–63), and does not apply to Early Christianity (nor, indeed, to the Orthodox Churches).

[41] The reverse is true of Rufinus' late fourth-century account of the *inventio*, however, which considers the cross only as material relic; see Drijvers, *Helena Augusta*, 79–80.

[42] Quoted in Drijvers, *Helena Augusta*, 81–2: '[...] in the days of your imperial father, Constantine of blessed memory, the saving wood of the Cross was found in Jerusalem (divine grace granting the finding of the long hidden holy places to one who nobly aspired to sanctity) [...].'

Remains of the Past in Old English Literature

refer to the relics of the cross, although Eusebius makes it appear as if it referred to the Holy Sepulchre.[43] If one follows this interpretation, the *Vita Constantini* is actively suppressing the discovery of the True Cross. And indeed: there is a rather striking discrepancy between Eusebius's and Cyril's accounts, which are separated by a gap of no more than about a decade. There is no shortage of plausible (and not necessarily mutually exclusive) explanations: for example, the authenticity of the relic may already have been contested at the time of its discovery.[44] Political reasons are another possibility: from the 320s, the sees of Jerusalem and Caesarea were struggling for dominance in Palestine (a struggle that Caesarea eventually lost in the fifth century, when Jerusalem became a patriarchate), so that the discovery of the True Cross, followed by the building of a basilica on the site in which the relics were displayed, would have been an event readily exploited by the bishops of Jerusalem (like Cyril) to boost the importance of their bishopric, while being downplayed by the bishops of Caesarea (Eusebius's see).

While the latter argument in particular is historically persuasive, the omission might also have to do with Eusebius's marked tendency to rate spiritual over material concerns.[45] According to Borgehammar, Eusebius regarded 'material things to be of value only insofar as they are able to elevate the mind. [...] Relics and holy places were not important, and could even be dangerous if over-emphasized'. Arguably, this was especially important in the case of the cross, since references to Christ's suffering might not only have entailed 'improper notions about the Deity', but even endangered the acceptance of the Christian doctrine as the newly adopted religion of the Empire:

> As a symbol, the Cross is a vehicle of revelation, telling about the sublime and spiritually 'safe' aspects of Redemption. It can be construed as a banner, a sign of victory over death and all evil; and in particular, in view of Constantine's use of it, it is a very opportune symbol of the defeat of paganism and the Christianization of the Empire. But as a beam of wood, together with rusty nails which once painfully had pierced human flesh, it makes Christianity seem dangerously primitive.[46]

Whatever the reasons for his silence, it is clear that Eusebius was less interested in the material side of sacred objects (and hence in the double nature of signs) than, for instance, Augustine. In light of this, it is all the more striking that Eusebius's account of Constantine's vision became

---

[43] *Ibid.*, 84–5.
[44] I here follow Drijvers's discussion, who quotes P. W. L. Walker and Ze'ev Rubin for the respective theories (*Helena Augusta*, 87–8).
[45] Borgehammar, *How the Holy Cross Was Found*, 116–17.
[46] *Ibid.*, 116–17.

such an integral part of the *inventio crucis* tradition, and indeed the means by which the double nature of the cross was integrated into the legend as a structural feature.

Artefact and Sign – The Cross's Double Materiality in the Acta Cyriaci *and* Elene

Having explored the tension between the material and spiritual aspects of the cross, I will now return to the Old English *Elene* and its probable source, the Latin *Acta Cyriaci*. In the first chapter, I discussed *Elene* as a narrative of *translatio* – the discovery and subsequent adulation of the True Cross and its relics, directed and supervised by Roman officials, serving to bolster Roman imperial claims. The concept of *translatio*, I argued, involves a specific form of temporality that, though obviously teleological and hence (in Cheah's words) 'circular and self-returning',[47] dispenses both with a clear logic of cause and effect and a direct form of sequentiality. In this section, I will examine *Elene*'s distinctive interplay of linear-historical and figural temporalities.

The poem's interest in figural relationships has been pointed out by a number of scholars, most prominently by Thomas D. Hill, who devoted several articles to the topic. Hill argued that *Elene* (and its sources) should be interpreted – and were interpreted at the time they were composed – 'as essentially symbolic rather than as historical narratives'. The legend, he says, 'was understood not as a straightforward historical event but as a symbolic event in which the history of the fourth century, the Passion of Jesus, and the ongoing tradition of Christian worship and praxis in the medieval world were linked together'.[48] Hill bases his concept of 'history' on a modern understanding of the term, however, noting, for instance, that there was 'no substantial Jewish community in Jerusalem' in the age of Constantine or that, historically speaking, the Judas of the legend 'cannot be the brother of Stephen the proto-martyr' and that the poem's author should have known better.[49] Yet as pointed out above, from a medieval theological perspective, historical and figural time did not constitute opposing principles. The events in the legend were no less historical from a medieval perspective because they had figural significance; indeed, they could only acquire their figural meaning by being part of the general scheme of the *historia sacra*.

[47] Cheah, *What is a World*, 7.
[48] Hill, 'Time, Liturgy', 158, 159; see also Hill, 'Sapiential Structure', 166; Irvine, 'Literary Theory'.
[49] Hill, 'Time, Liturgy', 158, 159.

Remains of the Past in Old English Literature

In what follows, I will contend that *Elene* negotiates the relationship between historical and figural time through the interplay of the cross's semiotic function as a sign and its material properties as a historical artefact. Drawing on Irvine's discussion of *Elene*, I will argue that whereas the *Acta* attempt to keep apart the material and the semiotic aspects of the cross by linking them almost exclusively to the *hoptasia* and *inventio* episodes, respectively, *Elene* brings the two aspects together, presenting the cross as a material object that also acts as a multivalent sign. At the same time, the poem also draws attention to the intermediary status of the cross as a *significabilium* that simultaneously acts as a *signum*, and hence to the temporal dimension of semiosis: as a sign, the cross is capable of highlighting its different material-historical configurations while also referencing an extra-temporal, spiritual truth. *Elene* thus emphasises two different temporalities interlocking in the cross, the historical and the figural; a feature that is given even greater prominence in *The Dream of the Rood*, discussed in the following section.

The *Acta Cyriaci* are perhaps the most influential version of the *inventio crucis* legend in the medieval West.[50] Despite the fact that *Elene* seems to be based on some version of the *Acta Cyriaci* – the closest known parallel being the one found in St Gall manuscript 225[51] – the two works employ very different strategies when it comes to addressing the interplay of semiotic and material aspects of the cross that has been introduced into the story by the combination of the *visio* and *inventio* accounts.

In the *Acta Cyriaci*, the distinction between these two configurations is expressed in fairly straightforward terms: in the context of Constantine's vision and his battle against the barbarians, the text uses the term *signum crucis* (or *signum crucis Christi*), whereas in those cases where the material artefact is concerned, it speaks of the 'wood of the cross' (*lignum crucis*) or, even more tellingly, simply of the 'cross' (*crux*). This suggests, first, that the *Acta* are not primarily interested in drawing attention to the concurrence of the semiotic and material aspects of the cross, but rather find each applicable in different contexts. Second, the parallel genitive constructions *signum crucis* [sign of the cross] and *lignum crucis* [wood of the cross] refer back directly to the artefact, that is, to the *crux* proper: just as the 'wood' in question is that of the True Cross, so is the heavenly apparition a sign pointing towards the one cross upon which Christ was put to death. In the *Acta*, the semiotic range of the cross as a sign is thus limited almost entirely to the object used in the crucifixion. This is

---

[50] See further Bodden (ed.), *Old English Finding*, 24–8. Quotations from the *Acta Cyriaci* follow Holder's edition (*Inventio sanctae crucis*), cited by line and using the readings from St Gall manuscript 225 (the version closest to *Elene*).

[51] Gradon (ed.), *Cynewulf's Elene*, 19–20.

208

Visions of the Holy Cross

true even of the passages that highlight the emblem's capacity to grant victory. Here, too, the sign of the cross appears to stand exclusively for the historical cross: the sign is a heavenly sign *from* God ('hoc signum celestis Dī est'; lines 33–4), but it does not, as far as the text is concerned, signify God or anything else apart from the cross. Rather, divine power is presented as mediated or channelled through the object: 'et dedit D[eu]s in illa die uictoriam regi Constantino *per uirtutem sanctae crucis*' [and God granted victory on that day to King Constantine *by virtue of the Holy Cross*; my emphasis; lines 26–7].

Unlike Eusebius, then, the *Acta Cyriaci* are chiefly concerned with the properties of the cross as a material artefact, or, more precisely, as a relic. As I pointed out in the first chapter, *Elene*'s description of the *inventio crucis* accords with Otter's list of core elements that typically characterise medieval *inventiones*.[52] The same holds true for the *Acta*: the search for the object is emphasised; there is an audience present; the location where the cross is hidden is indicated by a pleasant-smelling smoke rising from the ground; and when the finders are unable to ascertain which of the three crosses they have found was the instrument of Christ's Passion, a miracle confirms the identity of the 'true' one. Appropriately for a holy relic, this miracle is channelled through the object itself: one after the other, the three crosses are placed over a corpse; at the touch of the third, the dead man rises, confirming that this is the one upon which Christ was crucified. Its miraculous powers ascertained, the True Cross is adored by the onlookers; Aelena (Helena) bedecks it with gold and precious stones, places it in a silver reliquary and eventually builds a church over the spot where it was found. Later, another search reveals the nails with which Christ was fastened to the cross. Again, these relics are employed in a way that renders their salvatory properties especially effective: as in *Elene*, they are made into a bit for the bridle-chain of Constantine's horse, rendering the emperor invincible against all enemies.

Whereas Eusebius's account of Constantine's vision exclusively features the cross as a sign, ignoring not only the material dimension of the historical artefact but also that of the heavenly apparition (which is at least potentially material, too, as the *Acta Cyrici* suggest when they describe it as 'fashioned out of pure light' [ex lumine claro constitutum; lines 17–18]), the *Acta Cyriaci* clearly privilege the material properties of the True Cross as a relic. The semiotic dimension of the cross as a symbol is almost exclusively restricted to the historical artefact; only once does it feature as 'signum Xpi' [the sign of Christ], and St Galls manuscript 225, *Elene*'s closest parallel, even omits this single reference, using instead the expression 'signum crucis' (line 21).

---

[52] See Otter, *Inventiones*, 28–9; and Chapter 1, 30, of the present study.

Remains of the Past in Old English Literature

As Caroline Walker Bynum points out in the context of the late medieval adoration of material objects, attitudes towards the agency and power of sacred artefacts tended to be paradoxical, even within theological theorisations: although it was often maintained that such items 'merely referred beyond themselves or triggered a power other than their own', this was not reflected in actual practices, which often located the source of power within the object in question, and 'the same theologians who theorized relics and images as pointing beyond themselves vehemently condemned those who denied their veneration'.[53] As for bodily relics, their function as mediators channelling divine intercession is best understood as deriving from a metonymic relationship with the saint from whose body they stem. Even in the case of contact relics such as the True Cross, the relic's power is based on direct bodily contact.[54] The cross's potency thus derives from its association with Christ, and even if it could be interpreted typologically, that is, as standing for Christ himself, the relationship would not be purely semiotic but also at least partly based on an identity of sorts.[55] The *Acta Cyriaci*, whose primary focus is the *inventio*, consequently foreground the cross as a relic, downplaying its semiotic potential as a sign to signify anything apart from the True Cross: as far as the text is concerned, the 'signum crucis' always refers back to the material artefact.

Elene shares the *Acta Cyriaci*'s interest in the cross as a relic, but it complicates its source's neat division of semiotic and material aspects: in *Elene*, as Irvine rightly observes, the True Cross constitutes a relic that is simultaneously a multivalent sign.[56] The *Acta* use the expression 'signum crucis' almost exclusively in the context of Constantine's vision, and then always to signify the material object whose recovery it inspires, while consistently designating the relic itself with the term 'lignum crucis'. *Elene*, on the other hand, eschews a binary distinction between *signum* and *lignum*, opting instead to stress the concurrence of the cross's material and semiotic dimensions with a whole panoply of terms including (separately and in various compounds)[57] *rod* [rood, cross], *treo* [tree], *beam* [tree, wooden beam] and *galga* [gallows] when referring to the historical cross, and *tacn* and *beacen* [token, mark, sign, signal, emblem] in lieu of the Latin *signum*. *Elene*'s increased terminological repertoire is in keeping with the Old English poetic device of variation, the use of multiple near-synonymous words to describe the same object – a technique that not only

---

[53] Bynum, *Christian Materiality*, 30.
[54] Irvine, 'Literary Theory', 171.
[55] Kendall, 'Sign to Vision', 139.
[56] Irvine, 'Literary Theory', 171.
[57] Compounds include *sigebeam* [victory-tree], *wuldres treo* [tree of glory], *lifes treo* [tree of life], *rode treo* [rood tree], *mære treo* [victory-tree], *halig treo* [holy tree], *sigores tacn* [sign of victory] and *sigebeacen/sigorbeacen* [sign of victory].

Visions of the Holy Cross

affords greater stylistic freedom,[58] but also allows a poem to approach its subject matter from more than one angle, highlighting different aspects or characteristics and thus giving the impression of multidimensionality.[59] More importantly in our context, *Elene*'s expanded terminology blurs the distinction between different configurations (tree, wooden object, gallows, emblem, sign), thereby allowing the poem to negotiate the cross as an ambiguous entity whose material and semiotic aspects are not as easily divisible as the Latin text of the *Acta Cyriaci* makes it appear. In addition, whereas the *Acta* suggest that the cross as a *signum* always signifies the historical object, when *Elene* employs the words *tacn* or *beacen*, the nature of the referent frequently remains ambiguous or undisclosed: if the cross is a sign, what exactly does it signify?

As I argued in the first chapter, this uncertainty constitutes an important element in *Elene*'s depiction of the actual *inventio*. To recapitulate, when Judas first beholds the cross, still lying in the freshly dug pit, the poem states:

Þa wæs modgemynd   myclum geblissod,
hige onhyrded,   þurh þæt halige treo,
inbryrded breostsefa,   syððan beacen geseh,
halig under hrusan.

[Then was [his] mind much gladdened, [his] heart strengthened, through that holy tree, [his] heart inspired, when he saw the sign, holy under the earth; lines 839–42a]

At first glance, the use, within two successive lines, of the expressions 'halig treow' and 'beacen' (lines 840–1) appears to constitute no more than a typical instance of poetic variation, with both terms referring to the object just excavated. But if 'halig treow' and 'beacen' can both denote the same entity, then this means that this entity is both: the 'holy tree' is simultaneously a 'sign'/'token'/'emblem' – in effect, then, the two terms denote different aspects of one and the same thing. In suggesting that the cross is both a 'holy tree' and a 'sign', the poem draws attention to the artefact's ability to act as a *signum datum*, a thing signifying something else – although, strikingly, the text remains silent as to what the cross as a *beacen* signifies. I have argued in the first chapter that given the way Judas's prayer is phrased, and given that he is already on the verge of accepting the Christian truth, the text's choice of words mirrors Judas's perception of the object he has found – and, indeed, of the very discovery of the object – as a sign of God's power and grace. To him, the fact that

---

[58] See Sara M. Pons-Sanz, 'Old English Style', in Violeta Sotirova (ed.), *Bloomsbury Companion to Stylistics* (London, 2015), 569–82.
[59] Fred C. Robinson, Beowulf *and the Appositive Style* (Knoxville, TN, 1985).

Remains of the Past in Old English Literature

a fragrant smoke did indeed rise above the earth, just as he had asked, and that the spot indicated by the smoke does indeed contain a cross (or, rather, three crosses), signals God's capacity and willingness to respond to his prayer. The sight of the material object – an artefact that the miracle indicates must be the very object used to crucify Christ – also authenticates the historical account, proving to Judas that the Christian tradition (of which he has learned through his father and grandfather) is historically accurate. To Judas, the sight of the cross thus signifies both the theological and the historical truth of Christianity (and hence its superiority over the Jewish tradition), a realisation that finally accomplishes his conversion. And yet, even while I would argue that this is the most straightforward interpretation of the passage, the very fact that the text does not make explicit what exactly the *beacen* is supposed to signify emphasises the term's potential for being interpreted in a variety of ways. What is being highlighted, then, are not only to the mechanisms by which an object – even an object that is already a sign – can attain new meaning, but also the potential polyvalence of all *signa data*.

Both tendencies, the blurring of categories and the ambiguity surrounding the signified, are already apparent in the poem's description of Constantine's vision. The *Acta* describe the scene as follows:

> Illa uero nocte uenit uir splendedissimus et suscitauit eu[m], dix[it] q[ue] ei, Constantine noli timere sed respice sursum in celu[m] et uide[,] et intendens in caelu[m], uidit signum crucis Christi ex lumine claro constitutum et sup[er] litteris titulum scriptu[m] In hoc uince.

> [That very night there came a man surrounded by radiance and woke him, and said to him, 'Constantine, don't be afraid but look up into the sky and see', and looking at the sky he saw the sign of Christ's Cross, fashioned out of pure light, and above it was written in letters the title 'In this conquer'; lines 13–19.]

The corresponding passage in *Elene* is considerably longer:

> Þa wearð on slæpe   sylfum ætywed
> þam casere,   þær he on corðre swæf,
> sigerofum gesegen   swefnes woma.
> Þuhte him wlitescyne   on weres hade
> hwit ond hiwbeorht   hæleða nathwylc
> geywed ænlicra   þonne he ær oððe sið
> gesege under swegle.   He of slæpe onbrægd,
> eofurcumble beþeaht.   Him se ar hraðe,
> wlitig wuldres boda,   wið þingode
> ond be naman nemde,   (nihthelm toglad):
> 'Constantinus,   heht þe cyning engla,
> wyrda wealdend,   wære beodan,

212

Visions of the Holy Cross

duguða dryhten.   Ne ondræd þu ðe,
ðeah þe elþeodige   egesan hwopan,
heardre hilde.   þu to heofenum beseoh
on wuldres weard,   þær ðu wraðe findest,
sigores tacen.'   He wæs sona gearu
þurh þæs halgan hæs,   hreðerlocan onspeon,
up locade,   swa him se ar abead,
fæle friðowebba.   Geseah he frætwum beorht
wliti wuldres treo   ofer wolcna hrof,
golde geglenged,   (gimmas lixtan);
wæs se blaca beam   bocstafum awriten,
beorhte ond leohte: 'Mid þys beacne ðu
on þam frecnan fære   feond oferswiðesð,
geletest lað werod.'

[Then, during his sleep, a triumphant sign was revealed to the emperor
himself when he slept among the company, the revelation of a dream.
It seemed to him that a beautiful person in the form of a man, white
and bright of colour, a man unknown, appeared, unlike any he had
seen before or of late under heaven. He started from his sleep, covered
by the boar-banner. To him the angel hastened, the beautiful messenger of glory, and called him by name (the night-helm glided away):
'Constantine, the King of Angels, the Ruler of Destinies, has commanded
to offer you a pledge, the Lord of Peoples. Be not afraid, although a
foreign people may threaten you with terror, with harsh battle. Look
up to heaven, upon the guardian of wonders, there you find support, a
sign of victory.' He was immediately ready, by that holy command, to
unlock his breast, he looked up, as the messenger had bidden him, the
true peace-weaver. He saw bright ornaments, a beautiful tree of glory
over the roof of clouds, adorned with gold (gems glistened); the shining
beam was inscribed with letters, bright and light: 'With this sign you
will overcome the enemy in that terrible danger, hinder the harmful
troop.' Lines 69–94a.]

Elene expands the heavenly messenger's speech and provides a more
detailed description of the cross. Again, two different terms are employed
to express two configurations: 'treo' and 'beacen'. Constantine sees 'a
beautiful tree of glory' ('wliti wuldres treo'; line 89a) whose inscription
designates it a 'beacen', mirroring the use of the terms 'halig treo' and
'beacen' in the description of the *inventio* later in the poem – the description of the heavenly cross in the *visio* thus linguistically prefigures the
account of the *inventio*.

As in the later passage, we are left uncertain what the 'beacen' signifies.
In the *Acta*, we have seen, the heavenly cross is interpreted as a sign of
the True Cross, whose *inventio* it prefigures. In *Elene*, the situation is less

clear. The heavenly messenger who wakes Constantine to alert him to the vision introduces it as 'sigores tacen' [sign of victory; line 80], a phrase usually signifying Christ's victory over death, although in this case, and at this point in the narrative, it would also, and perhaps more obviously, signify the victory of the righteous emperor over his enemies; at least, that is how Constantine is bound to understand the message, given that he has not yet heard about the crucifixion (nor indeed about the Christian faith). For Constantine, then, the heavenly cross initially signifies no more than an abstract concept – victory – and, within the context of the battle at hand, a more concrete future event; namely, his own immanent triumph over the enemy.

Even so, the miraculous nature of the vision suggests to the emperor that there must be more to the sign than the heavenly messenger and the cross's inscription revealed: once returned to Rome, he immediately starts to enquire 'hwæt se god wære / [...] þe þis his beacen wæs' [what God it might be [...] whose emblem this was; lines 161b–2]. It is thus the obvious insufficiency of the explanation afforded by the messenger and the inscription that awakens Constantine's curiosity and leads, in due course, to his conversion. What is more, the use of the phrase 'wliti wuldres treo' in the description of the vision's heavenly cross not only prefigures Constantine's future knowledge of the crucifixion, which entails an awareness of the nature of the artefact from which its meaning as a sign emerges, but also extends the semiotic relationship between the heavenly *beacen* and whatever it signifies – God's victory over death, the emperor's victory over his enemies – by an additional step. In the *Acta*, the heavenly cross signifies the True Cross – a point made explicit by the expression 'signum crucis', literally the 'sign of the cross' – but the text does not mention any semiotic dimension that this True Cross itself might possess. It is *in* the sign of the cross ('*in* hoc [signo]', my emphasis) that Constantine will conquer, but what the cross itself means remains open. In *Elene*, too, the heavenly cross signifies the True Cross, but that True Cross is in turn invested with meaning: as 'sigores tacen' [a sign of victory; line 80], it signifies triumph in battle. In contrast to the *Acta*, then, which downplay the cross's nature as a sign by making the vision appear as if it exclusively referred to the relic whose excavation the text goes on to recount, *Elene* embeds the cross in a complex network of signification.

There is another significant difference between the *Acta*'s description of the *visio* and *Elene*'s; namely, with regard to the temporal dimension of the double-natured cross. *Elene* temporalises the semiotic relationship between the heavenly sign and the historical artefact through its description of the celestial apparition, whose visual details ('golde geglenged, (gimmas lixtan)' [adorned with gold (gems glistened); line 90] suggest that Constantine does not only see a vision of a cross-shaped sign, but indeed one that reflects the artefact's future state as a jewel-studded relic raised for adoration. The sign's materiality, too, is anything but unequivocal in *Elene*. Whereas in the *Acta Cyriaci* the cross in the sky is said to be 'fashioned out of pure light' ('ex lumine claro constitutum'; lines 17–18), *Elene* uses the phrase 'se blaca beam' (line 91). As in modern English, Old English *beam* is semantically ambiguous; 'se blaca beam' could thus denote either a brightly polished wooden beam or a shining ray of light. The additional descriptive elements – 'golde geglenged' [adorned with gold] and 'gimmas lixtan' [gems glistened; both line 90] suggest the former, implying that Constantine does not, in fact, witness a sign of light (in itself also material, but nonetheless only a sign referencing something else), but rather a vision of the *actual* wooden cross in its future state as exalted relic, covered with gold and gems – that is, in precisely the condition in which we encounter it later in the poem (lines 998b–1016) – and possibly encased in a reliquary, which would likewise take the shape of a cross, further blurring the distinction between a form of representation (in this case, the work of art symbolising the cross) and the relic that it contains.[60]

If we follow this line of argument, Constantine would be experiencing a prophetic vision of the exalted cross strikingly similar to the one that opens *The Dream of the Rood*, a poem found within a few folios from *Elene* in its manuscript context of the Vercelli Book. Read as a visual prophecy of the cross's future state, Constantine's vision pre-empts the story's outcome, narratively enacting the circularity attributed by Cheah to all teleology as 'the unfolding of, the return to, and the completion of an immanent end'.[61] In other words, Constantine first encounters the cross in a vision in which it appears as a relic adorned and possibly enshrined in a reliquary, a state that the emperor then strives to bring about. If the description of Constantine's vision linguistically prefigures the cross's *inventio*, the visual details supplied in the description suggest that it simultaneously prefigures its *translatio*, and that it does so in a material configuration that in fact postdates both events. From this perspective, all of Constantine's and Elene's subsequent actions can be regarded as being directed at realising and bringing to fruition a state of affairs already envisioned at the beginning of the poem, very much in keeping with interpretations of sacred history as the unfolding of a chain of events already predetermined – or at least anticipated – by God: a figural interpretation of providential history *par excellence*.

Elene's depiction of Constantine's vision thus expresses a complex semiotic operation that can be interpreted, in figural terms, as a postfigu-

---

[60] Irvine draws attention to the parallel between *Elene* and *The Dream of the Rood*, noting that the two poems here echo the language typically used to describe relics, but he does not address the temporal dimension of the description ('Literary Theory', 167).

[61] Cheah, *What is a World*, 7.

215

Remains of the Past in Old English Literature

ral image of the True Cross whose visual details prefigure its exalted state after the *translatio*. When read along these lines, the *visio*'s heavenly cross not only refers back to the True Cross and its role within sacred history – particularly with regard to the crucifixion – but also looks forward to events that at this point still lie in the future: Constantine's immanent military victory and subsequent conversion, the *inventio* and *translatio crucis*, and, inevitably, the ultimate victory of Christianity at the end of days, when all peoples will worship God, as envisioned in Isaiah 2.2–4:

> 2 et erit in novissimis diebus praeparatus mons domus Domini in vertice montium et elevabitur super colles et fluent ad eum omnes gentes 3 et ibunt populi multi et dicent venite et ascendamus ad montem Domini et ad domum Dei Iacob et docebit nos vias suas et ambulabimus in semitis eius quia de Sion exibit lex et verbum Domini de Hierusalem 4 et iudicabit gentes et arguet populos multos et conflabunt gladios suos in vomeres et lanceas suas in falces non levabit gens contra gentem gladium nec exercebuntur ultra ad proelium

> [2 And in the last days the mountain of the house of the Lord shall be prepared on the top of mountains, and it shall be exalted above the hills, and all nations shall flow unto it. 3 And many people shall go, and say: Come and let us go up to the mountain of the Lord, and to the house of the God of Jacob, and he will teach us his ways, and we will walk in his paths: for the law shall come forth from Sion, and the word of the Lord from Jerusalem. 4 And he shall judge the Gentiles, and rebuke many people: and they shall turn their swords into ploughshares, and their spears into sickles: nation shall not lift up sword against nation, neither shall they be exercised any more to war.]

The figural relationship between personal and universal conversion finds its most prominent expression in the figure of Judas Cyriacus, whose very name suggests a typological reading in that it harks back to Judas Iscariot, who, in the biblical narrative, betrayed Jesus to the Romans. As Irvine observes, while being 'at first presented as a deceitful rhetorician', *Elene*'s Judas Cyriacus 'undoes the treachery of the earlier Judas' through his later conversion.[62] As the antitype to the Judas of the Gospel, *Elene*'s Judas Cyriacus fulfils the earlier Judas's broken promise as a disciple of Christ. At the same time, the epithet 'Judas' links both bearers to the Jewish nation more generally. Hill points out that '"Judas" obviously suggests the "Judaei"', noting also that 'the Judas of the New Testament was traditionally interpreted as a type of the unbelieving Jews'.[63] Judas Cyriacus's conversion thus not only 'sets right' the earlier Judas's betrayal, but also

---

[62] Irvine, 'Literary Theory', 169.
[63] Hill, 'Sapiential Structure', 164.

Visions of the Holy Cross

prefigures the conversion of the Jews, which was regarded as the final prerequisite to be met before the second *parousia*.[64] Anagogically speaking, the heavenly cross of Constantine's vision can therefore be interpreted as gesturing even beyond the end of time, when the cross, as the tree of life, signifies salvation and hence the final victory over death.

Yet if the cross in *Elene* functions as a figural sign, the poem also acknowledges its material properties as a relic: like other relics, its touch has the capacity to heal and even to bring the dead back to life – in *Elene*, as in the *Acta*, the miracle that confirms the identity of the True Cross consists in just such a feat; and again like other relics, the cross is set up in a church for veneration, presumably to be touched and kissed so as to elicit divine intercession. *Elene*'s tendency, towards the end of the poem, to employ terms that stress the cross's semiotic nature – for instance, it is referred to as *sigebeacen* [a sign of victory; line 974a] when its discovery is made public – might seem to reduce this material potential, but on the level of narration, the poem time and again foregrounds the cross's materiality as an artefact and its potential power as a relic. In other words, even as *Elene* appears to follow the tendency adopted by early Christian writers to downplay the material-historical dimension of the cross (as noted by Drijvers and Borgehammar),[65] the poem in fact emphasises it.

The dual nature that characterises the cross as a historically contingent artefact and an extra-temporal sign extends to the Holy Nails. The repurposing of the latter as a bit for Constantine's bridle chain draws attention to their materiality as pieces of metal that can be reshaped into other metal objects, but it also stresses the fact that their sacred status survives their material transformation. At the same time, the poem emphasises that the product of this transformation can also be understood as a *beacen*:

> Cuþ þæt gewyrðeð þæt þæs cyninges sceal
> mearh under modegum midlum geweorðod,
> bridelshringum. Bið þæt beacen gode
> halig nemned, ond se hwæteadig,
> wigge weorðod, se þæt wicg byrð.

> [It will be known that this king's horse will be distinguished among the brave by its bit and bridle-ring. That emblem shall be named holy to God, and the fortunate one, honoured in war, whom that steed bears; lines 1191–5.]

---

[64] While this is not the place to discuss this issue, the disastrous consequences of this belief must not go unmentioned, from Luther's support of medieval pogroms against Jews should they be unwilling to convert to similarly apologetic attitudes towards the Holocaust within the twentieth-century Churches.

[65] Borgehammar, *How the Holy Cross Was Found*, 116–17.

Remains of the Past in Old English Literature

Nicholas Howe rightly observes that the use of the term *beacen* here suggests that 'the literal [...] [is] made figurative through this process [of transformation]. [...] The object made of the nails is at once a *midl* and a *bæcen*, a bit and a sign, that will ensure the triumph of the Christian emperor'[66] – as a sign, the bit attests, besides other possible meanings, that Constantine's rule and actions are divinely sanctioned. But when Howe contends that 'most astonishingly, [Elene] has transformed a literal object into a figurative sign', this seems to imply that the bit has lost its literal meaning as a material object,[67] which is clearly not the case: the bit is obviously more than an emblem; quite apart from its literal use in controlling the emperor's horse, employing the *actual* relics (rather than some symbolic representation) in the manufacture of the bridle suggests that there is an added value residing in their materiality, that the transformed nails are not merely 'holy signs' but *also* 'holy matter'. Unlike the cross-shaped standard that Constantine has his men carry into battle, which constitutes only a representation of the cross, the relic-enhanced bridle-chain will grant the emperor victory not because of its semiotic or representational value alone, but also by virtue of the transformed nails' nature as contact relics, which recall Christ's presence because they were touched by his blood.

Elene's presentation of the dual nature of the cross, which diverges significantly from the neat division employed in the *Acta*, thus emphasises both its material and temporal dimension as artefact and sign. In presenting the cross and its relics as material objects that also constitute figural signs, *Elene* incorporates two different temporal modes: on the one hand, the details of *Elene*'s rendering of Constantine's vision suggest a figural understanding of the heavenly cross that references past and future; on the other hand, as a poem concerned with the excavation of an object that was used in an execution more than 200 years in the past, and has since lain hidden in the earth, *Elene* acknowledges the cross's linear existence within historical time. In so doing, the poem sets side by side two different kinds of temporality: historical time, which is linear and unfolds in an irreversible succession of events; and figural time, which can cross-reference separate events in sacred time, moving forwards and backwards without regard for sequentiality. Unlike in the *Acta*, these two temporalities are not divided between the vision and the *inventio* episodes, but are enacted linguistically throughout the poem via the seemingly interchangeable use of the terms *tacn* and *beacen*, on the one hand, and *rod*, *treo*, *beam* and *galga*, on the other.

---

[66] Howe, 'Rome', 165–6.
[67] *Ibid.*, 166.

Elene's juxtaposition of historical and figural temporalities fits well with the poem's occupation with the theme of *translatio*, which I discussed at length in the first chapter. Wilcox notes that 'the *translatio imperii* served as a potential framework for all secular history and provided the basis from which medieval historians saw history as parallel linear series of spiritual and secular events'.[68] Like the figural unfolding of the vision of the four kingdoms in Daniel 7, a process in which each imperium can be understood as figured in the others, the *translatio imperii* is itself part of a figural vision of history: it intertwines continuous historical time, expressed in the direct succession of empires, and discontinuous figural time, in which the historically separate entities are figurally identical with each other. As I argued in the first chapter, *Elene* can be read as the foundation story of the 'Holy Roman Empire', an empire characterised by the coinciding of secular and religious authority under the same teleological impulse. During the Middle Ages and beyond, the Roman Empire was commonly interpreted as the culmination of all previous kingdoms, the last of the four before God's eternal fifth. In *Elene*'s retelling of the discovery of the True Cross, an artefact whose material properties as a relic and whose semiotic significance as a multivalent sign are used to emphasise the poem's political and theological message, the historical and the figural complement each other.

The Dream of the Rood

We find a similar preoccupation with figural and historical time in the poem known today as *The Dream of the Rood*. The text describes a nightly vision of the cross, told from an unnamed narrator's perspective.[69] However, most of its 150-odd lines consist of the prosopopoeic speech of the cross, in which the artefact relates to the dreamer the story of its own life: how as a tree in a forest it was cut down, shaped into a cross, used as a means of executing criminals and thus experienced Christ's crucifixion at first hand; how it was afterwards buried and eventually recovered, adorned with gold and silver and set up as an object for adoration (lines 28–77). In the second part of its speech, the cross explains the significance of the crucifixion as the event through which Christ overcame death, and exhorts the dreamer to proclaim the vision to other people. The text thus not only uses the persona of the cross to explain the figural significance of the historical event of the crucifixion, but it also employs a frame narrative

---

[68] Wilcox, *Measure*, 112.
[69] The Old English text of *The Dream of the Rood* is quoted from Michael Swanton (ed.), *The Dream of the Rood* (Manchester, 1970), omitting length marks and diacritics.

Remains of the Past in Old English Literature

to self-reflexively suggest a fictionalised context for its own production: the poem is (allegedly) the result of the dreamer's compliance with the cross's wish. The speech closes with a prophetic vision of the Second Coming (lines 78–121). In the remainder of the poem, the dreamer reflects on how the vision of the cross has fortified and comforted them in their belief and their hope for resurrection.[70]

The Dream of the Rood constitutes one example of the body of Old English devotional, introspective and sometimes penitential poetry that defies unequivocal assignment to a specific medieval genre. As pointed out earlier, it also stands in a complex intertextual relationship with *Elene*, which it precedes in its manuscript context, although the two poems are separated by a number of folios containing homilies. Different as they are, *The Dream of the Rood* and *Elene* share many elements and core concerns: both poems describe a nightly vision in which the cross, by way of its visual description, connects different historical moments in a scheme of figural temporality; both refer to the material history of the artefact in question, albeit with an emphasis on different historical moments (*The Dream of the Rood* focuses on the cross's early history and mentions its rediscovery only in passing, while *Elene* is concerned mainly with its *inventio* and *translatio*); and both feature the cross as a relic, possibly enshrined, and set up as a devotional object. On the level of language, the two texts employ the same strategy of referencing the cross's double ontological status through the seemingly interchangeable use of terms referring to its physical make-up and appearance (*rod*, *treow*) and its semiotic status as a sign (*beacen*). Already in the opening lines of *The Dream of the Rood*, the object of the dreamer's vision is described both as 'syllicre treow' [wondrous tree] and as 'beacen' [sign]:

> Hwæt! Ic swefna cyst   secgan wylle
> h[w]æt me gemætte   to midre nihte
> syðþan reordberend   reste wunedon.
>   Þuhte me þæt ic gesawe   syllicre treow
> on lyft lædan,   leohte bewunden,
> beama beorhtost.   Eall þæt beacen wæs
> begoten mid golde;   gimmas stodon
> fægere æt foldan sceatum,   swylce þær fife wæron
> uppe on þam eaxlegespanne.
> […]
> Hwæðre ic þurh þæt gold   ongytan meahte
> earmra ærgewin,   þæt hit ærest ongan

---

[70] For a discussion of narrative frames in *The Dream of the Rood*, see Carolyn Holdsworth, 'Frames: Time Level and Variation in *The Dream of the Rood*', *Neophilologus*, 66:4 (1982), 622–8.

Visions of the Holy Cross

swætan on þa swiðran healfe. [...]
[...] Geseah ic þæt fuse beacen
wendan wædum ond bleom;   hwilum hit wæs mid wætan bestemed,
beswyled mid swates gange,   hwilum mid since gegyrwed.
[...]
Ongan þa word sprecan   wudu selesta.

[So! I want to tell of an excellent dream that I dreamed at midnight, when speaking ones dwelt at rest. I thought that I saw a wondrous tree extend up high, wound with light, the brightest of beams [either timber or light]. All that sign was covered with gold; gems stood beautifully at the corners of the earth; of such there were five upon the cross-beam. [...] Yet through that gold I could perceive the old strife of wretched ones, that it once had begun to bleed on the stronger [i.e., right] half. [...] I saw that swift-changing sign shift its dress and colours; at times it was drenched with moisture, stained with the flowing of blood, at times adorned with treasure. [...] Then the heavenly piece of wood began to speak; lines 1–9; 18–23; 27.]

On the level of expression, the description of the dreamer's vision is highly reminiscent of Constantine's in *Elene*, where, as already noted, Constantine 'saw' ('geseah'; line 88b) 'a beautiful tree of glory over the roof of the clouds' ('wliti wuldres treo ofer wolcna hrof'; line 89), 'adorned with gold' and glistening gems ('golde geglenged, [gimmas lixtan]'; line 90) and described as a 'shining beam' ('se blaca beam'; line 91a) – despite the fact that its heavenly inscription or caption designates it a 'sign' ('þys beacen'; line 92b). These are not exact word-for-word parallels to the opening of *The Dream of the Rood*, but near-synonymous variants arranged in essentially the same sequence. Irvine explains this striking similarity by reference to 'an established poetic discourse derived from hymns on the cross and the language of the symbolism of reliquaries' on which the texts in question supposedly draw,[71] but the resemblance between the two poems is such that it seems almost as if one text were attempting to establish a direct correspondence without quoting the other verbatim. The occurrence in both poems of the ambiguous *beam* is particularly conspicuous, but the term's usage also reveals certain differences: in *Elene*, it is unclear whether the cross is corporeal (it is 'golde geglenged'; line 90a) or whether it is made of light (the letters with which the 'beam' is inscribed are 'beorhte ond leohte'; line 92a); the beam in *The Dream of the Rood*, meanwhile, appears to be unequivocally solid, covered with gold ('begoten mid golde'; line 7a), beset with gems ('gimmas [...] wæron / uppe on þam eaxlegespanne'; lines 7b–9a) and only garlanded with light

---

[71] Irvine, 'Literary Theory', 168.

Remains of the Past in Old English Literature

('leohte bewunden'; line 5b). But despite its unambiguously solid materiality, the vision's cross is constantly shifting its shape:

Geseah ic þæt fuse beacen
wendan wædum ond bleom;   hwilum hit wæs mid wætan bestemed,
beswyled mid swates gange,   hwilum mid since gegyrwed.

[I saw that swift-changing sign shift its dress and colours; at times it was drenched with moisture, stained with the flowing of blood, at times adorned with treasure; lines 21–3.]

In *Elene*, I have argued, the description of the heavenly cross in Constantine's vision resembles that of the rediscovered relic enshrined and set up for adoration, prefiguring the physical state that it will have assumed by the end of the poem. In *The Dream of the Rood*, by contrast, the dreamer appears to be seeing two different material configurations at once: 'hwæðre ic þurh þæt gold ongytan meahte / earmra ærgewin, þæt hit ærest ongan / swætan on þa swiðran healfe' [yet through that gold I could perceive the old strife of wretched ones, that it once had begun to bleed on the stronger [i.e., right] half; lines 18–20a]. On the one hand, the vision resembles a liturgical cross covered with gold and jewels; on the other, it has the aspect of the blood-stained instrument of the Passion. Seeta Chaganti argues that the dreamer's gaze 'through that gold' at the blood-stained object invokes the image of a reliquary, or indeed that of a monstrance that permits the worshipper to view the relic through an opening or transparent screen.[72] The Brussels Cross, an early eleventh-century wooden cross inscribed, intriguingly, with what seems to be a deliberate echo of lines 44 and 48 of *The Dream of the Rood*, was originally covered with a thin lamina of beaten silver and adorned with jewels; it also features a cavity that in 1925 still contained a wooden relic, now missing: presumably a piece of the True Cross, and potentially the very same given to King Alfred in 883 by Pope Marinus I.[73] Worshippers were thus able to see the 'original' wood through a slit in its precious covering. The opening section of *The Dream of the Rood* might be describing a similar situation. On the other hand, the wording of the following lines is more suggestive of alternating states than of one object contained within the other: the dreamer sees the cross (here described as a 'beacen') 'wendan wædum ond bleom' [shift dress and colours; line 22]; 'hwilum hit wæs mid wætan bestemed, / [...] hwilum mid since gegyrwed [at times

---

[72] Seeta Chaganti, 'Vestigial Signs: Inscription, Performance, and *The Dream of the Rood*', *PMLA*, 125:1 (2010), 48–72, at 60; see also Irvine, 'Literary Theory', 167, 173.

[73] Éamonn Ó Carragáin, *Ritual and the Rood: Liturgical Images and the Old English Poems of the* Dream of the Rood *Tradition* (Toronto, 2005), 339 and 353 n. 3.

Visions of the Holy Cross

it was drenched with moisture [...] at times adorned with treasure; lines 22–3].[74] The passage's contradictory language – at one point, the blood-stained cross is said to be seen *through* the gold ('þurh þæt gold'; line 18); a few lines later, it appears to alternate between two different forms or appearances – suggests an indeterminacy, a 'one *and* the other', that the narrator finds hard to put into words.

This indeterminacy may have to do with the quick succession of the alternating images, separate yet blurring into one. As it were, the poem's description of rapidly changing states suggests a temporal double vision, an almost cinematographic effect resembling such optical devices as the thaumatrope ('wonder-turner'), described by Jonathan Crary as

> a small circular disc with a drawing on either side and strings attached so that it could be twirled with a spin of the hand. The drawing, for example, of a bird on one side and a cage on the other would, when spun, produce the appearance of the bird in the cage.[75]

In the thaumatrope, the rapid alternation of two images, too rapid for the human eye to separate distinctly, produces a blurring of the two. Éamonn Ó Carragáin imagines a somewhat similar effect for the Brussels Cross when used in a ritual procession:

> When the reliquary-cross moves, the slight unevenness of the beaten surface catches the light in a multitude of shifting patterns: onlookers can still appreciate the effect, simply by walking around the reliquary as exhibited at Brussels. This cross must have seemed to come alive when, during a candle-lit procession, the light glinted, first on the massed rubies and diamonds of its front, and then on the gleaming silver and gold of its back. As the reliquary advanced, it gave visual reality to what the poetic image of 'an eager, restless symbol' ('þæt fuse beacen', *Dream* 22b) could imply.[76]

The Dream of the Rood, however, goes further than merely having the object seem to come alive by a play of light: the vision, which suggests both simultaneity and quick succession, appears like an attempt to describe

---

[74] This is something Chaganti herself notices when she observes: 'At one moment, the object appears as a cross reliquary, enclosed in gold and jewels. At the next, a Passion relic, the blood of Christ, becomes the outer covering for the object rather than a precious vestige contained within it' ('Vestigial Signs', 60). Chaganti does not follow up on the temporal implications of her observation, however; her interest is chiefly with the language of containment characteris-ing the passage.

[75] Jonathan Crary, *Techniques of the Observer: On Vision and Modernity in the Nineteenth Century* (Cambridge, MA, 1990), 105.

[76] Ó Carragáin, *Ritual*, 343.

Remains of the Past in Old English Literature

the delay experienced by the eye when trying to accommodate quick movement. In fact, whereas Crary reads the experience of temporality afforded by the thaumatrope and other related devices in the context of what he regards as a radical transformation in the nature of visuality in the late eighteenth and early nineteenth centuries,[77] I would argue that the early medieval *Dream of the Rood*'s description of changing material states suggests a very similar perception of visual temporality as that Crary claims for modernity.

But the cross's ever-changing nature implies not only an object locked in a temporality of its own, caught in a moment of continual transformation; its two material configurations also reference two distinct historical moments: that of the crucifixion, the blood still wet upon its wood, and that of its later exaltation as an object of veneration, covered with gold and jewels. The cross's oscillation between these two material-historical states recalls the mental operation required to establish the figural relationship between two historically distinct entities, whose simultaneity only exists in God's ever-present 'now'. In addition, the vision of the cross rising tall against the heavens has clear eschatological overtones: we find a similar image in the description of Judgement Day in the Old English *Christ III*, where the sign of the cross appears in the sky, summoning all human beings into Christ's presence to be judged (lines 1061ff.), a motif that goes back to Christ's eschatological prophecy in Matthew 24:30: 'et tunc parebit signum Filii hominis in caelo. Et tunc plangent omnes tribus terrae et videbunt Filium hominis venientem in nubibus caeli cum virtute multa et maiestate' [And then shall appear the sign of the Son of man in heaven: and then shall all tribes of the earth mourn: and they shall see the Son of man coming in the clouds of heaven with much power and majesty].[78] Like *The Dream of the Rood*, *Christ III* features a description of the bleeding cross:

> Ne bið him to are   þæt þær fore ellþeodum
> usses dryhtnes rod   ondweard stondeð,
> beacna beorhtast,   blode bistemed,
> heofoncyninges   hlutran dreore,
> biseon mid swate,   þæt ofer side gesceaft
> scire scineð.

---

[77] Ó Carragáin, *Ritual*, 343.

[78] Cf. *Christ III*: 'Ðonne sio byman stefen ond se beorhta segn, / ond þæt hate fyr ond seo hea duguð / ond se engla þrym ond se egsan þrea / ond se hearda dæg ond seo hea rod / ryht arǽred rices to beacne, / folcdryht wera biforan bonnað, / sawla gehwylce þara þe sið oþþe ær / on lichoman leoþum onfengen' (lines 1061–8); quoted from Krapp and Dobbie (eds), *Exeter Book*, 27–49 and 255–61 (notes).

Visions of the Holy Cross

[It will be no help to them that there our Lord's rood will stand present before all peoples, the brightest of signs, drenched in blood, with the heavenly king's pure blood, covered with sweat, that will shine brightly over the wide creation; 1081–8.][79]

Crucially, however, in *The Dream of the Rood*, the heavenly cross appears less as an instrument of punishment than as a sign of comfort and spiritual support. Although the speaking cross does invoke the image of Judgement Day in its speech, stating initially that 'no one there can be unafraid because of the word that the ruler speaks' ('Ne mæg þær ænig unforht wesan / for þam worde þe se Wealdend cwyð'; lines 110–11), only a few lines later it contends, in strikingly similar words:

Ne þearf ðær þonne ænig   unforht wesan
þe him ær in breostum bereð   beacna selest.
Ac ðurh ða rode sceal   rice gesecan
of eorðwege   æghwylc sawl,
seo þe mid Wealdende   wunian þenceð.

[No one there need be very afraid then, who earlier carries in his breast the noblest of signs. Yet through that cross every soul that intends to dwell with the Ruler will find the [heavenly] kingdom from the earthly path; lines 117–21.]

The dreamer, too, regards the cross as an image of consolation, expressing the hope that it will fetch their soul and speed it on its journey to the heavenly life (lines 135b–9a). Most telling in respect to the vision's eschatological temporality is the cross's statement that 'there now has come a time that all worship me far and wide, people on the earth, and all the great creation, prays to this sign' ('Is nu sæl cumen / þæt me weorðiað wide ond side / menn ofer moldan, ond eall þeos mære gesceaft, / gebiddaþ him to þyssum beacne'; lines 80b–3a). The referent of 'þyssum beacne' (line 83a) is ambiguous; it may be synonymous with the 'me' [me (that is, the cross)] of line 81a, or perhaps the universal worship described is itself taken as a sign of the approaching end of time. In any case, the lines constitute an obvious reference to Isaiah's prophecy of universal conversion, and hence have an apocalyptic overtone that chimes with the imagery of the whole passage.

---

[79]   The two poems also share the – perhaps entirely coincidental – characteristic of being transmitted in the immediate vicinity of 'Cynewulf' poems (*Elene* and *The Fates of the Apostles* in the case of *The Dream of the Rood*, and *Christ II* in the case of *Christ III*). Both *Christ III* and *The Dream of the Rood* have in the past been ascribed to Cynewulf, even though they lack the runic signature.

225

Remains of the Past in Old English Literature

The different aspects of the cross are thus directly linked to its temporality as a typological sign. Irvine notes that the 'multiple vision' of the dreamer – the bloodied implement of torture at the moment of crucifixion; the relic in its reliquary; the heavenly cross summoning the souls on Judgement Day – makes explicit the semiotic nature of the cross as a sign 'capable of yielding several layers of meaning simultaneously, according to the principles for signification understood for typological events or objects in sacred history'.[80] Like the objects named in Augustine's discussion of signification – the stone on which Jacob rested his head, the wood Moses threw into the bitter waters, the sheep Abraham burnt instead of his son – the cross is not merely a *res* in the strict sense of the term, but a *significabilium* used as a sign of something else – even though, initially, the poem neglects to tell us what that something is. It is only in the second part of the cross's speech, a passage wherein it provides its own exegesis, that the centrality of the crucifixion becomes apparent as the event through which the cross acquired special meaning and was thereby transformed from a mere thing into a thing that is also a sign:

> On me Bearn Godes
> þrowode hwile;   forðan ic þrymfæst nu
> hlifige under heofonum,   7 ic hælan mæg
> æghwylcne anra,   þara þe him bið egesa to me.
> Iu ic wæs geworden   wita heardost,
> leodum laðost,   ærþan ic him lifes weg
> rihtne gerymde,   reordberendum.
> Hwæt, me þa geweorðode   wuldres Ealdor
> ofer holtwudu,   heofonrices Weard,
> swylce swa he his modor eac,   Marian sylfe,
> ælmihtig God,   for ealle menn,
> geweorðode   ofer eall wifa cynn.

[On me God's child suffered for a time; because of that I now tower gloriously under heaven, and I can heal each and every one who holds me in awe. Long ago I became the harshest of punishments, loathsome to people, before I opened for them, the voice-bearers, the true path of life. So, the Prince of Glory honoured me above all wood, the Guardian of Heaven, in the same way as he also, almighty God, honoured his mother, Mary herself, over all womankind; lines 83b–94.]

Just as God singled out Mary among women (and, in Augustine's example, the stone upon which Jacob rested his head among others stones), so the cross – treated throughout the poem as identical with the

---

[80] Irvine, 'Literary Theory', 173. Irvine does not address the eschatological dimension of the passage, however.

Visions of the Holy Cross

tree from which it was fashioned and frequently referred to as 'treo' or 'wudu' [tree] – is singled out among other trees.[81]

In all these cases, the *res* in question is distinguished from other, similar entities through an event – a single, historically contingent moment – that transforms its meaning. In *The Dream of the Rood*, the cross expresses this transformation from *significabilium* to *signum* through a number of paradoxes that become comprehensible only when the temporal relationship between the statements is taken into account: 'On me Bearn Godes / þrowode hwile; forðan [...] ic hælan mæg / æghwylcne anra, þara þe him bið egesa to me' [on me God's child suffered for a time; because of that [...] I can heal each and every one who holds me in awe; lines 83b–6]; 'Iu ic wæs geworden wita heardost / [...] ærþan ic him lifes weg / rihtne gerymde, reordberendum' [long ago I became the harshest of punishments [...] before I opened for them, the voice-bearers, the true path of life; lines 87–9]. During the crucifixion, the cross was an instrument of death, but the event turned it into an instrument of life. Just as the visual appearance of the cross in the dreamer's vision indexes different historical-material configurations, so does the temporal logic underlying its paradoxical statements emphasise the temporality of its transformation, the before and after, and hence the supersessional logic of salvation history, in which death is overcome by life.

But then again, the cross's oscillation between different material-historical states, suggestive of a simultaneous vision and mirrored in the juxtaposition of paradoxes later on in the poem, collapses this linearity, highlighting instead the simultaneity of figural vision, its potential to open 'a window onto the whole panorama of correspondences in sacred history, the master narrative which is presented only in a partial and fragmentary form in any given biblical narrative', as Irvine puts it.[82] Irvine rightly calls attention to the vision's figural significance: by invoking crucial moments in sacred history, the alternation between different material states showcases the figural relationship that exists between them. As in the case of the thaumatrope noted above, where the spinning movement of two indi-

---

[81] In Irvine's words, 'what was once a thing, a tree in the forest, a piece of timber fashioned into an instrument of execution, is transformed through the narrative into a typological sign: a tree becomes *the* Cross with the full exegetical significance of the Cross uncovered in the conclusion to the narrative' (*ibid.*, 172). As Irvine notes, the slow unfolding of the Cross's autobiographical account enacts, in narratological terms, the hermeneutic process of typological interpretation that the reader must undertake to understand its significance: 'As the poem proceeds the reader constructs a sign, following the Cross's transformation from a tree in the forest and a gibbet or gallows to *the* Tree, *the* Cross, the unique instrument of human salvation' (*ibid.*, 174).

[82] *Ibid.*, 174.

227

vidual images creates a blurred vision of a single one, the rapid oscillation of different material states in *The Dream of the Rood* simultaneously suggests separateness and oneness, recalling the cross-temporal movement of figural interpretation that establishes a single, extratemporal truth. In the vision, the different material states are literally 'con-figurations', that is, historically distinct formations that combine to give shape to a third reality; namely, the temporality of figural history emerging from their relationship as type and antitype, a temporality that subverts the linearity of historical time.

That said, it would be short-sighted to reduce *The Dream of the Rood*'s temporal vision to the typological relationship between the various historical incarnations of the cross. As noted above, Auerbach insists that a figural relationship between two historically distinct entities does not eclipse their historical singularity.[83] In *The Dream of the Rood*, the concurrence of the different material-historical configurations of the cross invoked in the vision and the biographical account of the speaking object open up further temporal perceptions. More explicitly than in *Elene*, the cross's autobiographical 'life-story' provides a second, historical temporality, which sets a linear perspective against the cross-temporal figural one. The linearity of the biographical account emphasises the *longue durée* of the cross's existence as a historical artefact. Moreover, the poem's fictional ascription of a single, unified subjectivity that characterises the object throughout its journey contrasts with the purely spiritual nature that usually characterises typological relationships. *The Dream of the Rood* accords equal prominence to the two temporalities: in the description of the vision, none of the rapidly alternating forms of temporality appears to dominate, and in the cross's speech, the historical temporality of the biographical account and the figural significance revealed in the exegetical part are given roughly the same amount of space. This equality of historical and figural schemes is in keeping with Auerbach's interpretation of *figura*, according to which the figural connection does not eclipse the historical singularity of the historical entities involved.

Besides juxtaposing two different temporalities – the linear-historical one of the biographical account and the figural one that characterises the vision and the exegetical part of the cross's speech – *The Dream of the Rood* is also interested in the cross's material-temporal characteristics as a relic. This concern becomes especially apparent in the poem's emphasis on the cross's capacity for interceding on behalf of the worshipper. Relics, I have observed, grant believers direct contact with the saint by metonymically standing in for the whole person. It is this physical connectedness as parts of a former whole that makes it possible for them to channel the saint's

---

[83] Auerbach, 'Figura', 53.

Visions of the Holy Cross

power and thereby maintain beyond death their capacity for eliciting miracles and for coming to the aid of a supplicant. Relics can thus be understood as media through which a temporal operation can take place. On the one hand, they constitute human remains whose existence continues beyond the life of the individual person within linear, historical time; in allowing cross-temporal contact with the living saint, however, they effectively collapse this notion of linearity, bridging the span between the life of the saint and the present moment. It is not a figural relationship between object and saint that allows such posthumous interactions to take place, but rather a relationship based on material identity persisting over a long period. In *The Dream of the Rood*, the voice of the cross provides such a long-term identity: as the speaking artefact claims time and again, it is still characterised by the same subjectivity as the cross upon which Christ suffered, and even as the tree from which it was originally fashioned.

Posthumous interactions between saints and worshippers can take many different forms. Among the most frequent are visions, in which the saint gives advice or discloses events of the future, and acts of healing, often (though not always) accomplished through direct contact with relics or iconographic representations. *The Dream of the Rood* invokes this latter aspect when the speaking cross states that it has been endowed with the capacity for healing: 'ic hælan mæg / æghwylcne anra, þara þe him bið egesa to me' [I can heal each and every one who holds me in awe; lines 85b–6].[84] In this respect, the cross functions like any other sacred relic.[85] Nevertheless, *The Dream of the Rood* imagines it as a very unusual example of that category: albeit a contact relic by nature, hallowed by the touch of Christ's body and blood, it does not stand in as a substitute for or an extension of the person whose presence it recalls – it is not Christ who is speaking to the dreamer, but the personified cross. In the fictional account of the poem, the latter appears as an independent entity, capable of speaking, feeling and suffering, and, to all intents and purposes, acting with a will of its own: 'Þær ic þa ne dorste ofer Dryhtnes word / bugan oððe berstan' [There then I did not dare to bend or break; lines 35–6a]. In other words, where we should expect a relic of the Passion to bring the

---

[84] I have already quoted Bynum's observation that the distinction between relics and representations was never absolute; even a representation of the cross that postfigurally partakes in the reality of the 'True Cross' – whether in the form of an artwork or in the form of the mark of the cross traced with the finger – possesses the power to heal; see Bynum, *Christian Materiality*, 29.

[85] In addition, Ó Carragáin observes in the poem a strong kinship between the cross and the Virgin Mary, whose intercession on behalf of the sinful worshipper is also frequently invoked in early medieval prayers and penitential literature (*Ritual*, 308–16).

Remains of the Past in Old English Literature

worshipper into direct contact with Christ, we are confronted with the cross imagined as an independent persona.[86]

This alters the semiotic relationship between the relic and the person that it metonymically stands in for. As noted above, relics preserve the presence of their saintly source, and therefore operate as a *signum naturalis*, a *res* signifying another *res* to which it is connected by a material relationship, like smoke signifying fire. However, if the cross is imagined not merely as a relic preserving Christ's presence but as an independent being, it assumes a different quality of signification altogether: it functions as a *signum datum*, a *res* signifying another *res* to which it is not intrinsically related, and hence as a typological or figural sign representing Christ. Accordingly, *The Dream of the Rood* points to two different kinds of object at the same time, both of which can become media channelling divine power: (1) the devotional image, a work of art (for want of a better term)[87] that stands in a figural relationship with the entity it represents;[88] and (2) the bodily relic that metonymically preserves the saintly or divine presence. Strikingly, *The Dream of the Rood* collapses both possibilities into one. On the one hand, it presents us with a personified cross that stands in a figural relationship with Christ, whose bodily suffering it shares. As Tate has pointed out in a classic study, the tribulations of Christ and the cross mirror each other in a chiastic pattern, a rhetorical structure based on similarity rather than identity, that structurally reproduces the figure of the cross.[89] On the other hand, the cross's part in the crucifixion has turned it into a relic by contact, an artefact whose power and significance stem from the fact that it preserves the *material* presence of Christ. In the fictional account of the poem, the cross thus paradoxically appears and behaves as though it were a living person turned into a contact relic; in other words, it is presented as an entity whose *figural* identity with Christ is simultaneously also a *historical-material* identity by virtue of Christ's

---

[86] Perceptions of the nature of the cross appear to have been ambiguous outside the context of *The Dream of the Rood*, too. Drijvers quotes Paulinus of Nola, who called the cross 'inanimate' yet ascribed to it 'living power': 'Indeed this Cross of inanimate wood has living power, and ever since its discovery it has lent its wood to the countless, almost daily, prayers of men. Yet it suffers no diminution; though daily divided, it seems to remain whole to those who lift it, and always entire to those who venerate it' (*Helena Augusta*, 82).

[87] See Bynum for a discussion of the problems involved in referring to medieval visual objects as 'works of art' (*Christian Materiality*, 31–2).

[88] Typologically speaking, the cross's personification does not present a problem: persons, too, can function as antitypes (for example Adam and Jonah in relation to Christ).

[89] George S. Tate, 'Chiasmus as Metaphor: The "Figura Crucis" Tradition and *The Dream of the Rood*', NM, 79 (1978), 114–25, at 120–1; see also Chaganti, 'Vestigial Signs', 61.

Visions of the Holy Cross

touch during the crucifixion. In collapsing these two different tempo-ral-material possibilities into one, *The Dream of the Rood* highlights both the versatility of the cross as a sign and the difficulties that arise when imag-ining the instrument of the Passion as a singular historical-material entity. Where *Elene* presents the relationship between the material and figural aspects of the cross as complementary, *The Dream of the Rood* introduces an element of tension that characterises the cross's uneasy double nature as a contact relic, on the one hand, and a separate entity characterised by an independent subjectivity, on the other.

The Ruthwell Poem *as Riddle*

The tension between these two modes of conceptualising the cross is even more pronounced in the runic poem carved into the stone of the Ruthwell Cross, a text that presents us with a narrator-persona claiming identity both with the monument into which it is inscribed and with the True Cross that this monument represents.

Next to nothing is known of the early history of the object. Apart from a note made by Reginald Bainbrigg, an antiquarian and headmaster of Appleby Grammar School who visited Ruthwell in 1599 and 1601, it is first mentioned in a 1642 edict by the General Assembly of the Church of Scotland that commands it to be destroyed on account of its 'idolatrous' nature. This order was carried out before 1697, when William Nicolson, the soon-to-be bishop of Carlisle, saw the broken fragments.[90] In 1802, the monument was re-erected in the vicarage garden by the Reverend Henry Duncan, initially in the form of a pillar, to which a crosshead was added in 1823. Not all the original monument's fragments were found, however, and Duncan's reconstruction is anything but historically accurate: new stones were used to replace missing parts – most prominently the cross-beam, which displays modern iconography – and the entire monument was turned around so that the front and back, originally facing East and West, now look South and North, respectively. In the process, the front and back sides of the crosshead were mistakenly reversed, so that they no longer accord with the front and back of the shaft, as originally envis-aged. Other parts were possibly misplaced, too;[91] indeed, it has even been

---

[90] For detailed discussions of the monument's history, see Brendan Cassidy, 'The Later Life of the Ruthwell Cross: From the Seventeenth Century to the Present', in Brendan Cassidy (ed.), *The Ruthwell Cross: Papers from the Colloquium Sponsored by the Index of Christian Art, Princeton University, 8 December 1989* (Princeton, NJ, 1992), 3–34; Fred Orton, Ian Wood, with Clare A. Lees, *Fragments of History: Rethinking the Ruthwell and Bewcastle Monuments* (Manchester, 2007), 32–61.

[91] See Robert T. Farrell, with Catherine E. Karkov, 'The Construction,

Remains of the Past in Old English Literature

suggested that the original monument may have represented a simple obelisk rather than a cross, with the head added at some later point.[92] Even from a linear-historical perspective, the Ruthwell Cross thus constitutes a temporally ambiguous object – and as we shall see, the introduction of a figural perspective complicates the temporal perception of the monument even further.

In its present form, the monument is some eighteen feet high and consists of two parts of differently coloured sandstone, a column and a cross, both of which carry reliefs framed by raised borders inscribed with text (Figure 2).[93] The front and back of the monument each display four large panels with biblical scenes bordered by Latin descriptions in the Roman alphabet plus two smaller ones directly above and below the crossbeam. On the north face, these are (bottom to top): the Holy Family; the hermit saints Paul and Anthony; Christ acknowledged by the beasts in the desert; Saint John the Baptist bearing the Lamb of God; and, on the crosshead, below and above the crossbeam, two men and a bird on a branch. On the south face, we find the Annunciation; Christ healing the blind man; Christ and Mary Magdalene; Mary and Martha and, again below and above the crossbeam, an archer and a man with a bird. As mentioned, the top stone (that is, the one above the crossbeam) was mistakenly reversed in the reconstruction, so that the two men would originally have been on the

---

Deconstruction, and Reconstruction of the Ruthwell Cross: Some Caveats', in Brendan Cassidy (ed.), *The Ruthwell Cross: Papers from the Colloquium Sponsored by the Index of Christian Art, Princeton University, 8 December 1989* (Princeton, NJ, 1992), 35–47, at 43–4; and, in the same volume, Paul Meyvaert, 'A New Perspective on the Ruthwell Cross: *Ecclesia* and *Vita Monastica*', 95–166, at 100–4.

[92] Bainbrigg's account is somewhat ambiguous, as is the one given by Thomas Pennant in his best-selling travelogue *A Tour in Scotland, and Voyage to the Hebrides*, published in 1774. The former was interpreted by Fred Orton as the description of an obelisk rather than a cross, a reading rejected by Ó Carragáin. See Fred Orton, 'Rethinking the Ruthwell Monument: Fragments and Critique; Tradition and History; Tongues and Sockets', *Art History*, 21:1 (1998), 65–106; Orton, Wood, with Lees, *Fragments*, 46–61; Ó Carragáin, *Ritual*, 13–15 and 63 n. 10.

[93] For in-depth discussions of the types of stone used in the monument and its reconstruction, see Orton, Wood, with Lees, *Fragments*, 40–2; Farrell with Karkov, 'Construction', 41, fig. 2. To Orton, the obvious visual differences between the two kinds of sandstone constitute important evidence for his view that the column and cross parts did not originally belong together. However, Ó Carragáin has pointed out that medieval stone monuments were often covered with gesso – traces of which may, in the case at hand, still have been present in the nineteenth century – and painted in bright colours, which would have obscured the visual difference (*Ritual*, 27).

Figure 2 W. Penny, engraving published with Henry Duncan's 'An Account of the Remarkable Monument in the Shape of a Cross, Inscribed with Roman and Runic Letters, Preserved in the Garden of Ruthwell Manse, Dumfriesshire', *Archaeologia Scotica: or, Transactions of the Society of Antiquaries of Scotland*, 4 (1857), 313–36 (Plate XIII). Image © National Museums Scotland.

Remains of the Past in Old English Literature

same side as the man with the bird, and the archer would have been on the same side as the bird on the branch.[94] David Howlett interprets the man with the bird as Saint John with his eagle, and the two men as Matthew and the angel, arguing that the original crossbeam would probably have depicted the two missing evangelists with their attributes, Mark with the lion and Luke with the ox.[95]

The east and west faces of the monument, as far up as the crossbeam, are adorned with plant scrolls surrounded by a border inscribed with runes. Transcribed, these yield the following alliterative text in the Northumbrian dialect of Old English:[96]

East side
I. North border
[+ *ond*]geredæ hinæ ḡod almeʒttig [.] þa he walde on ḡalḡu gistiḡa
[God almighty prepared himself when he wanted to mount the gallows]
modig f[*ore allæ*] men
[brave before all men]
[*b*]uḡ[a] {*ic ni dorstæ*} [...]
[{I did not dare} to bow]

---

94 Meyvaert, 'New Perspective', 103; David Howlett, 'Inscriptions and Design of the Ruthwell Cross', in Brendan Cassidy (ed.), *The Ruthwell Cross: Papers from the Colloquium Sponsored by the Index of Christian Art, Princeton University, 8 December 1989* (Princeton, NJ, 1992), 71–93, at 74. For interpretations of the monument's iconographic programme, see Meyvaert, 'New Perspective', 95–166; Orton, Wood, with Lees, *Fragments*, 186–8; Margaret Jennings, 'Rood and Ruthwell: The Power of Paradox', *English Language Notes*, 31:3 (1994), 6–11, at 10; Ó Carragáin, *Ritual*, 79–222.

95 Howlett, 'Inscriptions', 76. Howlett's reconstruction is accepted by Ó Carragáin, *Ritual*, 143–4.

96 The Old English text is based on Ó Carragáin, *Ritual*, 79–81, 180–1, with <ʒ> substituted for <i>. Italicised letters represent letters still partially visible or, when put in square brackets, collated from earlier transcriptions or drawings. Curly brackets denote emendations based on the *Dream of the Rood*. When the available space on the border suggests that more text is missing, this is indicated by three dots in square brackets. A more recent, comprehensive reconstruction of what the original inscription may have looked like (including a number of conjectural additions) is offered in the poem's most recent edition (Kerstin Majewski, *The Ruthwell Cross and its Texts: A New Reconstruction and an Edition of the* Ruthwell Crucifixion Poem, Reallexikon der Germanischen Altertumskunde, Ergänzungsbände, 132 [Berlin, 2022]; the reconstructed poem can be found at 327). Incorporating only such readings as have been established with reasonable certainty, the text presented here omits a number of conjectures, even if these are supported by the available space.

Visions of the Holy Cross

II. SOUTH BORDER
[*ahof*] ic riicnæ k̄yniŋc .
[I lifted up a mighty king]
heafunæs hlafard hælda ic ni dorstæ
[I did not dare to hold Heaven's Lord]
[*b*]ismæradu uŋ̄ket men ba æt[ḡ]ad[*re*] [*i*]c [*wæs*] miþ blodi *b*ist[*e*]mi[*d*]
[men defiled the two of us, both together, I was drenched in blood]
bi{ḡoten of þæs ḡumu sida} […]
[{from that man's side}]

WEST SIDE
III. SOUTH BORDER
[+] kris*t* wæs on rodi .
[Christ was on the rood.]
hweþræ þer fus*æ* fearran kwomu
[Yet readily there came from afar]
*æ*þþilæ til anum ic þæt al bi[*heald*]
[nobles to the one, I beheld all that]
s[*aræ*] ic w[*æ*]s . mi[þ] so[*r*]ḡu[*m*] gidrœ[*fi*]d h[*n*]a[ḡ] {ic þam secgum til
   handa}
[Sorely I was troubled by grief, I bent {to the men's hands}]

IV. NORTH BORDER
*m*iþ s*t*re*l*um giwundad
[wounded by arrows]
alegdun hiæ *h*inæ limwœrignæ . gistoddu[*n*] him [*æt his lic*]æs [*hea*]f[*du*]m
[they laid the limb-weary down, stood at his body's head.]
[*bih*]ea[*ld*]u[*n*] [*h*]i[*æ*] [*þ*]e[*r*] {heafunæs dryctin} […]
[They beheld there the {Heavens' Lord}]

As noted above, this poetic inscription stands in a complex relationship, textually as well as regarding its modern reception, to the *Dream of the Rood*: although written in a different dialect – Northumbrian rather than West-Saxon – the runic text on the Ruthwell Cross is close enough to lines 39–49 and 56–64 of the *Dream of the Rood* to have given editors the confidence to use either poem to emend the other. However, there are also a number of differences. Most of these relate to the actual wording of what is, by all accounts, the same content, but some take the form of omissions, most significantly the instance in the speech of the cross wherein it identifies itself; namely, the half-line 'rod wæs ic geræred' [I was raised (as) a cross; *The Dream of the Rood*, line 44a], which in the *Dream of the Rood* forms a metrical unit with the half-line 'ahof ic ricne cyning' ('ahof ic riicnæ k̄yniŋc' in the inscription) [I lifted up a mighty king]. In the Ruthwell inscription, the first phrase is conspicuously absent, which not only renders the line

Remains of the Past in Old English Literature

metrically incomplete, but also suppresses the speaker's single unequivocal self-identification.

The exact relationship between the two poems is far from clear: on the one hand, they are too different to establish a direct influence of one upon the other; on the other hand, they are too similar not to suspect some kind of connection. Historically, the Ruthwell Cross is usually dated to the eighth century, while *The Dream of the Rood* is written in late West-Saxon and preserved in a tenth-century manuscript. The latter could therefore be an extension of the former,[97] or the former an abbreviation of an earlier form of the latter, or the two may simply partake in a tradition of similarly phrased devotional poetry of which only they (and the related inscription on the Brussels Cross) have survived. Some scholars have even suggested that the Ruthwell inscription may be later than the original monument and date to the tenth century.[98] Most runologists agree, however, that the language and form of the runic inscription point to an earlier date (although it needs to be said that the evidence used for dating is frequently circular and neglects the possibility of deliberate antiquarianism).[99]

[97] Kendall, for instance, hypothesises that the Ruthwell Cross – or, rather, a viewer's experience of engaging with it – could well have inspired *The Dream of the Rood*: '*The Dream of the Rood* can be thought of as the record of a visionary experience following upon an encounter with the sign of the cross, just as Constantine's dream vision was generated by his experience of the sign of the cross in the sky' ('Sign to Vision', 141–2). The relationship between the monument and the Vercelli poem, he notes further, is 'analogous' to the way the sign of the cross in the sky inspired Constantine's dream in the *Vita Constantini*; it resembles that between 'text and interpretation or commentary' (*ibid.*, 136).

[98] The theory that the inscription postdates the monument was first put forward by Raymond I. Page in an attempt to account for the unusual arrangement of the runes, which he found 'so odd [...] that I incline to think it may not be a part of the original design for the cross, and to wonder if these runes were added by a later carver who had less command over the space he had to fill'; Raymond I. Page, *An Introduction to English Runes* (London, 1973), 150. For more elaborate arguments that the inscriptions were added at a later date, see Paul Meyvaert, 'An Apocalypse Panel on the Ruthwell Cross', in Frank Tirro (ed.), *Medieval and Renaissance Studies: Proceedings of the Southeastern Institute of Medieval and Renaissance Studies, Summer 1978* (Durham, NC, 1982), 3–32, at 26 – later retracted in his 'Necessity Mother of Invention: A Fresh Look at the Rune Verses on the Ruthwell Cross', *ASE*, 41 (2012), 407–16 – and Patrick Conner, 'The Ruthwell Monument Runic Poem in a Tenth-Century Context', *RES NS*, 59:238 (2008), 25–51, at 26.

[99] Majewski cites a forthcoming study by Gaby Waxenberger, which suggests that the language and the runes corroborate a date around 750 (*Ruthwell Cross*, 21). For a discussion of the problems involved in using style as a means of dating, see Orton, Wood, with Lees, *Fragments*, 62–6. To my own concerns, the precise date of the cross is immaterial.

Visions of the Holy Cross

Yet whatever the two texts' exact relationship, it is obvious that the *Ruthwell Poem* – so much shorter and inscribed into a stone monument rather than written on a page – must be read in a context very different from that of *the Dream of the Rood*. Moreover, even if it were a case of one poem quoting the other, knowledge of the 'original version' cannot be presupposed: to most of its readers, at any given point in time, each of the two texts would have appeared self-contained. As Kendall points out: 'Suppose we knew nothing of [...] *The Dream of the Rood* [...] we would have no reason to suspect that the text was a fragment excerpted from a longer poem. It would seem more or less complete [...].'[100] So, suspending all knowledge of the *Dream of the Rood*, what does the *Ruthwell Poem* tell us?

To the Christian observer, provided that they are able to decipher the runes and understand the language, the references to 'God almighty' and 'Christ', as well as the terms *galga* and *rod* – conventional appellations of the cross in Old English – would immediately conjure up a crucifixion scene. The real question, then, is not about what is happening in the poem or about identifying Christ – as Fred Orton, Ian Wood and Clare Lees observe, it concerns the unnamed first-person speaker: 'Who speaks this "I"?'[101] From what the text tells us, the speaker is not merely an observer, but takes a more active role: 'I dared not withdraw', 'I lifted up a mighty king', 'I bent forward to their hands'. Indeed, the speaker implies a level of participation and suffering almost equal to that of Christ: 'men defiled the two of us, both together', 'I was drenched in blood', 'I was sorely troubled by grief', '[I was] wounded by arrows'.[102] These references suggest the True Cross itself as the speaker – who else carried Christ and was close enough to be drenched in blood? But this identification is veiled by the anomaly of a cross capable of feeling and expressing emotions, as well as by its being referred to in the third person rather than the first: 'þa he walde on galgu gistiga' and 'Krist wæs on rode' as opposed to **þa he walde on mec gistiga* and **Krist wæs on me*. In light of this, the missing self-identification of the cross noted above, with the resulting metrical inconsistency, looks very much like a deliberate suppression.[103]

---

[100] Kendall, 'Sign to Vision', 140.

[101] Orton, Wood, with Lees, *Fragments*, 168.

[102] It is not clear whether the last phrase refers to the preceding line – and hence to the speaker – or to Christ in the following line.

[103] This is admittedly only one of several metrical inconsistencies in the *Ruthwell Poem*, some of which result from damage to the monument, while other lines are 'are apparently deliberately incomplete, at least according to later, normative standards of metre' (Orton, Wood, with Lees, *Fragments*, 162). It should be noted, moreover, that the references to the cross in the third person also occur in *The Dream of the Rood*, where, however, the identity of the speaker is known from the outset – it is only in the *Ruthwell Poem*, where the speaker is never introduced, that these take on special significance.

Remains of the Past in Old English Literature

If the speaking cross's identity has been obscured on purpose, then it makes sense to read the poem as deliberately enigmatic and to regard the differences between *The Dream of the Rood* and the *Ruthwell Poem* as primarily a difference in genre; the former a dream vision, the latter a riddle.[104] Speaking objects are a common feature of many of the Old English Exeter Book riddles, where animals, natural phenomena and items of everyday use describe events from their 'lives' in the form of a first-person narrative, often (though not always) followed by an invitation to identify the speaker: 'Saga hwæt ic hatte' [Say what I am called].[105] It has become a scholarly commonplace to point out the similarities between these riddles and the runic inscription on the Ruthwell Cross, and to cite *The Dream of the Rood* as another example of a text involving prosopopoeic speech. In the latter poem, however, it is made clear from the outset who is speaking – unlike in the riddles and the Ruthwell inscription, where the speaker's identity is concealed.

The difference between the Ruthwell inscription and *The Dream of the Rood* is reinforced by their material presentation – that is, by the different material contexts in which the two texts have been transmitted and the different forms of (inter)mediality that characterise them:[106] whereas *The Dream of the Rood* is preserved in a codex of religious verse and prose, undistinguished from the rest, a text among texts, the *Ruthwell Poem* is set apart from the other writings on the monument by its different layout, language and script.

This last point requires elaboration. There is some disagreement among scholars as to the exact status of runes as a medium of writing after the conversion, and usage must, of course, have varied over time and between different contexts. That said, in early medieval manuscripts, runes seem to

[104] Orton, Wood, with Lees, *Fragments*, 156 and 167–9, respectively.
[105] Here quoted from Riddle 12, line 13b, quoted from Krapp and Dobbie (eds), *Exeter Book*, 186. On the association of the *Dream of the Rood* with the Exeter Book riddles, which rests chiefly on the poem's use of prosopopoeia, see Margaret Schlauch, 'The Dream of the Rood as Prosopopoeia', in Jess B. Bessinger, Jr., and Stanley J. Kahrl (eds), *Essential Articles for the Study of Old English Poetry* (Hamden, CT, 1968), 428–41; Peter Orton, 'The Technique of Object Personification in *The Dream of the Rood* and a Comparison with the Old English *Riddles*', *Leeds Studies in English*, 11 (1979), 1–18.
[106] For a recent discussion of the *Ruthwell Poem*, *The Dream of the Rood* and the related inscription on the Brussels Cross that highlights the way the differences between these texts and their material contexts generate independent meanings, see John Hines, 'The Ruthwell Cross, the Brussels Cross, and *The Dream of the Rood*', in Graham D. Caie and Michael D. C. Drout (eds), *Transitional States: Change, Tradition, and Memory in Medieval Literature and Culture* (Tempe, AZ, 2018), 175–92.

Visions of the Holy Cross

have been used chiefly for antiquarian and/or cryptographic purposes.[107] The latter function can be observed in a number of Old English riddles, in poems such as *The Husband's Message* and *The Ruin*, as well as in the Cynewulf signatures. According to John D. Niles, instances such as these can be regarded 'as a literary ploy, a special type of defamiliarization that appeals to writers who wish to cast a cloak of real or apparent mystery over their text'.[108] Similarly, Raymond I. Page has suggested that 'runes could be used in contexts where they stand distinct from Roman [letters], for display and riddling/cryptic purposes, as an unusual and "learned" script, to make certain passages stand distinct'.[109] In comparison to Roman letters, runes were possibly even more elitist in that even fewer readers would have been able to decipher them.[110] On the Ruthwell Cross, the presence of (exclusively) Latin inscriptions on the front and back suggests that the runes were certainly *not* employed because they constituted the most natural medium of writing; on the contrary, the use of a different, less usual and possibly 'marked' writing system separates and distinguishes the runic text from the Latin inscriptions and, I would argue, mirrors the riddlic quality of the language on the visual level of writing. The cryptic aspect is further emphasised by the unusual arrangement of the runes: on each side, the text runs first horizontally along the top bar, then vertically down the right border, in horizontal lines of two to four runes, then in the same fashion down the left border. This layout makes the text, in Page's words, 'maddeningly hard to read' even for experienced readers.[111] It is

---

[107] John D. Niles, *Old English Enigmatic Poems and the Play of the Texts* (Turnhout, 2006), 221. The earliest known cryptographic and ornamental use of Anglo-Saxon runes is in early eighth-century continental manuscripts; see David Parsons, 'Anglo-Saxon Runes in Continental Manuscripts', in Klaus Düwel (ed.), *Runische Schriftkultur in kontinental-skandinavischer und -angelsächsischer Wechselbeziehung: Internationales Symposium in der Werner-Reimers-Stiftung vom 24.-27. Juni 1992 in Bad Homburg*, Reallexikon der germanischen Altertumskunde, Ergänzungsbände, 10 (Berlin, 1994), 195–220, at 195–6; similar usage in manuscripts of insular provenience is late (tenth to eleventh century).
[108] Niles, *Enigmatic Poems*, 223.
[109] Raymond I. Page, 'Runic Writing, Roman Script and the Scriptorium', in Staffan Nyström (ed.), *Runor och ABC: Elva föreläsningar från ett symposium i Stockholm, våren 1995* (Stockholm, 1997), 119–35, at 135. See also Page, *Introduction*, 116–17.
[110] For a contrasting opinion, see Parsons, who assumes 'a widespread and essentially uniform runic literacy among the educated in eighth- and ninth-century Anglo-Saxon society' and explains the absence of runes in early insular manuscripts by arguing that, since runes were commonplace, they held no fascination for Anglo-Saxon scribes, whereas continental scholars would have been intrigued by the foreign script ('Anglo-Saxon Runes', 199, 215–16).
[111] Page, *Introduction*, 150. I made the experiment of arranging a translation of the poem in the same way and showing it to a number of people, all of whom took a long while to find out how the text worked. Ó Carragáin cites Roman and

Remains of the Past in Old English Literature

thus only after 'puzzling' over the runic inscription for a considerable amount of time that the reader will grasp the fact that it describes the crucifixion from the unusual perspective of the cross itself.

The text's veiling of its central concern with the crucifixion finds a parallel in the monument's pictorial programme. Just as the *Ruthwell Poem* fails to mention the identity of its speaker, and actually encrypts the entire account of the crucifixion scene, so do the reliefs and accompanying Latin inscriptions refrain from depicting the crucifixion, notwithstanding the fact that they predominantly show scenes from Christ's life. This is all the more surprising since, as Catherine Karkov has pointed out, 'the cross bearing the body of Christ in its multiple forms is at the centre' of the monument's imagery, even when that body cannot be seen, as in the Visitation panel or the depiction of Paul and Anthony sharing a loaf of bread in the desert – an obvious reference to the Eucharist.[112] There is, however, one exception that I have hitherto neglected to mention: an additional panel situated beneath the Annunciation, almost completely obliterated or left unfinished, with no trace of an accompanying text, showing a crucifixion scene (Figure 3). During the early Middle Ages, this panel was probably hidden, buried in the ground to provide the necessary hold for the monument. This is also how the Bewcastle Cross – in many respects the closest parallel to the Ruthwell Cross – is secured, and it was in the same manner that the Ruthwell Cross was initially re-erected in the early nineteenth century. Much speaks for the assumption that this is how the monument was originally conceived: the shaft broadens beneath the panel depicting the Annunciation and is much more roughly hewn, nor is there evidence of a block on which it could have stood – it was only when the monument was moved into the church that it was displayed in such a way as to make the base visible. Moreover, the mason John W. Dods had to carve away a considerable part of the original shaft in order to create a tongue with which it could be fitted into the pedestal: there would have been no need to do so if there had already been a tongue or corresponding hole in the

---

Greek examples of similarly (though not quite identically) arranged inscriptions, arguing that eighth-century readers would have been used to deciphering and processing inscriptions in *scriptura continua* through the act of *praelectio*, the meditation over a text until it is known by heart (*Ritual*, 44; see 52–3 and plates 6 and 8 for the discussion of the parallels). Compared to Ó Carragáin's examples, however, the sheer length of the Ruthwell text and hence the considerable number of runes involved, as well as its overall arrangement, would have rendered it inordinately more difficult to decipher.

[112] Karkov, *Art of Anglo-Saxon England*, 138, 140. Karkov's argument is more persuasive than Kendall's suggestion that 'the sculptural programme of the Ruthwell cross and the Latin inscriptions that accompany it [...] do not, for the most part, bear directly on, or derive from, the meaning of the cross as sign' ('Sign to Vision', 142).

Visions of the Holy Cross

Figure 3 The Ruthwell Cross, crucifixion panel © Crown Copyright: HES.

monument's shaft.[113] The absence of any reference to the crucifixion in the other panels grants this image a central place in the monument's overall design: placed on a part of the monument that was hidden but nevertheless central to its stability – the base that kept it from falling over – it wittily

---

[113] For discussions of Dods's account and drawing, see Farrell with Karkov, 'Construction', 38–43; Orton, Wood, with Lees, *Fragments*, 56–61. Although the fact that Dods had to carve out a tongue might contradict such an interpretation, Robert B. K. Stevenson has argued that the crucifixion panel was added in the late ninth century. He suggests that the shaft beneath the Annunciation and Holy Family panels was originally buried, but that the monument was raised in the late ninth century, at which point the crucifixion scene was added; Robert B. K. Stevenson, 'Further Thoughts on Some Well Known Problems', in Michael Spearman and John Higgitt (eds), *The Age of Migrating Ideas: Early Medieval Art in Northern Britain and Ireland* (Edinburgh, 1993), 16–26. Orton et al. propose that it was at this time that the monument was transformed from a column into a cross through the addition of the crosshead (*Fragments*, 56–7). One feels tempted to note that such a scenario would accord well with Page's, Maevaert's and Conner's suggestion that the runic poem could be a later addition. One might, for instance, hypothesise that the monument's iconographic and written programme was deliberately changed so as to take this transformation into account. My interpretation of the runic poem would be compatible with such a scenario but is in no way dependent on it.

Remains of the Past in Old English Literature

referred to the centrality of the crucifixion both to the Christian faith and to the monument's textual and pictorial programme.

The same can be said of the runic poem: by providing the very reference that is so obviously missing from the rest of the monument's visual and literary content, the text not only fits neatly into its overall programme, but in fact takes centre stage. Intriguingly, Christine Fell has observed that Old English *run* [rune] and related words such as *geryne* were frequently used to refer to Christian mysteries,[114] which not only militates against the notion of runes as a kind of pagan 'atavism' in vernacular culture, but also resonates with their specific usage on the Ruthwell Cross. The fact that the runic poem's meaning is hidden, both graphically and linguistically, can be read an allusion to the crucifixion, which is likewise a sacred mystery.[115]

The Ruthwell Cross as Figura

If the *Ruthwell Poem*, as an account of the crucifixion and a riddle on the True Cross, takes such a central place in the monument's programme, surely it is no coincidence that it is inscribed into an object that either was, or, as Orton, Wood and Lees more cautiously suggest, might have been conceived of as a representation of the cross?[116] Kendall argues that the runic poem 'is an expression, a translation into the vernacular, of the literal meaning of the cross as a sign of the crucifixion, a poetic version of what the cross says to the viewer who has ears to listen as well as eyes to see'.[117] However, the cross into which the poem is inscribed is not the 'true' cross but its representation; semiotically speaking, it is a thing (a stone cross) that is a sign signifying another thing (the 'true' cross), which signifies an event in sacred history (the crucifixion). Given this chain of signification, and given that the riddlic inscription is presented as the

---

[114] Christine E. Fell, 'Runes and Semantics', in Alfred Bammesberger (ed.), *Old English Runes and their Continental Background* (Heidelberg, 1991), 195–229, at 206.

[115] Arguably, the crucifixion, which points both to Christ's death and his resurrection, constitutes the most central of these mysteries. According to Jennings, 'the early Christians understood that their way of living in the world was characterized by the paradox of the cross in that the instrument of defeat had become the instrument of victory. [...] The cross was never presented as simply an instrument of suffering; belief in the cross necessarily included resurrection symbolism and assent thereto' ('Rood and Ruthwell', 7–8).

[116] 'Though there are few persons who would admit to *seeing* crosses *as* columns, there are many who tend to *see* columns *as* crosses, rather than as objects that may or may not once have been crosses' (Orton, Wood, with Lees, *Fragments*, 50).

[117] Kendall, 'Sign to Vision', 140.

Visions of the Holy Cross

speech of a narrative voice that refers to itself in the first person, one may well wonder about the identity of this 'I' that is speaking. 'The cross', of course – but which one? In other words, is the 'voice' whose words we read really that of the (absent) True Cross, or does it belong to the stone cross bearing the inscription?

Text-bearing objects that refer to themselves in the first person were quite common during the early Middle Ages, especially in Germanic-speaking regions – surviving artefacts include rings, knives and the famous Alfred Jewel, inscribed 'ÆLFRED MEC HEHT GEWYRCAN'.[118] Many of these inscriptions are runic, but the closest parallel to the text on the Ruthwell Cross is that on the aforementioned Brussels Cross, which is written in Roman letters:

+ DRAHMAL ME WORHTE
+ ROD IS MIN NAMA GEO IC RICNE CYNING
BÆR BYFIGYNDE B/LODE BESTEMED
ÞA/S RODE HET ÆÞLMAIR WYRICAN
OND AÐELWOLD HYS BEROÐO[R]
CRISTE TO LOFE FOR ÆLFRICES SAVLE HYRA BEROÞOR :-

[+ Drahmal made me
+ Cross is my name; long ago a powerful king
I bore trembling, drenched in blood;
Æþelmær ordered this cross to be made,
and Æþelwold his brother:
in Christ's honour, for the soul of Ælfric their brother.]

The similarities to *The Dream of the Rood* and the Ruthwell inscription are obvious: 'Geo ic ricne cyning' and 'blode bestemed' occur almost verbatim in both, with 'ahof' substituted for 'geo' and 'mid' [with] completing the instrumental dative construction 'blode bestemed' (*The Dream of the Rood*, lines 44 and 47).[119] In the Brussels inscription, the speaking 'I' paradoxically identifies both with the liturgical object ('Drahmal me worhte') and with the True Cross ('geo ic ricne cyning'). The poem on the Ruthwell Cross seems to invoke a similar situation: through the riddlic persona of the speaker, which speaks to the reader in the first person via the inscription, the poem appears to refer not only to the 'original' cross, but also to the monument – that is, to the True Cross's representation. Karkov argues that 'spoken words always suggest a body and a self that

---

[118] See, for instance, Swanton (ed.), *Dream of the Rood*, 66 n. 3.

[119] Majewski argues that due to the lack of space on the monument, the reconstruction 'hof' instead of 'ahof' is to be preferred (*Ruthwell Cross*, 314). Semantically, this does not make any difference.

243

Remains of the Past in Old English Literature

are present'.[120] In the absence of a frame narrative that introduces the speaker (such as we find in *The Dream of the Rood*), this means that it must be the monument itself, the silent bearer of the message, that is speaking to the observer, in the same way as the Brussels Cross and many other inscribed objects from early medieval England and Scandinavia proclaim their identity or affiliation in the first person. As Ó Carragáin observes, 'The runic verse *tituli* employ the rhetorical device of prosopopoeia to give the monument an articulate personality: they make this cross tell us, in the English vernacular, of itself'.[121] Kendall suggests that in religious settings, the notion of a 'speaking' object was not a purely literary conceit, but 'could express a deeper reality'. He cites as parallels portals of eleventh- and twelfth-century churches that '"spoke" in the voice of Christ or the Church', and whose voice worshippers would have experienced 'as something like "real presence"'. This sense of a 'real presence', Kendall argues, had its basis in medieval exegetical practices which posited a figural identity between the biblical event and its representation. [122] In the case of the Ruthwell Cross, the runic poem self-reflexively draws attention to the formal accord between its 'speaker' and the medium into which it is inscribed. If we read the poem as a riddle, as I suggested above, this means that the monument's literal *figura* holds the key: as in the process of riddling, where the solution already exists in the hints given by the text, the answer to the riddle of the *Ruthwell Poem* is 'already there' in the very form of monument.[123]

[120] Karkov, *Art of Anglo-Saxon England*, 145.

[121] Ó Carragáin, *Ritual*, 60.

[122] Kendall, 'Sign to Vision', 136, 138. As noted above, Kendall does not use the term 'figural', but alludes to the four senses of typological interpretation. Karkov proposes a different solution based on the Brussels Cross's function as a reliquary: 'Relics of the True Cross had the ability to turn the cross-reliquaries that contained them into further relics of the Cross, and thus the Cross itself' (*Art of Anglo-Saxon England*, 145). In the case of the Brussels Cross, the question is thus whether the speaker can identify with the True Cross because of the figural accord between the two objects, or because of the reliquary's capacity as a contact relic. Given that the inscription unequivocally refers to the circumstances of the representation's production, I tend towards the former. Karkov further hypothesises on the possibility of the Ruthwell Cross having served as a container for a relic of the True Cross. Since it does not provide an explicit self-referential comment like the Brussels Cross, the presence of a relic would alter the situation: the poem's speaking voice might be that of the relic. However, given that the evidence for such use is slight at best, I will not pursue this question further.

[123] Strikingly, while the Ruthwell Cross employs such extra-textual means to highlight the formal identity of the poem's speaker and the monument, in the *Dream of the Rood*, the speaker's identity is revealed by purely textual means, that is, in the frame narrative, rather than visually, as, for instance, in the cruciform

Visions of the Holy Cross

The double identification of the poem's speaker with both the True Cross and the monument as its representation is made possible through the figural relationship that exists between the two: the liturgical object, as the cross's *figura*, both represents the original and partakes in its reality. At the same time, the liturgical cross prefigures an even more universal truth; namely, the resurrection of the flesh at the end of historical time, which has yet to come to pass and whose full significance is still hidden. In addition, the cross as a Christian symbol and as a liturgical object signifying the True Cross is also part-fulfilment of the promise of universal conversion, since it represents one of the immediate effects of the crucifixion, namely the emergence of a Christian Faith and Church. Understood as a *figura*, the Ruthwell Cross is thus able to participate in salvation history by referencing the past and the future: the historical moment of Christ's crucifixion; Isaiah's prophecy of universal conversion, to be fulfilled before the end of historical time; and the resurrection of the flesh.

According to Schlie, it is this temporal relationship between phenomenal prophecy and the revelation of its significance that is expressed by Saint Paul in 1 Corinthians 13.9–12:[124]

> 9 ex parte enim cognoscimus, et ex parte prophetamus. 10 cum autem venerit quod perfectum est, evacuabitur quod ex parte est. [...] 12 videmus nunc per speculum in enigmate: tunc autem facie ad faciem. nunc cognosco ex parte: tunc autem cognoscam sicut et cognitus sum.

> [For we know in part, and we prophesy in part. [10] But when that which is perfect is come, that which is in part shall be done away. [...] [12] We see now through a mirror in a riddle; but then face to face. Now I know in part; but then I shall know even as I am known.][125]

Until the second *parousia*, human understanding of the figural relationship must by necessity remain fragmentary; any attempt to unveil it therefore appears as if one were looking 'through a mirror in a riddle'. It is tempting to see a connection between the *enigma* aspect of *figura* and the riddlic style of the *Ruthwell Poem*, whose speaker's veiled identity gestures towards the link between the True Cross and the monument as its *figura*. Indeed, the fact that the poem's solution is already present in the shape of its medium

---

acrostics of Venantius Fortunatus, Hrabanus Maurus, Alcuin and others (see Tate, 'Chiasmus', 120–1; Chaganti, 'Vestigial Signs', 61). However, it is intriguing that both the *Dream of the Rood* and the *Ruthwell Poem* make extensive use of chiasmus and thus structurally play on the form of the cross (Tate, 'Chiasmus'; Howlett, 'Inscriptions', 76–8).

[124] Schlie, 'Klosterneuburger Ambo', 206.

[125] Translation modified. Douay-Rheims translates the first part of 13.12: 'We see now through a glass in a dark manner; but then face to face.'

suggests a play on the hermeneutic process of riddling, a process in which the riddle's subject only comes into existence at the moment the riddle is solved, but is also already there, fragmented and veiled, in the textual hints that lead the reader to the solution.

In this dynamic structure, the monument takes a central place, since it is experienced by the viewer(s) as a sort of performance, one in which they likewise participate and one that reproduces, but also participates in, the process of salvation.[126] Several recent studies have highlighted the performative potential of the Ruthwell Cross. James Paz observes that the monument's design 'orchestrates' the viewers' movements as they move around it and let their eyes wander across the surfaces, while Karkov notes how the monument's programme requires the viewer to supply 'what cannot be seen', such as the unborn John the Baptist or the absent body of Christ: 'Like many contemporary sculptures, Ruthwell is not self-contained; it requires the physical presence of the viewer for its completion.'[127] The latter is arguably true of all works of art, but particularly so in the case of the Ruthwell Cross, where the double identification of the speaking voice with both the True Cross and its representation means that observers experience their encounter with the object as a performative situation in which the monument appears to be addressing them directly – at least if they have grasped the relationship between text, object and biblical event. Hines points out that the Old English texts on the cross 'invite the reader into a more immediately dramatic relationship with the monument itself in a way that the Latin texts never aim to bring about'.[128] In a strange parallel to the situation described in *The Dream of the Rood*, the viewer finds themselves on the same level as the dreamer in the frame narrative of the Vercelli poem. But where the latter is being lectured by the True Cross itself – if only in a vision[129] – in the case of the Ruthwell Cross it is a representation, a stone monument, that appears to be speaking to the reader through its inscription. And yet, from a figural perspective, the representation *is* the True Cross, in a fashion similar to later medieval mystery plays, where the performer *becomes*, figurally, the person they represent.

---

[126] Schlie argues that liturgical works of art constitute (postfigural) *figurae* of biblical events and are therefore experienced by the viewer as a performance that reproduces, and indeed makes present, the past. In witnessing this performance, the viewer participates in the process of salvation ('Klosterneuburger Ambo', 246).

[127] James Paz, *Nonhuman Voices in Anglo-Saxon Literature and Material Culture* (Manchester, 2017), 197–202; Karkov, *Art of Anglo-Saxon England*, 140, 142. Chaganti ('Vestigial Signs', 59) and Ó Carragáin (*Ritual*, 296–8) likewise emphasise the monument's performative potential.

[128] Hines, 'Ruthwell Cross', 187; see also 189–90.

[129] It could be argued that the cross in *The Dream of the Rood*, as a product of the *imaginatio*, is merely a representation, too.

Visions of the Holy Cross

In the case of the *Ruthwell Poem*, the identification even goes so far as to include the original object's historical perspective: its speaker *is* the True Cross, not its representation, and as such, the speaker – and hence the poem – lacks the temporal perspective of the monument, which, as a liturgical object, can place the crucifixion in the historical past. The material context may suggest that it is the monument that is speaking, but the narrator's perspective places the poem precisely at the moment of the historical event of Christ's Passion.[130] Although told in the past tense, the narrative has an immediateness to it that culminates in the incompleteness of the account, the strange silence, on the part of the speaker, concerning Christ's resurrection: the *Ruthwell Poem* ends with Christ being taken down from the cross, *limwærig*, 'dead'.[131] The speaker's historical knowledge, the poem suggests, goes no further than the time of Christ's temporary death; certainly, it does not extend as far as the resurrection. The speaker thus remains in doubt as to the outcome. The future – even that of the reader – has yet to come to pass, and the cross has no knowledge of it. From the reader's perspective, then, the cross is speaking from the past, in archaic writing and in a language shrouded in mystery. Both points are suggested by the contrastive use of Roman and runic letters: while the Latin

---

[130] Karkov seems to allude to the same paradox when she notes that the monument's inscription embeds the narrative voice's Old English language 'anachronistically into the chronology of the past, yet here eternally present, moment of the Crucifixion' (*Art of Anglo-Saxon England*, 145).

[131] This interpretation is impeded by the fact that the text at this point is truncated. Dickins and Ross estimate that there would have been enough room for another forty runes; see Bruce Dickins and Alan S. C. Ross (eds), *The Dream of the Rood* (London, 1963), 29, n. to line 64. These may have expressed something similar to Howlett's reconstruction of the last line (based on *The Dream of the Rood*): 'bihêaldun hiæ þer Hêafunæs Dryctin; ond he hinæ þer hwilæ restæ' [they beheld there the Lord of Heavens, and he rested himself there for a while] (Howlett, 'Inscriptions', 88); see also Majewski (*Ruthwell Cross*, 319–20), who reaches a similar conclusion: [*Bih*]ēa[*l*]*du*[*n*] [*h*]ī[*æ*] þē[*r*] [*heafunæs drihten, þā hē hwīlæ restæ*]. The expression *hwilæ restæ* in the second half-line, if part of the original inscription, might have highlighted the temporary nature of Christ's death. But *restan* also means 'to rest in death, lie dead, lie in the grave' (*BT*, s.v. *restan* I, 3) and *hwile* could also be understood to mean 'meanwhile, at the same time' (*BT*, s.v. *hwil*, example 6), although I admit to special pleading regarding the latter. In any case, it is uncertain whether the second half-line once formed part of the inscription; as outlined above, the Ruthwell text is prone to suppress important details. Moreover, even *The Dream of the Rood*, from which the Ruthwell text is commonly reconstructed, glosses over the resurrection. As Paz notes: 'Curiously, no mention is made here of Christ's physical resurrection. His animate-body-turned-inanimate-corpse simply vanishes from the poem at this point and it is instead the rood that is dug up and decked out in gold and silver' (*Nonhuman Voices*, 186).

247

inscriptions with their scriptural quotations would not have suggested a specific temporal context to the medieval reader, the runes would have had an archaising effect in that they would have been perceived, after the conversion, as belonging to an earlier stage of cultural development; as Niles points out, 'Since runes derive from a layer of culture older than the Roman alphabet which Christian missionaries introduced to Britain at the end of the sixth century AD, an Anglo-Saxon text that has been runified has at the same time been rendered more antique'.[132] The runic inscription, and hence the cross's speech, thus would have created (and still creates) the impression of being older than the monument, quasi contemporaneous with the biblical events themselves, and in that sense, what we encounter here – and what the early medieval viewer would have encountered, too – is an object that is already imagining itself as archaeological, an artefact from a distant past inscribed with archaic characters that describe an event long ago, and yet also make that event vividly present by addressing the viewer in their own present moment.

In this respect, the *Ruthwell Poem* differs from *The Dream of the Rood*, where the cross seems to be speaking from an extra-temporal perspective as a timeless symbol that views past, present and future all at once, as if it shared in God's extra-temporal eternity. The speaker of the *Ruthwell Poem*, by contrast, is not only arrested in a specific temporal moment, but even lacks the reader's historical hindsight. Unlike the pictorial programme and the Latin inscriptions, the Old English poem thus stresses the immanence of the historical object over the transcendental knowledge of the religious symbol. Historical time is presented as a process that privileges the later moment over an earlier one: the former possesses knowledge denied to the latter. The same is not true of the monument itself, however: as a symbol of the Christian hope of resurrection and a representation of the historical instrument of the Passion, the Ruthwell Cross possesses the very knowledge that the poem inscribed into it lacks. Strikingly, while *The Dream of the Rood* presents the cross's speech as part of a literary work that is removed from the reader by several layers of framing devices, the *Ruthwell Poem* feigns direct contact with its audience. The reader thus becomes, figurally, an observer of the crucifixion and, simultaneously, a witness of its historical impact, that is, of the spread of Christianity without which the present situation of liturgical enactment involving the reader would not have been possible. The temporal double vision experienced by the monument's observer reveals the tension inherent in the concept of *figura*.

---

[132] Niles, *Enigmatic Poems*, 223. In a similar vein, Lerer argues that runes, as an archaic script, were used by Anglo-Saxons to draw attention to the 'alterity of their own past' (*Literacy and Power*, 11–12).

Visions of the Holy Cross

Beyond a Figural Vision of History

I have argued above that as a model of history, *figura* is ultimately teleological but non-linear. This non-linear aspect is underlined by the reiterative nature of figural interpretation, in which temporally disparate
moments, figured in each other, repeat the same meaning over and over
again, paralleling Cheah's point about the iterative nature of teleology
more generally.[133] The disregard for sequential order makes it possible to
read the events both forward and backward, in spite of the transcendental
truth to which they ultimately refer.

The iterative dimension of the figural relationship between different
historical events is reinforced through the iterative practices of contemplation, devotion and interpretation that are performed and enacted by each
observer anew. Margaret Jennings points out that 'the church's public
worship, the liturgy is designed to be reiterative, to reflect repeatedly the
realities of the Christ and the Christian life'.[134] The figural relationship
between different historical events, albeit pre-existing in the similarities
between them, only comes into being through the act of expression. This
is pointed out by Niklaus Largier in his discussion of Tertullian's attack
on Marcion, Auerbach's central text for defining the Christian *figura*.
Largier contends that the 'similarities emerge at the moment when the
event enters written discourse, since for Tertullian they lie in the things
themselves that are perceived in the act of expression'.[135] He goes on to
argue that:

> [*Figura*] is not the event itself, but the sensual-concrete mode of expres-
> sion in which it appears in the narrative by way of the relationships
> of similarity and dissimilarity that determine the perception. [...] The
> events, persons, narratives that exist in the figural mode of expression
> are sensually-concretely real, and yet as such also veiled, opaque,
> incomplete, preliminary, incoherent, isolated, open, questionable, and
> without 'finality'. They are not reproduced, but represented/performed
> [*dargestellte*] reality.[136]

---

[133] Cheah, *What is a World*, 7.
[134] Jennings, 'Rood and Ruthwell', 6.
[135] 'Solche Ähnlichkeiten erscheinen, wo das Ereignis in die Schrift eingeht, da
sie für Tertullian in den Dingen selbst liegen, die im Ausdruck wahrgenom-
men werden.' Niklaus Largier, 'Zwischen Ereignis und Medium: Sinnlichkeit,
Rhetorik und Hermeneutik in Auerbachs Konzept der *figura*', in Christian
Kiening and Katharina Mertens Fleury (eds), *Figura: Dynamiken der Zeiten und
Zeichen im Mittelalter* (Würzburg, 2013), 51–70, at 67.
[136] 'Sie [die Figur] ist nicht das Ereignis selbst, sondern die sinnlich-konkrete
Ausdrucksform, in der sich dieses in der Erzählung in Ähnlichkeits- und
Unähnlichkeitsbeziehungen niederschlägt, welche die Wahrnehmung bestim-

Remains of the Past in Old English Literature

As a model of history, *figura* thus stresses the iterative aspect of cultural performance, while also preserving the singularity of each event. Historically concrete, singular events are perpetuated in other singular, historically concrete events – and yet, in their historical singularity, the events cannot be exact reproductions of each other: each iteration constitutes a difference.[137] This may not be readily apparent in the act of devotional performance, which must necessarily strive for stability, but it is quite obvious in the figural relationship between the work of art and the event it depicts. As a liturgical object and hence a symbolic representation, a *signum datum*, the Ruthwell Cross 'knows more' than the historical cross at the moment of the crucifixion. This temporal discrepancy is reflected in its design: the carved panels and accompanying Latin inscriptions, as well as the monument's status as a liturgical object, reveal it as temporally posterior to the event to which it refers. The Old English poem, on the other hand, pretending to be the original cross's speech at the moment of the crucifixion, adopts its temporally anterior and hence limited perspective. This discrepancy in historical knowledge reveals a tension within the concept of *figura*; namely, between the representational-symbolic, on the one hand, and the historically singular, on the other – a tension that the monument exploits to great effect.

Poem and monument, I have argued, draw part of their meaning from the tension between the historical and semiotic aspects of figural interpretation. This tension, we have seen, can be conceptualised in terms of similarity and dissimilarity. On the one hand, the formal accord that exists between the True Cross, the monument, and the poem's speaker suggests that all three are identical; it is this formal accord that makes it possible for the observer to perceive their figural relationship in the first place. The poem's mode of presentation, which veils, in riddlic fashion, the figural relationship conjoining these three entities, plays on *figura*'s complex hermeneutic dimension. On the other hand, by stressing the historical immanence of the speaker's perspective, the runic poem shows them to be historically separate, to possess each its own distinct, individual meaning. The tension between the poem's historically limited vision and the representational character of the monument as a whole highlights the tension between the historical and semiotic aspects of figural interpretation.

---

men. [...] Die Ereignisse, Personen, Geschichten, die uns demnach in der figuralen Ausdrucksform vorliegen, sind sinnlich-konkrete Wirklichkeit, als solche aber auch verhüllt, nicht transparent, unvollständig, vorläufig, abgerissen, einzeln, offen, fraglich, und ohne 'Endgültigkeit.' Sie sind nicht Abbilder einer Wirklichkeit, sondern dargestellte Wirklichkeit.' *Ibid.*, 67. In German, *darstellen* occupies a place that hovers semantically between 'represent' and 'perform'.

[137] In this respect, at least, *figura* resembles Derrida's notion of the 'trace' as discussed in Derrida, *Of Grammatology*.

Visions of the Holy Cross

Yet there is a further tension, or, one even might say, contradiction that marks the relationship between monument, poem and historical cross. For although the poem, on the one hand, pretends to be the speech of the historical cross, and the monument, on the other hand, suggests the speech is its own, in actual fact, it is of course neither. In reality (and here I mean not merely a modern, atheist form of reality, but also a reality experienced by medieval Christians), neither the True Cross nor the monument have an individual, independent subjectivity. The interpretive act that identifies the three entities as one requires a suspension of disbelief on part of the reader that marks the poem as fiction. It is in this respect that the poem goes beyond a purely figural – and, hence, providential – vision of history, thereby drawing attention to its own status as a work of art.

Conclusion

In this chapter, I have examined how three Old English texts – the narrative poem *Elene*, the lyrical *Dream of the Rood* and the runic inscription on the Ruthwell Cross – each in its own way exploits the tension-ridden interplay between a material-historical and a symbolic-representational perception of the cross. As a contact relic hallowed by Christ's blood, the latter is a material entity whose temporal existence far exceeds the lives of human beings. In preserving Christ's blood, the True Cross has the potential to recall Christ's presence and thus establish contact with the divine. As a symbol, whose material manifestations need not be materially identical with each other, the cross is primarily a representation that refers back to the 'true' instrument of Christ's Passion, but it also has the potential to act as a multivalent sign. As I have argued, a figural interpretation of the semiotic relationship between the True Cross and its representation makes it possible to see these entities as historically and materially distinct while also acknowledging the existence of a figural identity or accord between them, which in turn allows representations of the cross to partake in the spiritual significance of the original artefact and thereby become holy objects themselves: it is this figural accord that allows representations to connect worshippers with the divine.

The figural relationship between these historically distinct entities establishes a non-linear, figural temporality that complements but also complicates the linear historical temporality that each of them inhabits. The texts under consideration here acknowledge the existence of these two different temporalities while simultaneously revealing the potential tension between them.

251

Conclusion: Conceptualising Time and History through the Remains of the Past

While Sarah Semple has argued that early medieval engagements with the past by way of its material traces were 'widespread, varied, and long lived',[1] the same is true of the texts produced in that time frame. Bede, one of the earliest known authors with a distinct notion of an 'English' identity, produced – among other things – one of the most popular historiographical works of the entire Middle Ages, the *Historia ecclesiastica gentis Anglorum*, a text that has never been out of circulation (whether in manuscript or in print) since its completion in 731. Bede also wrote two important treatises on chronology, *De temporibus* and *De temporum ratione*. Some 150 years later, King Alfred not only had both Bede's *Historia* and Orosius's *Historiae adversus paganos* translated into Old English, but also appears to have instigated, directly or indirectly, the vernacular tradition of the *Anglo-Saxon Chronicle*. Moreover, early medieval Britain possessed a tradition of local hagiography that, unlike its more generic models of early Christian saints' lives, had a pronounced historiographical bent,[2] linking the biographies of local saints and church officials to political and ecclesiastical concerns.[3]

However, literary engagements with the past were not restricted to hagiography and historiography. As the texts discussed in this study demonstrate, poetry and prose in both Latin and the vernacular testify to an interest not only in the past itself, but also in different historical perspectives and their respective narrative potential, as well as in questions of temporality more generally, to which the works under consideration here yield a variety of individual and sometimes highly creative responses. These responses range from *Elene*'s exploration of the one-directional, though non-genealogical and potentially non-continuous nature of political and religious succession as expressed in the concept of *translatio*, via *The*

---

[1] Semple, *Perceptions*, 2. In the immediate context of this quote, Semple is specifically concerned with relationships between people and monuments; nonetheless, her study persuasively demonstrates the ubiquity, variety and longevity of engagements with the traces of the past in general.

[2] Michael Hunter, for instance, notes that 'Anglo-Saxon' historiography and hagiography are not usually easy to distinguish; Michael Hunter, 'Germanic and Roman Antiquity', 30–1.

[3] Important works of local hagiography include the early eighth-century *Vita Sancti Wilfrithi* and the *Vita Sancti Guthlaci*, Bede's own verse and prose *Lives of Saint Cuthbert*, as well as Ælfric's saints' lives of Æthelthryth and King Oswald.

Conclusion

Dream of the Rood's juxtaposition of linear-historical and non-linear figural time, to *Beowulf*'s implicit, but immensely potent histories of progress, whose dependence on rupture and radical periodisation strives to render the past obsolete.

As I have shown, these texts not only display an acute sense of the pastness and alterity of the past, but they also demonstrate complex modes of conceptualising the relationships between past, present and future. Nor does salvation history, the Middle Ages' own version of a supersessionist master narrative, prove quite as one-dimensional as has often been supposed: as has become clear in my discussion of historical and figural time, the concept was capable of incorporating multiple and potentially divergent historical perspectives, negotiating complex notions of temporality in the process. What I hope to have demonstrated, then, is that Old English literature was capable of combining and creatively adapting a broad variety of ways of conceptualising not merely history, but indeed the very processes by which historical thought operates. The texts examined display a deep and conflicted understanding of the philosophical implications of history and temporality; at the same time, they betray the capacity to explore these issues through sophisticated aesthetic means.

It is this fascination with the past and human beings' relationships with it that has been the principal theme of this study. Despite the diversity of the works that I have considered here, there is a strong common thread between them: they all develop their responses to history and temporality in conjunction with a specific literary theme, one that is centred on the depiction of what I have referred to as 'archaeological artefacts'. These objects, which are singled out as ancient, the remnants of a remote past, are as diverse as the historical perspectives to which their descriptions give rise; in turn, they elicit a rich variety of responses ranging from awe and incomprehension to the impulse to narrativise their histories, be it in the form of historical reconstruction (as in the case of *Beowulf*'s giants' sword or the prehistory of the Cross) or of deliberate, recognisable fiction (as I have argued of *The Ruin*'s pageants). The texts' 'archaeological imagination' connects the themes of materiality and temporality – in other words, the multiple perceptions of time associated with material objects – by foregrounding the longevity, but also the fragility of historical artefacts.

The central thesis of this book has been that the literary engagement with archaeological objects allowed texts to describe complex and sometimes contradictory temporal processes and experiences that they were unable or unwilling to conceptualise more explicitly. The assumption that literature is capable of expressing concepts that are otherwise difficult or impossible to theorise is common in the context of the literature of modernity, but is less so in the context of medieval texts. My emphasis on what one might call literary texts is not meant to deny the capacity of

253

other forms of literature to engage with these issues. Thus, even though Bede's *Historia ecclesiastica* may outwardly appear to follow a conventional teleological model that explains the displacement of the native Britons – Christian, but frequently sinful and heretical – as an instance of indirect divine intervention that ultimately led to the adoption of Roman orthodox practices throughout the island (despite an intermediary lapse into paganism), it implicitly acknowledges alternative historical models, such as the notion of a *translatio* of political and spiritual authority from the Romans to the 'English', or the different dating systems used throughout the work. The fact that medieval texts were capable of expressing complex and contradictory models of time on the level of narration without making them the object of explicit discussion may have to do with a tendency on the part of contemporaneous theology and historiography to eschew contradiction by treating potentially conflicting vantage points as distinct categories, as in the case of the four senses of typology. Perhaps the most important insight to be gained from these deliberations is that perceptions and conceptualisations of historical and temporal processes were variable and do not allow us to reconstruct a single, overarching medieval sense of history – even individual texts may permit different concepts of time and history to stand side by side, without attempting to reconcile them.

The present study does not claim to be exhaustive. There are other texts from early medieval Britain and beyond that involve similar, as well as divergent, discussions of the temporal nature of historical artefacts – as already pointed out in the introduction, it might prove particularly worthwhile to pursue a similar theme in the context of contemporary works in Latin. Nor does the engagement with 'archaeological artefacts' suddenly cease with the Conquest – another traditional narrative of rupture, and one that the present study is guilty of replicating. Monika Otter has discussed the multiple ways in which Latin historiographical texts from the twelfth century in particular (Geoffrey of Monmouth's *Historia regum Britanniae*, William of Malmesbury's *Gesta pontificum Anglorum* and *Gesta regum Anglorum*, Gerald of Wales's *Itinerarium Kambriae*, Matthew Paris's *Chronica maiora* and the *Gesta abbatum Sancti Albani*, to name but a few) use the *topos* of the *inventio* to reflect on the nature of historiographical writing. She has also drawn attention to the way that the late medieval *Saint Erkenwald*, an alliterative poem usually dated to around 1400 and preserved in a single manuscript of the late sixteenth century, uses the *inventio* model to stage a direct exchange between the past and the present. In this exchange, each gives something to the other: the past, by way of its material traces, provides the present with prestige, moral instruction and historical knowledge; the present, in receiving and incorporating these

Conclusion

traces, grants the past recognition, rehabilitation and meaning.[4] In a very tangible sense, then, *Saint Erkenwald* highlights some of the same issues as the Old English texts discussed in this study. Centred around a story set in seventh-century London, which involves the discovery of an unusually well-preserved tomb under the foundations of a pagan temple in the process of being reconstructed and converted into St Paul's Cathedral, the poem describes how the tomb's unknown provenance, the easily discernible but, to the sixth-century Londoners, incomprehensible inscription, and the richly dressed but unidentifiable corpse elicit awe, incredulity and an acute sense of the opacity of a past that refuses to yield its secrets.

Like *Elene*, *Saint Erkenwald* relies on a miracle to provide the present with information about the past: after London's bishop Erkenwald has spent a night in prayer, God grants the corpse speech and thereby enables it to disclose its identity. As it turns out, most of the historical details alluded to by the temporarily revived pagan judge are completely unknown to the seventh-century Londoners, including a British prehistory (modelled after the first books of Geoffrey of Monmouth's *Historia regum Britanniae*) that reaches back to the island's first human settlement by Trojan refugees. The fact that the newly converted Londoners have no knowledge of this past is explained by a rupture in Britain's cultural and political history: the coming of the pagan 'Saxones', who drove the native Christian British population into Wales (lines 7–10). Thus, like many of the texts discussed in this study, *Saint Erkenwald* conceptualises history – or, at least, British history – as layered, marked not only by separate historical periods but also by archaeological *stratae*: it is by digging deep under St Paul's foundations that the Londoners chance upon the traces of earlier times.[5] At the same time, the poem appears to comment on the possibility – or impossibility – of a transfer between the different historical layers: as Johnston points out, despite the fact that the miraculous dialogue between Erkenwald and the reanimated corpse promises unlimited access to information about the past, the poem nonetheless stages that past as largely beyond reach. Many historical details, such as the righteous judge's name or the meaning of the letters on the coffin, remain undisclosed; and even further: once the corpse has told its story and is miraculously and posthumously baptised by Erkenwald, it dissolves into dust (much like *Beowulf*'s giant blade).[6]

Intriguingly, the poem's Londoners are well aware of an array of strategies by which they might tackle the past's opacity: in order to gain information about the tomb, they try to decipher the inscription, they search

---

[4] Monika Otter, 'New Werke'. *Saint Erkenwald* is cited from J. A. Burrow and Thorlac Turville-Petre (eds), *A Book of Middle English*, 2nd edn (Oxford, 1996), 203–14.

[5] Johnston, 'Verfügbarmachung', 73–4.

[6] *Ibid.*, 74.

255

the city's historical archives, and they try to correlate the corpse's state of preservation, the depth of its burial and the lack of clues as to its identity with its relative age.[7] The finders' engagement with the corpse demonstrates a nuanced and sophisticated understanding of different temporal processes: for instance, while the citizens take the corpse's remarkable state of preservation as evidence that the burial must have occurred recently, Bishop Erkenwald points out that the body might have been embalmed. It is only the similarly good condition of the clothes that suggests the miraculous nature of the find – reminding us of a similar emphasis on the preservation of textiles and coins in the Legend of the Seven Sleepers. But despite these strategies, the past remains – at least initially – outside the grasp of the present: the tomb's inscription proves to be incomprehensible, not because it is illegible, but because it represents a language that the seventh-century Londoners can neither pronounce nor understand: 'Full verray were þe vigures, þer avisyd hom mony, / Bot all muset hit to mouth and quat hit mene shuld' [The shapes (i.e., of the letters) were perfectly distinct, as many could see; but everyone was at a loss to pronounce it (i.e., the text) or understand what it might mean'; lines 53–5].[8] As a matter of fact, not even the corpse's miraculous reanimation changes this state of affairs, since the question of the letters' meaning never comes up in Erkenwald's brief conversation with the corpse. Despite the potency of the miracle, many details of the past thus remain undisclosed – and intriguingly, it is precisely such details as the letters on the coffin or the corpse's name, which might have been recorded in the city's archives, which the poem's Londoners, thanks to their archaeological imagination, could reasonably expect to solve without the aid of divine intervention. Like several of the texts discussed in this study (such as *Elene*, *The Wanderer* or *Beowulf*), *Saint Erkenwald* thus presents historical knowledge – in the double sense of knowledge *of* and *about* the past – as something that becomes inaccessible over time, either because of temporal distance or through cultural and political ruptures. On the other hand, the fact that the Londoners tried various strategies to gain historical information shows that they believe that, in some cases at least, material remains may disclose their secrets.

Nineteenth-century historicism tended to regard an understanding of the alterity and pastness of the past – and hence its fundamental inaccessibility, despite attempts at historical reconstruction – as one of the prerequisites of a modern sense of history, one it denied to premodernity in general and the Middle Ages in particular. Engaging with the archaeological imagination of medieval texts allows us to challenge this assessment, which, although increasingly questioned in more recent

---

[7] Otter, 'New Werke', 407–8.
[8] Johnston, 'Verfügbarmachung', 74.

Conclusion

scholarship, nevertheless continues to influence current perceptions of premodernity (sometimes perhaps even inadvertently), and, in so doing, to question period boundaries on a fundamental level.

It is perhaps no coincidence that *Saint Erkenwald* is set in the same general period that produced the texts discussed in this study, that is, in pre-Norman 'England'. Indeed, the poem's very form – its use of alliterative metre – harks back to the formal features of Old English poetry and establishes a form of continuity across the political and cultural caesura of the Norman Conquest, a rupture frequently regarded as dividing English literary history into a 'before' and an 'after'. As it appears, then, even though the transmission of written texts in English ceased almost completely in the years after the Conquest, there may be more continuities than many scholars, until recently, were prepared to acknowledge. Whereas older studies habitually spoke of an 'alliterative revival' when referring to texts such as *Saint Erkenwald* or *Sir Gawain and the Green Knight* (another work at least potentially featuring an archaeological object, namely the 'Green Chapel', whose description is reminiscent of a prehistoric barrow),[9] recent scholarship has tended to imagine a less fractured English literary history, with Eric Weiskott observing a 'formal continuity between Old and Middle English alliterative meter, running directly through Lawman's *Brut* (ca. 1200) and other Early Middle English poems'.[10] Moving closer to our own present, Schwyzer has examined an impressive range of archaeological fantasies ranging from the works of Shakespeare to those of Thomas Browne.[11] The present study is an attempt to extend the discussion of literary engagements with materiality and its relationship with time and history to the English literature of the early Middle Ages.

---

[9] Bertram Colgrave, 'Sir Gawayne's Green Chapel', *Antiquity*, 12:47 (1938), 351–3. Johnston argues that 'the Green chapel [...] seems to be designed within a specifically archaeological frame of reference, inasmuch as it resembles a megalithic burial mound re-used and re-appropriated for different purposes'; Andrew James Johnston, 'Material Studies', in Leah Tether and Johnny McFadyen (eds), *Handbook of Arthurian Romance: King Arthur's Court in Medieval European Literature* (Berlin, 2017), 225–38, 234–5.

[10] Eric Weiskott, 'The Paris Psalter and English Literary History', in Irina Dumitrescu and Eric Weiskott (eds), *The Shapes of Early English Poetry: Style, Form, History* (Kalamazoo, MI, 2019), 107–34, at 108.

[11] Schwyzer, *Archaeologies*.

Bibliography

Primary Sources

Anderson, James E. (ed. and trans.), *Two Literary Riddles in the Exeter Book: Riddle I and* The Easter Riddle; *A Critical Edition with Full Translations* (Norman, OK, 1986).

Augustine, *City of God*, Loeb Classical Library, 411–17 (7 vols, Cambridge, MA, 1957–72).

——*De doctrina christiana*, ed. and trans. R. P. H. Green (Oxford, 1995).

Bately, Janet (ed.), *The Old English Orosius*, EETS SS, 6 (London, 1980).

Bede, *Bede's* Ecclesiastical History of the English People, ed. and trans. Bertram Colgrave and R. A. B. Mynors (Oxford, 1969).

—— The Ecclesiastical History of the English People: *With the* Greater Chronicle *and* Letter to Egbert, ed. Judith McClure and Roger Collins, trans. Bertram Colgrave (Oxford, 2008).

Berkeley, George, *The Works of George Berkeley, Bishop of Cloyne*, ed. A. A. Luce and T. E. Jessop (9 vols, London, 1955).

Bodden, Mary-Catherine (ed.), *The Old English Finding of the True Cross* (Cambridge, 1987).

Bradley, S. A. J. (trans.), *Anglo-Saxon Poetry: An Anthology of Old English Poems in Prose Translation with Introduction and Headnotes* (London, 1982).

Byron, George Gordon, *The Complete Poetical Works*, ed. Jerome J. McGann (7 vols, Oxford, 1986).

Dickins, Bruce and Alan S. C. Ross (eds), *The Dream of the Rood* (London, 1963).

Dobbie, Elliott Van Kirk (ed.), *The Anglo-Saxon Minor Poems*, ASPR, 6 (New York, 1942).

Dunning, T. P. and A. J. Bliss (eds), *The Wanderer* (London, 1969).

Fulk, R. D., Robert E. Bjork and John D. Niles (eds), *Klaeber's* Beowulf *and* The Fight at Finnsburg, 4th edn (Toronto, 2014).

Giambattista, Vico, *New Science: Principles of the New Science Concerning the Common Nature of Nations*, trans. David Marsh, 3rd edn (London, 1999).

Gordon, Ida L. (ed.), *The Seafarer* (London, 1960).

Gradon, Pamela O. E. (ed.), *Cynewulf's* Elene (London, 1958).

Henschen, Godefroid and Daniel van Papebroche (eds), *Acta Sanctorum: Maius*, rev. edn (7 vols, Paris, 1866).

Holder, Alfred (ed.), *Inventio sanctae crvcis: Actorvm Cyriaci pars I; Latine et Graece; Ymnvs antiqvs de sancta crvce; Testimonia inventae sanctae crvcis* (Leipzig, 1889).

Bibliography

Irvine, Susan, *MS E*, ASC, 7 (Cambridge, 2004).

Klaeber, Friedrich (ed.), Beowulf *and* The Fight at Finnsburg, 3rd edn (Boston, MA, 1941).

Klinck, Anne Lingard (ed.), *The Old English Elegies: A Critical Edition and Genre Study* (Montreal, 1992).

Krapp, George Philip (ed.), *The Junius Manuscript*, ASPR, 1 (New York, 1931).

——(ed.), *The Vercelli Book*, ASPR, 2 (New York, 1932).

Krapp, George Philip and Elliott Van Kirk Dobbie (eds), *The Exeter Book*, ASPR, 3 (New York, 1936).

Leslie, R. F. (ed.), *The Wanderer* (Manchester, 1966).

Magennis, Hugh (ed.), *The Anonymous Old English Legend of the Seven Sleepers* (Durham, 1994).

Matthew Paris, *The Life of Saint Alban*, trans. Jocelyn Wogan-Browne and Thelma S. Fenster (Tempe, AZ, 2010).

Miller, Thomas (ed.), *The Old English Version of* Bede's Ecclesiastical History of the English People, EETS OS, 95 (London, 1890).

Bokenham, Osbern, *Legendys of Hooly Wummen*, ed. Mary S. Serjeantson, EETS OS, 206 (London, 1938).

Schliemann, Heinrich, *Heinrich Schliemann's Selbstbiographie: Bis zu seinem Tode vervollständigt*, ed. Sophie Schliemann (Leipzig, 1892).

—— [as Henry Schliemann], *Ilios: The City and Country of the Trojans; The Results of Researches and Discoveries on the Site of Troy and throughout the Troad in the Years 1871–72–73–78–79, Including an Autobiography of the Author* (London, 1880).

——*Trojanische Alterthümer: Bericht über die Ausgrabungen in Troja* (Leipzig, 1874).

Skeat, Walter William (ed.), *Aelfric's Lives of Saints: Being a Set of Sermons on Saints' Days formerly Observed by the English Church; Edited from Manuscript Julius E.VII in the Cottonian Collection, with Various Readings from other Manuscripts*, EETS OS, 76 (2 vols, London, 1881).

Swanton, Michael (trans.), *The Anglo-Saxon Chronicles*, rev. edn (London, 2000).

——(ed.), *The Dream of the Rood* (Manchester, 1970).

Williamson, Craig (trans.), *The Complete Old English Poems* (Philadelphia, PA, 2017).

Secondary Sources

Abram, Christopher, 'In Search of Lost Time: Aldhelm and *The Ruin*', *Quaestio*, 1 (2000), 23–44.

Aravamudan, Srinivas, 'The Return of Anachronism', *Modern Language Quarterly*, 62:4 (2001), 331–53.

Bibliography

Arendt, Hannah, *The Human Condition* (Chicago, IL, 1958).

Arnold, Bettina and Henning Hassmann, 'Archaeology in Nazi Germany: The Legacy of the Faustian Bargain', in Philip L. Kohl and Clare Fawcett (eds), *Nationalism, Politics and the Practice of Archaeology* (Cambridge, 1996), 70–81.

Auerbach, Erich, 'Figura', trans. Ralph Manheim, in *Scenes from the Drama of European Literature* (New York, 1959), 11–76.

Baert, Barbara, *A Heritage of Holy Wood: The Legend of the True Cross in Text and Image*, trans. Lee Preedy (Leiden, 2004).

Baker, William, Andrew Gasson, Graham Law and Paul Lewis, *The Collected Letters of Wilkie Collins: Addenda and Corrigenda*, vol. 14 (London, 2023).

Bakhtin, M. M., 'Forms of Time and of the Chronotope in the Novel: Notes toward a Historical Poetics', in *The Dialogic Imagination: Four Essays*, ed. Michael Holquist, trans. Caryl Emerson and Michael Holquist (Austin, TX, 1981), 84–258.

Barad, Karen, *Meeting the Universe Halfway: Quantum Physics and the Entanglement of Matter and Meaning* (Durham, NC, 2007).

—— 'Posthumanist Performativity: Toward an Understanding of How Matter Comes to Matter', *Signs*, 28:3 (2003), 801–31.

Barthes, Roland, 'The Reality Effect', in *The Rustle of Language*, ed. François Wahl, trans. Richard Howard (Berkeley, CA, 1989), 141–48.

Bartosik-Vélez, Elise, '*Translatio Imperii*: Virgil and Peter Martyr's Columbus', *Comparative Literature Studies*, 46:4 (2009), 559–88.

Beaston, Lawrence, '*The Ruin* and the Brevity of Human Life', *Neophilologus*, 95 (2011), 477–89.

Bennett, Jane, *Vibrant Matter: A Political Ecology of Things* (Durham, NC, 2010).

Bennett, Paul, 'Canterbury in Transition: The Role of the Roman Theatre', in Andrew Richardson, Michael Bintley, John Hines and Andy Seamen (eds), *Transitions and Relationships over Land and Sea in the Early Middle Ages of Northern Europe* (Canterbury, 2023), 1–26.

Bhabha, Homi K., 'DissemiNation: Time, Narrative and the Margins of the Modern Nation', in *The Location of Culture* (London, 1994), 139–70.

Bishop, Chris, '"Þyrs, Ent, Eoten, Gigans": Anglo-Saxon Ontologies of "Giant"', *NM*, 107:3 (2006), 259–70.

Bloch, Ernst, 'Nonsynchronism and the Obligation to Its Dialectics', *New German Critique*, 11 (1977), 22–38.

Borgehammar, Stephan, *How the Holy Cross Was Found: From Event to Medieval Legend* (Stockholm, 1991).

Bowen, R. O., '*The Wanderer*, 98', *Explicator*, 13 (1955), 60–1.

Bradley, Mark (ed.), *Classics and Imperialism in the British Empire* (Oxford, 2010).

Bradley, Richard, 'Time Regained: The Creation of Continuity', *Journal of the British Archaeological Association*, 140:1 (1987), 1–17.

Bibliography

Brandl, Alois, 'Venantius Fortunatus und die ags. Elegien *Wanderer* und *Ruine*', *Archiv für das Studium der Neueren Sprachen und Literaturen*, 73:139 (1919), 84.

Burke, Peter, *The Renaissance Sense of the Past* (London, 1969).

—— 'The Sense of Anachronism from Petrarch to Poussin', in Chris Humphrey and W. M. Ormrod (eds), *Time in the Medieval World* (York, 2001), 157–73.

Burrow, J. A. and Thorlac Turville-Petre (eds), *A Book of Middle English*, 2nd edn (Oxford, 1996).

Bynum, Caroline Walker, *Christian Materiality: An Essay on Religion in Late Medieval Europe* (New York, 2011).

Campbell, Adrian, 'East, West, Rome's Best? The Imperial Turn', *Global Discourse*, 3:1 (2013), 34–47.

Campbell, Jackson J., 'Cynewulf's Multiple Revelations', *Medievalia et Humanistica*, 3 (1972), 257–77.

Cartlidge, Neil, 'Evidence of the Past in the Legend of the Seven Sleepers', in Jan-Peer Hartmann and Andrew James Johnston (eds), *Material Remains: Reading the Past in Medieval and Early Modern British Literature* (Columbus, OH, 2021), 57–77.

Cassidy, Brendan, 'The Later Life of the Ruthwell Cross: From the Seventeenth Century to the Present', in Brendan Cassidy (ed.), *The Ruthwell Cross: Papers from the Colloquium Sponsored by the Index of Christian Art, Princeton University, 8 December 1989* (Princeton, NJ, 1992), 3–34.

Ceram, C. W., 1949 *Götter, Gräber und Gelehrte: Roman der Archäologie* (Wien, 1949).

Chaganti, Seeta, 'Vestigial Signs: Inscription, Performance, and *The Dream of the Rood*', *PMLA*, 125:1 (2010), 48–72.

Chakrabarty, Dipesh, *Provincializing Europe: Postcolonial Thought and Historical Difference* (Princeton, NJ, 2000).

Chambers, R. W., '*Beowulf* and the Heroic Age', in Archibald Strong (trans.), Beowulf: *Translated into Modern English Rhyming Verse, with Introduction and Notes* (London, 1925), vii–xlix.

Chase, Colin (ed.), *The Dating of* Beowulf (Toronto, 1981).

Cheah, Pheng, *What is a World? On Postcolonial Literature as World Literature* (Durham, NC, 2016).

Cohen, Jeffrey Jerome, 'Old English Literature and the Work of Giants', *Comitatus: A Journal of Medieval and Renaissance Studies*, 24 (1993), 1–32.

——*Stone: An Ecology of the Inhuman* (Minneapolis, MN, 2015).

Colgrave, Bertram, 'Sir Gawayne's Green Chapel', *Antiquity*, 12:47 (1938), 351–3.

Conner, Patrick, 'On Dating Cynewulf', in Robert E. Bjork (ed.), *Cynewulf: Basic Readings* (New York, 1996), 23–55.

—— 'The Ruthwell Monument Runic Poem in a Tenth-Century Context', *RES* NS, 59:238 (2008), 25–51.

Copeland, Rita and Ineke Sluiter (eds), *Medieval Grammar and Rhetoric: Language Arts and Literary Theory, AD 300–1475* (Oxford, 2009).

Crabtree, Pam J., *Early Medieval Britain: The Rebirth of Towns in the Post-Roman West* (Cambridge, 2018).

Crary, Jonathan, *Techniques of the Observer: On Vision and Modernity in the Nineteenth Century* (Cambridge, MA, 1990).

Critten, Rory G., 'Via Rome: Medieval Medievalisms in the Old English *Ruin*', *JMEMS*, 49:2 (2019), 209–31.

Cross, Frank Leslie and Elizabeth Anne Livingstone (eds), *The Oxford Dictionary of the Christian Church*, 3rd edn (Oxford, 1997).

Cross, James E., '*Ubi Sunt* Passages in Old English: Sources and Relationships', *Årsbok: Yearbook of the New Society of Letters at Lund* (1958–59), 21–44.

Cubitt, Catherine R. E., '"As the Lawbook Teaches": Reeves, Lawbooks and Urban Life in the Anonymous Old English Legend of the Seven Sleepers', *English Historical Review*, 124 (2009), 1021–49.

Curtius, Ernst Robert, *European Literature and the Latin Middle Ages*, trans. Willard R. Trusk (Princeton, NJ, 2013).

Dailey, Patricia, 'Questions of Dwelling in Anglo-Saxon Poetry and Medieval Mysticism: Inhabiting Landscape, Body, and Mind', *New Medieval Literatures*, 8 (2006), 175–214.

D'Arcens, Louise, 'Introduction', in Louise D'Arcens (ed.), *The Cambridge Companion to Medievalism* (Cambridge, 2016), 1–13.

Davies, Joshua, *Visions and Ruins: Cultural Memory and the Untimely Middle Ages* (Manchester, 2018).

Davis, Craig R., 'Recovering Germans: Teutonic Origins and *Beowulf*', *Kritikon Litterarum*, 44:1 (2016), 125–42.

Davis, Kathleen, 'Old English Lyrics: A Poetics of Experience', in Clare A. Lees (ed.), *The Cambridge History of Early Medieval English Literature* (Cambridge, 2013), 332–56.

Dean, Christopher, '*Weal wundrum heah, wyrmlicum fah* and the Narrative Background of *The Wanderer*', *Modern Philology*, 63:2 (1965), 141–3.

Derrida, Jacques, *Of Grammatology*, trans. Gayatri Chakravorty Spivak (Baltimore, MD, 1976).

Deuel, Leo (ed.), *Memoirs of Heinrich Schliemann: A Documentary Portrait Drawn from His Autobiographical Writings, Letters, and Excavation Reports* (New York, 1977).

Dietler, Michael, 'A Tale of Three Sites: The Monumentalization of Celtic *oppida* and the Politics of Collective Memory and Identity', *World Archaeology*, 30:1 (1998), 72–89.

DiNapoli, Robert, 'Poesis and Authority: Traces of an Anglo-Saxon Agon in Cynewulf's *Elene*', *Neophilologus*, 82 (1998), 619–30.

Bibliography

Dinshaw, Carolyn, *How Soon Is Now? Medieval Texts, Amateur Readers, and the Queerness of Time* (Durham, NC, 2012).

—— 'Temporalities', in Paul Strohm (ed.), *Middle English* (Oxford, 2007), 107–23.

Dolezalek, Isabelle, 'Alternative Narratives: Transcultural Interventions in the Permanent Display of the Museum für Islamische Kunst', in Vera Beyer, Isabelle Dolezalek and Sophia Vassilopoulou (eds), *Objects in Transfer: A Transcultural Exhibition Trail through the Museum für Islamische Kunst in Berlin* (Berlin, 2016), 25–35.

Drijvers, Jan Willem, *Helena Augusta: The Mother of Constantine the Great and the Legend of Her Finding of the True Cross* (Leiden, 1992).

Dumitrescu, Irina, *The Experience of Education in Anglo-Saxon Literature* (Cambridge, 2018).

Dunleavy, G. W., 'A "De Excidio" Tradition in the Old English *Ruin?*', *Philological Quarterly*, 38 (1959), 112–18.

Earle, John, 'An Ancient Saxon Poem of a City in Ruins, supposed to be Bath', *Proceedings of the Bath Natural History and Antiquities Field Club*, 2 (1870–73), 259–70.

Easton, D. F., 'Priam's Gold: The Full Story', *Anatolian Studies*, 44 (1994), 221–43.

Eaton, Tim, *Plundering the Past: Roman Stonework in Medieval Britain* (Stroud, 2000).

Emerson, Oliver F., 'Legends of Cain, especially in Old and Middle English', *PMLA*, 21:4 (1906), 831–929.

Estes, Heide, 'Colonization and Conversion in Cynewulf's *Elene*', in Catherine E. Karkov and Nicholas Howe (eds), *Conversion and Colonization in Anglo-Saxon England* (Tempe, AZ, 2006), 133–51.

Fabian, Johannes, *Time and the Other: How Anthropology Makes Its Object* (New York, 1983).

Farrell, Robert T., with Catherine E. Karkov, 'The Construction, Deconstruction, and Reconstruction of the Ruthwell Cross: Some Caveats', in Brendan Cassidy (ed.), *The Ruthwell Cross: Papers from the Colloquium Sponsored by the Index of Christian Art, Princeton University, 8 December 1989* (Princeton, NJ, 1992), 35–47.

Fell, Christine E., 'Perceptions of Transience', in Malcolm Godden and Michael Lapidge (eds), *The Cambridge Companion to Old English Literature* (Cambridge, 1991), 172–89.

—— 'Runes and Semantics', in Alfred Bammesberger (ed.), *Old English Runes and their Continental Background* (Heidelberg, 1991), 195–229.

Felski, Rita, '"Context Stinks!"', *New Literary History*, 42:4 (2011), 573–91.

—— *Hooked: Art and Attachment* (Chicago, IL, 2020).

—— *The Limits of Critique* (Chicago, IL, 2015).

Ferhatović, Denis, *Borrowed Objects and the Art of Poetry: Spolia in Old English Verse* (Manchester, 2019).

Bibliography

Foley, John Miles, *The Singer of Tales in Performance* (Bloomington, IN, 1995).

Foucault, Michel, *The Archaeology of Knowledge* (London, 2007).

—— *The Order of Things: An Archaeology of the Human Sciences* (London, 2004).

Frank, Armin Paul, 'Transatlantic Responses: Strategies in the Making of a New World Literature', in Andreas Poltermann (ed.), *Literaturkanon – Medienereignis – Kultureller Text: Formen interkultureller Kommunikation und Übersetzung* (Berlin, 1995), 211–31.

Frank, Roberta, 'The *Beowulf* Poet's Sense of History', in Larry D. Benson and Siegfried Wenzel (eds), *The Wisdom of Poetry: Essays in Early English Literature in Honor of Morton W. Bloomfield* (Kalamazoo, MI, 1982), 53–65.

—— 'Germanic Legend in Old English Literature', in Malcolm Godden and Michael Lapidge (eds), *The Cambridge Companion to Old English Literature* (Cambridge, 2013), 82–100.

—— 'Sharing Words with *Beowulf*', in Virginia Blanton and Helene Scheck (eds), *Intertexts: Studies in Anglo-Saxon Culture Presented to Paul E. Szarmach* (Tempe, AZ, 2008), 3–16.

Frankis, P. J., 'The Thematic Significance of *enta geweorc* and Related Imagery in *The Wanderer*', *ASE*, 2 (1973), 253–69.

Frantzen, Allen J., *Desire for Origins: New Language, Old English, and Teaching the Tradition* (New Brunswick, NJ, 1990).

French, W. H., '*The Wanderer* 98: *Wyrmlīcum fāh*', *Modern Language Notes*, 67:8 (1952), 526–9.

Fukuyama, Francis, *The End of History and the Last Man* (New York, 1992).

Fulk, R. D., 'Cynewulf: Canon, Dialect, and Date', in Robert E. Bjork (ed.), *Cynewulf: Basic Readings* (New York, 1996), 3–21.

Garner, Lori Ann, *Structuring Spaces: Oral Poetics and Architecture in Early Medieval England* (Notre Dame, IN, 2011).

Ghosh, Amitav, *The Great Derangement: Climate Change and the Unthinkable* (Chicago, IL, 2016).

Gneuss, Helmut, *Handlist of Anglo-Saxon Manuscripts: A List of Manuscripts and Manuscript Fragments Written or Owned in England up to 1100* (Tempe, AZ, 2001).

Goez, Werner, Translatio Imperii: *Ein Beitrag zur Geschichte des Geschichtsdenkens und der politischen Theorien im Mittelalter und in der frühen Neuzeit* (Tübingen, 1958).

Gosden, Chris and Gary Lock, 'Prehistoric Histories', *World Archaeology*, 30:1 (1998), 2–12.

de Grazia, Margreta, 'Anachronism', in James Simpson and Brian Cummings (eds), *Cultural Reformations: Medieval and Renaissance in Literary History* (Oxford, 2010), 13–32.

Green, Martin, 'Introduction', in Martin Green (ed.), *The Old English Elegies* (Rutherford, NJ, 1983), 1–30.

—— 'Man, Time, and Apocalypse in *The Wanderer*, *The Seafarer*, and *Beowulf*', *JEGP*, 74:4 (1975), 502–18.

Greene, Thomas M., 'History and Anachronism', in Gary Saul Morson (ed.), *Literature and History: Theoretical Problems and Russian Case Studies* (Stanford, CA, 1986), 205–20.

Greenfield, Stanley B., 'The Old English Elegies', in E. G. Stanley (ed.), *Continuations and Beginnings: Studies in Old English Literature* (London, 1966), 142–75.

—— '*The Wanderer*: A Reconsideration of Theme and Structure', *JEGP*, 50:4 (1951), 451–65.

Grossi, Joseph, 'Barrow Exegesis: Quotation, Chorography, and Felix's *Life of St. Guthlac*', *Florilegium*, 30 (2013), 143–65.

Gurevich, Aron J., *Categories of Medieval Culture* (London, 1985).

Hall, Alaric, *Elves in Anglo-Saxon England: Matters of Belief, Health, Gender and Identity* (Woodbridge, 2007).

Hall, John R. Clark, *A Concise Anglo-Saxon Dictionary for the Use of Students*, 2nd edn (New York, 1916).

Hanning, Robert W., '*Beowulf* as Heroic History', *Mediaevalia et Humanistica* NS, 5 (1974), 77–102.

Harbus, Antonina, *Helena of Britain in Medieval Legend* (Cambridge, 2002).

Härke, Heinrich, 'Anglo-Saxon Immigration and Ethnogenesis', *Medieval Archaeology*, 55 (2011), 1–28.

Harris, Jonathan Gil, *Untimely Matter in the Time of Shakespeare* (Philadelphia, PA, 2009).

Hartmann, Jan-Peer, 'Monument Reuse in Felix's *Vita Sancti Guthlaci*', *Medium Ævum*, 88:2 (2019), 230–64.

Heckman, Christina M., 'Things in Doubt: *Inventio*, Dialectic, and Jewish Secrets in Cynewulf's *Elene*', *JEGP*, 108:4 (2009), 449–80.

Hegel, Georg Wilhelm Friedrich, *Vorlesung über die Philosophie der Weltgeschichte* (4 vols, Hamburg, 1988–93).

Hempelmann, Reinhard, *Sakrament als Ort der Vermittlung des Heils: Sakramententheologie im evangelisch-katholischen Dialog* (Göttingen, 1992).

Higham, Nicholas J., *An English Empire: Bede and the Early Anglo-Saxon Kings* (Manchester, 1995).

Hill, Thomas D., 'Sapiential Structure and Figural Narrative in the Old English *Elene*', *Traditio*, 27 (1971), 159–77.

—— 'Time, Liturgy, and History in the Old English *Elene*', in Samantha Zacher (ed.), *Imagining the Jew in Anglo-Saxon Literature and Culture* (Toronto, 2016), 156–66.

—— 'Wise Words: Old English Sapiential Poetry', in David F. Johnson and Elaine Treharne (eds), *Readings in Medieval Texts: Interpreting Old and Middle English Literature* (Oxford, 2005), 166–79.

Hines, John, '*But men seyn, "What may ever laste?"* Chaucer's House of Fame as a Medieval Museum', in Jan-Peer Hartmann and Andrew

James Johnston (eds), *Material Remains: Reading the Past in Medieval and Early Modern British Literature* (Columbus, OH, 2021), 240–57.

—— 'Literary Sources and Archaeology', in Helena Hamerow, David A. Hinton and Sally Crawford (eds), *The Oxford Handbook of Anglo-Saxon Archaeology* (Oxford, 2011), 968–85.

—— 'The Ruthwell Cross, the Brussels Cross, and *The Dream of the Rood*', in Graham D. Caie and Michael D. C. Drout (eds), *Transitional States: Change, Tradition, and Memory in Medieval Literature and Culture* (Tempe, AZ, 2018), 175–92.

—— *Voices in the Past: English Literature and Archaeology* (Cambridge, 2004).

Hodder, Ian, *Entangled: An Archaeology of the Relationships between Humans and Things* (Chichester, 2012).

Holdsworth, Carolyn, 'Frames: Time Level and Variation in *The Dream of the Rood*', *Neophilologus*, 66:4 (1982), 622–8.

Holtorf, Cornelius, *From Stonehenge to Las Vegas: Archaeology as Popular Culture* (Walnut Creek, CA, 2005).

—— 'The Life-Histories of Megaliths in Mecklenburg-Vorpommern (Germany)', *World Archaeology*, 30:1 (1998), 23–38.

Hope-Taylor, Brian, *Yeavering: An Anglo-Saxon Centre of Early Northumbria*, DoE Archaeological Report, 7 (London, 1977).

Howe, Nicholas, 'Anglo-Saxon England and the Postcolonial Void', in Ananya Jahanara Kabir and Deanne Williams (eds), *Postcolonial Approaches to the European Middle Ages: Translating Cultures* (Cambridge, 2005), 25–47.

—— 'The Landscape of Anglo-Saxon England: Inherited, Invented, Imagined', in John Howe and Michael Wolfe (eds), *Inventing Medieval Landscapes: Senses of Place in Western Europe* (Tallahassee, FL, 2002), 91–112.

—— *Migration and Mythmaking in Anglo-Saxon England* (New Haven, CT, 1989).

—— *The Old English Catalogue Poems* (Copenhagen, 1985).

—— 'Rome: Capital of Anglo-Saxon England', *JMEMS*, 34:1 (2004), 147–72.

—— *Writing the Map of Anglo-Saxon England: Essays in Cultural Geography* (New Haven, CT, 2008).

Howell, Naomi, 'Saracens at St Albans: The Heart-Case of Roger de Norton', in Jan-Peer Hartmann and Andrew James Johnston (eds), *Material Remains: Reading the Past in Medieval and Early Modern British Literature* (Columbus, OH, 2021), 145–71.

Howlett, David, 'Inscriptions and Design of the Ruthwell Cross', in Brendan Cassidy (ed.), *The Ruthwell Cross: Papers from the Colloquium Sponsored by the Index of Christian Art, Princeton University, 8 December 1989* (Princeton, NJ, 1992), 71–93.

Hume, Kathryn, 'The "Ruin Motif" in Old English Poetry', *Anglia*, 94 (1976), 339–60.

Bibliography

Hunter, Michael, 'Germanic and Roman Antiquity and the Sense of the Past in Anglo-Saxon England', *ASE*, 3 (1974), 29–50.

Ingold, Tim, 'The Temporality of the Landscape', *World Archaeology*, 25:2 (1993), 152–74.

Irvine, Martin, 'Anglo-Saxon Literary Theory Exemplified in Old English Poems: Interpreting the Cross in *The Dream of the Rood* and *Elene*', *Style*, 20:2 (1986), 157–81.

Irving, Edward B., Jr, 'Image and Meaning in the Elegies', in Robert P. Creed (ed.), *Old English Poetry: Fifteen Essays* (Providence, RI, 1967), 153–66.

Jennings, Margaret, 'Rood and Ruthwell: The Power of Paradox', *English Language Notes*, 31:3 (1994), 6–11.

Johnston, Andrew James, 'Anachronic Entanglements: Archaeological Traces in *Beowulf*', in Estella Weiss-Krejci, Sebastian Becker and Philip Schwyzer (eds), *Interdisciplinary Explorations of Postmortem Interaction: Dead Bodies, Funerary Objects, and Burial Spaces Through Texts and Time* (Cham, 2022), 97–112.

——'*Beowulf* and the Remains of Imperial Rome: Archaeology, Legendary History and the Problems of Periodisation', in Lars Eckstein and Christoph Reinfandt (eds), *Anglistentag 2008 Tübingen* (Trier, 2009), 127–36.

——'*Beowulf* as Anti-Virgilian World Literature: Archaeology, Ekphrasis, and Epic', in Irina Dumitrescu and Eric Weiskott (eds), *The Shapes of Early English Poetry: Style, Form, History* (Kalamazoo, MI, 2019), 37–58.

—— 'Global *Beowulf* and the Poetics of Entanglement', in Jan-Peer Hartmann and Andrew James Johnston (eds), *Material Remains: Reading the Past in Medieval and Early Modern Literature* (Columbus, OH, 2021), 103–19.

—— 'Material Studies', in Leah Tether and Johnny McFadyen (eds), *Handbook of Arthurian Romance: King Arthur's Court in Medieval European Literature* (Berlin, 2017), 225–38.

—— 'Medialität in *Beowulf*', *Germanisch-Romanische Monatsschrift*, 59:1 (2009), 129–47.

——*Performing the Middle Ages from* Beowulf *to* Othello (Turnhout, 2008).

—— 'St. *Erkenwald* und die Verfügbarmachung des Unverfügbaren', *Paragrana: Internationale Zeitschrift für Historische Anthropologie*, 21:2 (2012), 60–76.

——'Das Wunder des Historischen: Stephen Greenblatts' *The Swerve*', in *Aufklärung: Interdisziplinäres Jahrbuch zur Erforschung des 18. Jahrhunderts und seiner Wirkungsgeschichte*, 25 (2013), 287–303.

Karkov, Catherine E., *The Art of Anglo-Saxon England* (Woodbridge, 2011).

Kaske, Robert E., '*Beowulf* and the Book of Enoch', *Speculum*, 46:3 (1971), 421–31.

Bibliography

—— 'The *eotenas* in *Beowulf*', in Robert P. Creed (ed.), *Old English Poetry: Fifteen Essays* (Providence, RI, 1967), 285–310.

Keenan, H. T., 'The Ruin as Babylon', *Tennessee Studies in Literature*, 11 (1966), 109–17.

Kendall, Calvin B., 'From Sign to Vision: The Ruthwell Cross and *The Dream of the Rood*', in Catherine E. Karkov, Sarah Larratt Keefer and Karen Louise Jolly (eds), *The Place of the Cross in Anglo-Saxon England* (Woodbridge, 2006), 129–44.

Kiening, Christian, 'Einleitung', in Christian Kiening and Katharina Mertens Fleury (eds), *Figura: Dynamiken der Zeiten und Zeichen im Mittelalter* (Würzburg, 2013), 7–20.

Klaeber, Friedrich, '*Aeneis* und *Beowulf*', *Archiv für das Studium der Neueren Sprachen und Literaturen*, 126 (1911), 40–8, 339–59.

Klein, Stacy S., 'Reading Queenship in Cynewulf's *Elene*', *JMEMS*, 33:1 (2003), 47–89.

Köberl, Johann, 'The Magic Sword in *Beowulf*', *Neophilologus*, 71 (1987), 120–8.

Koselleck, Reinhart, *Futures Past: On the Semantics of Historical Time*, trans. Keith Tribe (New York, 2004).

Lapidge, Michael, 'The Career of Aldhelm', *ASE*, 36 (2007), 15–69.

—— 'Hypallage in the Old English *Exodus*', *Leeds Studies in English*, 37 (2006), 31–9.

Largier, Niklaus, 'Zwischen Ereignis und Medium: Sinnlichkeit, Rhetorik und Hermeneutik in Auerbachs Konzept der *figura*', in Christian Kiening and Katharina Mertens Fleury (eds), *Figura: Dynamiken der Zeiten und Zeichen im Mittelalter* (Würzburg, 2013), 51–70.

Latacz, Joachim, *Troia und Homer: Der Weg zur Lösung eines alten Rätsels*, 6th edn (Leipzig, 2010).

Latour, Bruno, *We Have Never Been Modern*, trans. Catherine Porter (Cambridge, MA, 1993).

Lavezzo, Kathy, *The Accommodated Jew: English Antisemitism from Bede to Milton* (Ithaca, NY, 2016), 28–63.

Lee, A. T., '*The Ruin*: Bath or Babylon? A Non-Archaeological Investigation', *NM*, 74 (1973), 443–55.

Leo, Heinrich, *Carmen Anglo-Saxonicum in Codice Exoniensi servatum, quod vulgo inscribitur 'Ruinae'* (Halle, 1865).

Lerer, Seth, *Literacy and Power in Anglo-Saxon Literature* (Lincoln, NE, 1991).

—— '"On fagne flor": The Postcolonial *Beowulf*', in Ananya Jahanara Kabir and Deanne Williams (eds), *Postcolonial Approaches to the European Middle Ages: Translating Cultures* (Cambridge, 2005), 77–102.

Liuzza, Roy M., 'The Tower of Babel: *The Wanderer* and the Ruins of History', *Studies in the Literary Imagination*, 36:1 (2003), 1–35.

Bibliography

Majewski, Kerstin, *The Ruthwell Cross and its Texts: A New Reconstruction and an Edition of the* Ruthwell Crucifixion Poem, Reallexikon der Germanischen Altertumskunde, Ergänzungsbände, 132 (Berlin, 2022).

Malamud, Margaret, '*Translatio Imperii*: America as the New Rome *c.* 1900', in Mark Bradley (ed.), *Classics and Imperialism in the British Empire* (Oxford, 2010), 249–83.

Manetti, Giovanni, *Theories of the Sign in Classical Antiquity*, trans. Christine Richardson (Bloomington, IN, 1993).

Meller, Harald and Kai Michel, *Die Himmelsscheibe von Nebra: Der Schlüssel zu einer untergegangenen Welt im Herzen Europas* (Berlin, 2018).

Mellinkoff, Ruth, 'Cain's Monstrous Progeny in *Beowulf*: Part I, Noachic Tradition', *ASE*, 8 (1979), 143–62.

——'Cain's Monstrous Progeny in *Beowulf*: Part II, Postdiluvian Survival', *ASE*, 9 (1980), 183–97.

Meyvaert, Paul, 'An Apocalypse Panel on the Ruthwell Cross', in Frank Tirro (ed.), *Medieval and Renaissance Studies: Proceedings of the Southeastern Institute of Medieval and Renaissance Studies, Summer 1978* (Durham, NC, 1982), 3–32.

——'Necessity Mother of Invention: A Fresh Look at the Rune Verses on the Ruthwell Cross', *ASE*, 41 (2012), 407–16.

——'A New Perspective on the Ruthwell Cross: *Ecclesia* and *Vita Monastica*', in Brendan Cassidy (ed.), *The Ruthwell Cross: Papers from the Colloquium Sponsored by the Index of Christian Art*, Princeton University, 8 December 1989 (Princeton, NJ, 1992), 95–166.

Millns, Tony, '*The Wanderer* 98: "Weal wundrum heah wyrmlicum fah"', *RES NS*, 28:112 (1977), 431–8.

Miyashiro, Adam, 'Homeland Insecurity: Biopolitics and Sovereign Violence in *Beowulf*', *Postmedieval*, 11 (2020), 384–95.

Moorehead, Caroline, *The Lost Treasures of Troy* (London, 1994).

Muir, Richard, *The New Reading the Landscape: Fieldwork in Landscape History* (Exeter, 2000).

Murphy, Patrick J., *Unriddling the Exeter Riddles* (University Park, PA, 2011).

Nagel, Alexander and Christopher S. Wood, *Anachronic Renaissance* (New York, 2010).

Near, Michael R., 'Anticipating Alienation: *Beowulf* and the Intrusion of Literacy', *PMLA*, 108:2 (1993), 320–32.

Nederman, Cary J., 'Empire and the Historiography of European Political Thought: Marsiglio of Padua, Nicholas of Cusa, and the Medieval/ Modern Divide', *Journal of the History of Ideas*, 66:1 (2005), 1–15.

Neidorf, Leonard (ed.), *The Dating of* Beowulf: *A Reassessment* (Cambridge, 2014).

Niles, John D., *Old English Enigmatic Poems and the Play of the Texts* (Turnhout, 2006).

Nolan, Maura, 'Historicism after Historicism', in Elizabeth Scala and Sylvia Federico (eds), *The Post-Historical Middle Ages* (Basingstoke, 2009), 63–85.

Nora, Pierre, 'Between Memory and History: Les lieux de mémoire', *Representations*, 26 (1989), 7–24.

North, Richard, *The Origins of* Beowulf: *From Vergil to Wiglaf* (Oxford, 2006).

Ó Carragáin, Éamonn, *Ritual and the Rood: Liturgical Images and the Old English Poems of the* Dream of the Rood *Tradition* (Toronto, 2005).

Ohly, Friedrich, 'The Spiritual Sense of Words in the Middle Ages', trans. David A. Wells, *Forum for Modern Language Studies*, 41:1 (2005), 18–42.

Olsen, Alexandra Hennessey, '"Thurs" and "Thyrs": Giants and the Date of *Beowulf*', *In Geardagum: Essays on Old and Middle English Language and Literature*, 6 (1984), 35–42.

Oosthuizen, Susan, *The Emergence of the English* (Leeds, 2019).

Orton, Fred, 'Rethinking the Ruthwell Monument: Fragments and Critique; Tradition and History; Tongues and Sockets', *Art History*, 21:1 (1998), 65–106.

——and Ian Wood, with Clare A. Lees, *Fragments of History: Rethinking the Ruthwell and Bewcastle Monuments* (Manchester, 2007).

Orton, Peter, 'The Technique of Object Personification in *The Dream of the Rood* and a Comparison with the Old English Riddles', *Leeds Studies in English*, 11 (1979), 1–18.

Osborn, Marijane, 'The Great Feud: Scriptural History and Strife in *Beowulf*', *PMLA*, 93:5 (1978), 973–81.

Otter, Monika, *Inventiones: Fiction and Referentiality in Twelfth-Century English Historical Writing* (Chapel Hill, NC, 1996).

——'"New Werke": *St. Erkenwald*, St. Albans, and the Medieval Sense of the Past', *Journal of Medieval and Renaissance Studies*, 24 (1994), 387–414.

Owen-Crocker, Gale R., *The Four Funerals in* Beowulf *and the Structure of the Poem* (Manchester, 2000).

Page, Raymond I., *Anglo-Saxon Aptitudes: An Inaugural Lecture Delivered before the University of Cambridge on 6 March 1985* (Cambridge, 1985).

——*An Introduction to English Runes* (London, 1973).

——'Runic Writing, Roman Script and the Scriptorium', in Staffan Nyström (ed.), *Runor och ABC: Elva föreläsningar från ett symposium i Stockholm, våren 1995* (Stockholm, 1997), 119–35.

Panofsky, Erwin, *Renaissance and Renascences in Western Art* (2 vols, Stockholm, 1960).

Parsons, David, 'Anglo-Saxon Runes in Continental Manuscripts', in Klaus Düwel (ed.), *Runische Schriftkultur in kontinental-skandinavischer und -angelsächsischer Wechselbeziehung: Internationales Symposium in der Werner-Reimers-Stiftung vom 24.-27. Juni 1992 in Bad Homburg,*

Bibliography

Reallexikon der germanischen Altertumskunde, Ergänzungsbände, 10 (Berlin, 1994), 195–220.

Patenall, Andrew J. G., 'The Image of the Worm: Some Literary Implications of Serpentine Decoration', in J. Douglas Woods and David Pelteret (eds), *The Anglo-Saxons: Synthesis and Achievement* (Waterloo, CA, 2006), 105–116.

Paz, James, *Nonhuman Voices in Anglo-Saxon Literature and Material Culture* (Manchester, 2017).

Pons-Sanz, Sara M., 'Old English Style', in Violeta Sotirova (ed.), *Bloomsbury Companion to Stylistics* (London, 2015), 569–82.

Ramey, Peter, 'The Riddle of Beauty: The Aesthetics of *Wrætlic* in Old English Verse', *Modern Philology*, 114 (2017), 457–81.

Rancière, Jacques, 'The Concept of Anachronism and the Historian's Truth', trans. Noel Fitzpatrick and Tim Stott, *InPrint*, 3:1 (2015), 21–52.

Regan, Catharine A., 'Evangelicism as the Informing Principle of Cynewulf's *Elene*', *Traditio*, 29 (1973), 27–52.

Renoir, Alain, 'The Old English *Ruin*: Contrastive Structure and Affective Impact', in Martin Green (ed.), *The Old English Elegies* (Rutherford, NJ, 1983), 148–73.

Robinson, Fred C., Beowulf *and the Appositive Style* (Knoxville, TN, 1985).

Rosa, Hartmut, *Social Acceleration: A New Theory of Modernity*, trans. Jonathan Trejo-Mathys (New York, 2013).

Rumsey, Alan, 'The Dreaming, Human Agency and Inscriptive Practice', *Oceania*, 65 (1994), 116–30.

Salih, Sarah, 'Found Bodies: The Living, the Dead, and the Undead in the Broad Medieval Present', in Jan-Peer Hartmann and Andrew James Johnston (eds), *Material Remains: Reading the Past in Medieval and Early Modern British Literature* (Columbus, OH, 2021), 21–37.

Savoy, Bénédicte, *Africa's Struggle for Its Art: History of a Postcolonial Defeat* (Princeton, NJ, 2022).

Scheil, Andrew, *The Footsteps of Israel: Understanding Jews in Anglo-Saxon England* (Ann Arbor, MI, 2004).

Schiffman, Zachary Sayre, *The Birth of the Past* (Baltimore, MD, 2011).

——'Historicizing History/Contextualizing Context', *New Literary History*, 42:3 (2011), 477–98.

Schlauch, Margaret, '*The Dream of the Rood* as Prosopopoeia', in Jess B. Bessinger, Jr, and Stanley J. Kahrl (eds), *Essential Articles for the Study of Old English Poetry* (Hamden, CT, 1968), 428–41.

Schlie, Heike, 'Der Klosterneuburger Ambo des Nikolaus von Verdun: Das Kunstwerk als *figura* zwischen Inkarnation und Wiederkunft des Logos', in Christian Kiening and Katharina Mertens Fleury (eds), Figura*: Dynamiken der Zeiten und Zeichen im Mittelalter* (Würzburg, 2013), 205–47.

Bibliography

Schmidt-Biggemann, Wilhelm, 'Geschichte, Ereignis, Erzählung: Über Schwierigkeiten und Besonderheiten von Geschichtsphilosophie', in Andreas Speer (ed.), *Anachronismen: Tagung des Engeren Kreises der Allgemeinen Gesellschaft für Philosophie in Deutschland (AGPD) vom 3. bis 6. Oktober 2001 in der Würzburger Residenz* (Würzburg, 2003), 25–50.

Schwyzer, Philip, *Archaeologies of English Renaissance Literature* (Oxford, 2007).

—— 'The Return of the King: Exhuming King Arthur and Richard III', in Jan-Peer Hartmann and Andrew James Johnston (eds), *Material Remains: Reading the Past in Medieval and Early Modern British Literature* (Columbus, OH, 2021), 78–100.

Semple, Sarah, *Perceptions of the Prehistoric in Anglo-Saxon England: Religion, Ritual, and Rulership in the Landscape* (Oxford, 2013).

Serres, Michel, with Bruno Latour, *Conversations on Science, Culture and Time*, trans. Roxanne Lapidus (Ann Arbor, MI, 1995).

Sharma, Manish, 'The Reburial of the Cross in the Old English *Elene*', in Samantha Zacher and Andy Orchard (eds), *New Readings in the Vercelli Book* (Toronto, 2009), 280–97.

Shippey, Tom A., Beowulf *and the North before the Vikings* (Leeds, 2022).

——*Poems of Wisdom and Learning in Old English* (Cambridge, 1976).

—— and Andreas Haarder (eds), Beowulf: *The Critical Heritage* (London, 1998).

Shryock, Andrew and Daniel Lord Smail, 'Introduction', in Andrew Shryock and Daniel Lord Smail (eds), *Deep History: The Architecture of Past and Present* (Berkeley, CA, 2011), 3–20.

Stephens, Walter, *Giants in Those Days: Folklore, Ancient History, and Nationalism* (Lincoln, NE, 1989).

Stevenson, Robert B. K., 'Further Thoughts on Some Well Known Problems', in Michael Spearman and John Higgitt (eds), *The Age of Migrating Ideas: Early Medieval Art in Northern Britain and Ireland* (Edinburgh, 1993), 16–26.

Stierle, Karlheinz, '*Translatio Studii* and Renaissance: From Vertical to Horizontal Translation', in Sanford Budick and Wolfgang Iser (eds), *The Translatability of Cultures: Figurations of the Space Between* (Stanford, CA, 1996), 55–67, 313–15.

Strange, James F., 'Archeological Evidence of Jewish Believers?', in Oskar Skarsaune and Reidar Hvalvik (eds), *Jewish Believers in Jesus: The Early Centuries* (Ada, MI, 2007), 710–41.

Strohm, Paul, *Theory and the Premodern Text* (Minneapolis, MN, 2000).

Stuhmiller, Jacqueline, 'On the Identity of the *Eotenas*', *NM*, 100:1 (1999), 7–14.

Swanton, Michael, *English Poetry before Chaucer* (Exeter, 2002).

Tambling, Jeremy, *On Anachronism* (Manchester, 2010).

Bibliography

Tate, George S., 'Chiasmus as Metaphor: The "Figura Crucis" Tradition and *The Dream of the Rood'*, *NM*, 79 (1978), 114–25.

Thornbury, Emily V., *'Eald enta geweorc* and the Relics of Empire: Revisiting the Dragon's Lair in *Beowulf'*, *Quaestio*, 1 (2000), 82–92.

Tolkien, John Ronald Reuel, Beowulf *and the Critics*, ed. Michael D. C. Drout (Tempe, AZ, 2002).

—— *'Beowulf*: The Monsters and the Critics', in *The Monsters and the Critics and Other Essays*, ed. Christopher Tolkien (London, 1997), 5–48.

—— 'On Translating *Beowulf'*, in *The Monsters and the Critics and Other Essays*, ed. Christopher Tolkien (London, 1997), 49–71.

Traill, David A., *Schliemann of Troy: Treasure and Deceit* (London, 1997).

—— 'Schliemann's discovery of "Priam's treasure": A Re-examination of the Evidence', *The Journal of Hellenic Studies*, 104 (1984), 96–115.

Trilling, Renée R., 'Ruins in the Realm of Thoughts: Reading as Constellation in Anglo-Saxon Poetry', *JEGP*, 108:2 (2009), 141–67.

Wallace, Jennifer, *Digging the Dirt: The Archaeological Imagination* (London, 2004).

Weiskott, Eric, 'The Paris Psalter and English Literary History', in Irina Dumitrescu and Eric Weiskott (eds), *The Shapes of Early English Poetry: Style, Form, History* (Kalamazoo, MI, 2019), 107–34.

Weiss-Krejci, Estella, 'The Plot Against the Past: Reuse and Modification of Ancient Mortuary Monuments as Persuasive Efforts of Appropriation', in Marta Díaz-Guardamino, Leonardo García Sanjuán and David Wheatley (eds), *The Lives of Prehistoric Monuments in Iron Age, Roman, and Medieval Europe* (Oxford, 2015), 307–24.

Whatley, Gordon, 'The Figure of Constantine the Great in Cynewulf's *Elene'*, *Traditio*, 37 (1981), 161–202.

Whitelock, Dorothy, 'The Numismatic Interest of the Old English Version of the Legend of the Seven Sleepers', in R. H. M. Dolley (ed.), *Anglo-Saxon Coins: Studies Presented to F. M. Stenton on the Occasion of his 80th Birthday, 17 May 1960* (London, 1961), 188–94.

Wilcox, Donald J., *The Measure of Times Past: Pre-Newtonian Chronologies and the Rhetoric of Relative Time* (Chicago, IL, 1987).

Wilhelm, Friedrich, 'Über fabulistische Quellenangaben', *Beiträge zur Geschichte der deutschen Sprache und Literatur*, 33 (1908), 286–339.

Williams, Howard, *'Beowulf* and Archaeology: Megaliths Imagined and Encountered in Early Medieval Europe', in Marta Díaz-Guardamino, Leonardo García Sanjuán and David Wheatley (eds), *The Lives of Prehistoric Monuments in Iron Age, Roman, and Medieval Europe* (Oxford, 2015), 77–97.

Wilson, Peter H., 'Bolstering the Prestige of the Habsburgs: The End of the Holy Roman Empire in 1806', *International History Review*, 28:4 (2006), 709–36.

Bibliography

Znojemská, Helena, '*The Ruin*: A Reading of the Old English Poem', *Litteraria Progensia*, 8 (1998), 15–33.

Zollinger, Cynthia Wittman, 'Cynewulf's *Elene* and the Pattern of the Past', *JEGP*, 103:2 (2004), 180–96.

Online Sources

Bosworth, Joseph and T. Northcote Toller (eds), *An Anglo-Saxon Dictionary Based on the Manuscript Collections of the Late Joseph Bosworth* (Oxford, 1898); Supplement, ed. T. Northcote Toller (Oxford, 1921); Revised and Enlarged Addenda, ed. Alistair Campbell (Oxford, 1972), online edition <https://bosworthtoller.com> [accessed 26 February 2024].

Poppe, Patrick, '"Translatio Europae?": Kulturelle Transferdiskurse im Kontext des Falls von Konstantinopel' (PhD dissertation, Saarbrücken, 2019) <http://dx.doi.org/10.22028/D291-27907> [accessed 29 February 2024].

Weber, Robert and Roger Gryson (eds), *Biblia Sacra iuxta vulgatam versionem*, 5th edn (Stuttgart, 2007), <https://www.bibelwissenschaft.de/bibel/VUL/GEN.1> [accessed 25 February 2024].

Index

Abraham 198, 201, 226
Acre 80
Acta Cyriaci 33 n. 20, 37 n. 30, 40, 42
    n. 45, 45 n. 48, 69, 76, 196, 197,
    207–15, 217, 218
    see also under Constantine I, cross,
    St Helena, *inventio crucis*,
    miracles, *visio Constantini*
Acta Sanctorum 37 n. 30
actor-network theory 59
Adam 94, 230 n. 88
Ælfric, abbot of Eynsham 103 nn.
    59–60, 153 n. 41, 162
    De septem dormientium 153, 162
    Inuentio S. Crucis 34
    Life of St Æthelthryth 252 n. 3
    Life of St Oswald 252 n. 3
    Lives of the Saints 153 n. 41
Aeneas 75, 81, 151
Æthelberht, king of Kent 115
Æthelthryth, St 31
Albinus, abbot of St Augustine's
    Abbey (Canterbury) 42
Alcuin 245
Aldhelm, abbot of Malmesbury
    Abbey and bishop of
    Sherborne 74, 136
    De virginitate 34
Alexander the Great 77
Alfred Jewel 243
Alfred the Great, king of
    Wessex 90, 222, 252
Allen, Hope Emily 12
alliterative revival 257
anachronism 8, 14, 16, 18, 21–3, 74
    n. 119, 142–52, 154, 164–5, 167,
    168 n. 79, 176, 179, 182–91, 247
    n. 130
anachrony (Nagel and Wood) 21,
    23, 145 n. 17, 148, 150, 151,
    154, 158, 161–4, 165, 183, 188,
    191

Anatolia 76
Andreas 10, 36, 84 n. 6, 98, 101,
    103–4, 113
Andrew the Apostle, St 101
Anglo-Saxon Chronicle 252
    MS Laud Misc. 636
        (E, 'Peterborough
        Chronicle') 32
    MS Cotton Domitian A VIII
        (F, 'Canterbury Bilingual
        Epitome') 33 n. 23
Antioch 31
antiquity
    classical antiquity 19, 25, 64, 67,
        68, 69, 77, 78, 149, 150, 151,
        176, 202
    late antiquity 64, 146, 154
Apocalypse 97–8, 129, 225
Aquinas, Thomas, St 162 n. 63, 204
archaeology
    as modern academic discipline 1,
        3–6, 9, 17, 26–9, 32, 51, 57, 62,
        82, 114, 158
    colonial/imperial archaeology 63,
        69
    popular perceptions of 28–9
Arthur, legendary king of Britain 62
Asia Minor 35 n. 26, 75 n. 121, 76
asynchrony 12–15, 18, 22, 149, 151,
    152, 154 n. 46, 155, 160–1, 165
Athens 26–7 n. 3
Auerbach, Erich 23, 202, 204, 228,
    249
Augustine of Canterbury, St 101
Augustine of Hippo, St 1–6, 10, 103
    n. 60, 184 n. 109, 193, 197–200,
    204–5, 206, 226
    De civitate Dei 1–4, 66 n. 92, 90
        n. 28
    De dialectica 194
    De doctrina christiana 194,
        197–200

Index

see also semiotic theory

Babel, Tower of   90–3, 96–7, 103, 119
    n. 104, 135 n. 150
    conflation with Babylon   90 n. 28,
    103 n. 60
Babylon *see under* Babel
Bainbrigg, Reginald   231, 232 n. 92
Bakhtin, Mikhail   87–8
Bancroft, George
    History of the United States   65
Barad, Karen   11, 134
Barthes, Roland   167
Bath (city)   102, 135, 136
Bede   3–6, 10, 39, 41–2, 45, 89, 90 n.
    26, 102, 136, 201, 252
    Commentary on Genesis   201 n. 27
    De temporibus   252
    De temporum ratione   252
    *Historia ecclesiastica gentis
        Anglorum*   3–6, 10, 18, 34–5
        n. 25, 39, 41–2, 45, 89, 90 n. 26,
        254
    Vita sancti Cuthberti (prose)   18,
        130, 252 n. 3
    Vita sancti Cuthberti (verse)   18,
        252 n. 3
Benedictine reform   38 n. 33
Bennett, Jane   11
Beowulf   4, 7, 10, 21–3, 74, 75 n. 120,
    101, 102–3, 104 n. 62, 105, 106,
    112, 113, 137 n. 158, 152, 158,
    160, 163–91, 253, 255, 256
    Beowulf (character)   106, 163, 166,
        167, 168–9, 170–1, 172, 174,
        177–9, 182, 183 n. 107, 187–9,
        191
    Brosinga men   163, 177
    dragon   166, 172, 174, 178, 187–8
    dragon's hoard   7, 10, 22, 105,
        106, 158, 163, 164, 165, 172–4,
        178–9, 191
    fag flor   164–5, 178
    giants' sword   4, 7, 10, 22, 103,
        113 n. 85, 152, 160, 163–4, 165,
        170–3, 179–85, 189, 191, 253,
        255

Grendel   22, 152, 168, 170–1, 177,
    181–3, 186–8, 191
Grendelkin   22, 152, 163, 182, 185,
    189, 191
Grendel's mother   22, 103, 152,
    163, 170–1, 182–3, 186–8
Hama   177
Heorot   164–5, 168–9, 174, 178,
    186, 187, 191
Heremod   171
'Hrothgar's Sermon'   170–1
Hrothgar   164, 168, 170–1, 182–3,
    186, 187, 191 n. 123
Hrunting   163, 177–8, 182
Hygelac   166, 167, 177
Ingeld   168, 188
'Lay of the Last Survivor'   22–3,
    105, 172, 174, 178–9
layered past, depiction of   166–76
    periodisation in   174, 178–9,
    185–90
Scyld Scefing   173–4
'Song of Creation'   187
stanbogan   164
stanfah stræt   164, 165, 178
Unferth   163, 177, 182
Wealtheow's necklace   163
Wealtheow   163
Wiglaf   163, 178
Berkeley, George
    *On the Prospect of Planting Arts and
        Learning in America*   65–6, 67
Berlin
    Ethnological Museum   63
    Kunstgewerbemuseum   63
Bewcastle Cross   240
Bhabha, Homi   13, 71
Bible   2, 3, 22, 151, 183, 201
    Old Testament   70, 78, 80, 201,
        204
    Daniel
        Daniel 2   66 n. 92
        Daniel 2.41   81
        Daniel 7   66, 219
    Enoch   103, 181, 185
    Exodus 15.25   198
    Genesis

276

Index

Genesis 3.19 94
Genesis 6.4 84
Genesis 6.4–7 103, 151, 181, 185
Genesis 22.11 198
Genesis 22.13 198
Isaiah
Isaiah 2.2–4 216, 225, 245
Isaiah 13.19–22 112 n. 82
Jeremiah 50–1 112 n. 82
Numbers 13.33 151 n. 36
Zechariah 14.20 70
New Testament 78, 80, 201, 202, 204, 216
1 Corinthians 13.9–12 245
2 Corinthians 3.5–6 195 n. 8
Matthew 24.30 224
Bingham, Hiram 29
Bithynia 35 n. 26
Bloch, Ernst 13
Bokenham, Osbern
Legendys of Hooly Wummen 31
Vita Sanctae Margaretae 31
Bonneval 32
Bosphorus 77
Britain
early medieval 1, 2, 3–4, 7, 18, 33–5, 40, 68, 74, 77, 89–90, 99, 103, 114, 128, 135–6, 154, 165, 178, 181, 197, 248, 252, 254–5
prehistoric 113 n. 86, 114, 117
Roman 3, 10, 34–5, 40, 89–90, 99, 102, 107, 113, 128 n. 131, 135–7, 164–5, 178
Trojan past, alleged 68–9, 255
Browne, Thomas 257
Brussels Cross 222–3, 236, 238 n. 106, 243–4
Brutus (legendary founder of Britain) 68
Burckhardt, Jacob
Civilization of the Renaissance in Italy 142
Byron, George Gordon (Lord Byron)
Darkness 97–8
Byzantium 76–7

Caesar, Gaius Julius 77, 78, 142
Caesarea 40, 206
Cain 170, 182, 184, 187
Canterbury 115
Carlisle 130
Carter, Howard 29
Casa Santa di Loreto 80 n. 130
Castor (monastery) 32
ceaster 83–5, 99, 101–2
Ceram, C. W.
Götter, Gräber und Gelehrte: Roman der Archäologie 29 n. 9
Chakrabarty, Dipesh 13–14, 63, 71 n. 110, 185
Chapman, Mark David 60 n. 76
Charlemagne 67 n. 98
Cheah, Pheng 203, 207, 215, 249
Chester 102, 135, 136
Chicago 143, 148, 189
Christ II 225 n. 79
Christ III 224, 225 n. 79
Christ, Jesus 12–13, 14, 23, 39, 42, 46, 47, 51 n. 62, 52, 54, 56, 57, 60, 70 n. 107, 72, 80 n. 130, 153, 156, 192, 195, 196–7, 199 n. 22, 200, 201, 204, 206, 209–10, 214, 216, 218, 219, 223 n. 74, 224, 229–30, 232, 235, 237, 240, 242 n. 115, 244, 246–7, 249, 251
Christopher, St 165
chronotope (Bakthin) 87–8
Church of Scotland 231
Cicero 67 n. 97
Clement of Alexandria
Stromata 196
Coel/Cole, spurious British king 35
colonialism 13–14, 62–4, 68–9, 71, 73, 147, 186
neo-colonialism 64
Constantine I, emperor 19, 33–6, 39–40, 144, 196–7, 205–6, 207
as character in *Acta Cyriaci* 208–9, 210, 212
as character in *Elene* 39, 40–1, 42–3, 46–7, 51, 52, 55, 56 n. 66, 57–8, 60, 69–72, 73, 74 n.

277

119, 79, 80, 82, 101 n. 52, 194,
212–16, 217–18, 221
Constantinople 63, 77
Constantius II, emperor 205
Constantius, Flavius Valerius
'Chlorus', emperor 34–5
Cotton Tiberius B.v *mappa mundi* 77
Council of Trent 205 n. 40
cross
as sign 23–4, 53, 192, 194–7,
199–200, 201 n. 27, 205–7, 226,
231, 240 n. 112
in *Acta Cyriaci* 208–11, 213–4,
218
in *The Dream of the Rood* 225–8
in *Elene* 46–7, 49, 60, 79 208,
210–18
as speaking object
in *The Dream of the Rood* 23, 34,
219–31, 235, 237 n. 103, 238,
243–4, 246, 248
in *Ruthwell Poem* 235–8, 240,
242–8, 250–1
as tree of life 48, 60, 192, 210, 217,
192
in eschatological visions 224–6
cross symbols/
representations 24, 41,
192–5, 222–3, 229 n. 84, 236,
242–5, 248, 251
in *The Dream of the Rood* 222
in *Elene* 41 n. 41, 218
in Legend of the Seven
Sleepers 156
True Cross 19, 23–4, 32–4, 37 n.
30, 38, 39, 46, 59, 70 n. 106,
192–3, 195–7, 199–200, 205–6,
210, 229–31, 242–3, 244 n. 122,
145–7, 250–1, 253
in *Acta Cyriaci* 208–11, 213–14,
217–18
in *The Dream of the Rood* 23, 34,
193–4, 219–20, 224, 229–30
in *Elene* 19, 23, 34, 36, 38–9,
42–3, 49–58, 69–72, 74, 81–2,
193, 207–8, 210–19

as relic 69, 194–7, 199–200,
204–6, 210, 222, 244 n. 122, 251
in *Acta Cyriaci* 209–10,
214–15
in *The Dream of the Rood* 220,
222, 223 n. 74, 226, 228–31
in *Elene* 19, 23, 42, 48–9,
54–8, 81, 207, 209–10,
214–15, 217–18, 219–20, 222
translatio/exaltatio
crucis 215–16, 220
in *The Dream of the Rood* 220
in *Elene* 55, 58, 70–1, 215–16,
222
see also inventio crucis
crucifixion 13, 23, 36, 42–51, 53, 55,
56, 57, 60, 69 n. 104, 74, 78–81,
82, 192, 194, 197, 199 n. 22,
200, 208, 214, 216, 219, 224,
226–7, 230–1, 237, 240–3, 245,
247, 248, 250
Cuthbert, St 130
Cyneburh, St 32
Cyneswith, St 32
Cynewulf 32, 37, 38 n. 33, 60, 71,
225 n. 79, 239
Cyril of Jerusalem
Catecheses 69–70 n. 106, 205–6

Danube 40, 101 n. 52
Dardanelles 26 n. 3
De falsis deis 103, 184
Decius, emperor 152, 154, 155, 157,
158, 160–1, 162
deep history (Shryock and
Smail) 107–9, 120, 138, 141,
174
deep past 106–8, 109, 116
deep time 117, 137–8, 178
denial of coevalness (Fabian) 13,
64, 117, 146–7, 186, 189, 190
Derrida, Jacques 86, 139, 250 n. 137
Dickens, Charles 60 n. 76
Dinshaw, Carolyn 11–15, 18, 60,
151–3, 155, 161
Diocletian, emperor 35 n. 26
Dods, John W. 240–1

Index

Dream of the Rood, The   23, 34, 36, 193, 208, 215, 219–31, 234 n. 96, 235–8, 243–4, 244–5 n. 123, 246–8, 251–2
  as dream vision   34, 193, 238, 236
  eschatological vision   224–5
  relationship to Brussels Cross   222–3
  relationship to *Elene*   220
  relationship to *Ruthwell Poem*   235–7, 246, 248
  temporalities in   219–20, 222–4, 226–228, 230–1
  see also under cross, *inventio crucis*
Drepanum (Hersek)   35 n. 26
Duncan, Henry   231, 233

Eadgar, king of England   136
Ealdred, abbot   6
early modern period   4, 16, 64, 66, 75 n. 121, 146
Eboracum *see* York
Ecgfrith, king of Northumbria   130 n. 136
Edda   169 n. 81
Eddius Stephanus
  Vita Sancti Wilfrithi   252
Egypt   29 n. 11, 64, 159
Elene   7, 10, 19–20, 23, 33 n. 23, 34–60, 69–82, 101, 103, 193–4, 197, 207–22, 225 n. 79, 228, 231, 251–2, 255–6
  as archaeological narrative   43, 55–6
  as history of conversion   51–4, 56, 69, 71–4
  as imperialist narrative   69–81
  linear-historical and figural temporalities   207–8, 215–6
  precariousness of historical knowledge   42–51
  relationship to *The Dream of the Rood*   220
  see also under Constantine I, cross, St Helena, *inventio crucis*, Judas Cyriacus, miracles, *visio Constantini*

Eliot, George
  Middlemarch   26 n. 3
enta geweorc (*eald enta geweorc, enta ærgeweorc, giganta geweorc*)   10, 20, 83–6, 96, 99–107, 113, 116, 119, 123, 125, 135–7, 140–1, 180–1
Ephesus   152, 154–7
episteme (Foucault)   9 n. 22
Erkenwald, bishop of London   255–6
Eucharist   193, 240
Eusebius of Caesarea   40, 199, 205–7, 209
  Chronicon   34 n. 25
  Vita Constantini   40, 196, 205–7, 209
Eutropius
  Breviarium   34–5 n. 25
Exeter Book (Exeter Cathedral Library MS 3501)   19, 86, 93, 122, 136

Fabian, Johannes   13, 64, 117, 146–7
Fates of the Apostles, The   36, 225 n. 79
Felix, *Vita Sancti Guthlaci*   18, 74, 252 n. 3
Felski, Rita   8–9, 17 n. 48, 58–9
figura (Auerbach)   23–4, 37, 50 n. 60, 194–5, 202–4, 207–8, 215–19, 224, 227–30, 232, 244–8, 249–51
  figural time *see under* time
Flavia Maximiana Theodora, empress   35 n. 26
Flavius Josephus   67
Flood (Genesis 6–9)   22, 103, 151–2, 163–4, 170, 180, 181–6, 188–91
Florentine, St   32
Franz Ferdinand, Archduke of Austria   59
Fukuyama, Francis
  The End of History and the Last Man   98

Genesis A   90–2

Index

Genesis B 94
Geoffrey of Monmouth
    Historia regum Britanniae 68–9,
        254–5
Geoffrey of Vinsauf
    Documentum de modo et arte dictandi
        et versificandi 154
Gerald of Wales 62
    Itinerarium Kambriae 254
    on King Arthur's exhumation (in
        Speculum ecclesiae and *Liber de*
        Principis Instructione) 62
Germany 29 n. 11, 63, 68
Gesta abbatum Sancti Albani 6, 159,
    254
giants
    alterity of 105–6, 186 n. 114
    association with craft and
        technology 103–4
    in Augustine, *De civitate Dei* 1–3,
        10
    in *Beowulf* 102–3, 105, 152, 164–6,
        170–1, 174, 180–7, 189
    in the Bible 22, 100, 103, 135 n.
        149, 151, 165, 180–1, 183–4
    in classical literature 180
    in Germanic legend 180
    in *Maxims II* 84–5
    in Old English texts 99–107, 137
    in *The Ruin* 125, 126 n. 123, 133
    in *The Wanderer* 109, 116
    postdiluvian survival 151, 152,
        165, 183–5, 188, 191
    see also enta geweorc
Glastonbury 62
Greece 67–8, 75, 76
Greenblatt, Stephen
    The Swerve 30
Gregory of Nyssa
    Vita Macrinae 70 n. 106
Gregory of Tours
    De gloria martyrum 152
    Passio septem dormientium 152–3
Grendel, Grendelkin *see under Beowulf*
Guinevere, legendary queen 62
Guthlac A 19
Guthlac B 19

Guthlac, St 18

hagiography 18, 30, 32, 36, 194, 252
Harris, Jonathan Gil 15–16, 18, 149,
    187–8
Hegel, Georg Wilhelm Friedrich 63
    Lectures on the Philosophy of
        History 147
Helena, St 19, 33, 34–6, 40 n. 40, 47,
    196
    as character in *Acta Cyriaci* 209
    as character in *Elene* 19–20, 35,
        42–50, 52, 55, 57, 58, 69–74, 76,
        78–80, 215, 218
heliotopism 67
Henry II, king of England 62
Hersek (Drepanum) 35
Hisarlık 25, 27, 29 n. 10
historia sacra 8, 13–14, 23, 39, 50, 53,
    78, 80, 171, 194, 201–3, 207,
    215–16, 226, 227, 242, 245, 253
historian 3, 6, 21, 65, 68, 119, 142,
    150, 165, 166, 219
historical consciousness 8, 21, 121,
    140, 142–5, 148, 156, 166, 190,
    254, 256
historical determinism 78, 147, 188
historical knowledge 20, 21, 22–3, 38,
    41, 43–6, 49–51, 55, 79–80, 102,
    106–7, 108, 125, 134, 136–8,
    140–1, 166, 168–9, 171–3, 247,
    250, 254, 256
    loss of 43–4, 46, 55–6, 108–9, 118,
        120–1, 134, 136–7, 141, 159,
        172–3, 178–9
historical progress 8, 13, 14, 22, 23,
    39, 130, 137 n. 158, 140, 144–7,
    156, 186–7, 189–90, 248, 253
historicism 12, 13–4, 17, 63–4, 151,
    256
historiography 3–4, 6, 8, 13–14, 22,
    29, 33, 34, 38–41, 64–5, 68–9,
    80, 82, 99, 108, 136, 138, 140,
    149 n. 24, 150, 160, 167, 252,
    254
holy images *see* sacred images

Index

Holy Nails 36, 38, 49, 51, 52, 55, 58, 70–1, 74, 80–1, 206, 209, 217–18
  as relics 55, 69, 70, 80–1, 218
  inventio 70
  translatio 81
holy objects *see* sacred objects
Holy Sepulchre 206
Homer 2, 26 n. 3, 27–8, 61, 63, 75–6, 77 n. 123, 202
  Iliad 57, 61, 75, 77
  Odyssey 75
hoptasia see *visio Constantini*
Horace 67 n. 97
Hrabanus Maurus 245 n. 123
Huneberc
  Life of St Willibald 153 n. 41
Husband's Message, The 239

Imperium Romanum see Roman Empire
incarnation 14, 39, 80, 192, 204
India 13–4, 185
Indiana Jones (Steven Spielberg) 29
intra-action (Barad) 134
inventio crucis 19, 23, 32–5, 192, 194, 196–7, 205–6, 230
  in *Acta Cyriaci* 33 n. 20, 196–7, 208–10, 217–8
  in *Elene* 19, 36, 49–50, 52–4, 57–8, 69–70, 72, 74, 81–2, 207, 208, 209, 211, 213, 215–17, 219–220
  in *The Dream of the Rood* 220
inventio
  of arguments (in rhetoric) 38
  of relics 6, 30–2, 55, 56–8, 62, 81–2, 209, 254
Inventio sanctae crucis (legend) 33–7, 196, 199 n. 22, 207, 208
  see also *Acta Cyriaci*
Isidore of Seville 103 n. 60
Italy 31, 64, 75, 80

Jacob 198, 199, 200, 201, 216, 226
Jacobus de Voragine
  Legenda aurea 153
James of Sarug 152

Jerome 34 n. 25, 42, 79 n. 125, 162
Jerrer, Georg Ludwig
  Weltgeschichte für Kinder 27
Jerusalem 19, 33 n. 20, 36, 37 n. 30, 42, 46, 47, 49, 50, 52, 58, 69–72, 73, 76–81, 196, 205–6, 207, 216
John of Garland
  Parisiana poetria 154 n. 48
John the Baptist, St 232, 246
Jonah 201, 230
Judas Cyriacus, legendary first bishop of Jerusalem 33 n. 20, 37 n. 30, 207
  as character in *Elene* 41, 42, 43–6, 48–56, 69, 72–4, 78, 80, 211–12, 216–17
Judas Iscariot 216
Judea 69, 76
Judgement Day 14, 37, 126, 224–6
  see also parousia
Junius Manuscript (Bodleian Library MS Junius 11) 90
Justin
  Epitoma historiarum Philippicarum 64
Jutland 166

Kempe, Margery 12–13, 15, 60
Kent 42
Klaeber, Friedrich 75 n. 120, 169

Langley, Philippa 61
Latour, Bruno 15–16, 145–6, 150, 190
Laȝamon
  Brut 257
Legend of the Seven Sleepers 152–3
  Ælfric, *De septem dormientium see under* Ælfric
  Anonymous Old English Legend of the Seven Sleepers 21, 22, 148, 152–63, 190–1, 256
    as asynchrony tale 152–5
    sleepers as relics 22, 158, 161–2
Leicester 29, 61
Lennon, John 60 n. 76
Leutze, Emanuel Gottlieb 65

Index

Lewis, C. S.
 *The Voyage of the Dawn
  Treader* 191
Liber Eliensis 31
Life of King Edward 153 n. 41
London 16, 255–6

Macarius of Jerusalem, St 205
Machu Picchu 29
Macrina the Younger, St 70 n. 106
Malone, Kemp 166
mappa mundi see Cotton Tiberius B.v
  mappa mundi
Marcion of Sinope 249
Margaret of Antioch, St 31
Marianus I, pope 222
Marínus, bishop of Ephesus 161
Martin of Opava/Martin von
  Troppau 67 n. 98
Mary and Martha (Luke
  10.38–42) 232
Mary Magdalen 232
Mary, Virgin 12, 226, 229 n. 85
materiality 2, 4, 8, 9, 10–11, 15–17,
  23–4, 31, 33, 36, 38, 53–6, 62,
  81, 84, 86, 88, 98, 122, 125, 134,
  153–4, 158–61, 192–7, 200, 202,
  204–12, 215, 217–20, 222, 224,
  227–31, 251, 253, 257
 durability of matter 10–11, 95–6,
  98, 109, 118, 122, 125, 129, 134,
  141, 153, 159–60, 253
 material evidence 1–3, 27–8, 30,
  62
Matthew of Vendôme
 Ars versificatoria 154
Matthew Paris
 Chronica maiora 254
 see also Gesta abbatum Sancti Albani
Maxentius, emperor 40
Maximian, emperor 35 n. 26
Maxims II 10, 83–6, 99, 101–2,
  103–4, 106, 107 n. 70, 112
medievalism 119–20, 128 n. 131
Mediterranean 64, 68, 75, 76, 154
Meller, Harald 29
Michael, George 60 n. 76

Middle Ages 1, 6–9, 12, 14, 21, 24,
  57, 62, 65. 66, 119–20, 140, 142,
  144–6, 152–3, 196, 201, 219,
  252–3, 256
 early Middle Ages 1, 2, 3–4, 6–7,
  9, 40, 41, 72 n. 116, 77, 114–15,
  128, 135, 151 n. 36, 240, 243,
  257
 late Middle Ages 4, 8, 66 n. 93, 67
  n. 98, 75 n. 121, 135, 193, 195
Milvian Bridge, Battle of 40
miracles 30–1, 195, 229, 57
 in *Acta Cyriaci* 209, 217
 in *Elene* 49–52, 54–5, 69, 82, 211,
  217
 in *Saint Erkenwald* 255–6
 in the Legend of the Seven
  Sleepers 158, 161–2
modernity *see* Western modernity
monstrance 195, 222
monument reuse *see* reuse
Moscow
 Pushkin Museum 63 n. 83
Moses 198–9, 201, 226
multitemporality *see under*
  temporality

Nebra Sky Disc 29
Nebuchadnezzar 66 n. 92
Nennius
 Historia Brittonum 35 n. 27, 68–9
Nero, Claudius, emperor 142
new historicism 30
new materialism 11, 134
Nibelungenlied 191 n. 124
Nicolson, William, bishop of
  Carlisle 231
Nimrod 103. 135 n. 150, 165, 184
Ninus, Assyrian king 64
Noah's Ark 183
Nora, Pierre 96 n. 39, 140
Norman Conquest 257
Northumbria 114, 130

Old English elegies 88, 122 n. 112,
  124 n. 119

Index

Old English Orosius, The   90–2, 96,
     98, 103, 184
Old English riddles   85, 132, 238–9
Old English wisdom/catalogue/
     sapiential poetry   84–5
Origenism   161
Orosius, Paulus
     Historiae adversus paganos   90, 252
     see also *Old English Orosius*
Otto von Freising
     Chronica sive historia de duabus
          civitatibus   66
Ovid   202
Ovide moralisé   202

Palestine   206
Panofsky, Erwin
     Renaissance and Renascences in
          Western Art   143–4
Papua New Guinea   117
Paris (city)   67
Paris, Gaston   142
parousia   73, 203, 204, 217, 220, 245
Paul and Anthony, hermit
     saints   232, 240
Paulinus of Nola, St   230 n. 86
Pennant, Thomas
     A Tour in Scotland, and Voyage to
          the Hebrides   232 n. 92
periodisation   9 n. 22, 21–3, 109,
     142, 145–52, 173–4, 179,
     185–91, 253, 255, 257
Phoenix, The   113
Pilate, Pontius   80 n. 130
Pliny   2
polychronicity (Serres)   15–16, 18,
     21, 22, 87, 90, 115, 132–3, 138
polytemporality *see* temporality
Pompeius Trogus
     Historiae Philippicae   64
Priam of Troy   25, 28 n. 8
     'Priam's Treasure'   25, 26 n. 2, 59,
          63, 68
Procopius   35 n. 26
prosopopoeia   91, 219, 238, 244
Proust, Marcel
     À la recherche du temps perdu   149

purification (Latour)   150

Ragnarök   169
Rancière, Jacques   142
reality effect (Barthes)   167
regime of truth (Rancière)   142, 146,
     185, 190
relic   6, 20, 30–2, 36, 54–7, 60, 62, 64,
     70, 81, 161, 162, 193, 194, 195,
     199–200, 206, 210, 215 n. 60,
     217, 228–30
     see also under Cross, Holy Nails,
          Legend of the Seven Sleepers
reliquary   195, 209, 215, 221–3, 226,
     244 n. 122
Renaissance   16, 21, 143–5, 147, 150
repatriation   62–3
reuse
     of material objects   7, 16–7, 20,
          114–16, 118, 127, 154, 164
     see also spolia
Richard III, king of England   3, 5 n.
     9, 29, 61
Roman Empire (*Imperium*
     Romanum)   3, 20, 36, 39–40,
     66–8, 69–72, 74–6, 78, 89, 101,
     128, 153, 160, 196, 206, 219
     Holy Roman Empire (*Sacrum*
          Imperium Romanum)   66, 74,
          219
Rome (city)   19, 36, 38 n. 33, 39,
     42, 46–8, 52, 67, 69, 71–2, 74,
     78–81, 90 n. 26, 144 n. 15, 159,
     214
Romulus   74
Ruin, The   6, 10, 20–1, 84 n. 3, 86, 88,
     95, 98, 99, 101–2, 103–4, 106,
     121–39, 141, 239, 253
     as meditation on
          transience   121–3
     imaginary recreation of
          past   133–4, 136–8
     implied narrator   123–4
     longue durée of successive
          cultures   125–9
     multitemporal vision   129–33

Roman provenance of
  ruins 128–30, 135–7
ruins 3, 6, 20–1, 77 n. 123, 85–7,
  88–93, 96–9, 101–2, 106, 109,
  111 n. 80, 112 n. 82, 113–16,
  118–25, 127–41
  marking historical change 86–7,
    119, 125, 129, 138
  marking longevity of
    matter 95–9, 118, 122, 125,
    129, 139
  marking *romanitas* 89–90, 99,
    101–2, 113–16, 128–30, 135–7
  marking transience 20, 88, 90,
    92–3, 95–8, 118–23, 139–141
runes 34, 132 n. 140, 172, 238–9,
  242, 248
  rune stones 159
  see also under Ruthwell Cross
Russia 63
Ruthwell (Dumfriesshire) 231
Ruthwell Cross 23–4, 193, 231–48,
  250–1
  as representation of True
    Cross 242, 245
  crucifixion panel 240–2
  runic inscription 234, 236–40, 247
    n. 131, 248
Ruthwell Poem 23–4, 193, 234–8, 239
  n. 111, 240, 242–8, 250–1
  as riddle 238–40, 142–3
  relationship to *The Dream of the
    Rood* 235–7, 247–8

sacred history *see historia sacra*
sacred images 60, 193, 210, 230
sacred objects 31, 36, 60 n. 74, 61,
  70, 192–3, 194–5, 205, 206, 210,
  217, 251
Sacrum Imperium Romanum see under
  Roman Empire
St Albans 6
Saint Erkenwald 24, 254–7
St John Lateran 80 n. 130
salvation history *see historia sacra*
Saxony-Anhalt 29
Scaliger, Joseph Justus

*Opus novum de emendatione
  temporum* 149
Scandinavia 159, 165, 167, 169 n.
  81, 174 n. 92, 244
Schliemann, Heinrich 25–8, 29, 30
  n. 12, 56, 57, 58, 60–1, 63, 68
Schliemann, Sophia (née
  Engastroménou) 25–7
Seafarer, The 93–5, 97–8, 122, 129 n.
  134, 130, 133 n. 143
semiotic theory
  medieval/Augustinian 194,
    197–200, 204–5, 242
Serres, Michel 16, 18
Shakespeare, William 29 n. 11, 150,
  257
sign theory *see* semiotic theory
Sir Gawain and the Green Knight 257
spolia, spoliation 113, 115–6, 118,
  154, 191 n. 123
  see also reuse
Staffordshire Hoard 5
Stephen the Protomartyr, St 207
Stoppard, Tom
  Arcadia 98 n. 42
Swedes 106, 167, 179
Sylvester I, pope 80

Tambora, Mount 98 n. 42
teleology 8, 14, 19, 65, 129, 138, 203,
  207, 215, 219, 249, 254
temporality 2, 9, 10–21, 23–4, 30,
  33, 36, 39, 42, 55, 59–60, 86–8,
  92, 93, 108–9, 115, 116–18,
  120, 125, 127 nn. 126–7, 130,
  139–40, 145 n. 17, 149, 150–2,
  161, 163, 168, 173, 183, 186–9,
  192, 194, 202–3, 207–8, 214–15
  n. 60, 217–20, 223–9, 230, 232,
  245, 247–51, 252–4
  asynchronous temporalities 12–15,
    18, 22, 149, 151–2, 154 n. 46,
    155, 160–1, 165
  multiple temporalities 11–12,
    15–16, 86–7, 129, 130 n. 136,
    131–3, 138, 141, 150–1, 253
  polytemporality 15–16

Index

queer temporality 12
temporality of explosion 188
see also asynchrony, polychronicity
Tertullian
  Apology 196 n. 9
  De corona 196 n. 9
thaumatrope 223–4, 227
Theodosius II, emperor 152, 161–2
Thorkelin, Grímur Jónsson 166
time 10, 19, 21, 87–8, 133, 138 n.
  159, 179, 202, 254, 257
  cyclical time 14–15, 121, 129–31,
    138
  figural time 151, 203, 207–8,
    218–20, 228–9, 232, 245,
    249–51, 253
  historical time 1, 2, 3, 8, 10, 13,
    17, 21, 22, 23, 28, 39, 43–4, 50,
    55, 59, 88, 91, 92, 117, 120, 121,
    124, 125, 129–31, 134, 140,
    141, 145, 150, 151 n. 34, 153,
    155, 162, 163, 166 n. 71, 169,
    179, 192, 194, 201, 203, 207–8,
    218–19, 228–9, 245, 248, 253,
    255, 256
  empty homogeneous, historicist
    time 12, 13–14, 64, 117,
    142–3, 145–9, 155, 203
  literary presentation of 87–8
  mythical time 116–17
  perceptions or experiences of 2,
    11–15, 19, 44, 117, 151, 155,
    253
  see also deep time
timelessness 11, 15, 23, 126 n. 126,
  151, 248
Tintin (Hergé) 29
Tolkien 29 n. 10, 174–6
  The Lord of the Rings 4
  'The Monsters and the
    Critics' 154, 166–9, 174–5,
    176, 184, 189–90
trace (Derrida) 86, 91–3, 99, 118,
  121, 138–9, 151, 178, 250 n. 136
translatio 19, 36, 64, 68, 74–5, 78,
  207, 219, 252

translatio imperii 19–20, 38, 64–9,
  74–6, 78, 80–1, 128, 219, 254
translatio religionis 19, 38, 64, 66,
  69, 78–81, 252, 254
translatio reliquiae 30, 31–2, 52, 62,
  64, 70, 80–1, 215–16, 220
translatio sapientiae/studii 64,
  66–9, 80
translatio Troiae 75 n. 121
Trojan War 20, 27–8, 44–5, 50, 74–8,
  80–1
Troy 25–8, 29 n. 9, 56, 57, 61, 63,
  68–9, 74–8, 81, 82, 255
  Ilion, Ilium 77
True Cross *see under* cross
Turkey 63
Tutankhamun 29
typology 35 n. 27, 47, 192, 194–5,
  197, 200–4, 210, 216, 226–8,
  230, 244 n. 122, 254

United States of America 65, 68
untimeliness (Harris) 149, 150, 151
USSR 63

Vainglory 133 n. 143
Valla, Lorenzo
  De falso credita et ementita
    Constantini donatione
    declamatio 144
Valley of the Kings 29 n. 10
Venantius Fortunatus 245
Vercelli Book (Vercelli, Biblioteca
  Capitolare CXVII) 34, 36,
  215
Vercelli homilies 36
Verulamium *see* St Albans
Vico, Giambattista
  Principi di Scienza Nuova d'intorno
    alla Comune Natura delle
    Nazioni 149
Vienna
  Heeresgeschichtliches
    Museum 59 n. 72
Vikings 40 n. 38
Vimpos, Theokletos, bishop of
  Athens 26 n. 3

285

Index

Vincent of Beauvais
Speculum historiale 67 n. 98
Virgil 202
Aeneid 20, 68, 74, 75, 76
visio Constantini (hoptasia) 39, 47,
196–7, 205, 206–7, 208–9, 236
n. 97
in *Acta Cyriaci* 197, 208–10,
212–15, 218
in *Elene* 39–40, 42, 47, 51–2, 56
n. 66, 57, 71, 197, 210, 212–17,
221–2
Vita Sancti Cuthberti 18, 130

Wales 35 n. 27, 62, 255
Wanderer, The 7, 10, 20–1, 44 n.
47, 86, 88, 93, 95–9, 101–2,
103–4, 106, 109–23, 124 n. 119,
129–30, 134, 137–8, 139, 140,
141, 256

as meditation on durability of
matter 95–9, 118, 121
as meditation on transience 20,
93, 95, 109, 118–21, 130
ruin imagery 21, 86, 88, 93, 96–9,
109, 116, 118, 120–2
serpentine pattern 20, 109,
110–14, 117–18
Western modernity 11–14, 67, 117,
147, 150, 167, 185, 189, 190
William of Malmesbury
Gesta pontificum Anglorum 254
Gesta regum Anglorum 254
William of St Albans
Passio Sancti Albani 159
work of giants *see enta geweorc*
World War I 59, 63 n. 83, 68
wrætlic 83–4, 86, 104, 123, 135, 141

Yeavering 114
York 34

ANGLO-SAXON STUDIES
Please see the Boydell & Brewer website
for details of earlier titles in the series.

Volume 24: The Dating of *Beowulf*: A Reassessment, *edited by Leonard Neidorf*

Volume 25: The Cruciform Brooch and Anglo-Saxon England, *Toby F. Martin*

Volume 26: Trees in the Religions of Early Medieval England,
Michael D.J. Bintley

Volume 27: The Peterborough Version of the Anglo-Saxon Chronicle:
Rewriting Post-Conquest History, *Malasree Home*

Volume 28: The Anglo-Saxon Chancery: The History, Language and
Production of Anglo-Saxon Charters from Alfred to Edgar, *Ben Snook*

Volume 29: Representing Beasts in Early Medieval England and Scandinavia,
edited by Michael D.J. Bintley and Thomas J.T. Williams

Volume 30: Direct Speech in *Beowulf* and Other Old English Narrative
Poems, *Elise Louviot*

Volume 31: Old English Philology: Studies in Honour of R. D. Fulk, *edited by
Leonard Neidorf, Rafael J. Pascual and Tom Shippey*

Volume 32: 'Charms', Liturgies, and Secret Rites in Early Medieval England,
Ciaran Arthur

Volume 33: Old Age in Early Medieval England: A Cultural History,
Thijs Porck

Volume 34: Priests and their Books in Late Anglo-Saxon England,
Gerald P. Dyson

Volume 35: Burial, Landscape and Identity in Early Medieval Wessex,
Kate Mees

Volume 36: The Sword in Early Medieval Northern Europe: Experience,
Identity, Representation, *Sue Brunning*

Volume 37: The Chronology and Canon of Ælfric of Eynsham, *Aaron J Kleist*

Volume 38: Medical Texts in Anglo-Saxon Literary Culture, *Emily Kesling*

Volume 39: The Dynastic Drama of *Beowulf*, *Francis Leneghan*

Volume 40: Old English Lexicology and Lexicography: Essays in Honor of
Antonette diPaolo Healey, *edited by Maren Clegg Hyer, Haruko Momma and
Samantha Zacher*

Volume 41: Debating with Demons: Pedagogy and Materiality in Early English Literature, *Christina M. Heckman*

Volume 42: Textual Identities in Early Medieval England: Essays in Honour of Katherine O'Brien O'Keefe, *Edited by Jacqueline Fay, Rebecca Stephenson and Renée R. Trilling*

Volume 43: Bishop Æthelwold, his Followers, and Saints' Cults in Early Medieval England: Power, Belief, and Religious Reform, *Alison Hudson*

Volume 44: Global Perspectives on Early Medieval England, *edited by Karen Louise Jolly and Britton Elliott Brooks*

Volume 45: Performance in *Beowulf* and Other Old English Poems, *Steven J. A. Breeze*

Volume 46: Wealth and the Material World in the Old English Alfredian Corpus, *Amy Faulkner*

Volume 47: Law, Literature, and Social Regulation in Early Medieval England, *edited by Anya Adair and Andrew Rabin*

Volume 48: The Reigns of Edmund, Eadred and Eadwig, 939–959: New Interpretations, *edited by Mary Elizabeth Blanchard and Christopher Riedel*

Volume 49: Emotional Practice in Old English Literature, *Alice Jorgensen*

Volume 50: Old English Studies and its Scandinavian Practitioners: Nationalism, Aesthetics and Spirituality in the Nordic Countries, 1733–2023, *Robert E. Bjork*

Printed in the United States
by Baker & Taylor Publisher Services